# promise me the stars

NORAH WILSON

This book is a work of fiction. References to real people, establishments, organizations, or locations are intended only to provide a sense of authenticity, and are used fictitiously. The characters and events portrayed in this book are fictitious, and are not to be construed as real. Any similarity to real persons, living or dead, is coincidental and not intended by the authors.

Published by:
Norah Wilson / Something Shiny Press
P.O. Box 30046, Fredericton, NB E3B 0H8

Edited by Lori Gallagher
Cover by The Killion Group, Inc.
Book Design by Author E.M.S.

ISBN-13: 978-1-9276513-0-8

# – one –

SCOTT STANDISH looked at the clock on the wall behind the counter of the truck stop diner. Six twenty. He'd made pretty good time. In less than two hours, he'd be back in Harkness, New Brunswick.

It was a cold, dark, late-October morning, but even at this early hour, he was just one of many patrons. Hands wrapped around a steaming coffee, he leaned over his now empty plate. He'd just finished putting away trucker-sized portions of fried eggs, sausage, home fries and toast. But he'd eaten it because his body needed the fuel, not because he was particularly hungry. Every damned bite had stuck in his throat.

What a crazy few days it had been.

At his brother's behest, he'd gone home for the Thanksgiving weekend and ended up staying more than a week beyond that. He'd known something was up when Titus had insisted both he and their sister Ember come home for the holiday. He just hadn't known what. Turned out Titus hadn't either. At least not all of it.

Scott balled his paper napkin up and dropped it onto the plate.

The homestead stuff wasn't the only reason that breakfast of champions now felt like lead in his gut.

"More coffee, Sunshine?"

It took him a moment to realize the waitress—a tiny woman who couldn't have been more than a year out of high school—was speaking to him. The nametag on her pale yellow uniform read *Madonna,* and the hot black coffee waved lazily against the sides of the pot as she swirled it invitingly. He smiled. *Sunshine?* At twenty-eight, he had a good decade on her. And he sure as hell didn't feel like any kind of sunshine. Especially after yesterday.

"Can I have it to go? Black. And I'll take the bill too, please."

With a snap of pen across the order pad, she handed him the bill, then hustled off to get his coffee for the road. When she returned less than a minute later with his double-cupped joe, he stood and handed her a twenty, waving off the change.

"Wow, thanks."

He knew from Duchess at the diner in Harkness how hard servers worked. And in a rough place like this, he could imagine some of the crap these waitresses had to put up with. Of course, if he ever tried to over-tip Duchess, she'd likely cuff the back of his head. The thought made him smile. "Thanks for the excellent service."

"Have a good day," she called after him as he headed out the door.

Early as it was, the gas pumps were already busy. As he trudged past them, he noticed a display of ice scrapers and snow brushes. They'd soon be in demand. He pulled his jacket closer against the chill as he rounded the building to the parking lot where he'd left Titus's old truck. Two men walked toward the diner, passing a cigarette between them. The air was suddenly pungent as Scott passed them.

*Weed.*

He was pretty sure that was the least of the drugs that could be found back here. To his left the big trucks parked, the eighteen wheelers. Easy place for an enterprising drug dealer to ply his trade. Drug testing generally kept drivers for the major trucking companies clean, but there would always be drivers working for small companies who didn't employ drug-testing. Having done some short-haul trucking himself, Scott knew some of the latter group would be on their CBs right now, looking for "Lucille." Lucille being the speed or cocaine they wanted to score to help them stay awake longer, or maybe weed to help them unwind and sleep.

He didn't partake himself. Hell, he barely even drank. None of the Standish men were regular drinkers. Although he, Titus and Uncle Arden had tipped a few back the other night. He smiled at the memory.

Scott had left Montreal at eleven o'clock at night, Eastern Time, partly to avoid the traffic he knew he'd encounter if he left the congested city in daylight, and partly because he couldn't stay there another night. Naturally, he'd tell Titus he'd left considerably earlier. Yeah, he'd gotten that whole *not a click over the speed limit* lecture from his brother, and to a lesser extent, from his uncle. But on the Trans-Canada Highway, the old pickup had practically *begged* to be let off leash.

Well, who was he to refuse such a fine old vehicle?

It wasn't like he was in Titus's baby, the new F-250 Super Duty. And strange as it seemed, he swore he could almost feel a kinship with that old truck. Feel the need for speed, the need to break out and run, just to prove it could.

Reaching the truck, he noticed the tarp he'd used to wrap the load—motorcycle parts Titus had asked him to pick up—had come untucked. He flipped it up, checked that the boxes were still there, then tucked it back into place. The lot had security cameras, but one never knew.

Load secured, he climbed in behind the wheel and keyed the ignition. The faithful old truck roared to life, but instead of pulling away, Scott scanned the radio channels. He'd been listening to rock music most of the way home, but the signal had been getting increasingly fuzzy. Now, as he cruised through the stations, he hit upon a piece of classical music. The only "classic" he knew was classic rock, but this piece was…nice. Soothing. Just for a moment, he closed his eyes.

For a few precious seconds, his mind was clear, at ease. Sleepy. But then it was once again on *her*. April Morgan. The woman he'd left behind. The one he'd never see again.

Dammit, his leaving had hurt her. He'd seen it in her eyes, right there behind the determination not to show it.

Christ, it wasn't like they were lovers or anything. They'd both been clear about that from the start. Montreal was a temporary stop for him. Like every other place had been. Like every place ever would be.

Then there was April's daughter, Sidney. Or Sid the Kid, as Scott called her. She'd spent nearly every day of her summer vacation at his side. When school started up again, that bright ten-year-old still managed to wriggle out of it from time to time. When she *did* go, she'd race from the bus to find him, watching as he worked around the Boisvert estate. She was curious, bright, and full of questions. Questions he'd found himself looking forward to answering, or trying to answer. Until she'd asked about the stars.

*How do you know the stars will come back? I see them at night, but they're gone in the morning. What if...what if sometime they just go away forever?*

*But they don't go away at all,* he'd explained. *Not really. You just can't see them during the day.*

*What if you're wrong, Scott?*

He hadn't known how to answer.

*Thunk.*

His eyes flew open. What the hell was that? A soft but definite noise from the back of the truck.

He turned around in the seat and looked out through the back window. The tarp was still drawn taut over the load. Thank God. He hadn't drifted off. No one had ransacked Titus's parts while he'd dozed.

A couple passed between his truck and the Nissan Xterra on his passenger side, heading toward the diner. The mother had a toddler on her hip. When they got far enough away, he noticed they had two other kids in tow. Boisterous kids brandishing inflatable bats who ran ahead, whacking car fenders. The father caught up to them, confiscating the blow-up toys.

Mystery solved. One of them must have whacked the truck.

Wide awake now, Scott flipped back the tab on the plastic cup lid and took a cautious sip of his coffee. Then, with stars still dotting the dark sky above, he reversed out of his parking space and made his way back to the highway.

An hour and forty-five minutes later, Scott pulled into the yard. And as he always did, he breathed a little deeper. He looked over the straw-covered fields. Titus and Ocean had done a good job of getting things ready for winter. Scott would have been happy to help, but Ocean's mother Faye had suddenly needed a ton of work done at her house down the road. Some of those odd jobs could have waited, but Scott knew Faye just wanted to throw Titus and Ocean together alone. Apparently the strategy had worked. His brother and Ocean Siliker were now pretty much inseparable. It was just a matter of time before Titus popped the question.

Between Titus and Ocean and Ember and Jace, there was so damned much giddy happiness around, it was hard to take sometimes.

He got out of the truck and stood there a moment, his gaze going to the orchard now. They'd done a good job with it too, sanitizing the ground beneath the early-ripening trees, putting vole guards on the younger trees and such. But most of the trees were still heavy with fruit. The crop would be ready to pick soon.

The farm was his responsibility now, at least until after Christmas. He'd volunteered to stay on with Uncle Arden for a few months to give Titus a break. It was the least he could do after all the years Titus had put in. Except his brother hadn't left much for him to do. Thank God there were repairs that needed doing to the old farmhouse. It would be hard enough to stay put here. He couldn't do it and be idle. He needed projects.

A movement to his left caught his eye. He turned to see Titus had come out of the old machine shed. Swinging both doors wide, he waved at Scott. "Might as well back it right in."

Of course. The motorcycle parts. Titus would be anxious to unload them. Probably anxious to check the old truck over too.

Scott hopped behind the wheel again, drove over to the machine shed and backed the truck in.

"Keys?" Titus held his hand out.

Scott grinned and dropped them into his waiting palm. "Good morning to you too."

Titus pocketed the keys. "I didn't expect you till early afternoon."

Scott stretched his back, then his arms. Damn. He'd driven from one end of this country to the other, and the long drives never usually bothered him. He was well used to the rambling life. But as he rubbed a hand over the back of his neck, he felt the tension in his muscles.

"I got an earlier start than planned."

Titus moved to the back of the truck and began untying one corner of the tarp. "How was the drive?"

"Beautiful. I love driving at night. Traffic was light, sky was clear."

"The highway between Edmundston and here?"

"Good. They seem to have filled a lot of potholes this past summer."

Titus nodded. "You must have been able to pick up some time there?"

*Ah, yes.* Fishing to see how hard he'd pushed the truck.

Knowing a non-answer would drive his brother crazy, he said, "Where's Uncle Arden?"

"Just hitting the shower now. He slept in this morning. First time in years."

Scott felt a chill. "Is he sick?"

"Nah. He was out late. Over at Faye Siliker's."

"Getting out of the house to give you two lovebirds some room, huh?" Scott opened the truck's door again and rescued his cup—less than an inch of cold coffee in the bottom of it.

Titus barely blushed, an indication he was getting used to this girlfriend thing. "Yeah, I think you're right. He goes over to Faye's a lot, but this is the first time he stayed out so late," Titus said. "It was almost midnight when Ocean and I got back to town. When I dropped her home, we found Dad and Faye sitting on Faye's porch swing."

"That's not a bad thing."

"Preaching to the choir, bro. After seeing Dad so depressed for all those years after Mom died, it's great to see him finally doing things with a friend."

Scott smiled, but it was for Titus's benefit. All those years Titus had been stuck here, having put his chosen career on hold to take care of the farm and his parents. Meanwhile, Scott had bailed.

But didn't he always?

"So what kept you out of town until midnight? Were you out on an S&R call?" He guessed not. In fact, he guessed search and rescue had been the last thing on Titus's mind when he'd come home so late.

"Nah. Haven't been called out for weeks now." He'd been working on the knots closest to the cab, but his hands stilled. "Ocean and I took a drive up to Rockland Lake."

"Would have been a beautiful night for it."

Titus chuckled. "Did I mention I was with Ocean? Any night would have been a beautiful night for it."

Scott grinned. It looked good on his brother, this love. And no one had been more surprised than Titus to find that the thing he was looking for was right here in Harkness.

Behind him, Scott heard the screen door on the house creak open, then bang shut.

A few seconds later…*woof…woof!*

"Hey there, Axl," Scott bent and patted his thigh in that *come here* way. The old mutt trotted up to him, tail waving. "Aren't you looking chipper."

"I'm giving him a new joint supplement along with the fish oil. Must be working."

Scott bent to give the dog the good scratching he loved, but Axl ignored him. Moving to the back of the truck, the dog began sniffing, his head bobbing almost comically as he scented the air. Then Axl jumped his front paws up onto the tailgate and strained toward the tarp. He whined.

*Clunk.*

Scott's adrenaline shot through the roof. Yeah, he'd definitely heard it this time. So had Titus, judging from the way he was pulling the last few ties on the tarp.

Ember appeared around the corner. "Hi, Scott."

"Stay back," Titus commanded.

"What the—"

"Just wait by the door, Ember."

Scott had no idea whether she obeyed Titus's command or not. He couldn't take his eyes off the truck. Shit! Had someone crawled under the tarp at the truck stop? Someone dangerous? He and Titus and a geriatric Axl could be the only things standing between some fugitive and their sister.

Dammit, why hadn't he checked that noise out at the truck stop instead of assuming one of those kids had bopped his truck with their toy? How stupid could he be?

Pretty damned stupid, as it turned out.

Titus pulled the tarp away, then jumped back. "What the hell? A *stowaway*?"

Not just any stowaway. *Sidney Morgan.*

She sat up, shivering.

Ember elbowed her way between Scott and Titus to see for herself. “Omigod, it’s a *kid*.” She was up on the truck, examining the little girl in a flash. “You poor thing. You’re freezing.” She looked up. “Titus, grab her. We need to get her in the house and warmed up.”

Scott stepped forward. “I’ll do it. She trusts me.”

Titus’s eyes widened even further. “You know her?”

Scott went to the side of the truck and picked Sidney up. She immediately snaked her arms around his neck and clung so tightly, she almost cut off his air supply. “I do.”

“Here, wrap her in this.” Ember held out a sleeping bag, the one Sid must have huddled in all the way from Montreal. “Now get her inside and I’ll see to her,” she said with the same doctor-in-charge voice.

He draped the sleeping bag around Sid’s trembling form and headed for the house.

*Oh, Sid. What have you done?*

# – two –

April Morgan studied herself in the mirror. A woman dressed in a crisp, black chef's jacket smiled back. Or was that a grimace? She'd been practicing for so long she wasn't sure.

She nodded, tilted her head slightly to the left, and continued rehearsing the words she so desperately hoped she'd have the opportunity to say to the client. *"Pleased to meet you. The breakfast spread? Yes, that's one of my own jam recipes. One hundred percent original. And you're right—you did detect a hint of butterscotch. Why, thank you, Ms. McCoy.* At this point, she always imagined Ms. K.Z. McCoy, style-maker, would invite her to use her first name, or rather, her initials. *Thank you, K.Z. And please, call me April.*

Argh! Who was she kidding? She was the kitchen help. It didn't matter that she could rival most formally trained chefs out there. K.Z. would be sampling her food, but all the glory would be going to the Boisverts. It was their residence. Their business. Their chance to meet the famous K.Z. McCoy. CEO, and majority shareholder of K.Z.'s Corporate Kitchen, seller of healthy, high-end foods to corporations concerned about their workers' health.

The Boisverts ran an exclusive alternative healing resort and spa. *A place of tranquility, beauty, and rejuvenation*, as Mrs. Boisvert liked to call it. Of course, only the wealthy could afford to experience that healing and restoration. But price notwithstanding, with a positive recommendation from K.Z., the place would be swamped with a certain type of employer, anxious to impress their senior team with an exclusive corporate retreat.

Not for the first time, April wished she'd been able to find a photograph of K.Z. McCoy. Rightly or wrongly, she'd always felt you could deduce certain things from how people looked, or maybe more accurately, how they chose to present themselves to the world. But as hard as she'd scoured the Internet, she hadn't unearthed a single photo of the woman. Yes, K.Z. was definitely a woman, but that was about the only detail April knew, beyond how influential her company was. And if it weren't for the pronouns—the *she* and *her*—employed on the K.Z. Corporate Kitchen site, she wouldn't even know that much.

Yes, first impressions mattered. She smoothed her hands over the sides of the fitted black jacket. With average height and dark brown hair that was rarely out of the French twist she wore it in, she knew she looked older than her twenty-seven years.

*Oh God, my eyes.*

She'd slept so poorly. She pulled in a deep breath, let it out slowly.

Sidney probably hadn't slept any better, since she hadn't stirred yet. Of course, Mondays were never her daughter's favorite day. But there was more to it than that.

April sighed. She should be in the kitchen right now, preparing to dazzle Ms. McCoy, who would arrive in less than an hour for breakfast. Dr. and Mrs. Boisvert wanted everything to be perfect. This was their big chance.

And for April herself, it was a chance to have her unique creations sampled by the best in the business. Just the thought made her heart beat faster. In her wildest dreams, she imagined herself running her own business.

Except for a single woman with a child to support, some dreams were just too wild.

*Callum Martin.* Handsome, charming, underhanded. He'd swept her off her feet. Stolen her heart. She hadn't listened to the bells and whistles going off in her mind.

He had been her first. First boyfriend, first love. First everything, after getting out of her parents' household in Dartmouth to attend St. Francis Xavier University in Antigonish on scholarship. Her father had made it clear they wouldn't put a cent to her education, but at seventeen, she'd been undaunted. She'd already perfected a half dozen jam and jelly recipes and was determined to get her business degree, start her own business.

Then, on a blustery winter morning, she peed on a stick.

Nearly eight months later, Sidney Kathleen Morgan had come screaming into the world.

That had been ten years ago.

Oh, that precious baby was her prize. Her life. Her shining star. But that beautiful baby was also her responsibility and hers alone. Two weeks after she told Callum she was expecting, he was gone. No goodbye, no explanation, and definitely no forwarding address.

She'd had to drop out of university once the baby was born. She hadn't been home for months, but finally, her parents had gotten word. Her roaring father had ordered her home with *the little bastard.* He and April's mother would raise it. Adopt it.

That's right—*it*.

That was the day she cut her parents out of her life.

There was a reason Kathleen, her older sister, had run away at sixteen, never to be heard from again. And why Harley, her entitled, older brother—Sarah and Dick Morgan's only male offspring—had never left the nest. A chip off the old block, he was just as misogynistic and nasty as their father. But somehow, he'd found a wife. Harley and his family now lived in the Morgan household in Dartmouth, while Dick and Sarah had moved to a condo.

April had raised Sidney Kathleen—her little Ladybug—on her own.

But she was still determined to work in the food industry.

She'd started out as a dishwasher in one of Halifax's smaller downtown restaurants, a family-owned business. She'd worked her way up to prep cook, then line cook, for those part time hours she put in. She'd soaked up everything the chef was prepared to teach her, not to advance with her job, but because it had fascinated her. She read more online. Studied food safety. Analyzed recipes and perfected some of her own. Then the owners had retired, closing the restaurant. In one fell swoop, she'd lost her job and the tiny apartment she rented above the restaurant. That was six years and three positions ago.

This job with the Boisverts wasn't much, but she'd needed someplace that could also supply housing. And it was safe. Secure. But in taking the job, she'd uprooted Sidney from her school, her friends. The job also kept her so busy, she didn't have as much time for Sid as she'd like.

*Time*. Crap! She needed to be downstairs.

But first, she'd look in on Sidney.

She knocked on the door. "Ladybug? You awake?"

Silence. Sid silence—and that, as she knew, could last for a spell.

They shared a small, upstairs apartment in the Boisvert home with two closet-sized bedrooms, and cupboard-sized closets. Because there was just the two of them, they always left their bedroom doors open. Except for last night.

Yes, Sid was getting older, but April knew it wasn't just a general tween desire for privacy. Her little girl's heart was breaking though she wouldn't admit it in hundred years.

April's throat started to ache. Her own heart had taken a pretty good thumping too.

She usually let the alarm clock do the job of waking her brilliant and independent daughter. Though since summer, Sidney hadn't needed the alarm. She'd gotten in the habit of getting up at the crack of dawn to work around the estate with Scott Standish. Or the *butt crack of dawn*, as Sidney liked to say. Yes, that had been just one of Scott's colorful contributions to her daughter's vocabulary.

As April stood there debating whether or not to enter her daughter's room, the clock radio alarm went off. When the radio played on without any sounds of stirring, April knocked gently on the door.

"Sidney, time to get up. School day." When there was no response, April knocked a little louder on the door. "Sidney?" Still no action. *Dammit, April couldn't be late this morning.*

"I'm coming in." With that warning, she walked into the room and groaned.

Her daughter had never scored high marks for tidiness, but this was ridiculous. Her laundry basket had been turned upside down. Dresser drawers stood open, spilling socks and clothing.

Still no movement from the little girl tucked so tightly under those blankets. Precious seconds ticked by. Praying for patience, April sat down on the bed. "Come on, sleepyhead. School. I know you're upset. I know you miss—"

The words she was going to say died on her lips as she put her hand on her daughter's shoulder beneath the bedding. Except it wasn't her daughter. She pulled the blankets back to find a pillowcase stuffed with a Barney doll.

She tore the covers back. More stuffed animals, two small cushions, and a balled-up Montreal Canadiens jersey.

*Oh, God, no!*

Where was her child?

She tried to stem the flood of panic with logic. This was not an abduction. Clearly her daughter had snuck out under her own steam. But where was she?

Oh crap, she had to find Sidney before she got herself into even more trouble. Was this about school? This wouldn't be the first time she'd played hooky.

"Oh, Sidney, honey, where are you?" Tears choked her voice.

April had to go downstairs and get to work, like *now*. But how could she? She had to find Sidney. Every possible scenario as to where her girl could be ran through her head.

She tightened her fists in frustration, her trimmed nails digging little half-moons into the palms of her hands.

As much as she hoped Sidney was somewhere within the relative safety of the estate, she also dreaded that thought. The Boisverts were a nice enough couple, but they had absolutely no interest in children. There was also a definite division between the family and staff. The little suite April and her daughter occupied had its own private entrance at the back of the house. Sidney knew she wasn't to wander alone. As defiant as she'd gotten in the last couple weeks, surely she wouldn't defy that rule…again.

She hoped.

Ten days ago, Sidney had snuck into Dr. Boisvert's parlor. Though she hadn't taken anything, she'd moved some things around. She hadn't intended to rearrange the objects on his desk, but in the process of picking things up, inspecting them and putting them back down, they didn't necessarily get back in their precise place. If that hadn't been enough to give her away, she'd started his Newton's cradle pendulum balls in motion.

April had made Sidney apologize, and had apologized for her. Sid was just a little girl curious about the oddities on the desk. That wasn't how Dr. Boisvert saw it, however. He was adamant it not happen again. Or else…

*Oh, Ladybug! We can't move again so soon.*

April had been more concerned about her daughter than angry with her. Normally, she didn't have to worry too much about that sort of thing. Sid was mature for her age. Smarter than most ten-year-olds.

But she was still a child. And, heaven help her, she was missing!

*The phone.* She could call her daughter. And if Sid was being stubborn and refused to answer, she could still get a general location. She'd been thinking about loss or theft when she'd installed the app, but maybe it could help her find her daughter.

She ran to the small kitchen and grabbed her phone off the top of the fridge. Her daughter's name popped up immediately. As the phone rang, April's eyes fell on the school photo of Sidney pinned to the fridge with magnets. The strangest, most lonesome feeling invaded her gut. That sweet face, those wide brown eyes. Nut brown hair just a shade lighter than April's own dark brown, bangs brushed to the side.

The muffled sound of Sidney's ringtone—a few distinctive notes from her favorite Taylor Swift tune—sounded from within the suite. *Oh no!* She dashed back into her daughter's room and tore the bedding completely off the bed. Sidney's phone clunked to the floor, face up.

She bent to pick it up. *Mom* appeared on the caller ID.

The panic she was trying to hold down flared. She'd left her phone. Sidney had gone off God only knew where, leaving April with no way of contacting her. No way to know if she was safe.

Unless she hadn't gone anywhere. Maybe she'd just…slipped outside. There was no point getting worked up until she knew she needed to.

Except that didn't make sense. She wouldn't create that elaborate dummy in her bed just to slip out this morning. She'd have done it last night, so her disappearance would go unnoticed if April checked in on her.

Her daughter's phone stopped ringing and the *Mom* call

went into voice mail. April hung up her own phone. Focusing on her daughter's phone, she scrolled through the call history. Nothing more recent than three days ago, and all the calls had been to April's phone.

She checked her own phone's history. Nothing recent but for Sid's calls a few days ago. No missed calls.

"Oh, Sid."

Maybe there was something else on the phone, some clue that would help her. She hit the home button and caught her breath at what she saw. Her ten-year-old daughter had managed to install a custom wallpaper. Clearly she'd also figured out how to hide most of the apps in a single file to declutter the screen enough to display the picture. It was a shot of April in the Boisvert's kitchen, but she wasn't alone. Scott Standish was there with her. He was looking down at her with the biggest smile on his face, and she was grinning right back.

She swallowed hard. If only Scott were here, he'd help her find Sidney. He'd know where to look.

*If only he hadn't left.* Sidney had been so happy having him around.

But Scott wasn't here. There'd be no help from that quarter.

She pushed the self-pity away and went back to exploring the phone. She found nothing on there that she hadn't approved. A quick look at the browser history was equally unenlightening.

Think, April. Okay, nothing on the phone. Maybe she'd left a note.

Wait, the journal!

April pulled out the night table's drawer and there it was, the beautiful journal with the Ladybug on the cover that she'd given Sidney for her tenth birthday.

She ran her hand over the cover. The words *SID'S JOURNAL* were scrawled across the cover, and beneath, a white piece of paper had been glued into place. The words on the paper read: *Sid the Kid - Ha Ha! You are STAR-TACULAR!*

That's what Scott had written on the birthday card when he'd given her his gift—a telescope. A kid's one, but still an extravagant gift. Sidney had absolutely loved it. She'd shot into Scott's arms for a long, tight hug. He'd smiled, looked at April as he'd hugged her back. But there'd been something in that smile—an unease. A worry.

As she looked at the journal now, it broke her heart how carefully Sidney had cut Scott's handwriting out—an almost perfect circle—and how neatly she'd glued it to the cover.

Blinking rapidly, she opened the journal and some tiny papers fluttered to the floor. She bent and picked them up. There were three of them. The first was a phone number on a slip of paper along with the handwritten words *Daven Dog Rescue*. A second, similar slip read *Rescue Mission—Dagwood the Rottie-Lab X*. The final slip had a Visa credit card number on it, one she didn't recognize.

*Oh God, could it be Dr. Boisvert's credit card?* She looked again at the slips of paper. Sidney was such a dog-lover. The first thing she did whenever they moved was to look up the local shelters. She loved to follow the dogs on the shelters' websites and celebrated every time one was adopted. Could she have used Dr. Boisvert's credit card to sponsor a dog?

She sank down onto the bed. If she'd gotten her hands on a credit card…

Taking a deep breath, she began flipping through the journal's pages. Her daughter hadn't written much, but she'd drawn and colored lots of pictures. There were some photographs too, which had been cut out and pasted into the journal. They appeared to have been taken with her phone, so Sidney must have found a way to download them and print them off. She had to have done that in Dr. Boisvert's office.

April stopped flipping when she came to one photo that

pierced her heart. It was from Sidney's birthday. She'd taken a selfie. Her image was in the foreground, all smiles and red cheeks and wind-blown hair. And in the background, April and Scott in an unguarded moment, completely unaware that the picture was being taken. Sid had drawn a red-marker heart around them.

They were looking into each other's eyes. About to steal a quick kiss while Sidney wasn't looking.

Such a dangerous game.

Sidney had captured the moment perfectly. She'd also captured what April had allowed herself to feel that day—happy, safe.

But even in that moment, she'd known she was deluding herself. Scott was a rambler. Always would be. She had scolded her fluttering heart for that smallest bit of hope.

Scott Standish was the most unsafe man she knew—at least for her little world.

And yet, she wished he was here.

"Oh, Sidney." This wasn't just a kid playing hooky. "What have you done?"

The phone rang. Even without the two distinct rings of the house line, she knew it had to be Mrs. Boisvert.

She picked up the phone.

"Miss Morgan, come down here immediately. This is not the day to be sleeping in. We're behind schedule for our preparations."

"I'm sorry, Mrs. Boisvert, but—"

"No buts, Miss Morgan. I expected you to present yourself straight away. We've so much to do."

Bracing for Mrs. Boisvert's wrath, she clenched the receiver harder. "I'm sorry, I can't. Sidney seems to have disappeared."

"Oh, that imp! You must control her, Miss Morgan. Tell her we have no time for her games this morning."

"I'm afraid it's more than a game. I think she slipped out in the night. She made up the bed to look as though she was in it, and she took some of her things."

"Oh, dear. She's really run away, then?"

Hearing the words spoken by someone else made her stomach lurch. She pinched the bridge of her nose. "I'm afraid so."

"I'm so very sorry," the older woman said, her voice soft with sympathy. "Of course you must focus on finding her quickly. I'll have Claude Fournier call you straight away. He can review the security tapes with you. Perhaps you can see how she got off the estate or what direction she took."

Recognizing the name of the security person, April wilted with relief. "Thank you."

"But you understand what this will mean, no? Bad enough to have young Sidney's antics disturbing the tranquility we strive to create, but this morning…" Mrs. Boisvert drew an audible breath and expelled it. "I fear that we will fail to impress Ms. McCoy."

April massaged her temple. *Oh, Sidney.* "I understand. As soon as I've located my daughter, I'll start packing."

# – three –

POOR APRIL. It was still early in Montreal, but not so early she wouldn't have noticed her daughter's absence. She must be frantic. Scott stepped out onto the porch, out of earshot of Sid and the others, and hit April's number. He paced as he waited for it to connect.

She answered on the first ring. "Scott!"

"Sid's safe, April." He went down the steps to the front yard. "She's here with me. I know it's a lot to take in, but the important thing is she's safe."

"Oh thank God!" Her voice quavered with relief, then dissolved into sniffles.

Scott closed his eyes, relieved he wasn't there to see her cry. A woman's tears—even his sister's—always bothered the hell out of him. But sharing the stage with that guilty relief was the conflicting desire to jump back in the old truck and drive like a bat out of hell to wipe every one of those tears away.

"We just found her minutes ago," he said. "She stowed away in the back of the truck. Rode all the way to Harkness like that. I hadn't a clue."

"I was just about to call you. I'm sitting here with the Boisverts' security person scouring surveillance tape. We just finished watching her disappear behind your truck with a big bundle in her arms."

"Yeah, that would be her sleeping bag. She managed to get under the tarp and wriggle all the way up to the front of the truck bed."

"Is she all right?"

"Cold and hungry, but she's fine. And she's in great hands. My sister Ember, the doctor, is with her right now."

"Scott, I… Did she tell you why she ran away?"

Silence. No, Sid hadn't told him, but he could guess. "We haven't talked about it yet. I wanted to call you right away because I knew you'd be worried."

"This is my fault. I knew she was upset over…things."

The *things* she was talking about included his leaving. From what April had said, when he'd come home to Harkness for Thanksgiving, Sid had started acting out more and more. When he'd left Montreal last night for good…

"But *running away*? Scott, what was she thinking? She's only ten!"

He rubbed the back of his neck. "Let me talk to her for a bit, April. See what I can figure out."

"Okay, good idea. She might open up to you."

She paused, and he could hear her rapid breathing.

"April?"

"It just seems like I can't get through to her anymore." The words came out in a rush.

"I didn't mean—"

"It's okay, Scott. It's the truth." After another pause, she said, "Tell her I love her."

"I will. And I'll call you afterward."

"Thanks."

Not quite ready to hang up, he searched his mind for something else to say. "So, how's that breakfast going for the Boisverts' special guest? That's today, right?"

The seconds ticked by.

Okay, dumb question. She'd just said she'd been going

over security tapes. She probably hadn't been anywhere near the kitchen yet today.

"I have to go," she said at last. "Call me when you've talked to Sid."

"I will, April. In the meantime, try not to worry."

Shoving his phone into his pocket, he went back inside. When he entered the kitchen, Titus, Ember, and Arden all shot him a look. Sidney sipped her hot chocolate, both tiny hands wrapped around the oversized mug.

Arden nodded. "Good to have you home again, Son."

"Good to be back." The words flowed out like he meant them. And he did, at this moment, stowaway notwithstanding. But he had no illusions these next months were going to be a picnic. He hadn't been home more than a few days at a stretch since he'd graduated high school. Since Margaret Standish got sick.

He glanced at Sid. Ember had insisted the kid have a chance to warm up before facing any third-degree grilling. Sid was now dressed in a pair of Ember's old fleece pajamas—Christmas ones. As if that wasn't enough, Ember had practically swaddled the girl in her red and black flannel house coat. Now Sidney sat cross-legged on one of the old kitchen chairs, her feet and knees tucked in under the flannel, the red collar pulled close around her neck. To her obvious pleasure, Axl laid his head on her knee, and she stroked that old head gently.

"Could I have another grilled cheese?" Sid looked down at the empty plate in front of her—well, empty if you didn't count crusts—then looked toward Scott.

"I'll get it, Scott," Ember volunteered. "You've got to be exhausted." She got up and went to the stove.

"Thanks." Scott sat down at the table, but rather than taking the seat his sister had just vacated beside Sidney, he sat across from her.

He was beat. He was also worried about Sidney, and her mother too. And he was more than a little freaked out when he thought about what harm could have come to the kid. Riding in the box of a truck, in the cold, traveling at high speeds on the freaking highway. No restraint in the event of an accident. He took a deep breath, dialed his emotion back.

"Hungry, huh?" he said.

"Starving," she said.

"Maybe next time you'll pack a lunch before you stow away," Titus offered. He and Uncle Arden stood on the other side of the kitchen

"I bought a Mars bar when we stopped at the Gas and Grub."

"*You what*?" Scott was pretty sure his heart stopped for a moment.

She shrugged. "You were sitting at the counter with your back to the door, so you didn't see me. I just slipped in, bought my bar and slipped out." She slid her hands together in a pretty good imitation of a *slick as anything* move.

"I wouldn't be so proud of that fact if I were you, young lady," Uncle Arden said. "That was a dangerous thing to do."

Dangerous? That was putting it mildly. If something had happened to her out there, he'd never have forgiven himself.

"Well, I didn't just get out because I was hungry," she said. "I had to pee too."

"You shouldn't have been there in the first place," Scott said. "Not in the Gas and Grub. Not in the truck."

She looked down at Axl. The old dog gently whined, either in encouragement or sympathy. His tail thumped softly on the floor. She patted his head. "At least you don't hate me."

"Whoa!" Ember said. "Who said anything about hating you?"

"Sid, we're just concerned," Scott said. "Very concerned. And your mother—"

She stiffened, then sat up straight. “No need for concern,” she said in her best adult voice. “I’ll finish up my breakfast and be on my way.”

Titus snorted. “On your way?”

Ember shot him a glare, then turned to Sid. “That won’t be happening.”

“But—”

“I’ve already called your mom, Sid,” Scott said. “She knows you’re here.”

She deflated back against the seat and crossed her arms over her chest. She didn’t even uncross them when Ember slid that second grilled cheese onto her plate. “Why’d you have to call her?”

“Because you’re a minor,” Titus said.

“She’s going to ruin everything!”

“Well, it’s either her or Police Chief Buzz Adams. Under the law, we’re legally required to—”

Ember set a hand on Titus’ shoulder and shook her head. Scott shot him a quelling look for good measure.

He turned back to Sid. Tears shone in the little girl’s eyes, but her jaw was set tightly.

Poor kid.

Scott had been on that hot seat himself a few times in his younger years. Like when his Harkness mother had found that half pack of smokes he’d hidden in the laundry hamper. Or the time he’d laid a thumping on Dundas Bloom. Though on that occasion, he’d actually sat up a little straighter on the hard oak chair whilst Arden gave him a talking to about *right place, right time*.

He didn’t think a person could sink any lower into that old kitchen chair than Sid did now. And his heart went out to her. She still wasn’t talking.

“Titus, why don’t we go unload the truck?” Arden said, clamping a hand on his son’s back.

“What?” Titus said, then recovered. “Right. The truck.”

"And Ember," Arden said, nodding toward the kitchen clock. "Look at the time."

She took the hint too. "Whoops. I'd better get going. Gotta meet Jace."

*Jace.* Scott caught himself tensing at the name of the man who'd caused his sister so much pain. He had to remind himself that was in the past. Ember was engaged to Jace now. He would soon be part of the family, had proved himself more than worthy.

"Well," Arden said. "We'll leave you two to talk, Son."

"Thanks, Uncle Arden."

Titus and Ember abandoned the kitchen quickly. But Arden, instead of heading out the door, went to the fridge.

He pulled out a wrapped piece of blueberry pie. Delaying his departure for a few seconds more, he warmed the pie in the microwave. When it dinged, he grabbed a fork from the utensil drawer and set the pie down in front of Sidney. "That'll warm you up, sweetheart," he said.

Sid blinked rapidly. "Blueberry's my favorite," she whispered.

"I had a hunch." Smiling, Arden retrieved his jacket and orange vest. With a *you-got-this* nod to Scott, he left the house, leaving Scott alone with Sid.

It was quiet for a moment while Scott debated what to say, but it was Sid who broke the silence.

"Is he going hunting?"

*Hunting?* Ah, the orange vest. "No, Uncle Arden doesn't hunt anymore. Hasn't for a long time. But other people do, and if you want to go for a walk in the woods or fields during hunting season, you wear the orange vest for safety."

Frankly, Scott was thrilled to see Arden heading out for a morning walk. Walking was something that had helped pull him back up from his depression. Beyond the blast of endorphins it produced, just being in nature, with it smells and sounds, was incredibly peace-inducing. Scott saw a lot of those walks in his own future.

"What about the dog?" She looked down at Axl. "Does he go walking in the woods too?"

"Sometimes. When he's feeling good."

"Does he wear a vest too?"

"During hunting season, yeah. Uncle Arden keeps it in the pocket of his own vest, I think."

"So why do you call him Uncle Arden?"

"Arden's his name."

"But why don't you call him *Dad?*"

Scott raked a hand through his hair. "I'm adopted. I told you that. But he's my uncle."

"He calls you *Son.*"

Dammit, he was supposed to be probing her about why she'd run away, and here she was practically making him squirm in his chair. If there was one thing he'd learned from these past months with Sid tagging around behind him, it was that kids often saw the adult world in black and white. Not much room for nuance.

Besides, how could he explain something to Sid that he didn't even understand himself?

He'd come to call Margaret Standish, his adoptive mother, *Mom* within months of landing in Harkness from the only home he'd ever known in Minnesota. She'd been nothing like Beth Wheaton-Standish, his birth mother, but somehow the transition to calling her Mom had been easy. Maybe because he knew how important it was to her.

Yet he'd never been able to bring himself to call his uncle and adoptive father *Dad.* Arden had unfailingly treated him exactly the same as he'd treated Titus or Ember. And he'd tried just as hard as Margaret Standish had to make him feel at home.

He'd even told Scott that he was welcome to call him Dad, but only if he wanted to. He'd only said it the once, and he'd never pushed.

Scott shook his head. God, he must be more tired than he'd thought.

"Sid, why are you here?" he asked.

She shrugged. "I've never been to New Brunswick."

"Ha-ha, very funny."

She shrugged again, but the gesture was tight, almost jerky.

"Why did you say your mom would ruin everything?"

"Huh?"

"Come on, Sid. Don't play dumb with me. What did you mean? Ruin what?"

"I can't tell you." She bit her lip.

"Can't or won't?"

She just looked at him with those big brown eyes, so like her mother's.

He sighed. "I wish you'd talk to me, Kid."

Her stare sharpened. "Maybe you're not wishing hard enough."

Scott studied her for a moment. The others had left so they could have this heart-to-heart, but he wasn't doing such a hot job. What would Uncle Arden do in a situation like this?

"Are you going to eat that pie?" he asked.

She started to push her plate toward him. But her hand stilled, then switched over to the grilled cheese plate. She pushed that his way instead.

When Axl whined hopefully, Sid looked down at him. "Cheese isn't really good for dogs. It can give them diarrhea if they get too much lactose."

"How'd you know that?"

"I like dogs. A lot."

"Well, Axl can handle a little cheese. He's used to getting some with pills. Maybe you could give him one of the crusts."

"Really?"

"Sure."

She tore a crust from the sandwich and fed it to Axl, who took it gingerly from her hands, then gobbled it quickly.

"There, you've fed him something. Now you're fast friends."

She smiled down at the dog, then went to work on her pie, ignoring Scott completely.

He pulled out his phone. "Okay, let's call your mom. We'll have to make arrangements to get you home."

Her head came up. "I'm not going home."

"You have to, Sid." He started to punch in a number. "Your mom's worried sick. She loves you, and—"

"Wait!" She leaped up, leaned across the table, and grabbed his hand before he could complete the call.

"Why?"

"Can I at least go to the bathroom before we call her? And I want to change back into my own clothes. I just feel weird in these."

"Okay, fine."

Feeling weird or not, she ate the last bit of blueberry pie. Then she put her fork down. Her eyes narrowed assessingly. "Crust was a little too crumbly," she said. "Probably cut the butter in too much. But otherwise, good pie."

Scott would have smiled if he wasn't trying to be stern. She was just like April. She could taste something and spiel off the list of ingredients that had gone into it, or speculate about what had gone wrong in the making of it. Except Sid was more vocal about it than her mother.

"Where are your clothes?" he asked.

"In the dryer warming up."

"Great." Pocketing his phone, he went to the laundry room, a small room at the back of the house with access to the back porch and the seldom-used clothes line. He stopped the dryer and pulled out her clothes.

Back in the kitchen, he handed the warm bundle to her. "You can change in the bathroom. Upstairs at the end of the hall."

"Thanks." She tucked the clothes under her arm and picked

up her knapsack. "I'll be right back." Sidney looked at the dog. "Bye, Axl."

The old dog hung his head.

"He'll be here when you come down," Scott said.

She walked into the living room.

He heard three easy steps on the stairs, then fast heavy *thump thump thumps* as she ran up the last of them.

Axl looked toward the ceiling and whined. He swung his head toward Scott.

"Don't give me that look. I'm not being too hard on her."

*Was he?* He hadn't a clue.

Scott poured himself a coffee from the pot on the counter. Well, half a coffee. Replacing the empty carafe, he turned the burner off, then rolled his neck. What he really needed was a catnap, but he doubted that would be happening. So bring on the caffeine.

Mug in hand, he crossed to the window overlooking the winter-ready fields. Tall, imposing Harkness Mountain beyond. Maybe he'd take a hike up there before the snow fell. At least up to Crooked Man Cave.

Jesus, he'd spent more time in Harkness in the last few weeks than he had in the last few years. And was set to spend a lot more time here. He'd told Uncle Arden he'd stay until the first of January.

His gaze dropped from the mountain on the horizon to the land in the foreground. His responsibility for the next few months, even though there'd be precious little to do once the apples were picked. Arden had delayed opening to u-pickers when they thought they'd be leaving. His plan had been to tell folks they could help themselves to the crop when it ripened, as a goodbye gesture. Now that the farm was back in Standish hands, they'd be opening it to u-pickers the first of the week. And when they'd had a go at the fruit, he'd get a few good paid pickers in to deal with the rest.

He almost wished it were earlier in the season so there'd be more to keep him occupied outdoors. Still, there were projects aplenty he could do inside the house, starting with that fireplace flue.

He tried to push his thoughts in that direction, toward the jobs that needed doing, but they kept leaping back to Sid.

To her beautiful mother…

Axl woofed.

"Easy, boy." He bent to scratch the old dog's head. "I know things are in a bit of turmoil right now, but they'll smooth out. You'll see."

Axl whined, apparently unconvinced.

Scott drained his mug, swished it out under the tap, then filled it with water. Now this was something he missed when he traveled. Most of Harkness was on the town water supply, but the Standish property had its own deep well. Nothing tasted better. He took a slow cold drink, then just about choked on it as he looked out the window.

Behind him, Axl was barking like hell.

Dammit, Sid.

There she was—no coat, no hat. God, her sneakers were still by the door. She had to be in her sock feet. Wearing the clothes he'd just dug out of the dryer, she was hightailing it across the field.

Scott was out the door and after her in a flash. Less than a minute later, he caught up to her. "Hey," he said, laying a hand on her shoulder. "Whoa up, little lady."

"No!" She shrugged out from under his hand. "This is important. It's a matter of…everything!"

"I don't understand. Where do you think you're going?"

She turned and glared at him for all of two seconds. Then she burst into tears. Scott's heart just about broke at the sight.

"I can't tell you," she said.

And no matter how gently he asked as she cried in his arms, she didn't.

# – four –

APRIL WISHED she had some hard liquor in the place. She didn't indulge often, but if she'd had some whiskey on hand this morning, she might have knocked one back before calling her brother.

"I suppose I'll have to let the two of you stay, but you'll have to help around the place. And there will be parameters. My house, my rules. None of your…shenanigans."

On second thought, it was a good thing she hadn't had a belt of whiskey. Otherwise, she might have given in to the temptation to congratulate Harley on being as big a piece of shit as ever.

She hadn't talked to her brother in at least five years, apart from his annual drunken New Year's call that always left her feeling exhausted and vowing not to answer next year. And if it wasn't for that faint hope there'd finally be news of their long-gone sister, Kathleen, she'd probably be able to hold to that vow. As for her parents, she didn't speak to them at all.

But she couldn't say anything to get Harley's back up. She had to think of Sid.

"Of course, your rules. Thanks, Harley. It shouldn't be for long. Just until I can land another position and then Sidney and I will be out—"

"Right. The child." He sighed dramatically.

She cringed. Sidney hated being called a child.

"What is she now? Six? Seven?"

"Ten."

"That's a hard age."

If she'd told Harley her daughter was thirty-two, he'd be saying it was a hard age. She took a deep breath. "Every age has its ups and downs, I guess."

"Is the girl—"

"Sidney."

"—well behaved?"

"Oh, she's very well behaved."

"Because, you know, my house…"

"Your rules." She closed her eyes tightly. Hadn't she heard that from her father every day for the first seventeen years of her life? Her stomach roiled. "Got it, Harley."

"All right then."

"Thanks. I really appreciate—"

He hung up.

This day just was not getting any better.

There was a low *tap tap* on the door and it was all she could do not to groan. Even before a third tap landed, she knew who it was knocking.

"Come in, Mrs. Boisvert."

The door opened slowly, and a trim, petite, and heavily made-up woman entered.

April desperately wanted to be alone, but she dredged up a polite smile. By the look on Mrs. Boisvert's face, she wasn't any keener on being here in this little suite than April was to have her there. Which reminded her…

"The place is clean," April said. "I'll still run a wet mop over the floors before I leave."

The older lady made a dismissive gesture. "Oh, please don't bother. Its fine, I'm sure. That's not why I'm here."

Oh, great. What now? She'd already alerted the Boisverts to the slip of paper she'd found with the credit card number on it.

It *was* theirs, and Sidney *had* used it online. As April suspected, she'd used it to make a donation on behalf of a dog that was at risk for euthanasia if the funds for its expensive medical treatments couldn't be raised. Fortunately, the Boisverts had agreed not to alert the credit card company or the authorities in exchange for restitution, which April had already made.

Wasn't it enough that she'd lost her job? Missed her chance to impress K.Z. McCoy? That her little girl had run away? Had Mrs. Boisvert come to heap on recrimination? Tell her what a terrible parent she was, raising a delinquent?

Whatever she had to say, April would meet it head on and deal with it politely and with dignity. "Would you like to sit down?"

"Thank you." Mrs. Boisvert sat on one of the cushion-covered kitchen chairs but didn't tuck herself into the table.

April waited for her former employer to speak. She'd be damned if she opened yet another conversation with an apology. Yes, she was sorry that her daughter had used Dr. Boisvert's credit card. Sorry that she'd caused so much trouble by running away. And April was *very* sorry she hadn't been in the kitchen to cook for K.Z. McCoy. But as sorry as she was, she wasn't prepared to grovel.

She'd need to save all of that for placating Harley. And if Mrs. Boisvert thought for one moment she was going to sit here and listen to one more bad word about Sidney, well she could stick that in her—

"I'm so very sorry about all this. I can see you've been crying. I know your daughter is safe in New Brunswick, but it's obvious how heavily the whole affair is weighing on your heart."

April hadn't expected a show of sympathy. A genuine show. "Thank you."

"Such a nice young man, Scott Standish. He told me he's putting off that big job in Alberta to help out at the family farm for a few months."

He was? He hadn't mentioned that to her. She figured he'd be off to Alberta as soon as he delivered those motorcycle parts for his brother. Of course, he hadn't confided much in the few days he'd been there. Which was okay with her. The parting two weeks ago had been wrenching enough. She couldn't afford to let him get close. He seemed to be thinking along the same vein because he hadn't tried to get her alone. April counted it a partial success. While she'd stayed out of his arms, there'd been major eye contact. And thanks to Sidney's efforts, they'd been thrown together regularly.

"Can I offer you some tea, Mrs. Boisvert?" Not the smoothest change of subject, but hopefully it would work. "I haven't quite finished packing up the kitchen. I have lemongrass and decaf English breakfast."

She shook her head. "No. Thank you, dear. But it's very gracious of you to offer, considering…"

*Gracious?* "Mrs. Boisvert, I don't blame you. I know I let you down this morning. And Sidney—"

"It's Jean, you know," she said. "Dr. Boisvert can be very unforgiving. If it were up to me, I'd give you another chance. You're such a wonderful cook, April. I'm so sorry to lose you."

"Thank you. I wish it had worked out here."

"Me too." She drew a deep breath. "Well, I really cannot stay. Jean and I are going into the city for the evening. But I wanted to tell you that if you need a reference, please contact me rather than my husband."

April managed a light tone. "He didn't like my cooking?"

Mrs. Boisvert smiled. "Seriously, April, you have a great talent. Dr. Boisvert loved everything you cooked. Everyone loved it. And your jellies and jams…superb. You should go into business for yourself."

April almost laughed. Or almost sobbed—she wasn't sure which. Her little dream was farther away than ever. "Oh, I don't think so."

"The entrepreneurial road is not for everyone, that's for

certain," she said, getting to her feet. "I'd better get going before Dr. Boisvert comes looking for me."

April stood. "Thanks for stopping by."

"*Bon chance ma chère*. I'm so sorry it didn't work out. If I hear of anything, I'll let you know, if that's all right?"

"Yes, please. You have my cell number?"

"I do."

With a last nod, Mrs. Boisvert left and April went back to her packing.

And her thoughts.

Her daughter was safe, and that was more important than anything else in the world. But that didn't stop her from worrying. From missing Sidney like crazy. Like she'd been gone for a hundred years. Or from grasping tight to the balled up tissues in her hand, ready to cry again.

When was Scott going to call? He'd had plenty of time to talk to Sidney, hadn't he?

She packed a few more of her well-seasoned sauté pans into the box, topped it with crumpled paper, then closed it up. Grabbing the huge tape dispenser, she taped the box closed. Then she turned back to cupboards and the dishes standing ready for packing. The little suite had been furnished, with a cupboard full of dishes, but like most women, April had her special ones. Nothing expensive or extravagant, but they were the first set of dishes she'd ever owned, bought when Sidney was just a baby. The beautiful chocolate fondue set that Scott had bought for her.

Despite herself, tears welled again.

She was not one to cry easily, or often, but today she couldn't seem to stop. She'd cried tears of fear, tears of relief. Tears of frustration and sorrow and yes, a little self-pity. How could she have any tears left?

She knew what was behind Sid's running away—Scott Standish. Sid had been missing him since he'd left before Thanksgiving.

She should have done a better job preparing her daughter for Scott's return, drilling it into her that he was only here to put some finishing touches to a couple of jobs around the place. For his part, Scott could have called ahead to alert her so she could try to manage the situation better. But he hadn't. He'd just shown up three days ago, and Sidney had greeted him with such hope. Stupid, childish hope.

How could she blame her daughter, though, when she'd felt that same spurt of hope herself when he'd walked through the door? Hope that he'd stay. Hope that he'd be with her. Of course, April had quashed it ruthlessly.

Sidney had hugged Scott like there was no tomorrow. Or like she had on her birthday.

The three of them dining at Pizzeria Napoletana on rue Dante for Sid's favorite thin-crust pizza, then home for the Morgan gals traditional birthday cake—banana, with a slathering of April's own homemade strawberry jam between the layers. Topped with cream cheese icing and sprinkled with chopped pecans.

Naturally, there had been ten candles. Sid had blown them all out in one breath.

"What'd you wish for, Sid the Kid?"

"Can't tell." She grinned like the Cheshire cat, as if she had the biggest secret in the world, or more likely, had made the best wish ever.

Then there'd been the gifts. April had given her the ladybug journal and the complete Harry Potter collection, which Sidney was finally old enough to read. She'd loved them, but her enthusiasm had paled compared to her reception of Scott's gift—the telescope. She'd been over-the-moon elated and had thrown her arms around in him in a big hug.

Scott had hung around to set up the telescope and help Sidney find and identify some stars with the aid of the amateur astronomy guide he'd also given her.

Two days later, his brother had called—he was needed at

home. With the job ninety-nine percent finished, he'd left the next day.

*Poor Sid.* She'd been angry, outraged. She'd tossed that journal—the one she'd so carefully glued Scott's star-tacular card to the cover of—right out the window of their suite. April had retrieved it, but she hadn't seen Sidney add to it since. No scissors and pencil crayons spread out over the table. No sticky glue or glitter to be scrubbed off the vinyl tablecloth.

April went to the fridge and removed the picture of her daughter in the magnetic picture frame. It was one of those school portraits, and wisps of flyaway hair that should have been airbrushed away stood out from her head. Her smile was beautiful, though.

April pressed the picture to her chest, heart aching for her daughter. She understood what it was like to have someone you love leave. Which was why she'd made no attempt to track April's father down and bring him into their lives. And why she'd tried so hard to keep Scott at a safe distance.

She totally got it. The bitter disappointment, the devastation, the anger.

But to do something so stupid as stowing away in the back of a truck? What if there'd been an accident? She'd have been tossed out like a rag doll. Or impaled with some motorcycle part. Oh God, she must have been so cold.

What if—

April's phone rang and she dived for it. Scott, finally!

"Scott? Is Sid okay?" she said immediately. "Did she say anything? You told me your sister's a doctor? Did she—"

"Take it easy, April," he said, his own voice calm and slow. "She's fine. Ember checked her out and she's none the worse for wear. She was hungry and cold. But she's fine."

"Where is she right now? Is she there with you?"

"Not this minute, no. She's upstairs in my sister's room."

"Napping?"

"Not exactly. I'm giving her a time out."

Under different circumstances, the comment would have made April grin. Scott meting out discipline? Now, though, it just sharpened her anxiety. "Why? What's she done?"

"She tried to run away again."

"From the farm?"

"Yes. She snuck out while I thought she was upstairs changing clothes. I don't know what's gotten into her."

"Where did she think she was going?" Dear God in Heaven, what was going on with her daughter?

"I caught up with her and asked her the same thing, but she wouldn't talk to me. Says she won't talk to you, either." She could hear the frustration in his voice. "I know she can be stubborn, but April, this is…"

"Beyond stubborn." She felt tears well again but battled them back. What if she ran away again? She knew nothing about the country. "Is she alone?"

"Don't worry. She won't take off again. Our old dog is babysitting her."

"Axl?"

"You remember."

"Oh yes." She remembered he'd named his dog Axl. That his mom, Margaret, had gotten the dog for a newly-orphaned Scott when he'd come to Harkness to live with them. She also remembered Scott liked old black and white movies. That his big brother, Titus, had taught him how to throw a punch, and that in his younger, wilder days, he'd had occasion to throw a few. He loved dill pickle chips but never adopted that Canadian taste for ketchup chips. That some nights he'd sneak out of the house and wander to a place he called Slamm's Landing—best place ever to think about your life. On clear nights when the sky was cloudless, you could practically reach up and touch the stars. Oh, and Crooked Man Cave was apparently just as good.

April remembered everything he'd said on those late nights when they'd traded stories. She also remembered sharing something else with him. Soul-stirring kisses, on that little sofa in the living room, while Sid slept soundly in her own room.

She wet her lips. “What do you mean, babysitting?”

“He tried to warn me when she got out the first time. Whined and barked, but I ignored him.”

“Did you say she was upstairs? And aren’t the stairs hard for Axl?”

“He seems to be managing them okay, and he really likes her,” Scott said. “He’s not going to be happy with me when I take her back.”

“About that…”

“Don’t worry, I’ll keep an eagle eye on her the whole way. We’ll leave early in the morning and should be back in Montreal by—”

“No, I’ll come get her. I’ll come to Harkness.” She blurted out the words so quickly, they surprised even her. But it made sense. She’d have to drive through New Brunswick anyway to get to Nova Scotia where Harley lived. She looked around the apartment. There wasn’t much to pack.

“Are you sure?”

“I’m sure.”

“So you’re going to drive down here, then back home?”

She bit her lip. “Close enough.” She couldn’t tell him she was going to stay with Harley. She’d told him a little about growing up in the Morgan household, and he’d try to fix everything for her. Try to help because that was just the kind of man he was.

“Well, it’ll be good to see you, April.”

Her throat ached, not just from the crying now. Because, dammit, it would be good to see him too. Painful but good.

Oh, it would be so, so easy to let herself love him. When he was around, he was good, steady, and steadfast. But he was still a rambling man. Next stop, northern Alberta.

So all she said was, “Take good care of my little girl. I’ll see you soon.”

"Try not to worry. I'll keep her safe until you get here. Drive carefully. And whatever's bothering her…we'll figure it out."

"Bye, Scott."

"Bye, April."

Two silent seconds later—with so much unspoken between them—she disconnected the call.

# – five –

SID SAT perfectly still on the third step from the top of the staircase, leaning forward. Close enough to listen in on Scott's conversation with her mother, yet near enough to the landing that she could dart back up and into Ember's room where she was supposed to be serving her time out.

For eavesdropping purposes, it wasn't ideal. She had to really strain to hear his words. But if she slid her butt any further down the stairs, poor old Axl—her newly acquired canine shadow—might head down after her. He'd had a hard enough time climbing up the stairs, she didn't want to see him struggle back down, or maybe even fall. She also didn't want his noisy, thumping steps to give her presence away. She glanced back at the dog, who sat at the head of the stairs as though debating whether or not to start down.

She held up her hand in a clear *stop* gesture and whispered, "Stay, boy." Axl's response was to thump his tail on the floor. *Darn it!*

"Hush, Axl!" she whispered, a little louder this time, but he only thumped harder.

She tried turning away and ignoring the dog. Thankfully, that worked. Axl stopped wagging and laid his head down, the breath whooshing out of him in a kind of groan.

She'd missed some of the exchange, dang it. She ducked

her head even lower, listening hard. Had Scott moved outside? Or into another room, beyond her hearing? Then she heard his voice again.

"Try not to worry. I'll keep her safe until you get here. Drive carefully."

Here? Her mother was coming *here*, as in Harkness, New Brunswick?

That meant there was still time. There was still a chance! She knew it.

And Sid knew something else—she'd been right to stow away in the back of Scott's truck. As cold and dark and grease-stinky as it had been, she'd done the right thing. Okay, yeah, it had been a dangerous thing to do. She'd never admit it, but she'd been petrified going into that truck stop when it was still dark outside. But she'd do it all over again for this chance. There was no better place to wish on the stars than Harkness, New Brunswick. That's what Scott had told her, and Scott never lied, even when the truth sucked.

Now, here she was in Harkness, and her mother was coming! Her plan was working already.

It would have been best to get to Slamm's Landing, but that wasn't going to happen. She realized that now. It had been silly to try, especially without her sneakers. And yeah, that whole not-knowing-where-the-heck-it-was thing.

Scott had been so disappointed with her when she'd sneaked off. It made her stomach hurt just to think of that look on his face. But she couldn't tell him what she was trying to do. If he knew what she was wishing for, it could spoil everything. Everyone knew telling your birthday wish could ruin it, and this was so much bigger, so much more important than anything she'd wished for before. She just couldn't risk it.

But it was looking like she didn't have to get to Slamm's Landing after all. Because earlier today, she'd wished on those Harkness stars even though she couldn't see them in the daytime sky, and now her mother was coming here!

Sid bit her lip. Her wishing might have worked to get her mom here, but that was far from a guarantee that they'd stay. She couldn't slack off. She had to keep wishing and wishing and wishing.

Everything depended on it.

*Everything.*

# — six —

TWO DAYS later, Scott Standish sat on the back step, sneaking an early morning cigarette. He glanced at his watch—not yet five o'clock. Real early. Cold too.

He exhaled the smoke, then drew and exhaled another breath, watching the white cloud of vapor hang in the air a few seconds, then vanish. It had been this cold the other morning when Sid had been riding in that back of that truck. Poor mite. She'd pressed herself right up against the box. Between that and the tarp, she hadn't been in the direct wind, but there would have been lots of cold air eddying around back there. And her with nothing more than the clothes on her back and a child's sleeping bag that had no doubt been purchased more for its Disney print than its insulating power. Thank God for Ember. Her assessment was mild hypothermia. He'd been distressed by her deep shivering and chattering teeth, but Ember had been glad to see it. Something about her heat regulating system still working. And she'd come around quickly.

If anything had happened to that little girl, he never would have forgiven himself.

There was a bump on the kitchen door behind him. Automatically, he cupped his cigarette in his hand, hiding it down by his leg. The noise came again and he recognized it as Axl scratching to be let out.

He crossed the porch and opened the door. Axl lumbered across the porch and down the wide steps to the lawn, sniffed a bush, and then peed.

Scott lifted his cigarette and took another haul. God, twenty-eight years old and still sneaking smokes.

Arden always pointedly ignored the lingering scent in the air or the grinding of boot to ground to extinguish a suddenly dropped cigarette. That was guilt-inducing enough, but it was the wrath of his doctor sister he most wanted to avoid.

It wasn't like he lit up all the time. Just when he had something on his mind.

It was a wonder he hadn't smoked a pack since yesterday. Or that he'd slept at all. What little sleep he'd gotten had been filled with dreams of April.

He thought he'd left those behind when he left Montreal this last time. The dreams had persisted for the nearly two weeks he'd been home, but he'd put that down to knowing he was going back to Montreal to finish things up. His brain wouldn't let her go, knowing he'd see her again. But when he'd said his final goodbye, he'd fully expected to be on his way to April-free sleep.

Then Sid had popped up from beneath that tarp like a jack-in-the-box, and his mind had hopped right back on that treadmill.

He took a final haul from the cigarette, then bent and ground it out in the dirt. Picking it up to dispose of in the garbage, he called to Axl. "Come on, boy. Let's go inside and I'll feed you."

The dog glanced at him, chuffed out his own breath of white vapor, then moseyed to another bush.

"Fine. Stay out then."

Axl swished his tail, then headed toward the barn and whatever mischief he could get into at this early hour. Hopefully, he wouldn't surprise a skunk.

Scott glanced at his watch again to check the time.

*She'd be here soon.*

The thought filled him with an anticipation that scared the shit out of him.

Scowling, he turned on his heel and went inside.

The sound of an approaching vehicle brought Scott's head up, but even before he saw it, he realized it wasn't a car's engine. A few seconds later, the milk truck lumbered into view, headed out to Escher's dairy farm.

There wasn't much on the Shadow Road—just Standish Farm, a few scattered homes, and near the end, Bram Escher's dairy farm—but it was a through road, so it did get a little traffic. This morning, with each car that passed, he'd looked up from what he was doing outside the old storage shed to see if it was April.

So had his sidekick.

Sid had bunked down with Ember last night and had crept down the steps, fully clothed, at six o'clock. Scott had made her poached eggs on toast, which she'd devoured. Afterward, with a cup of milk, she'd demolished a handful of Mrs. Budaker's gingersnaps, which she pronounced "really quite good." And Scott hadn't even had to pry the cookies from Titus's cold, dead hand. He'd handed them over to Sid voluntarily. Wonders would never cease. The whole head-over-heels-in-love thing had had amazing effects on his big bro.

Titus wasn't the only one who'd mellowed. Sid was positively civil this morning. And very talkative. Probably a product of nerves. She was definitely a little bit anxious, knowing her mom was coming.

April had decided to make it a two-day trip, stopping for the night in Rivière-du-Loup. Mother and daughter had spoken on the phone last night. Judging by Sidney's demeanor, that second conversation had gone better than the first. Scott had overheard Sid's end of the latter talk, and while it was clear April couldn't wait to be reunited with Sid, the kid was definitely in hot water.

At least Sid was talking. Not about why she'd run away; she still refused to discuss that topic. But everything else under the sun was apparently fair game as they sorted through the cans of exterior paint Titus had bought in the spring with such good intentions.

"So why'd you name him Axl?" Sidney asked.

"Who?"

She rolled her eyes. "Axl, silly."

He loosened the lid on a full can of red exterior barn paint and popped the top off, depositing it beside the can on the makeshift sawhorse-and-plank table. "Titus suggested the name and we went with it. He used to listen to this metal band—"

"Guns N' Roses! He's named after *that* Axl? Axl Rose?"

Scott's eyes widened. "You know Guns N' Roses?"

She propped her hands on her hips, a gesture so like her mother's that she must have picked it up from April. "I'm not a child."

"Of course not. You're a…hmmm…"

"A kid."

He grabbed a stir stick and started to stir the paint, gazing down into the can so she wouldn't see his grin. Apparently, there was a critical distinction between being a child and being a kid that he'd failed to comprehend.

"How long before we can paint?"

"Soon. But I'd like the wood to be a little dryer." He kept stirring. "When the temperature drops at night, there's some condensation that forms."

"Dew, you mean?"

"Sort of. But when it gets as cold as it was last night, it's more of a light frost. I'm using latex paint, and it'll stand a little water, but the dryer the surface, the better."

"The sunny side looks dry," she observed.

"It probably is, but generally, we try to stay out of the sun when we're painting so the paint doesn't dry too fast."

"So you move around the building with the sun?"

"You could do," he agreed. "But we're a small crew, and it's a tall barn. We'll finish that north side first, probably over the course of a few days, then I'll move the staging around to the west side. When we finally make our way around to the east face, we'll probably paint later in the day, when the sun has moved around."

She frowned. "There's a lot more to it than I thought there'd be."

"Yeah, but it's such a big job, you want to do it right. Otherwise, you'll wind up having to do it again sooner than you want to 'cause the paint didn't adhere well and starts peeling, or just plain looks crappy."

"I hope the painting is more fun than the scraping was yesterday."

He laughed at her scrunched-up nose. He didn't enjoy scraping off the old paint either. It sucked. "Yeah, it's *way* more fun. And really cool to be able to see your progress. But like we talked about, you can only do it for short intervals and you have to take frequent breaks."

"Right. 'Cause repetitive stress injuries are really bad for growing bones."

"Exactly." He was glad to know that she'd absorbed Ember's lecture. He'd taken it to heart too, as witnessed by the egg timer he'd swiped from the kitchen so he wouldn't forget to enforce the breaks. His ass would be grass if he let the kid hurt herself.

"Yup, it's a big job." Her gaze went to the Far South Barn, the job in question, and she nodded in a determined way—one he was familiar with. "Good thing I'm here, huh?"

"You bet." Truthfully, he *was* glad she was here—not so much for the help, but for the company. It also made it easier to keep tabs on her.

"Wanna help me carry some of this stuff down to the barn?"

"Load me up."

He handed her two paint brushes, two paint pails with plastic liners in them, and some well-spattered drop cloths, which she tucked under her arms. Usually he didn't bother with drop cloths outside, but with a kid painting, he figured the risk of a spill probably went up.

"Race ya!"

Sidney took off toward the barn, her brown hair swinging behind her. He grinned, then scraped off his stir stick and replaced the cover on the paint can. She was such a little live wire. And she was charming Uncle Arden too.

Yesterday, after her short stint at scraping the barn, Arden and Faye had driven her to Crandler. They'd treated her to lunch at Chloe's Back Porch. She'd come home raving about the biscuits, but opined there'd been too much basil in the sausage soup. Her foodie critiques had cracked everyone up, but they'd all had the good judgment not to laugh. Even Titus.

Titus still wasn't Sid's biggest fan—he couldn't fathom why she wouldn't explain her reason for trying to run away, or more to the point, why Scott accepted her refusal. The guy could be a bit rigid sometimes. Still, even he was warming up to the kid. Uncle Arden and Faye had stopped by Titus's new bike repair shop and Sid had come home with a temporary tattoo of a motorcycle on her right bicep. She'd flexed it proudly. It looked a lot like his old Bonneville, actually. Sid explained it was a custom temporary tattoo his brother had ordered for promotional purposes, a redundant explanation, considering that the words *Classic Bikes by Titus* were emblazoned beneath the bike image.

That was yesterday. She'd been glad to escape the bulk of the scraping. Today, Sid was all his.

And that was kind of okay.

He grabbed some supplies, snagged the gallon of paint and headed toward the barn. By the time he caught up to her, she'd put the stuff down carefully on the ground and had opened the smaller paint brush. He'd bought it new for her, knowing the bigger ones they usually used would be too heavy. She was running the soft bristles over the palm of her hand, back and forth. She'd done the same thing at the Boisverts' once, peeling the cardboard cover off a new paintbrush for him. Of course, there he hadn't been able to let her help for obvious reasons, liability being chief among them, but she'd watched from a safe distance. She'd become his shadow.

"Mom's here!" The new paintbrush hit the ground and Sid took off running toward the familiar Hyundai with Quebec plates that had pulled into the yard.

*April.*

Scott put his own burdens down and wiped his brow. Ran a hand through his hair. Then did it again. And though he didn't run like Sid had, he was glad to see April. More than he should be. Oh, hell, way more than he *wanted* to be.

He walked over to the two Morgan women, who were still hugging beside the little car.

April finally drew back from her daughter.

"Hi, Scott." She met his gaze over Sid's head. "Thanks for taking care of my girl."

"No problem. Good to see you again, April."

"You too."

Her smile was genuine, despite the long haul she'd just made in that tiny Hyundai. It didn't boast a lot of room at the best of times, and right now, it was jam-packed. He leaned closer to see what was taking up all the space.

*What the hell?* It looked like she had her whole world packed up in there. If she was going to head straight back to

Montreal today or tomorrow, there shouldn't be anything more in the car than an overnight bag on the back seat, and maybe a bag for Sidney too. But the car had been efficiently packed to the top of the seat in the back with boxes. A clean plastic bag with winter coats was stuffed down into the footwell of the front passenger side. Scott guessed if he popped the small trunk, he'd find it full too.

He looked back at April, a question in his eyes. With her daughter still wrapped in her arms, she bit her lip and shook her head slightly. Enough that only he'd notice.

After one more squeeze, Sidney pulled back from her mother. "So how much trouble am I in?"

April looked down at her daughter. As happy as the two had been to reunite—and Scott could only imagine April's relief—there would be consequences.

"A fair amount, Sidney Kathleen Morgan."

Yikes. Three-name trouble.

"And not just for running away," April added. "I know about the credit card you *borrowed.*"

*Credit card?* This was news to Scott.

"The Boisverts were pretty unhappy—Dr. Boisvert especially."

"They were going to kill the dog if they didn't get enough money for the surgeries he needs! I had a…*moral responsibility* to save his life."

"That's not going to wash," April said. "Moral responsibility and stealing credit cards? They don't go hand in hand."

"But Dagwood…"

"I get it, Sidney. And I know how much you love dogs, but what you did was wrong."

"Sorry, Mom." She said it like she meant it.

"We'll talk. And we'll figure out how you're going to pay me back."

Sid's eyes widened. "Pay *you* back?"

"Every last cent. Who did you think would be footing that huge bill, Sid?"

"So Dr. Boisvert was pretty mad?"

"Wouldn't you be if someone stole from you?"

Sidney's' bottom lip trembled as she looked from her mother to Scott. She blinked back the tears and lowered her head. "Will I have to go to…youth jail?"

"No. But Sid, this is not a path you want to be traveling."

Scott felt sorrier for April than he did for Sid. She didn't like this situation—this discussion—any better than her daughter did. But she had to be tough. It wouldn't do Sid a bit of good to be let off the hook.

God, this whole situation reminded Scott of the time he and Vaughn Lewis had *borrowed* his grandmother's scooter. School had just let out for the summer and the boys were thirteen and bored. It was a lax time for chores; spring activity on the farm was behind them and the harvesting activity was yet to come. Girls were out of reach. So taking Vaughn's grandmother's wheels for a spin out to Rockland Lake while she'd gone to play bingo at the Legion had seemed like a great idea. Not so much, as it turned out. They'd wiped out half way there—the bike's front wheel was completely ruined, the rim bent beyond repair.

Grandma Lewis had laughed it off. No harm—she was getting too old to drive it anyway, she assured Arden when he'd come to retrieve Scott. But that wasn't the way his uncle had seen it. For the rest of the summer, every Tuesday right after lunch, he'd driven Scott over to Mrs. Lewis's house to mow and rake her lawn. It took him all afternoon.

And every Tuesday that summer, as he'd sweated and swatted at the clouds of mosquitoes that rose up from the grass, he'd chafed at his punishment. *It wasn't like the old lady would be missing that ancient scooter.*

Then there was his first year of high school, the year he'd gotten into so many fights with Dundas Bloom. It seemed like

Uncle Arden got called to meet him at the principal's office a lot that year. But this time, the activity had been extracurricular. Scott had found himself on the town's train bridge with a can of orange spray paint and too much time on his hands. The trains rarely ran through Harkness anymore, the bridge over the Prince River seldom used. So he'd decided to spruce up the black-painted bridge with a dash of orange.

Who'd ever know it was him?

Arden knew. He'd noticed Scott's orange fingertips that night, and seen the train bridge art the next morning. Scott really was sorry, embarrassed—it had seemed like a good idea at the time. Though the railroad crew had painted over it within hours the next day, Scott was still in trouble. Still had to be responsible. He had to apologize in person to the stationmaster, pay for the paint used to cover it up. Oh, but that wasn't all. He was grounded for a week, missing his first-ever high school dance.

He'd learned his lesson—do the crime, do the punishment.

He'd been pretty pissed at his uncle on both occasions. And though the anger wore away, it had taken a few years before he got it—until he understood it all. And only now did he get a glimpse of how Arden must have felt.

"Dr. Boisvert's gonna kill me, isn't he?" Sidney said.

"No, he won't."

"Bet he'll yell at me."

April bit her lip, looked at Scott as she answered Sidney. "He won't."

They weren't going back. Scott knew it and marked April with a serious, questioning look. She shook her head in a *don't-say-a-word* way. Her eyes were filled with worry, tiredness. Almost an air of defeat.

"Sid, do me a favor?" Scott said.

"What?"

"There are a couple more paintbrushes—yellow-handled ones—in the storage shed. I was thinking they might work better on those shingles. Think you could go ask Uncle Arden to help you find them?"

"Sure." She started to bolt again but stopped herself. She turned to her mom, her face serious. "I really am sorry, Mom."

April nodded. "I know."

As soon as Sid was out of earshot, April turned to Scott. "Yellow-handled ones, huh? That makes a difference?"

"Thought we could talk."

"So you sent her on a wild goose chase?"

He shrugged. "They're really there, stashed away somewhere. But when Sidney goes in and tells Uncle Arden I sent her looking and that you've arrived…"

"Ah, a delay tactic. He'll know to not find them too quickly."

"Yes."

April smiled weakly. "I've been so worried. I was scared she'd try to run again, and not knowing the area…I've been imagining the worst."

"We've kept a good eye on her. Dad's in the kitchen, and then there's her shadow." He nodded toward the back step where a tail-wagging Axl got up and followed Sidney into the house. "He keeps an even closer watch than we do."

"She's always loved dogs."

"Maybe they'll let her have one wherever you're going?"

"Where we're going? What makes you think we're going anywhere?"

Scott put his hand on the hood of the Hyundai. "I know this isn't just packed for a road trip."

She bit her lip, glanced toward the house. "Can we talk someplace more private?"

"There," he said. "The Far South Barn." He led her across the grass to the outbuilding. Skirting the pile of painting supplies he'd just deposited, he opened the door for her. She preceded him in, then stopped.

"Give it a minute and your eyes will adjust." He stepped in behind her and closed the door.

It was a bright day outside, but the well-maintained barn had very little light coming in. High windows allowed a few streams of it to fall down into the room. The loft was a different story. Though those wide doors were closed now, on more than a few mornings he'd watched the sunrise from there.

"What a beautiful old building."

He murmured an agreement, but couldn't take his eyes off her face as she looked around. She seemed to be drinking the place in. The soft lighting, the smells, the motes of dust dancing in the focused streams of sunlight

"Lots of memories here, I bet." With a soft smile on her lips, she turned her face up to him.

Memories? Yeah, the place was steeped in them.

And he was about to make another one.

He pulled her to him.

They'd agreed not to do this. Every time they'd fooled around, one or the other of them had pulled back, remembering why it was such a disastrous idea. But as with those other times, she went into his arms easily, eagerly. When he covered her mouth, she met his demand with a matching hunger.

Just like that, he was kissing her like there was no tomorrow.

# — seven —

APRIL WAS drowning, but she didn't care. She wrapped her arms around his neck and went up on tiptoe, the better to press her breasts against his lean strength. He groaned and pulled her hips closer. Another wave of desire washed over her when she felt his hardness against her belly, but she recklessly submersed herself in it.

Then he was moving her, backing her up. Within seconds, she found the small of her back bumping up against something. Before she could figure out what it was, he lifted her and deposited her onto a hard surface. A wooden sideboard or storage cabinet of some kind, she thought. He urged her legs apart and moved between them. With his hands now free, they roamed her body at will. From her hair to her nape. From her breasts to the outsides of her thighs. She gloried in every sensation. Then he lifted her T-shirt out of the way and bent to press a hot, open-mouthed kiss to the top of her left breast above the lacy cup of her bra.

For whatever reason—maybe the cool air on her midriff—she finally came to her senses.

She gripped his shoulders, pushing him away. "Stop." She sucked in a shuddering breath. "Scott, we can't…"

"Right." He stepped back, turning away to adjust himself.

Oh, God, what was she thinking? As if her life wasn't

already complicated enough. The troubles with Sidney. This move to Nova Scotia to live with her jerk of a brother. The fifth move in her daughter's young life. Not to mention losing her job and her one and only chance to meet K.Z. McCoy. Top that off with how she felt about Scott…

He was a man who lived life on the road; she was a mother. She would not feel for him. *Could not* feel for him. It would be sheer stupidity. And so dangerous for Sidney's heart. For her own.

April eased herself off the sideboard—it was definitely a sideboard, rustic and rough and probably built expressly for the parties held here—and smoothed her clothing. Well, best it could be smoothed after so many cramped hours in the car.

Scott pulled a deep breath and ran his hands through his hair.

"I'm sorry," she said. "I shouldn't have—"

"No, I'm sorry." He waved off her apology. "You're tired after that drive, emotional from the reunion. Unsettled, literally. I shouldn't have kissed you."

"I'm glad you did." She forced a smile. "I know it doesn't change things, but I can't say I regret it."

He smiled back at her. "Me either."

"So." She cleared her throat. "This is the famous Far South Barn, huh?" She walked a little deeper into the near-empty expanse, giving herself a moment to settle before she turned back to face him.

"Famous?" Scott smiled. "I don't know about that. Maybe in Harkness."

"Well, Harkness is the Heart of the Prince Region, isn't it?" She cocked her head. "Unofficially."

Scott lifted an eyebrow.

"You mentioned it to me once. Harkness is the heart of the Prince Region, and the Standish Farm the heart of Harkness.

"You've got a good memory."

*Especially when it comes to you, Scott Standish.* But she couldn't have him thinking that. She shrugged. "Can't help it." She tapped her head. "This brain is a steel trap."

"Is that how you dash off those dishes without cracking a recipe book? From memory? Or is it all improvisation?"

"All cooks improvise with some elements, but the core of the dish is usually a carefully tested recipe."

"Ah, I remember. We've had this discussion before. You have to have the science down before you dabble with the art, right?"

"Exactly." She looked around the barn. "You know, I can almost picture this place full of people, dancing, drinking punch…"

"The band always sets up there," Scott pointed to a raised section of flooring at the narrow end of the barn farthest from the door.

The place actually reminded her of every elementary school gym she'd ever seen. Except currently, there were no parents sitting in folding chairs, their winter coats unzipped as they waited for the curtain to open at the Christmas concert. She remembered all of Sid's concerts. Her kindergarten class's song-and-dance routine to the tune of *Jingle Bell Rock.* The time the two of them had sat up nights attaching silver glitter to stars bound for the stage backdrop, and red and green sequins to an elf hat. *We Wish You a Merry Christmas* sung through a toothless grin that made it sound more like *with you a Merry Chrithmath.* April had sat all by herself in those various gymnasiums with all the other moms, dads, grandparents, and aunts.

"And see all these tables along this wall?" He gestured to a row of five mismatched tables and sideboards—one of which she'd just been sitting on—lining the wall behind them.

"That's where you set up the meals?" She could picture it so clearly, those surfaces laden with food and punch bowls. If she were handling it, she'd move one of those tables to relocate the liquid refreshments to a separate area. That would clear some of the congestion around the buffet tables.

"Yup. It's officially a potluck, but we'd always provide a few main course dishes. Folks would bring lawn chairs and we'd line them up along the walls. Of course, the kids never really needed chairs. Too much room to run, and too much energy to sit still. And the atmosphere..."

"What?" she prompted when he let his words trail off.

He shrugged. "There's an excitement. An air of anticipation. You just know something's going to happen."

April drew in a breath and let it out slowly as she looked around the barn. Her eyes had adjusted now to the low lighting. The beauty. She could see it—how the place would take on that atmosphere.

"Anyway, the kids run from one end of the barn to the other. We have games for them. Little contests and stuff."

"It's beautiful here." When she turned back around he was staring at her, a serious look on his face.

"April, what's going on? Why is the car packed?"

She raised a finger to her lips in a shushing gesture, then crept to the barn door and opened it. Light spilled in as she looked around the yard. No sign of Sid. She closed the door again.

When she turned back around, Scott was watching her quizzically.

"Sorry about that. I just didn't want Sidney to overhear me."

"That bad?"

"The Boisverts fired me."

He didn't look surprised. Why should he be? Sidney stealing Mr. Boisvert's credit card to rescue that dog from euthanasia. Running away, disrupting the Boisvert's courtship of a critically important potential client.

"That sucks, April. I'm sorry."

She shrugged as if it was nothing. But it was—they both knew it.

"So they just told you to get out. No notice?"

"They gave me severance pay," she said. "And a week to clear out, but since I was driving down here anyway for Sid, I just left. We'll just keep going."

"Keep going where?" His eyes narrowed.

April paused. "Dartmouth," she whispered.

"Jesus, April. *Him?* Your brother." His jaw tightened. While Scott had shared tales from his childhood, April had shared with him a couple of her own. Only life as a Standish in Harkness had been significantly different than life for a female child under Morgan rule.

"Harley's a jerk, but it's just for a little while. Just until I find a good position."

"A position good enough to support you and Sid both," he said, his tone thoughtful.

"Sidney needs the stability. I've tried to give her that."

"You have given her that."

"She's never had a truly permanent home."

"She's had you."

April shook her head. "I know. And I know I've been a good mom. At least I've tried to be. But lately…maybe I've been working too hard at the Boisverts. Didn't pay her enough attention. Kids need that."

"That and a dog."

April laughed darkly. "A dog. Well, that's the last thing Harley would have in his house. Anything that might make a mess doesn't get through the front door." She cringed at that, thinking of Sid's *science projects* spread out over their kitchen in Montreal. Her sneakers and socks, under the dining room table. Marshmallow fights.

"Then maybe the two of you shouldn't use that front door."

"You think he'd make us use the back door?" Her stomach knotted. "Oh, God, he might. That sounds like something he would do."

She put her head in her hands. What the hell was she going

to do? She was so tired. Her muscles ached from the drive and she was scared for the future. For Sidney's future. Tears stung her eyes.

"Hey, don't cry."

She felt the warmth of his hands gripping her shoulders. Earlier his touch had been charged with the potent electricity of desire. Now, it offered only comfort as he urged her into his arms.

"I'm sorry, April. I didn't mean it like that." He folded her tighter against him. "I don't think even Harley would do that."

For a few seconds, she just stood there and breathed him in—the fresh smell of his recently laundered flannel shirt mixed with the clean, male scent that was all his. Reluctantly, she lifted her face from his chest to look up at him. "Then what *did* you mean?"

"I meant, stay here. Rent free. With us."

*With us?*

"Here? Scott Booker Standish, if you think I'm looking for charity from you, then you don't know me very well."

He grinned, no doubt at the full-name treatment. She usually reserved that for her daughter, but if he thought for a minute that—

"Charity? Oh, sweetheart, that's not what I had in mind."

Argh! If all Standish men were this damned cryptic, it was a wonder they'd managed procreation. "Maybe you'd like to elaborate about what you *do* have in mind?"

"Stay here. Let us hire you for the next couple of months."

"But I know nothing about farm work."

Those dimples flashed again. "No, not as a farmhand. I meant doing domestic stuff. Kitchen help—at least for a while. Titus is going to be busy building up his motorcycle restoration business. Ember'll be opening a medical practice and working long hours. It's soon going to get busy with apple-picking, and I'm going to be juggling some house repairs over the next two months. With all of us going full tilt, we could use the help."

"A couple of months?"

"Well, that's how long I'll be here. Two months. Till the first of January, basically."

"Scott, I—"

"Don't say no until you've had a chance to think about it, April. I think it could be good for both of us. I'm in charge of the farm for the rest of the year. Ember and Titus are going to be too busy to do much around here. And while Uncle Arden can make a basic meal, that'll get old fast. I really will need the help keeping this place going."

"I don't know." She chewed the inside of her lip. "I'm not looking for a handout."

He laughed. "A handout? You're kidding, right? You don't know the appetite we Standish men have."

"Don't I? I've fed you, remember."

"What do you say, April? Stay here and help us for a while. You can look around for something else from here—not from that asshole's place in Dartmouth."

"I don't know…"

"It's a real job offer, April. Not charity. If we don't hire you, we'll just give the job to someone else."

Her heart pounded. Every fiber in her being wanted this—wanted to say yes. Wanted to stay here on this farm, in this heart of Harkness, even if just for a while. Stay here with Scott. But she wasn't sure if that was a good thing or not.

"And another thing," Scott said. "Sidney can take care of Axl for a little while. She would probably love—"

"You bet I'd love that!" The barn door flew open, and Sidney, face red from the cold wind and the sun, burst in. She held yellow-handled paintbrushes in each hand.

"Sidney Morgan, were you eavesdropping?" April asked.

"No, I was listening. There's a difference. But the point is…can we, Mom? Please?"

Scott looked at April. "What do you say?"

# – eight –

SCOTT SHOVED the carafe into the coffee maker and hit the button to start the second pot of the morning. The first one had gone down quickly over introductions and small talk.

"So, I was just telling April that we need some domestic help with cooking and such," he said. "Since she's an experienced chef, I told her the job is hers if she'll take it." He glanced around at everyone. Titus's eyebrows shot up, but that was the only indication any of them gave that Scott had just dropped a bombshell. "Can you help me persuade her? She seems to think this is a charity offer."

He glanced at April, who clutched her near-empty coffee cup like a lifeline.

Ember was the first to react. "Well, you certainly have my vote, April. I hope you'll decide to stay with us. Scott has raved about your cooking." His sister downed her coffee and leaped up from the table. With a wink at Sid, she grabbed her jacket from the hook on the wall. "I'm heading over to the clinic if anyone needs me."

"It's been nice to meet you, Ember," April said. "Scott's told me so much about you. About all the family."

"Well, only believe the good stuff. Unless it's about Scott, or Titus, then only believe the bad."

"Hey, watch it," Titus said.

Ember laughed. "Anyway, I'm meeting with the decorator around eleven. She's bringing fabric samples for the drapes and color chips for the paint."

Their sister was all smiles as she talked about the practice she was opening in MacQueen Square. Ember's fiancé Jace had bought the small, six-unit strip mall. It was two streets west of Main, but still within the downtown. Every unit was vacant right now apart from the one Ember had leased, but Jace aimed to change that. Having a doctor's office anchoring one end would certainly help, given the traffic it was bound to generate. Jace had scooped the property right out from under WRP Holdings, paying the former owner, Jim Wistaff, handsomely enough to beat his stepbrother's offer. Terry had been furious. Make that even more furious—he was still pissed off at Jace for undermining him on the sale of the Standish Land. And pissed off at every single Standish. They were sworn enemies now.

Scott found himself smiling.

Ember pulled on her coat and wrapped a cherry-red scarf around her neck. "Seriously, it would really be a great relief if you took the job."

"Thank you," April said.

"I'm off. Bye, guys!" With her usual speed, Ember swept out to a chorus of goodbyes.

"This is all happening so fast," April murmured.

Scott could very easily have added an *amen* to that. Now that April and Sid were here, he was loath to see them go. Especially to her idiot brother, Harley.

"It makes perfect sense to me," Arden said. "We could sure use the help around here."

"He's right," Titus said, weighing in. "Between Dad and me, we can boil vegetables and fry up steaks, but that's about the extent of our culinary skills. So if you're half the cook Scott's been bragging you up to be, you've got my vote too."

"Oh my gosh, Titus, you're in for a treat!" That

enthusiastic endorsement came from Sidney herself. Everyone looked her way

"Is that so?" Titus drawled.

Sidney had perched herself on a tall stool beside the kitchen counter. "You've never tasted blueberry pancakes until you've tasted Mom's. Oh, and do you guys like bacon?"

Scott, Titus, and Uncle Arden exchanged glances. Almost simultaneously, they nodded.

"Well, you haven't lived until you've had one of Mom's Caesar salads from an oven-warm bacon bowl. It's crazy good." She looked around the room, nodding encouragingly.

"My mouth's already watering," Uncle Arden said. "Maybe we could have that with supper on Friday?" He smiled at April. "I mean if you'll take the position."

*Thank you, Uncle Arden.*

"I really don't know what to say," April said.

"I do," Sid put in. "We'll stay, Arden."

"Whoa there a minute, Sidney," her mother said. "Not so fast." She shook her head in an *is-this-really-happening* way.

Scott couldn't blame her. In the last forty-eight hours, her world had turned upside down.

"It really does sound like a great offer," April said. "Sidney would have to be enrolled in school…"

"No problem," Sid said. "I'm smart as hel—uh, heck. I can handle this, Mom."

April waved her off, as if handling it hadn't been a worry. As if her daughter's ability was a given. "I know how smart you are, Sid. But…"

"But I've changed schools before."

"I know, Ladybug. Too many times."

Scott knew she'd be more than fine. She *was* smart as hell. If he knew Sid the Kid, she'd be leading the class by Christmas.

*Then what happens for Sidney? For April?*

He shook the thought away.

"So what would the job entail, exactly?" April's hands were folded in front of her on the kitchen table. Neatly. Definitely in down-to-business mode.

Thankfully, Uncle Arden was quick to answer.

"Meal planning, shopping to stock the stuff you need, cooking, maybe some cleaning," he said.

She frowned. "I can't see that filling *all* my time."

"Don't forget the Halloween party!" Sidney said.

"Halloween party?" That was the first Scott had heard of a Halloween party in…well, years. By the look on everyone else's face, he was pretty sure it was the first any of them had heard about it.

The surprise must have registered with Sidney too. She looked at Scott.

"You said the party was a yearly event here. A big one. There was bobbing for apples, and pin the tail on Frankenstein, and that the old folks would bring real caramel apples—Mom makes those. And fudge. She makes that too. Almost everyone dressed up, even the adults. Don't you remember?" She looked at him imploringly.

"I do." He grinned. "One year Titus dressed up as Batman. Split his tights bobbing for apples. And all I can say is thank goodness for the cape."

Sid giggled.

Titus shook his head. "Ah, that never gets old, does it? Oh wait, it *is* old. Like almost fifteen freakin' years."

Arden put a hand on Titus's shoulder before the sibling one-upmanship escalated. "You know, boys, we're sprucing up the Far South Barn anyway. I know it'll be busy with the apple-picking, but with April's help, we could get the place ready for a little Halloween event. Maybe something small scale."

From Scott's experience, no matter the intentions, there was no such thing as *small scale* when it came to parties in the Far South Barn. Not when word got around that one was happening. And if they went ahead with it, it would be the first Halloween party in that barn since the Standish kids were in high school. Once his mom, Margaret, had taken ill, that one tradition had ended.

For the community's sake, Titus had ensured that the Christmas dances continued, usually with a crap-load of help from Ember. Scott felt that familiar dusting of guilt. He could have done more; should have done more. While Arden approved, he hadn't had the heart to participate at those events, beyond making a brief appearance. The Halloween event, on the other hand, had been easy to let go. With the Standish kids grown and two out of three of them no longer living in Harkness, it just seemed like too much work.

Scott was glad to see Uncle Arden offering to resuscitate the tradition, apparently happily. That was huge, given his ambivalence about anything that happened in that barn now that Margaret was gone. Sid the Kid seemed to have found an ally.

"A Halloween party?" Titus shrugged. "Yeah, that'd be doable, as long as someone is prepared to do the planning and preparation."

"Excellent." Arden rubbed his hands together. "It also sounds like a good way for our Sidney to make some new friends." He turned to April. "I mean, if you intend to stay."

"Do you really need the help?" She addressed the question to Arden, not Scott.

Scott held his breath as he waited for Arden to answer.

"I know you think we're trying to help you out here," Arden said. "And if it *does* help, so much the better. But you'd really be helping us out too. There's lots to do around here, and this place can use a woman's touch." He looked at his sons sharply. "If either of you tell your sister I said that, I'll skin you both."

Scott looked at April. She met his gaze with those beautiful, changeable brown eyes. At that precise moment, they looked the color of copper pennies. She drew a deep breath and he knew she was going to accept. His heart started thumping crazily, but he couldn't have said whether the spike was from pleasure or trepidation.

April looked at Sid. "You really want this, don't you, Ladybug?"

Axl had been sitting by Sid's stool. As if he could feel the shift, the dog's tail started wagging even before his new friend's feet hit the floor. Sid launched herself into her mother's arms. "Oh, yes! Can we please?"

"We can," she said. "But only until Christmas."

Sid pulled back. "Why just till Christmas?"

"Because…I have another job starting then."

That's the first Scott had heard of it. "Oh, yeah? Where's that?"

She wet her lips. "I…I applied to a small resort in Northern Ontario. They have a position coming available in the new year and they want me to fill it."

"In Northern Ontario?" Arden looked to almost shudder. "Pretty cold part of the country."

"Where specifically?" Titus asked.

April shrugged. "Small town. I don't recall right off."

*Not the best lie Scott had ever heard.*

"But you don't have to take it," Sidney pointed out. "We don't have to leave at Christmas."

April sent Scott a pleading look.

True, he'd only offered her the position for the next two months, but mostly because he didn't think she'd accept anything longer term. But just because *he* was leaving after Christmas didn't mean she had to go too. He just sort of figured there'd be time enough to talk about an extension down the road if he could only get her to accept the job now. Once she settled in, she'd be comfortable here in Harkness in her own right and wouldn't need him around.

But she didn't know that, of course.

When this master plan had come together in his mind, he wasn't sure. But the more he thought it through, the more he wanted to make it happen. For April and Sid.

And crap, was she lying about having that job lined up in Northern Ontario for him? So that Sid wouldn't blame him when the job expired and they had to move on.

Unless…maybe she didn't *want* to stay past Christmas?

He searched her face. She seemed to want him to back up the two-month term, so he did. "That's all the job here is for, Sid, to get us over a hump. You must have missed that part of the conversation when you overheard your mother and me talking."

Titus and Uncle Arden said nothing.

April telegraphed her thanks with her eyes. Well, at least he'd made one of the Morgan girls happy.

"This sounds like our respective problems are solved—a match made in Heaven, as they say," Arden said. "That is if you'll say yes."

April looked at each of them, ending with her daughter. "Sidney, if we stay, there'll have to be a few conditions."

"Like what?"

Scott knew what was coming.

"No more running away," April said sternly. "That's the big one. I've never been so worried in all my life as when I found you missing. And then there was the little thing with sending all that money to the dog shelter."

"Did the Boisverts fire you?"

"Leaving was my decision," she said quickly. "But Dr. Boisvert was very upset."

He knew she hated to lie, especially to her daughter. She really wasn't very good at it. Color rose in her cheeks.

Sid dropped her gaze. Axl nudged her hand and she sank her fingers into his fur. From the rise and fall of her little chest, Scott could see she was near tears.

"You two must want to talk," Scott said. "Have some alone time."

The phone rang—thankfully not the search and rescue distinct ring. Arden excused himself to go answer it.

"I'll give you a hand with the painting, bro," Titus said.

"That'd be great." He nodded at April and Sid, "Later ladies."

The two men walked in silence to the Far South Barn. But it was a silence Scott didn't figure would last. He was right.

As soon as they reached the barn, Titus said, "So where are we going to keep everybody?"

"Keep them?"

"Sleeping arrangements," Titus said. "I know Ember doesn't mind sharing the room with Sidney—she's been spending most of her nights with Jace anyway."

"Does Uncle Arden know this?"

Titus cast him a get-real look. "She's twenty-eight, Scott."

True, but she was still their kid sister.

"Maybe we could move things out of Mom's old sewing room?" Titus said. "Fix it up temporarily for April. Pretty small room, though. Probably wouldn't hold more than a single bed and a dresser."

"She can sleep in my room," Scott said.

Titus raised an eyebrow.

"I'll sleep in the loft." He nodded up toward the hay mow. "I do that half the time when I'm home anyway." He'd bought a latex foam mattress, lugged it up there, and laid it out on a sleeping platform he'd constructed. The air was fresher out here, especially when he threw open the wide hayloft windows to stargaze. When he left again, the mattress and blankets could be quickly rolled up and shoved into the truck bed chest he'd bought secondhand for rodent-safe storage.

"That'd work," Titus conceded. He strode over to the staging Scott had erected yesterday, testing its strength. Apparently, it met his approval. He turned back to Scott. "You know you're going to be April's employer, right?"

"You think she can't do the job?"

He shook his head. “I’m sure she’s more than capable of taking care of things around here. You didn’t exactly look underfed when you got here.”

“Then what are you saying?”

“I’ve never been accused of understanding women—”

“I know. Everyone’s surprised as hell you ended up with a great gal like Ocean Siliker.”

Titus smiled. “She’s a keeper.”

A *keeper*—oh God, why did that word send cold fingers up his spine? Why did it give him the urge to get out while the getting was good? Like he would be the end of December. His mind flashed to April, Sidney—and having to say goodbye to them all over again.

Titus continued, “But I’m guessing she’d be out of here in a flash if she thought it was some sort of pity project.”

“She would.” He cast Titus a look. “By the way, thanks for backing me up in there when I dropped that on you guys.”

“No problem. But my point is you can’t be with her while she’s working here. No hanky-panky.”

“Hanky-panky?” Scott snorted. “What are we? Twelve? And what makes you think I’m interested in her that way?”

“’Cause you’re not a fool. Well, not much of one. She’s beautiful, purportedly talented in the kitchen, and it would seem she’s currently in need of help or shelter. At least two of those things are in your romantic wheelhouse, and I’m not talking about her cooking.”

“She’s also a single mother who has no interest in a temporary hook-up with a rolling stone like me.”

“Then I guess we can add smart to the list of her attributes.”

“Gee, thanks, brother.”

“You said it yourself—not much future for her in that kind of relationship, especially with the kid in tow. I was just thinking you don’t want her feeling this job you offered her comes with any…expectations.”

"Of course it doesn't!"

He held up his hands. "Glad to hear it. But I saw the way you looked at her. Maybe I don't know much about women, but I know *you*. You've got feelings for April. And the child."

"Kid."

"Come again?"

"Sid's a kid. Not a child. There's a difference, evidently."

Titus scratched a hand along the back of his neck. "The thing is, I know you didn't hire April thinking there was any expectation of sex. Just make sure *she* knows."

Scott nodded. "Got it."

"Another thing," Titus said. "I know you're running the farm now for the next few months. Thank you again for that. I'm enjoying the break."

"Least I could do."

"Dad's got a handle on the bookwork," Titus continued. "But where are April's wages going to come from? Have you thought of that?"

He had. "They'll come out of mine."

There had always been a 'wage' paid from the farm to the family in proportion to their responsibility. Even as kids, allowances were given based on how much they contributed. Want more—do more. Ember had worked sixty-hour weeks on her summer vacations in high school to earn what she could for university. When Scott had been saving for his first dirt bike, he'd put in just as many. That was the way it was on the farm too when they were grown. Titus was temporarily stepping down from managing the place, handing over the small salary to Scott, along with the responsibility.

"Even if you split it fifty/fifty with her, that's not going to be much of a salary—for either of you."

"We won't be splitting it," Scott said. "She can have it all."

# – nine –

"IT'S A start, right?" Sidney put the question to the Harkness sky, awash with more stars than she'd seen in her life.

She pulled Scott's jacket a little bit tighter. Her fall coat was in the wash. She'd gotten some grease on it from her travels in the back of Scott's truck, and her mother insisted it needed laundering before her first day of school. So when she'd headed out the door after supper, Scott had stopped her and handed her his coat. She'd swung it on gladly, practically disappearing into it.

Even with the oversized coat, the cold of the wooden steps beneath her butt worked its way through.

She'd thought about setting up her telescope, seeing if Scott wanted to come out and look at the sky with her like he had on her birthday. Not that she needed the help with the setup anymore; it was simple. But in the end, she decided against it.

She'd save that nocturnal sightseeing for another time. A more important time.

She listened to the evening sounds around her—that wind rustling through the trees, a distant dog's low woofing from somewhere up the road. It was only six forty, and already the sky was dark—the stars were coming out. She'd missed that very first one…

So she'd try again tomorrow.

For once, Axl wasn't beside her. There'd been quite a crowd for supper—Titus and his girlfriend Ocean. Ocean's mom, Faye. Ember and Jace, Scott, Uncle Arden, her mom. With the extra table scraps Axl had scored, he was now sound asleep on the rag rug in the hall.

Sidney had felt awful when her mom had told her how worried she'd been to find her gone. But the smile on her face at suppertime had been real. Sid knew the difference. She wasn't just smart about book stuff and memorizing facts. She was smart about people stuff too.

Where to explore...

Sidney pushed to her feet and walked around the house. This late in the fall, the leaves that remained were dried out and crunched under her sneakers as she shuffled through them. That was fine. There was a beauty to the brown curled leaves as much as to the red, gold and yellow ones. And besides they were louder. And you could kick them higher when you walked.

She didn't explore far, mainly because she wanted to keep the light of the house in sight. The curtains were drawn back on the kitchen window and the brightly lit square of glass felt like it was both watching over and welcoming back.

She ended up at the edge of the lawn, where a single big apple tree stood. Scott had called it a Bramley. She remembered everything he'd told her. These were the apples that his Harkness mom, Margaret, had made all those pies from.

She moved closer until she stood under the tree's gnarled branches. Most of the apples had already been picked from this particular tree. There were still plenty of apples on the trees in the actual orchard, though. Mostly Sandows, Scott said, because they were the easiest to grow without chemical spraying. Something about not being scabby. She'd thought that was pretty funny—apples with scabs—but he assured her it was true, that it came from a fungus.

Scott had said he'd take her to pick some. They'd need a

fair bunch for bobbing at the Halloween party, and her mother would need some for the candied apples she was going to make.

It probably wouldn't be a bad idea to take a really nice, shiny apple for the teacher. She was going to get registered for school tomorrow morning. From her many experiences changing schools, she knew they might not let her join the class straight away. Sometimes they took her in just as soon as the paperwork was signed if the class wasn't too big. Sometimes they had to do some juggling to squeeze her in. She hoped she got to stay tomorrow.

Her stomach fluttered thinking about it. She was happy to be here in Harkness, excited to start school. But nervous too. It was always good to get the first day over and done with.

Sidney trailed her left hand along the rough bark of the apple tree as she walked around it, under the dark, low branches. She stopped, facing the mountain. Harkness Mountain. That place with all the trails, the slopes and that little cabin Scott's great-grandmother and her sisters used to grow flowers in as a side business years ago.

Yeah, right! She wasn't so young as to believe that! They wouldn't grow flowers up there. Tomatoes, maybe, but flowers? Doubtful.

She was pretty sure everything else Scott had told her about this place, about growing up in Harkness, was true. She'd listened to him all summer long. She turned her head slightly west, looked past the house. A cold night was settling in over the straw-covered fields, and she shivered inside Scott's coat.

The Bone Road was that way. When Scott was fourteen, that's where he'd spilled his first dirt bike. His Harkness Mom never knew. If she had, she'd never have let him ride again. But Uncle Arden came across him and Titus when they were trying to secretly repair the bike before anyone learned about the accident.

She pivoted to look at the Far South Barn. Though it was too dark to see the effects, the south-facing side had got a pretty coat of red paint today. Scott and Titus had done most of the work, but she'd done quite a bit too. She could have done a lot more, but everybody was so worried she'd get carpet tunnel or something. And so weird—she'd tried both a yellow-handled and a red-handled paintbrush and couldn't tell the difference.

She stepped out from under the apple tree branches. Just then, someone opened the door to let Axl out, and she heard a burst of laughter coming from inside. Holding still, she watched Axl. He lifted his nose and sniffed the air a few times, chuffed a cold breath. Scott said the old dog was half-blind, but there was nothing wrong with his sniffer! After marking his territory on several bushes, he started making his tail-wagging way over to her.

She hurried to meet him so he wouldn't have to walk so far.

She'd head inside in a few minutes. She'd have a bath, get her clothes out for her first day of Harkness school, then try to sleep. Except in her experience, the harder she tried to sleep, the harder it was to actually do. Maybe she'd let her mother make her warm milk.

Reaching the dog, she plunked down on her knees on the lawn. Immediately, she felt the cold damp coming through. Axl sat and she stroked his neck the way he liked.

"You know, Scott was right." She looked up at the sky.

*On a clear night in Harkness, the sky's so full of stars, you wouldn't believe it,* he'd told her. *And there are a few places where I swear you can reach out and touch them.*

Obviously, she knew he didn't mean you could literally touch them. But she didn't doubt for a second that it would feel exactly like that.

That was the important thing.

"Sidney Kathleen! Come in now," her mom called in a

sing-song voice—one Sid hadn't heard in a very long time. The one she used when she was really happy.

Well, Sid was happy too.

Maybe, just maybe, her plan would work.

"Coming!"

She got to her feet, as did Axl. "Guess what, Axl? I know what I'm going to be for Halloween."

Axl woofed, which make Sid laugh.

"C'mon, boy." Giddy with happiness and the fresh, cold air, she ran for the house.

# – ten –

"SO IS that everything on the list?" April asked, which struck her kind of funny considering it was *her* list. Ember had confiscated the precious *Need for Halloween Party* checklist when she and Ocean had picked her up at the house after lunch. Once she'd started brainstorming, it had been hard to stop. She'd been like the proverbial kid at...well, Halloween. But Arden had nodded over every one of her party suggestions. He'd even added a couple of his own, which she was happy to see.

They'd just come out of a store called Drummond's Meat and Produce. Donny—who was about the most courteous and sweet young man April had ever met—had already loaded the SUV with the goods they'd bought. While the three women had been browsing a small giftware section of the store, Donny had come right up to Ember, given her a hug, then asked for the car keys. She hadn't hesitated to hand them over so Donny and his helper could load the vehicle.

And there was a lot to load.

There were the old standbys, of course—pumpkins for carving, and she couldn't wait to try her hand at making old-fashioned popcorn balls. They'd have apple bobbing too, but the Standishs had that covered.

April used her own money to buy a few unique items. She

was acutely conscious of the need to stretch her severance pay, but she had a new recipe in mind for Halloween.

All in all, there was nothing too extravagant; nothing too fancy. And well within Arden's budget. Something to please everyone, and all of it sure to please the kids. April had been thinking of one kid in particular.

The last few days since she'd landed in Harkness, her little girl had been so happy. They'd even had one of their old-fashioned mother-daughter evenings—popcorn and a movie. Just the two of them, sitting up on the bed in Scott's old room, giggling at the hapless villain and cheering on the heroes. It had been awhile.

And the highlight so far for April? Calling Harley to tell him she and Sidney wouldn't be coming to stay with him after all. He'd actually been a little pissed. No doubt he'd been looking forward to lording it over her, rubbing her nose in her misfortune. Her inadequacy.

"Next on the agenda—and no need to consult the list for this one—coffee."

Ember's announcement pulled her thoughts away from her brother.

"Oh thank God!" Ocean said. "I'm going through caffeine withdrawal over here. How about you, April?"

"No coffee for me, but I'd kill for a cup of tea. I love tea."

"Oh, God," Ocean stopped in her tracks. "Did you tell my Mom that? She'll think you're a long lost daughter. Mom loves her tea."

April laughed. "It didn't come up. We were too busy talking recipes." Faye Siliker was quite the kitchen chef herself.

"I knew you and Faye would hit it off." Ember unlocked the SUV and climbed into the driver's seat. April reached for the back door, but not quickly enough.

"You ride in front," Ocean said.

"But you've taken the back seat all day," April said.

Ocean climbed right in. "Well, that's because I don't want you to miss the big city lights of Harkness. The action on the strip."

"We have a strip?" Ember said. "I've been gone longer than I thought."

April smiled. Or rather she continued to smile as she walked around the car and climbed into the front seat beside Ember. It had been a pretty full afternoon. She so hoped the party would be a success.

While they'd made the rounds shopping, Ember had dropped off posters for a half-dozen storefront windows. Yesterday, Ember and Ocean had called a bunch of friends and neighbors, urging them to call their friends too. Between the phone campaign and the posters, they were sure to get a good turnout.

They'd even put up posters at the elementary school. Yesterday, when April had enrolled Sidney, she'd given a copy of the poster to the principal, Eden Makepeace. As soon as she realized it was a Standish community party, she'd sent the secretary to make copies for every classroom.

"That family really is the heart of this town, you know," the young principal had said. "I went to school with Titus. Well, I was a year behind him, but I remember him. Scott and Ember too, but they were three years behind me. And I remember those community parties…"

Oh, how April had wanted to ask what Scott had been like in those younger years. Titus had told some of the more outlandish and embarrassing tales, but what had he *really* been like?

"Did I mention Ms. Makepeace put your poster up in every classroom?" April said.

"What'd I tell you?" Ember grinned. Sending the poster to school had been her idea. "The school's always been good about that. Whenever Mom heard of a new kid moving to town, she'd come up with some excuse to host a party for all the kids, even if it wasn't Halloween."

"She sounds wonderful," April said.

"She really was."

"You must miss her terribly,' Ocean said.

"I do. All the time," she said simply. "Whenever life knocked me around a little, I could always turn to her for a hug. But when the hardest knock came…"

"She wasn't there to hug it better." April hadn't had that kind of relationship with her mother, which only made Ember's loss seem all the more poignant. Her heart ached—for both of them.

"Exactly. But it does get better. When we first lost her, I didn't think I'd have a dry-eyed day ever again," Ember said. "But there was med school, and life. It hit Dad especially hard."

April turned to look at Ocean. "What about you? You must have lost your father."

"My sister and I never knew him. Not really. He left when Mom was pregnant with River. I wasn't even two at the time. And yes, our mother is nuts. She really did name us Ocean and River."

"She's not *nuts*," Ember said, maneuvering out of Drummond's packed parking lot. "She's just…fun."

April noted Ember turned right on Capital Street, working on her mental map of Harkness.

"She is that." Ocean chuckled. "Anyway, Mom rarely talked about our father, and only when we asked. She always answered our questions, but it made us feel weird to ask after a while, so we stopped. I honestly don't even know whether he's alive or dead."

Whoops. She hadn't meant to open a painful topic. She twisted in her seat to face Ocean. "I'm sorry. I shouldn't have pried."

Ocean waved off her concern. "Oh, it's not a sensitive subject. It just…is what it is."

April sat back in the seat. Sid had asked about her

biological father a few times when she was younger. Those had been hard conversations. She knew there'd be more in her future as Sid entered her teens. She knew, too, that the conversations would get even harder.

"What I think is weird—well, once I got old enough to think about it—is that Mom never dated. I mean—never, ever."

"You guys must be so glad they found each other then," April said.

"Um, glad that who found whom?" Ocean asked.

"Faye and Arden. They seem so happy together. Such a sweet couple."

Ember nearly drove off the road. Well, one wheel hit the gravel before she righted things. "Sorry. Didn't mean to jostle you guys. But, April, honey, you couldn't be more wrong about Dad and Faye."

"Seriously, that's not even...possible," Ocean said. "I mean, *seriously*."

April half turned in the seat again, her gaze going from one woman to the other. Ember's hands were white on the steering wheel, and Ocean was sitting forward in the seat now. "Why isn't it possible?"

"For starters," Ember said. "Dad's nearly seventy."

"Mom too."

"And...?" April pushed.

"And that's too old," Ocean said.

April grinned. "No, it's not."

Ocean looked at Ember. "You're a doctor. Tell her that's too old."

There was a pause.

"Ember?"

Ember cast a glance at Ocean in the rearview mirror. "They have been playing a lot of Scrabble lately. Dad never used to be a big fan of Scrabble."

"And what's with all the chickweed tea in the pantry?"

April said. “I’m guessing that’s not a traditional Standish drink. Sounds like something a tea person might like?”

“Yeah, I’ve noticed the tea.” Ember chewed her lip. “Maybe there *is* something going on. I mean, they’ve been friends forever.”

“That’s all there is to it.” Ocean spoke the words, but she didn’t sound a damn bit convinced anymore. “Scrabble. Tea. Pies. Maybe that’s how their generation dated. Yeah, I’m guessing not so much in the hanky panky department.”

“Well, there’s always Viagra,” April offered.

For a second, April thought Ember was heading toward the ditch again, but the abrupt turn took them into the gravel parking lot of a small building with wide windows in the front. *I’m a Little Tea Shop*, the sign read.

For the few seconds it took for Ember to park the car, nobody moved. Or spoke.

April’s gaze shot to Ember’s face. “Guys, I’m sorry. If I’ve spoken out of line—”

“Don’t apologize,” Ocean said. “There’s no such thing as out of line with us. It’s just…weird to think about.”

The three women got out of the car.

“Your mom and my dad,” Ember said. “I had no idea.”

Ocean shook her head. “Me neither. But you know, I did find a man’s sweater folded on a chair in mom’s room the other day when I was looking for Tylenol. I never thought much about it. But now…”

“Red sweater?” Ember asked.

“Yes.”

“He’s been wondering where it got to.”

“Oh God, Titus!” Ocean burst out laughing. “I cannot wait to see the look on his face when I tell him that his dad and my mom are—”

“You’re going to tell him?” Ember asked.

“I *was* going to.” Ocean glanced at April. “Are you going to tell Scott?”

She shrugged. "Um, I wasn't planning to. And we're friends, not a couple."

Ember and Ocean exchanged a look without breaking stride. Then Ocean laughed. "Who do you think we are? Titus?"

April frowned in confusion. "Sorry?"

"My brothers might be oblivious when it comes to this sort of thing, but we're not." Ember's eyebrows drew together. "Well, at least I didn't *think* we were..."

Ocean waved a dismissive hand. "Okay, we may have missed Faye and Arden, but just because they're...well, our parents." She pushed the door to the tea shop open and they went inside. "But you and Scott? There's definitely some chemistry there."

April felt the heat rise in her cheeks and was grateful that Ocean was already off and searching for a suitable table. They found one near the window and settled on elegant bistro chairs. Thankfully, the waiter, a handsome middle-aged gentleman, bought her some more time by coming to greet them.

"Hey, Stephen," Ocean and Ember said almost simultaneously. They introduced him to April as a friend of the Standish family.

After bantering with Ember a moment, he handed them small menus. "I'll be back in a few minutes to take your orders, ladies."

April immediately got lost in the menu. Everything came in single serving and sliver size.

*Caramel lemon squares.*

*Peanut butter brownies.*

*Cranberry-lemon cheesecake.*

A thought hit her. Cranberry cheesecake would make a perfect flavor for a breakfast bar. With maybe just a pinch of finely shredded coconut into the mix. And chia seeds. Oh! Maybe instead of a bar, a breakfast spread for bagels. She could use cottage cheese and Greek yogurt instead of cream cheese for a healthier—

"Oh!" Ocean started digging, frantically, through her purse. "I need a pen."

April and Ember started reaching for their own purses.

Stephen materialized at their table, handing Ocean both his pen and a slip of paper torn from his order book. By the look of it, he'd done this before.

"Thanks." Madly she scribbled down a few words. Smiling, she handed the pen back. "If I don't write an idea down when I think of it, I'm afraid I'll lose it."

"You're entirely welcome. Now, are we ready to order?" he asked. "I can recommend the cheesecake."

Ocean glanced at April. "I write here once in a while and can second that recommendation."

"That's what I'm having," Ember said, handing Stephen her menu. "But don't bring me one of those slivers. I want a real slice."

He grinned. "So, single servings all around?"

"Suits me," Ocean said, then glanced at April.

April bit her lip. "Actually, I'd like the sliver size, but I'd also like a sliver of the cranberry-lemon square and the chocolate-raspberry mousse cake."

"Got it," he said. "Now, what can I bring you to drink?"

The three women placed their orders. Within minutes, Stephen was back with the desserts, promising the coffee and tea to follow.

April took a small bite of the cranberry-lemon cheesecake. She closed her eyes and let it sit on her tongue a minute. Just a hint of sweet perfectly balancing the tartness. The lemon? Maybe a bit overdone. But pretty damn close to perfect. She chewed it slowly.

When she opened her eyes again, Ocean and Ember were staring at her—smiling.

"Sorry." She picked up her napkin and wiped her mouth. "I must look like an idiot."

"Um, no more than I look like an idiot when I scream for a

pen as if the fate of the world depended on it. Which it kind of does. My fictional world, anyway." Ocean took a bite of her own cheesecake. "God, this is soooooo good."

"You look like someone who has a passion for food, April," Ember said. "I love seeing passion in people."

April grinned. "You could say that. And passion sounds so much better than obsession."

The girls laughed.

Over Ember's shoulder, April caught sight of a school bus rolling by outside. Maybe Sidney was on it. She was having fun with Ocean and Ember, but she would have liked to be there to greet her daughter when she got off the bus. But Scott had promised he'd be home to do it, and she knew Sidney would love that, having some time to hang with Scott for a bit before April got home.

She bit her lip. She so hoped Sidney had a good day at school. And that they'd be able to offer her some enrichment education. She really was a smart kid; she deserved it.

"Okay, maybe that multiple sliver thing was a better idea," Ocean said. "That raspberry chocolate mousse cake looks killer."

April took a bite. Mmm, another winner. "It *is* killer." She pushed the plate closer so the other ladies could take tiny tastes. "I bet you could make a good gluten-free version with almond flour."

"Wow, I'd love to try that," Ocean said. "I don't have a particular problem with gluten, but I'm always looking for ways to limit it, you know?"

"Me too," Ember chimed in. "I love carbs, and they love me right back. I can tell because of the way they want to stick with me."

"I hear you," April said. She went on to talk about the challenges of keeping a balanced diet when she spent so much time experimenting with recipes and tasting the results.

And as they talked, she found herself relaxing into it a little. This must be what it was like to have sisters.

No, this was *exactly* what it was like to have a sister.

Kathleen had been quite a bit older than April, but April had loved her so much. She'd have sworn they were close. Yet when her sister left, she'd never looked back. Never called April, never sent a card.

Forget about sisters. It had been so long since April had even one real *friend*. Oh, she always had lots of people in her life—bosses, co-workers, neighbors, even other young mothers. But none of those relationships had progressed beyond casual friendships because in the back of her mind she knew the status quo could be very temporary.

The thought was like a dark cloud hovering. She reached for her tea, took a big sip, and laughed at something Ocean said. And if her smile came a little harder, no one seemed to notice.

# – eleven –

SCOTT WASHED his hands at the kitchen sink. Flipping the tap off with his elbow, he grabbed a hand towel and dried them.

His gaze went to the window and fields outside. It was great to see the berry fields covered in straw, ready for the winter. The apple orchard…well, that was another matter. The u-pickers would start turning up on Monday. After they'd had a go at the apples, Scott would hire a few pickers to harvest the rest. Some would go straight to market, some would go into cold storage, and some would be pressed for sweet cider. He'd helped with those activities growing up, but this would be the first time he was in charge of it all.

And there it was, right on schedule. The tug-of-war between wanting to immerse himself in the farm—in his family—and wanting to be gone. He knew how that battle would eventually shake out.

But for two months? He could do it.

Grabbing the cutting board and his favorite knife, he went to work on some white onion. He knew he wasn't cutting them as finely as April would, but they'd do. He looked at the basket of Roma tomatoes beside the cutting board and smiled—they'd be next. At his suggestion, April was planning a huge spaghetti supper tonight. He'd thought he'd give her a head start while he babysat Sidney.

Babysat? He wondered what Little Miss I'm-a-*kid*-not-a-*child* would think of that term.

He stuck with a much safer question: "How's the homework going?"

She looked up from the pages of her textbook. Math. Not his favorite subject, despite the fact that carpentry required hella math. Try to square a wall without knowing the Pythagorean Theorem, or evenly place multiple windows without math skills. But he was pretty sure he could handle the grade five stuff if she needed help. If he knew Sid, though, she wouldn't need or appreciate help. She was one smart cookie. In fact, she'd shown him how to complete a function table earlier.

Twice.

"Fine," she said. "It's almost done. And it's pretty easy."

"All of it, or just the math?"

"All of it, but especially the math."

"Why's that?" He halted his chopping long enough to glance over at her. "Is it stuff you already learned?"

"No. It's just easy. School's kind of boring that way." She sat up straighter. "Thunderchicken said they have a tutor coming in to see me tomorrow."

*Thunderchicken*? "I think you mean Mrs. Thorburn."

He turned back around to the chopping board so she wouldn't see his grin. So the kids were still calling her that behind her back—same as they were when he had Mrs. Thorburn in grade five. Call him juvenile, but it still seemed funny.

"Okay, Mrs. Thorburn," Sid corrected. "Anyway, she said she found someone to give us some math and science enrichment.

"Us?"

"Yeah, there's another girl who's pretty good at school too," Sid said happily.

"What's her name?"

"Danika Kelly. Do you know her?"

*Kelly.* Not a common Harkness name. He'd gone to school with a Robert Kelly. Could that be his little girl? "I might know her father. Is he a mail carrier?"

"Yep, he delivers the mail in his car. Danika says it has a flashing light on top, almost like a police car."

"Cool."

"Yeah. She's really nice. She gave me this." She reached into her pencil case and pulled out a brand new pencil—fresh eraser, never been sharpened or chewed. Purple with yellow happy faces wearing sunglasses dotted along the length of it.

"Sounds like you've made a friend already," Scott said.

Sid shrugged, seeming to pull back into herself. "We'll see."

Poor kid. She'd settled in so well and so quickly, he'd almost forgotten how cautious the little girl could be. Any other kid would be ready to declare they'd found their new BFF, but not Sid. Not yet. She was reserving judgment. He couldn't blame her. How could she do otherwise when it could all disappear at the snap of someone's fingers?

"So Thunder—I mean, Mrs. Thorburn—found the two of you a tutor. That's great news."

"Yep. We're starting tomorrow. There's a letter in my backpack for Mom."

The kitchen door opened and Ember and April burst in, laden with parcels and packages.

"Hey, Mom, look what my new friend gave me." Sid jumped up to show her the pencil and launched into a report of all the good things that had happened on day two of Douglas Street Elementary School. "Oh, and you know what else? I think every kid in Harkness is planning on coming to our party."

*Our party?* For a girl who didn't trust easily, Sid seemed to be making herself at home here.

"All of them? That's a lot of kids." April moved to the counter, nabbed a piece of raw onion and popped it into her mouth. She was smiling. Energized. She'd clearly had a great time with Ember and Ocean.

"Hey, I'm working here," he said. "Don't be messing with perfection."

"Yeah, right."

"Did you get the Halloween stuff?" Sid asked.

"Did we ever! I hope you're keen on helping me after supper for the next couple nights, Ladybug. Lots of fudge to be made."

"No problem. We have to dip candy apples too, right?"

"Right."

"And you wanted me to help you decorate the Far South Barn, right?"

Before April could answer, Ember jumped in. "Sorry, kiddo. The barn is a big no."

April glanced from Ember to Scott, her confusion plain. "Why not?"

"No kids allowed until we open the doors on Halloween night," Scott explained. "No exceptions."

"Even kids that are staying here?"

Ember laughed. "Oh, Sid, even if you'd been *born* here. It's tradition."

"Rats. I wanted to help decorate."

April laid a hand on her daughter' shoulder. "You can help me with the cooking, like I said. But homework comes first—don't hurry it."

"I'm just about done. Oh, and that reminds me." Sid scooted back to the table and pulled the folded envelope from her backpack. She handed it to her mother, then sat back down. "Mrs. Thorburn sent a letter home."

"*Thunderchicken?*" Ember said. "She's still teaching?"

Scott lifted his eyebrows. "Excuse me?"

"Uh…Mrs. Thorburn, I mean. Wonderful lady."

"I already heard the nickname, Ember," Sid said, in a very grown-up way.

"Well, it's not a nice one to repeat," April said.

"I know. Scott already told me that. I won't."

April opened the letter; she read the contents quickly. "Seems you've got yourself a tutor." She smiled. "Faye Silkier."

"The lady who was here the other night? That Faye?" Sid smiled. "Arden's g—"

"Well, you probably should call her Mrs. Siliker at school, huh?" Scott said.

"For sure. This is going to be so great. I'm going to text Danika right now and—"

"Finish your homework first," April said sternly, even as she started to put the grocery items away—some in the fridge, others on the huge counter to be squared away in various cupboards. From what he could see, they'd be eating well in the days to come.

There wasn't a Standish alive that couldn't rustle up a mean grilled-cheese sandwich. And, a little-known fact—Scott had worked as a camp cook one winter. Nothing like the kind of meals April put on, or the desserts she could make, but he could put a meal together. Even bake a little. He watched her unpack several bags of sugar. Probably destined for fudge. His mouth watered at the prospect.

"Funny Ocean never mentioned Faye was going to tutor Sidney," Ember said.

"Maybe she doesn't know yet," Scott said.

"I wonder if she told Arden?" Sidney asked.

Scott shrugged. *Heck if he knew.* But, what was that little look between April and Ember? "Why would she?"

"I kind of wanted to tell him myself," Sid said, then shot a look at her mother. "I don't bother him, Mom."

"Sweetie, of course you don't."

"No way would hanging with you bother Dad, Sid," Ember said. "He's not much of a talker but he's a heck of a good listener." She smiled. "He used to love to watch me do my homework."

"Did he watch Scott and Titus do theirs?"

"Sure. But I was better at it than they were, so he watched me more."

Just like he went to every one of Scott's football games, and took every chance he got to check out what Titus was working on in the garage. Uncle Arden's interest had only served to make each of them even better, his attention all the encouragement they'd needed.

But Scott knew where Sid's worry that she was bothering his uncle came from. The Boisverts hadn't exactly been the kid-friendly type. Not that they were bad to Sidney, but the older couple were very much of the children-are-to-be-seen-and-not-heard mentality. And that was *before* Sid got creative with their credit card.

"Well, you can tell Uncle Arden about your new tutor when he gets home. He's over at Faye's right now, but that lady knows how to keep a secret," Scott said.

*And Uncle Arden was pretty good at acting surprised.*

"So, Scott," Ember said. "What do you think Dad's doing over at Faye's? I mean, again."

"Playing Scrabble, I think. Though I don't remember him liking the game when we were growing up. Probably because you always cheated, Ember."

"Cheated?" She gave an exaggerated huff. "Latin isn't cheating."

He wasn't so sure about that. "Anyway, he seems to enjoy it now. He was over there until almost nine o'clock last night." He shrugged. "Some men discover golf in their retirement. Maybe Uncle Arden found Scrabble?"

With one final chop, the onions were done. Okay, more of a flourish than a chop. His mouth was watering already in anticipation of the spaghetti.

"Scrabble? Scott I think—" Sidney's words were cut short.

Scott turned around to see the three females looking at him, with identical grins on their faces.

"You think what?" he said.

"Should we tell him?" Ember asked. She looked at Sid, then April.

Scott looked down at himself. Was there something on his shirt? He raised a hand to his mouth. Something in his teeth?

"Let's not," Sid said.

April nodded firmly. "I agree. Let's not."

"I haven't a clue what you three are talking about," he said, half annoyed.

"And we're not telling." Ember grabbed a piece of raw onion.

"My homework's done," Sid announced. "I'm gonna go change." She got to her feet and gathered up her things, precious new pencil packed away in her pencil case. "Then I'll come down and help you with supper."

"Why don't you go out and play for a bit?" April said.

"Maybe you can check out the old tire swing hanging from the second oak tree out back," Ember suggested.

Sid's eyes widened. "I didn't know if I was allowed on it or not."

"Of course you are," Ember said. "I mean, if your mom says it's okay."

April looked at Scott.

"It's safe," he said. "The limb is strong and the rope will hold two adults, let alone one Sid the Kid."

April nodded. "It's okay by me, then. But don't wander further away."

"Okay!" With all the energy of a happy ten-year-old, Sidney darted out of the room. A second later she was *thump thumping* up the stairs.

April grabbed an apron from a hook near the stove and hung it around her neck. The strings were so long, she passed them behind her, then back in front, tying them at her waist. God, she was the only woman in the world who could make that look sexy.

"I've got the onions chopped," he announced.

She blinked. "Oh, and how did you do that when I just picked them up at Drummonds?"

"These were in the cupboard." He gestured to the mountain of onion on the cutting board.

"I thought they must be for something else."

She didn't look as thrilled as he'd hoped. And that little line between her eyebrows hadn't been there when she'd first gotten home from shopping.

This couldn't be about the onions, could it? Granted, he didn't chop them as finely as she did, but it hadn't seemed to matter before. He'd helped her make a meal in that little kitchen in Montreal—plenty of times.

She put her hands on her hips. "I thought that was my job."

"It is but—"

"Then why are you doing it?"

Ember jangled her keys, no doubt to remind Scott and April that she was still there. "I'll get the rest of the stuff out of the car."

"Let me help you," April said.

"No. I've got it. And I'll take my time so…"

He watched Ember close the door behind her. Jesus, how much trouble was he in? He turned to April. "You're mad about the onions?"

"No, I'm not angry." She shook her head. "I'm more troubled."

"But I used to help you in Montreal." He'd enjoyed those relaxed times, working together in the kitchen.

"Yes, when we were both off duty. In my personal kitchen, not the Boisverts commercial kitchen."

"I was just trying to help. I knew you were making—"

"*I'm* the help. Scott, if you didn't need me in the kitchen why did you hire me?"

"All this over the onions?"

"It's not just the onions." She faced him squarely. "Last

night you made the garlic bread. This morning you were up frying bacon before I was out of the shower."

"I'm just used to doing these things, April. I'm here, so why not help? I enjoy it."

"I know. I get that. You're not trying to be anything but your awesome, helpful self. But I'm concerned. Why'd you hire me? Am I…are Sidney and I…is this some sort of pity project?"

Oh, hell. "Of course not. Sorry, April. How about I stay out of the kitchen completely?"

"I'm not saying that." She walked over to him. "I like having you in the kitchen. And thanks for looking after Sidney after school."

"Glad to do it."

"But…" She reached to fix the flap over the pocket on his Levis shirt and smiled up at him. "But this is my job, and I want to do it well."

"Ah, so that's it—you think I'm going to screw up the spaghetti sauce."

"You just diced up a sweet onion, which is really better for eating raw with sandwiches or fresh salsa or something. My spaghetti sauce calls for yellow onions, which are sharp enough to cut through the sweetness of the tomato sauce."

"I'm an idiot."

"Oh, the sweet onion would do in a pinch. The spaghetti sauce would be all right, but—"

"But you quite properly take pride in what you do, and all right doesn't cut it."

"Exactly."

"Sorry," he said. "I know this is nothing like at the Boisverts'. I just have to remind myself that things are different."

"Not everything, surely?"

She went up on tiptoe and pressed her lips to his. Even with Titus's warnings ringing in his ears, he closed his arms around her reflexively and drew her against his body, kissing her back. When her hands went around his back, he wanted so much to maneuver her up against the cupboard and kiss her senseless. But he couldn't. Damn it all to hell.

He put his hands on her waist and moved back to insert some space between them. "We can't do this, April."

"You're right—Sidney will be back down any minute." She unlinked her hands from behind his neck, but let them slide slowly, lingeringly down his chest and abdomen as she stepped back.

Scott groaned. Damn, how he wanted her! "That wasn't what I meant."

Her eyebrows drew together. "What did you mean?"

*Thump, thump, thump.*

Two seconds later, Sid was back in the kitchen.

"Off to the tire swing?" Scott asked.

"Nope." Instead of heading for the door, she reached for one of her mother's aprons—a light yellow one with wide pockets in the front. Sidney wrapped the strings around herself twice before knotting them in the back. "Actually, I thought I'd work off some of my debt, if that's okay with you, Mom?"

Debt? Right. The credit card.

"Good idea," she said. "Get out the chopper. You can start on the yellow onions."

This would be so good for them, spending time in the kitchen. Back in Montreal, April had confided how she wished she had more time with Sidney.

"Great." Sid looked at Scott. "What are you going to do with the onions you chopped, Scott?"

"Umm…"

April laughed. "How about we make some quiche?"

"Yes!" Sid said. "Oh, can I take a piece in my lunch?"

"Sure," April said.

"After the onions, want me to FIFO the fridge?"

"That'd be great, sweetie."

"Um…*what* the fridge?"

"FIFO. It's an acronym for first in, first out," April supplied. "Whether it's a fridge or freezer, or dry goods in a pantry, the oldest stuff needs to be rotated to the front and the newest stuff placed at the back, to minimize spoilage."

"Makes sense," he conceded. "But why haven't I heard the term before, given all the time I spent in your kitchen?"

"Prolly 'cause we do it automatically," Sid said. "Nobody has to talk about it." She went to the sink, adjusted the taps to the perfect temperature, then began scrubbing her hands.

Scott grinned—Sid the Kid was truly her mother's daughter. "Well, it looks like you ladies have everything under control," he said, heading for the exit. "I'll leave you to your work."

"You can help me later," April called after him.

He paused in the doorway and looked back questioningly. "With what?"

"Halloween stuff. Tonight, after supper. Maybe even later than that. Say…after Sid's in bed."

He gave April a pulse-stirring smile. "Deal."

# – twelve –

APRIL WAS a few minutes late, but there was no way she was leaving that kitchen less than pristine. The supper dishes had been done and put away an hour ago, every last bit of leftovers stowed in the fridge, and the prep done for tomorrow's breakfast. They'd be having quiche with their sausage and toast.

As for the toast, they'd be trying out her new chunky cranberry spread with lemon zest and freshly grated Ceylon cinnamon.

She hadn't stopped thinking about making that breakfast spread since she left the tea shop earlier. So after supper, while Sidney had gone out to play on the tire swing, she'd taken a stab at it, keeping the quantities small to avoid excessive wastage. Rarely was she satisfied with her first attempt to formulate a recipe. This time was no different. Each effort got closer. When Sidney came in, she tried the fourth attempt, pronouncing it "pretty good." As her daughter went through to join the others in the living room for the post-dinner *Jeopardy!* routine, she'd gone back to the drawing board. Two tries later, she got it right. *Hallelujah!* The Greek yogurt and cottage cheese base finally came together with the other ingredients for an experience that was at least as good as cream cheese.

She hoped everyone would like it.

Arden especially. He was an incredibly kind man, and she respected that. Then again, she wouldn't have expected anything else from Scott's father—er, uncle. She wondered if Scott had any idea how much he was like Arden. Steady, strong, caring. There was one huge difference, however. Arden had been perfectly content to spend his days on the farm.

She put the kitchen back to rights, turned off the lights and headed into the living room to join everyone.

The show was well underway when she sat down beside Scott on the small sofa. Ember winked at her as she did. In April's defense, it was the only place left to sit in the family room unless she parked herself on the floor beside Sidney. Arden and Faye occupied the other sofa and Ember, the recliner.

Titus and Ocean had decided to snag some alone time over at the Silikers', with Faye being out of the house for the evening.

Arden and Faye. The girls had agreed not to tell Titus and Scott, just to see how long it took them to figure it out for themselves. Ocean had also agreed not to let on to her mom that she knew anything. Naturally, Sidney was in on it too. Earlier tonight, when Arden had ushered Faye into the dining room, she'd given her daughter a wink and put her finger to her lips in that don't-tell way. Sidney had looked full to bursting with the secret, but she also looked happy, thrilled to be part of this *just between us girls* knowledge.

Scott leaned close keeping his voice down so as not to distract anyone from the television. "That was an awesome supper."

"See what I mean about the onions?" she murmured.

"I do indeed."

Sidney was on the floor at their feet, currently cheering on the market analyst from Ann Arbor, Michigan who had a significant lead.

As Scott and Ember had informed her, *Jeopardy!* was a long-standing Standish family tradition. A take-no-prisoners, every man and woman for themselves, all-out competition that had been going on for years.

The bragging rights were obnoxious.

"Final Jeopardy! is coming up," Uncle Arden announced loudly, sitting up straight on the sofa. "Everyone has ten thousand dollars, except for Sidney."

From what Scott had told her, April knew Arden hadn't much formal schooling, having dropped out to help with the farm, but he was well-read. And apparently no slouch at *Jeopardy!*

April laughed. "I just got here. How'd I get ten grand?"

"We don't really keep score until the end," Arden said. "Then everyone gets ten thousand for the final round."

"Hey, what about me?" Sidney asked. "How come I don't get ten thousand dollars?"

"Because you're ten years old," Scott answered. "And by Standish rules, you get fifteen thousand if you're under fourteen."

"Sweet!" Sidney sat up and gave a fist pump. She looked so excited, for a moment, April wondered if her daughter didn't think it was real money they were playing with. "I'll bet—"

"Don't tell," Scott said.

Sidney frowned. "But how do you know how much I bet?"

"Because you're going to write it down." Ember jumped up and handed out the blank recipe cards and stubby pencils she'd evidently been holding on her lap. So that's what was in the pencil case. "Write down your wager, and when Alex reads the question…"

"Got it," Sid said.

Sid had slid in a couple of correct answers earlier, in the category of desserts. At the commercial break, she'd run out to the kitchen to give April a breathless recap. April suspected

Faye could easily have answered those questions, judging by her baking skill. That carrot cake she'd brought over tonight had been scrumptious—moist, with a good crumb and properly spiced. But Sid had been first on the draw.

"You ready for this?" Scott asked her.

April grinned at the glint of challenge in his eyes. "Absolutely."

The category was American Vice-Presidents. The question, a hard one.

*Crap!*

She gave it a pure guess…*John C. Calhoun.*

And she was right! So was the happy market analyst who survived to play another night.

April wasn't sure who was happier—she with her imaginary win, or the woman on TV who'd just made some real dough. Faye and Scott got the answer too. Arden, Ember, and Sidney missed with Burr, Clinton—George, not Bill—and Gore respectively.

But who had outbet whom?

It was a sweet, sweet victory for…Scott Standish. He'd outbet April by thirty-two dollars. *Thirty-two measly dollars!* He had bragging rights for the night.

"That was fun!" Sidney said. "Do you really do this every night?"

"Every weeknight," Arden said.

"And I can play again?"

"Absolutely."

"But for now, you'd better get to bed," April said to her daughter.

Sidney's jaw dropped. "Mom! You know I'm ten years old, right? It's too early."

"I do know that, Sidney Kathleen. But nine o'clock is perfectly reasonable. Besides, I thought you wanted to get up early to walk down to your friend's place to see the new kittens and board the bus with Danika?"

“Oh, right. I wasn’t thinking.”

It took very little digging on Scott’s part to find out Danika’s father was his former school mate. They lived about a quarter of a mile down the Shadow Road. April was so glad her little girl had already found a friend.

“I’m looking forward to working with you two young ladies tomorrow,” Faye said. “Ms. Makepeace tells me both you and Danika are math and science whizzes.”

“We’re excited too, Faye—*Mrs. Siliker*.”

Faye beamed her approval and Sidney soaked it right up.

“You taught Danika’s dad years ago,” Sidney said. “She told me.”

“I also taught your principal.”

Sidney’s eyes widened. “Really?”

“Really. I can’t wait to get started. The math will take care of itself, but science-wise, is there anything you’re particularly interested in learning more about? I intend to ask Danika too, of course. Maybe we can come up with some subjects we’ll all enjoy exploring.”

Sidney perked up. “I’ve always been interested in space stuff.”

“Oh, like black holes?” Faye rubbed her hands together in anticipation. “Such a fascinating phenomenon.”

“And stars,” Sidney said. “They’re interesting too. Did you know that our sun is actually a G2 yellow dwarf star?”

“Indeed,” Faye said. “And destined in a few billion years to grow into a red giant, when all the hydrogen has burned off. Eventually, when the core condenses, it’ll become a white dwarf star.”

“That’s so cool!”

“Very cool,” April agreed. “But it’s off to bed for you now, Ladybug. Tomorrow’s an early start.”

“Okay.” Sidney jumped up and headed for the stairs. She had one foot on the bottom step when she turned around. “Whoa, I almost forgot!” She crossed the room again to give her mother a hug where she sat on the couch. April squeezed her back and released her.

Sidney straightened then paused.

Back in Montreal, it was nothing for her to hug Scott goodnight too. Not every time he was over, but on those evenings after special outings. And of course, on her birthday, when he'd given her that telescope and she'd made that secret wish. She'd thrown her arms around him without hesitation.

But this was different.

"'Night, Scott," she said. "'Night everyone."

"I'll be right behind you, Ladybug," April said. "Don't forget to brush your teeth."

"I won't." Night time or not, Sid wasn't slowing down—she ran the stairs two at a time.

April stood. "Thanks for letting me join you tonight."

"Wasn't it fun?" Faye said. "You're obviously a good competitor. Next time you'll have to join us for the whole show."

"Thank you." Unless she had a recipe to work out or something complicated to prep for the next day, she should be clear of the kitchen in time to participate.

"Yeah, you rock at this," Ember said. "Do you come from a family of *Jeopardy!* freaks too?"

Ember's innocent question made April want to sink right through the floor. Her family enjoying a rousing game of *Jeopardy?* Not in this lifetime. Sarah and Dick Morgan had had rules. Stifling rules, and remorseless punishments. She'd been afraid to breathe too loudly. The only one allowed to make noise was Harley. And her parents, who drank and fought continuously. Her older sister Kathleen had left as soon as she was able to. She'd run away and never come back. Harley—the Morgans' only male offspring—had been the only valued, if not adored, child. None of them had been adored.

She wasn't sure how many seconds had ticked by in her reflective pause.

"I think it's been a long day for April," Scott said, shooting his sister a look. "Let's—"

"No," April said. "We didn't watch *Jeopardy!* We weren't much for TV."

Ember looked momentarily confused, but she obviously got Scott's *don't push it* message. "No doubt that's why you knew the Final Jeopardy! answer," she said. "'Cause you were busy reading books instead of rotting your brain in front of the television."

April grinned. "Well, I did read every book in our community's tiny library by the time I was fifteen." In fact, the library had been her retreat from the harsh reality of her home life.

"Good for you," Arden said. "Margaret made sure our kids were readers, so we never overdid the TV around here, either. But you *will* find it on every night at the same time. Same channel, same show, since the mid-eighties." Arden smiled, but there was a seriousness in his eyes. "I really hope you'll join us."

"Me too." Scott reached for her hand and squeezed it.

"We'll see." April pulled her hand away and stood. "I'm thinking I'll be pretty busy getting things ready for the festivities. Speaking of which..." She turned to Scott. "Still willing to give me a hand decorating the barn?"

"Wouldn't miss it. I'll go on out now and you can come along when Sid's settled."

"Want some more help?" Ember asked.

"No," Scott said quickly. "I think April and I have it covered."

Ember smiled but resisted the urge to tease her brother. "Sounds good. Jace will be waiting for me anyway." She met April's gaze. "Let me know if I can do anything?"

"I will," April said.

"I don't know who's more excited for this, me or Jace." Ember's eyes softened. "It's been a long time since he's been to a Standish party."

A long time? Try a whole decade. April's throat tightened. Scott had told her about Ember and Jace's teenage romance and how they'd been torn apart by Jace's brother's machinations. They'd only just worked through it and were crazy in love again.

The fact wasn't lost on anyone in the room.

Arden cleared his throat. "That'll be a fine sight to see, the two of you in the old barn."

"Are you dressing up?" Faye asked.

"We are."

Arden lifted an eyebrow. "I'm not going to even ask about costumes."

Ember stood and crossed to her father's side. She bent down and kissed his cheek. "Ask away, I won't tell you."

"Anthony and Cleopatra?" Faye ventured. "I've always loved couples costumes."

"Nope," Ember said.

"Prince William and Princess Kate?"

Before Ember could respond, Sidney shouted from upstairs. "Mom!"

*Yelling in the house?* April cringed. Her gaze shot to Arden. "I'm so sorry about that."

He waved her off. "Good to have young voices in the house again."

April dashed up the stairs.

She knocked on the door to Ember's room, which, by the look of things, was already showing signs of Sidney's influence. Her daughter had definitely made herself at home. Her book bag was on the window seat, as were her clothes for tomorrow—she always got them out before she went to bed. The pencil Danika had given her was resting on the side table.

Sidney sat in the twin bed, the one Titus had moved into the room, with Axl curled up at her feet.

Between Titus and Ember, they'd shifted Ember's bed back against the wall and installed the twin bed by the window so Sidney could have the prime piece of real estate. They'd also dispensed with the bed frame at Sidney's request, setting up the box spring and mattress directly on the floor so the arthritic old dog could climb up on it.

April's gaze landed on the vanity between the two beds, noticing for the first time that her daughter's hairbrush, scrunchies, cherry lip balm, folded bits of paper, and other miscellaneous things were strewn on it.

"Um, Sid…"

She must have seen her looking. "That was Ember's idea, that we share the vanity."

April looked closer. Okay. There was a clear dividing line on the vanity top. Left side: foundation, eyeliner, night cream in an opaque blue jar. Other grown up things. On the right, kid's stuff.

"That was very kind of her," April said. "I hope you thanked her."

"I repeat—I'm ten years old now. Of course I thanked her."

April gave Sidney her *enough* look—or, as Sidney liked to call it, her *Hulk* frown. "You're pushing it, Kid."

"I'm not just a kid you know." Sidney lay back on the pillow and pulled the blankets around her.

"No?"

"I'm Sid the Kid again."

April bit her lip. It wasn't permanent. It was only till Christmas. She'd told the Standishs that was as long as she could stay, and that was certainly all she'd be needed for. Granted the two days she'd been here had proven that there was enough to do, at least for the time being. But there was no way—for the tidy sum they were paying her—that her presence could be justified over the long term.

Besides, how could it be right here without Scott?

But she didn't have the heart to say any of that. The last thing her daughter wanted right now was a reminder of what she already knew in her heart.

Truth be told, Sidney hadn't been the only one who'd listened to Scott's tales about his Harkness home. And while her daughter might have retained every detail of the place, April had memorized every detail of the man. April had imagined this place so often, imagined Scott at the center of it. The old farmhouse, the barn, the land. She'd fallen into that dangerous dream more nights than she cared to remember. And now she was living it.

But this happiness she'd felt these past days would be short-lived. This warmth. This life. This time with Scott.

*So why not make the most of it?*

The treacherous thought slid through her, making tendrils of excitement unfurl in her belly.

She'd been celibate since before Sidney was born. Ten long years. Not necessarily lonely years; she'd been too busy to dwell much on the lack of a partner or a sex life, and it had been years since she'd even given a man a second look.

Until Scott.

The two of them had been doing this dance for months, drawn together like magnets, powerless to resist the attraction, but one or the other of them always pulled away before things got too heavy. April had been left behind by a rambling man once, and it wasn't going to happen again. And Scott was too good a man—too honorable—to take advantage of her vulnerability.

But what if she were to leave him? He was here until the new year; she could leave right after Christmas…

*Semantics*, her cynical side said. *You'd be leaving because you know he won't stay. Just beating him to the punch.*

*No, I'd be leaving to get on with life.*

This was just a…temporary rest stop. A chance to work on things with Sidney in a more forgiving, family-friendly environment. To gather herself, make a plan. She would find a job to go to, a real one. A good one. While she was here, she could bank most of her salary, add to their little nest egg. She'd be leaving on her own terms.

And in the meantime, why not enjoy everything Harkness had to offer?

"What are you thinking 'bout?"

April looked down at her daughter. "Nothing, sweetheart. Just…stuff."

"Fun night, huh?"

April smiled. "It was."

"I'm going to study up. Really, I mean, I'm going to look up one really cool thing a day. Like, a fact on history, or football or spiders or something."

*Spiders.* How random was that?

"You never know when a category will come up. I bet you if I study a whole bunch of stuff, someday I'll be as good as Faye and Arden."

"They've been playing a long time."

"I'm in no hurry."

April loved to see her enthusiasm, but damn. Looked like she'd have to raise the temporariness of their Harkness stay after all.

"Sidney, don't get too…comfortable." She practically cringed at the way that sounded. "Um, what I mean is…we're only here for a few months."

"Oh, you never know."

"Yeah, Sid, I do know. We're here just until Christmas. Period. End of story." God, she hated to do this—hated to say this. *Don't like your teacher too much. Don't love that dog. Don't expect forever. Scott will not be your dad.*

"You know what would be fun?" Sid said, changing the subject. "If we had, like, a way to keep a record of the wins, then had a trophy or a plaque or something! Like at the end of the season."

April sighed. She'd have to work on this with Sid, but not tonight. Not at bedtime. But there *was* something else that needed raising. "Honey, Ember won't be home tonight, so you've got the room to yourself."

"How come?"

"She's staying with a friend."

"Cool. Could I leave the closet light on? Do you think Ember would mind?

April smiled. "I'm sure she wouldn't mind. But you have to do something for me?"

"What?"

"You've got to promise me—no sneaking out."

The smile dropped from Sid's face. "I said I was sorry."

"I don't doubt it. But Sidney, while I'm out in the barn, getting it decorated for Halloween, I need to know you're safe in here. Get it—*in here*."

She smiled. "Don't worry, Mom. I'll stay put."

"Thank you." April bent and kissed Sidney on the forehead. "If there's anything you need, Arden and Faye will be right downstairs, okay?"

"'Kay."

"Goodnight, sweetie."

"'Night, Mom."

With another quick kiss, April got up. Leaving the closet light on, she left the bedroom, pulling the door closed behind her.

There was something she needed herself…and that was her arms around that man out there in the barn.

# – thirteen –

"HAND ME that other staple gun, would you please?" Scott called down. "This one's not getting the job done. I need the heavier one."

April complied, grabbing the tool from the work table, reaching up as far as she could while he reached down from his perch on the ladder.

"Thanks. You know you really don't have to hold onto the ladder, I've done this a few times."

There it was again, the slight jarring vibration as she resumed her place at the base of the extension ladder. One foot on the floor, the other jacked up on the lowest rung.

"Just being cautious," she said.

"Overcautious."

"Well, that's too bad. You're not going to fall while I'm around."

Scott grinned as he turned back to his task.

*Ka-thunk*. The heavier gun worked perfectly.

He'd already gotten a good start on attaching the first set of pumpkin lights when April arrived.

She looked beautiful tonight. She'd walked into the well-lit barn, her cheeks rosy from the cold, a happy smile at the ready. Earlier her hair had been tied back in a ponytail—her norm for when she worked in the kitchen. Now it was down, flowing loosely around her shoulders. She'd put on lipstick too. Or what passed for lipstick for her. More like a barely-tinted gloss, he suspected. But just the fact that she'd put it on…

God, how that aroused him.

He forced his attention back to the job. Having done this before, he knew there were enough lights to go all the way around the perimeter of the barn. When he'd told April that, she'd taken one look at the remaining strands of lights neatly coiled on the floor, glanced around the barn, and said, "I don't think so."

Now, half an hour and countless ladder moves later, here they were, working on the last section of the final beam.

*Ka-thunk, ka-thunk, ka-thunk,* and the last string was tacked. Sweet.

"Okay, so you were right," she acknowledged. "There was enough to go around with what?—a whole six inches to spare?"

"Hey, six inches is more than enough, or so I've been told."

She snorted at the innuendo. Thank God. He hadn't meant to say that. Had intended, in fact, to avoid the topic of sex altogether.

"Ready for the extension cord?" she asked.

"Yes, please."

She retrieved the heavy duty orange cord from the floor and handed it up. He plugged the last string into the cord, then looked down. "Can you step back a little? I want to let the cord down."

"Rapunzel, Rapunzel, let down your hair."

He grinned. "Yeah, my long, orange, indoor/outdoor hair. I always wondered what it'd be like to be a ginger."

She giggled. The sound made him want to do it again, make her laugh. It wasn't a side of April Morgan that many people saw. With that laughter on her lips and crinkles around her eyes, she was the most beautiful, most desirable woman on earth.

And off limits for so many reasons.

*Damn you, Titus Standish, and you're sage advice.*

Except that really wasn't fair to his brother. Long before Titus had laid eyes on April, Scott had mentally put her in the off-limits category. He did not want to line up with those guys who'd hurt her. Starting with the asshat who'd abandoned her when she got pregnant at seventeen and ending with those few jerks who'd tried to rush her into bed. It seemed some men—including some of her bosses—thought her single mother status translated into easy. She'd corrected that assumption, and each time, the guy's interest had evaporated once he realized casual sex was off the table.

No small wonder she'd sworn off dating. He totally got it, the reluctance to have a succession of men rotate in and out of her daughter's life. And for the most part, he'd managed to leave her alone.

Except when he hadn't.

But that had to stop. The flirting, the kissing…

She stepped back as requested. "Drop away."

He released the coiled extension cord. The pronged end and a few feet of cord hit the floor.

Hands free now, he climbed down the ladder. April had picked up the cord and now stood beside the receptacle, poised to plug it in.

"Okay, plug that puppy in and let's see the big light show."

"On the count of three—one, two…oh, wait!" She put the cord down, darted over to the light switch, and turned off three of the four overhead lights. "That's better." She went back and picked up the extension cord again. "Ready?"

He laughed. "Yes, ma'am."

She plugged the cord in and the strings of small, grinning pumpkins leaped to orange life from the rafters.

"Wow." She stood up, her luscious lips curving in a delighted smile. "Just…wow."

"I take it you approve?"

"Very much."

For reasons he didn't care to analyze, her pleasure made him feel way happier than it had any right to. "I'm glad."

"What about the little ones, though?" She dropped her gaze from the lights to his face. "Do they ever get spooked by the lights?"

"We leave the bright overhead lights on for the wee ones who come right after supper. Then as the older kids come and the little ones have gone, we start dimming them." He moved to his left and hit the dimmer switch. The room's one remaining light dimmed in response. "Like this."

"Cool."

"It's an every-hour-on-the-hour sort of thing. The kids love it. By the time the teenagers are dancing at the end of the party, its orange lights only."

"Ah, the teen dance."

Her eyes took on a faraway look, as though she might be remembering some dimly lit gymnasium. Instantly, his mind supplied a picture of a younger April with some guy's arms around her, slow dancing to Aerosmith's *I Don't Want to Miss a Thing.* The guy's hand sliding down her back to rest on the top of her buttocks…

"How long does it go?"

He blinked. "Sorry, what?"

"The dance. How long does it go on?"

"About an hour," he said. "Everything wraps up with the last waltz."

"With the overhead lights off?"

"Yup."

"Turn them off now so I can see the effect."

He hit the switch to kill the last overhead light.

"Wow," April breathed. "You guys must have been the most popular family in the region. Safe fun for all age levels." She tilted her head. "I'm guessing everyone knew enough to behave?"

He brought the lights back up to their lowest setting. "You bet they did. No one under the influence permitted. No exceptions."

"Anyone ever try to defy that rule?"

"Once in a while. Most notably, Terry Picard." His gut tightened at the thought of that jerk. How he'd tried to get his hands on their land. Their homestead.

"Picard? Any relation to Ember's boyfriend, Jace?"

"Brother. Stepbrother, actually. But Jace is nothing like Terry, thank God."

"So what did he do? This Terry guy?"

"You know Ember and Jace were high school sweethearts, right?"

April nodded. "So you told me."

"They'd just started going out. Grade ten, I think. Jace was fine. He knew the rules about no alcohol, and I don't think he was much of a drinker anyway. Couldn't have been if he was dating Ember. Anyway, this particular Halloween, Terry decided he would crash the party. Made a total ass of himself. Honestly, I think he was always jealous of Ember dating Jace. Couldn't stand the fact that the most beautiful girl in town didn't have the time of day for him." He let his gaze linger on April's face, those intelligent brown eyes, those full, kissable lips glistening with that touch of lip gloss. "Well, she used to be the prettiest girl in the region."

"*Used to be?*"

"Yeah. Until you came to town."

Her gaze flew to meet his, desire leaping to instant life in her eyes.

Dammit, there he went again. He wasn't supposed to be stirring things up with her. He needed to pull back, *right damned now*.

Her lips parted on a sigh. Suddenly, she was closer. A lot closer. She put her hand on his chest, no doubt feeling the hard pounding of his heart.

He closed his hand over hers, intending to remove it. Intending to step back.

But then she spoke. "Scott…"

The way she said his name, as though it were something wondrous, sent a tidal wave of yearning through him. His puny resistance evaporated like a puff of vapor.

Releasing her hand, he pulled her into his arms and captured her mouth.

Her lips were full and lush beneath his and tasted faintly of vanilla. And when her arms went around his neck, he pulled her even closer. She pressed herself eagerly against him, her breasts soft against his chest, her hands clutching at his shoulders.

He kissed her until he was drunk on her taste, her smell, the warm solidity of her body. He kissed her until she sagged weakly against him. Only then did he release her mouth. Reddened and swollen from his kisses, her lips looked lusher than ever.

Then those lips started moving.

"Make love to me, Scott."

# – fourteen –

ONE MINUTE she was in his arms and the next she was standing there by herself. He couldn't have backed away any faster if she said she had the plague.

"Scott?"

He ran a hand over the back of his neck. "We can't have sex."

"Why not?"

"It wouldn't be…prudent."

*Prudent?*

"Scott Standish, if I didn't know better, I'd think you'd been talking to Titus." No disrespect to Scott's older brother, but even in the short while she'd been there, she could see he was a bit of a stiff. Not even Ocean—who was madly in love with the guy—would deny that he was a stickler for rules. The kind of guy who'd use the word *prudent*. "Is this because I'm working for you?"

"Of course not!"

She crossed her arms in front of her. "Really?"

He hesitated. "Okay, yes, it *is* because I'm your employer. But only partly. Mostly it's because I'd be bad for you April."

"Why?"

"You know why. I can't seem to stay in one place for long." He shrugged. "I just can't seem to do…close."

In that moment, she felt his pain. If things could be different—if *he* could be different—he would. She put a finger to his lips "Don't say another word. I'm not trying to pin you down, Scott."

"Never thought you were. I didn't mean it like that."

"I know. I just..." She combed her hair back with her fingers, buying time. How could she couch this delicately? Or at least so he'd understand. "I've never wanted any man like I've wanted you. You know that, right?"

His eyes darkened. "April..."

"I don't know when or if I'll ever want a man again the way I want you."

"And if I was a different man, I'd grab you up so quick." The anguish in his words tore at her heart. "You are the most amazing woman, and you know I adore Sid. But—"

"That's not what I'm asking for, Scott. This time here in Harkness, it's like a little bubble for me and Sid, between where we came from and where we're going. Soon enough, we'll be off to the new job. A new life. Once we leave after Christmas, we won't see you again."

"April. I'm—"

"Hear me out." She held up a hand to stop him. "I look back, and I see years and years of celibacy. I look forward and see more of the same, until Sidney is older, and until I'm better established financially. And I've never minded. Well, not much. Not until you."

"I'm not a good choice, April. I...I'm not good for anyone."

"Ah, but you're the one I want." She gave him a gentle smile. "Chemistry like this is such a rarity, at least for me, and I think for you too."

"You're right about the attraction," he said, his voice gruff. "I swear, there are times I want to kiss you more than I want to breathe."

Desire flared in her eyes. "And that's why we've never

been able to stop this back-and-forth dance, no matter how many times we tried." She tilted her head. "What do you say? Don't you want to finish the dance?"

"God, yes! But—"

"I know." She stepped closer, put a hand on his chest. "I know you're not going to stay. Not here, not anywhere. Well, guess what? I'm not staying either. But I'm hoping that when I drive away, I'm going to have some memories that are mine alone."

"What about Sid? Isn't it...dangerous?"

"Believe me, I've thought about that. But I think that ship has already sailed. No matter what happens or doesn't happen between you and me, leaving here—driving away from you, your family, Axl—is going to be desperately hard for Sid. I knew that when I agreed to take the job."

"You're right." His brows drew together in a frown. "I didn't really think about that before I strong-armed you into staying."

"Nobody strong-armed me," she said quickly. "The decision was mine. And I made it because even though leaving will hurt, I have to believe this time in Harkness is going to be good for her. Lord knows *something* had to change. For God's sake, Scott, she ran away from home. Ran away from *me*. Sid and I obviously have to work on our relationship, and this is a great environment to do that."

He took her hand from where it rested on his chest, running the pad of his thumb over her knuckles. Just that small contact sent sparklers of excitement zinging through her.

"If we do this, Sid can't know about it."

Yes! He was going to accept her proposal. She knew it. "Agreed," she said. "It would just set up unrealistic expectations. You know Sidney. She still believes in magic, believes that wishes come true if only you wish hard enough."

"And you? What do you believe?"

"I believe wishes are a luxury grownups can't afford."

"Maybe you're not wishing right."

She smiled up at him. "You know what I wish, Scott Standish?" She moved closer. "I wish you'd stop talking and kiss me."

Desire blazed from his eyes, but he grasped her arms to keep her from closing the distance between them. "This…us. This physical relationship. I don't want you to think…"

"That you're coercing your new employee? Trading on sexual favors?" She smiled, noting the way his gaze dropped to her lips. "I'll say it again: this isn't part of the deal. It's completely outside the working relationship. It's just…us, here."

The hands that held her at bay suddenly yanked her against him. His kiss was hard and demanding and positively thrilling. Hooking her fingers in his belt loops, she urged him closer, exulting in the growing swell of his erection.

He lifted his head. "God, I can't believe we're doing this. I've wanted you so long."

Her answer was to pull his face back down and kiss him as fiercely as he'd just kissed her.

Then he was backing her up. She went with it, letting his hands on her hips guide her. Was he thinking about the sideboard? The one he'd deposited her on that first day? Would he lift her up there, strip her pants off and spread her legs… Her insides went liquid with need.

Then she felt something hard against her butt and shoulders. Something that definitely was not the sideboard. She broke the kiss to see that he'd backed her up against the ladder to what used to be a hayloft. Of course! That's where he often slept, even when no one was occupying his bedroom in the house. To be closer to the stars, he'd said, but she knew it was to escape the claustrophobia of being there in Harkness.

"Climb."

The command in his voice sent another bolt of excitement to her core.

She wasn't fond of heights, but as she climbed the ladder, she was conscious that he was right behind her. If she slipped, he would catch her. He would always keep her safe.

*Not so safe for your heart, though.*

She shook the thought away. Not because it wasn't true, but because it wasn't relevant. Just as it was too late for her daughter to avoid some anguish when they left here, it was too late for April to shield her heart. His leaving Montreal had shown her that. Even if she'd chosen to walk away untouched, it wouldn't stop the heartache. So why not have him while she could?

As she stepped from the ladder into the loft, she caught her breath. It was beautiful. The rough-hewn floorboards had been painted white, giving the place an airy feel, even though the walls and rafters were unfinished. The focal point was the bed and night table, which stood in the midst of all that otherwise empty space. She crossed to the bed, neatly made with a Hudson's Bay point blanket as the coverlet. The classic style, of course, off-white with those primary colored stripes. It looked perfect in the rustic setting.

He went to one side of the room and opened two huge wooden doors. She felt the cold, fresh evening air move into the space and went to stand beside him.

"Omigod, the stars! Look at them. So beautiful."

"Not half as beautiful as you."

She glanced up to see the hungry way he was looking at her. Her breasts tingled with the need to have his hands on them. She started to move closer, intending to take his hand and place it exactly where she wanted it, but then it hit her—they didn't have any protection.

She froze.

"April, what is it?"

So much for her poker face. "I was just thinking...we don't have condoms."

His eyebrows shot up, then came down in a frown. Then

his face cleared. He strode purposefully over to a big aluminum bin standing against the far wall, the type of storage chest you usually saw in the box of a pickup truck to hold tools and such. He lifted the lid and pulled out his backpack. Unzipping the side compartment, he fished around inside.

"Bingo." He held up two condoms. "But I better date check 'em. They've been riding around with me for a while." He moved to the edge of the hay mow to catch more light from the overhead fixtures. "And we have a winner. Well-traveled, but plenty of shelf-life left."

"Good." Suddenly nervous now that the last potential obstacle had been removed, April walked over to the bed and trailed her fingers over the woolen Hudson's Bay blanket. She glanced up at him. "What about mice…any chance we'll be getting in bed with some?"

He grinned. "No. The mattress is solid latex foam, which they don't seem to like very much. But to be safe, it gets rolled up and stored in there when I'm not here." He nodded toward the aluminum storage unit. "And there's no box spring for the little guys to get up inside of. Just a wooden platform." The sexy smile he gave her made her toes fairly curl. "It'll just be you and me, April."

"Good." *Wow, April. Scintillating conversation, there.*

"You know, we don't have to do this." He was studying her face now. "You can still change your mind. You can *always* change your mind."

In that moment, she almost loved him. Standing there beside the wide, inviting bed, sporting a hard-on beneath those faded Levis after she'd practically jumped him, and he was offering to pull back. Her nerves dissolved in the face of his consideration.

"Thank you, but I'm not changing my mind." She toed off her runners. Then, taking a deep breath, she reached for the hem of her heavy sweater and pulled it over her head.

His gaze clapped onto her chest and the plain nude-colored,

seamless T-shirt bra. If her decision hadn't been so spur-of-the-moment, she'd have worn something sexier. Her black pushup bra did wonders for her modest breasts. But he didn't seem to mind the lack of lace or seductive construction.

"Let me take it off."

She shivered as he came to stand just inches from her. As his arms went around her, she breathed him in, the scent of his soap, his skin. The clean, outdoorsy smell of his gray chamois shirt. She felt his right hand find the bra's clasp, releasing it. She let him peel it from her. He deposited it on the nightstand and stepped back to look his fill.

Despite all the times they'd come close to this, he'd never seen her breasts. Her bra, yes, and one of them fairly transparent. But never her bare breasts.

"You are so beautiful."

He lifted a hand to cup and lift one breast. Her dark nipples contracted, hardening into tight nubs.

She lifted his other hand and guided it to the other breast. He laughed, his breath warm on her face. Then he bent to suckle one of those nipples, sending bolts of desire straight to her womb. Her body sagged and he guided her back to the bed.

They went down in a tangle of limbs. His mouth was on hers now, kissing her urgently. She tore at his shirt, helping him strip it off. Then they were both wriggling out of their jeans. He cursed as he fought to get his boots off, then the Levis. She laid back and watched him, smiling at his struggle. Finally naked, he rolled toward her. She went into his arms easily.

There was silence in the old barn then, save for their breathing. As hands sought heated skin and learned dips and curves, their breathing accelerated, growing harsh in the silence. April was poised to take his rock-hard cock into her when he remembered the condom. He got it open and on without losing a beat, and when he slid home inside her, she had to bite down on a shout of delight at the all-but-forgotten sensation.

*This*. This is what she dreamed of those nights when Scott had slept in the suite at the end of the hall in the Boisverts' home. How many times had she woken drenched in sweat, her thighs damp from the yearning? And now he was between her thighs, propped on his arms, pinning her to the foam mattress. Fucking her with slow, deliberate strokes.

She dug her nails into the points of his shoulders and lifted her hips to meet each thrust. "Faster." She heard the naked plea in her voice but didn't care. "Harder."

With a growl, he complied. Short minutes later, she tipped over the edge, convulsing around him. He followed quickly, with an exultant cry.

She was vaguely aware of him getting up. Disposing of the condom, she supposed. Then he was back, drawing the covers over their cooling bodies. She snuggled into him, resting her head on his arm. She really should get up, dress. Sneak back into the house.

He kissed her forehead. "You okay?"

She smiled. "I'm so much better than okay."

"Good. Stay and watch the stars with me for a bit."

She really shouldn't. "Okay."

"Let me get the lights."

He slipped out from under the covers again. This time, she was very much aware as he strode naked to a beam on the hay mow's edge and the junction box with the light switch mounted on it. She'd spent enough time looking at his butt—in work pants, in blue jeans, in motorcycle chaps—to know it was truly world class, but it gave her great pleasure to see it bared. Then the light went out and he was just a blur of white making his way back to bed.

They settled together again beneath the blankets. Outside the big doors, the sky was a gorgeous blanket of stars, pinpricks of light in a luscious, dark fabric.

"Oh, a falling star!" she said. "Quick. Make a wish."

# – fifteen –

IT WAS almost midnight and Scott lay looking out at the star-filled sky with a sleeping April nestled into his shoulder. The temperature had plunged in the last few hours. They were snug enough beneath the sheet, cotton thermal blanket, and woolen topper, but mainly because they were sharing body heat. He really should get up and close the big double doors.

He always slept so much better out here, and it wasn't entirely owing to the fresh air. This was one of the few places on earth where it felt like nothing came between him and the stars.

But he wasn't alone tonight.

*Make a wish,* she'd said. For once, he'd been tempted to wish he could stay. But what was the point of wishing for the impossible? Staying would require he be someone fundamentally different.

Tenderly, he kissed her hair as she slept, taking the scent of her shampoo into his lungs. What the hell had he done? She was so lovely, beautiful through and through. He wouldn't hurt her for the world—this woman who'd melted so perfectly into his arms.

She sighed in her sleep, burrowing closer. And oh God, just that innocent sound made him harden.

*Easy. Give the girl a break.*

With the long days she put in, she needed her rest. She was up every morning at dawn, even back in Montreal. She worked damned hard. But it wasn't just a physical strength and stamina she brought to her job; she put her whole heart into it. And yeah, he had to admit there was little else in this world more attractive than a woman engrossed in her personal passion.

*Passion.* She had plenty of that. He suspected it had only grown stronger for all the years of denial. They way she'd spent herself so completely with him tonight… It humbled him.

God, he was the luckiest man in the world.

Or the biggest bastard.

He eased himself out of bed, slowly and quietly so as to not disturb her.

*Brr.* He was used to the cold, had put in winters in some of the world's most frigid places. When he was twenty-two, he'd driven a bus in the Yukon, shuttling workers from camp to the job site in weather cold enough to freeze the tossed dregs of your hot coffee before it could hit the ground. It had never really bothered him. You just dressed for it, and made damned good and sure you didn't get caught out in it.

He reached for his jeans and tugged them on. A shiver persuaded him to shrug back into his shirt too.

He padded to the window, his feet cold on the painted boards. Down below, the yard was quiet. Well, mostly quiet. As he watched, a skunk—its white stripe giving it away—waddled away from the lawn toward the apple orchards. He gave a silent thank you that Axl wasn't out, and then another thank you when the yip of a coyote sounded from the brush-filled field across the road. Years ago, that might have been enough to rouse Axl from his sleep to give a warning growl. And if the noise persisted, he'd bark hard enough to wake the household. But these days, Axl's hearing wasn't what it used to be. Though sometimes he suspected the old dog only pretended not to hear, particularly when it involved a command to leave something alone.

"Are you leaving?"

At April's soft voice, he turned. In the dim light, he could see she'd sat up in bed.

"Of course not. I wouldn't leave you here to wake up by yourself. But we should go in soon."

"Come back to bed for a while?"

"I will. Just give me a sec."

He closed up the doors, then moved to locate the portable space heater. It was easy to find: just head toward the corner until his bare feet found the ceramic tile he'd laid down to insulate the old boards from the heat source. He found the electrical outlet and plugged the heater in. It came to immediate, glowing life. By its orange glow, he made his way back to the bed.

"Looks like you're occupying more than your share of the middle, Miss Morgan. I never pegged you for a bed hog."

"Undress."

At the sultriness in that single word, his heart leaped. But rather than reveal how powerfully her command had affected him, he just let his smile widen and reached for the buttons of his shirt.

She didn't smile back. Her eyes were too busy drinking him in as he stripped off his shirt. He shucked off his jeans and kicked them away to stand naked before her. She watched with avid interest as he crawled into bed beside her.

She slid her arms around his neck, pressing her breasts into him and twining a leg with his. The heat from her body felt scorching against his cooler flesh.

"You've got a second condom, right?"

He could help but flex his hips against her. "I do."

"Can I put it on you this time?"

"You absolutely can."

# – sixteen –

SIDNEY HAD been counting down the hours since breakfast. And the days since they'd agreed to stay with the Standishs.

This was it—finally October 31st. She was pretty sure every kid at school would be coming to the party, at least for a bit.

Danika had walked back to the Standish place with her after school. Sid's mom had made them an early supper, and now Danika was in the upstairs bathroom down the hall, quietly singing a Katy Perry song as she applied the sparkles to her cheekbones and glitter to her piled high black curls. She'd raided her aunt's makeup bag, and spent about ten bucks of her birthday money—Danika's birthday was in October too—at the dollar store.

Mid-tune, Danika changed to a Taylor Swift song. Most times, Sidney wouldn't have minded her singing. In fact, she'd often urged her friend to sing louder. She had a beautiful voice and Sid figured she shouldn't be shy about showing it off.

But at that very moment, as Sidney sat at the top of the stairs straining to hear the conversation going on downstairs, she wished Danika would give it a rest. She knew she shouldn't be doing it. Her mom would so not be impressed. She did not approve of *eavesdropping*, as she called it. But she literally couldn't help it! All because of what she'd thought she'd heard a few moments ago—by accident—and what she was hoping to hear again.

"There's enough red licorice there for the next three Halloweens," Scott said.

There were six full boxes of it on the kitchen table, Sidney knew. She and Danika had lined all the late-donated treats up this afternoon, after they'd finished their homework. The slender boxes of licorice—donated by Arden's friend from the pharmacy—were right there beside a larger box full of divinity fudge, compliments of a Mrs. Budaker, the lady who made those gingersnaps for Titus all the time.

"Licorice?" Titus said. "Oh, man, keep that stuff away from Axl. Last time he got into red licorice, I was dealing with a vomiting dog in the middle of the night."

"I'll tell him not to keep you up so late tonight."

"Me? No way. You're home—you're on dog duty. Where is he by the way?"

"Up in Sidney's room."

Yes!

There it was again. She *had* heard it right the first time.

*Sidney's room.*

Scott said it just now, and a few minutes ago when Ocean had called Titus on his cell, Titus had said practically the same thing: *Hey, babe. Can't wait to see you too. Yes, the girls are super excited. They're up in Sid's bedroom now getting their costumes on.*

She clenched her hands, restraining her giddiness.

She couldn't tell her mom. Not that she'd be mad, exactly. But she wouldn't like it. Sidney bit her lip. She knew her mother didn't want her to hope; didn't want her to even wish it.

"Tada!"

Sidney turned to look at Danika. Her friend stood in the hallway now, striking her best sea queen pose—one hand on her hip, chin held high. In the other hand, she held an awesome trident, which was really a plastic devil's pitchfork from the dollar store that they'd covered with tinfoil. She'd also attached a bunch of plastic fishes to her sea foam-green chiffon skirt using fishing line that was practically invisible. As she walked toward Sidney, the fishes clattered together.

Sid stood. "You look awesome!"

And she did. Everything was perfect—from the orange and white clownfish tucked into her hair to the matching orange sneakers on her feet. Then there were the fingernails—Sidney was pretty sure her friend wasn't sporting those half-inch pearly green nails when she'd walked into the bathroom.

"Wow! Are those press-ons?"

Danika splayed her polished nails proudly. "Yup. Aunt Natalie's. I love them! Aren't they amazing?"

"Totally. Especially for a sea queen."

"Your turn. I can't wait to see your costume!"

"It's so cool. You're gonna love it." She led her friend back into her room. "Ember helped me with it."

"Is she really a doctor?"

"Ember? Yeah."

"And she's setting up practice here? In Harkness? That's what I heard."

"Yes."

"Dad was saying that was really good for the region."

Axl was lying on Ember's bed. He lifted his head up then lay it back down on her cloud-covered comforter. He closed his tired eyes but thumped his tail all the same when Sidney stopped to pet him on the head.

"Poor Axl. He looks tuckered right out." Danika said.

Sid giggled. "*Tuckered right out*?"

"Exhausted. Really tired. Too pooped to party. Haven't you ever heard that expression before?"

"Nope."

Danika shrugged. "Maybe it's a Harkness thing. Or an old people's thing."

Sid moved her hand to scratch under Axl's graying chin. "He's really old. Scott got him when he was just a kid."

Danika sat on the edge of the bed and started scratching Axl behind the ear. The old dog practically squirmed in pleasure.

"Honestly, I worry about him climbing the stairs so much. Sometimes, I try to sneak up here when he's sleeping on his bed in the living room, but he always follows me. It's like he has a sixth sense or something."

"My dad says dogs are kind of psychic," Danika said. "But I think Axl does it just because he likes you."

"Buddy Boy's like that with you," Sidney said.

Buddy Boy was Danika's whippet. That dog could run like the wind. Poor Axl would be lamed up for a week if he tried to run even a little bit. Though she'd never say that in front of Axl. She wouldn't want to hurt his feelings.

"Yeah," Danika said. "He's a good dog."

"You're so lucky. I wish I could have a dog."

"Maybe someday you will."

*That would take one heck of a wish...*

Sid crossed the room to the closet beside the vanity, but before she could open the door, Danika said. "Wait!"

"What?"

"Let me get the door for you. I'm a magic sea queen, after all," Danika pointed the pronged end of the trident at the closet doors, and said, "Abracadabra!"

"Hmm, that didn't work," Sid said. "Try spinning around really fast."

"Okay." She spun multiple times and the plastic fish rattled up a storm.

As Danika was spinning, Sidney grabbed the knob on the bi-fold door and pulled it open. "Hey, look. It worked!"

She stopped. "It's magic!"

Danika dissolved in a fit of giggles, and Sidney laughed too. But in her head, the word was still echoing.

*Magic.*

Obviously, it wasn't really magic. Sid had opened the door herself and they both knew it. But the word caused her to think about something Scott had told her about that maybe *was* real magic. Just the memory of it made her shiver.

It was back in August. They'd been fixing the Boisverts' gazebo. Scott was in charge of hammering the thin sheets of lattice work into place, while Sid was in charge of handing him the tiny nails, one at a time.

As always, he'd told her it was a good thing she was there to help. But as always, it wasn't all work. They'd talked. She told him stuff; he told her stuff.

*There's this place along the Prince River, Slamm's Landing.*

*"That's a weird name."*

*"Well, that's just what I called it. I came across the place when I was hiking. I must have been sixteen or so."*

*"Oh, so back in the day?"*

*"That's right; back in the day." He'd smiled. He always smiled when she said things like that. 'Back in the day' or 'groovy' or 'hip'. So she did that a lot. "There's a big, flat rock on the bank, and the river is really fast there. Rapids, I guess you'd say. And the trees are set back so that you can get a real good look at the sky. When I was young, I used to bike out there in the summer. I'd get up on that rock and look right out over the river."*

*"Was it a special spot?"*

*"Very special. I just knew there was nobody else for miles around. Just me, the river, and the big, blue dome of sky. I loved that feeling."*

*"Ever go at night?"*

*"Yep, a few times on clear, starry nights. Though I shouldn't have. Looking back, it was dangerous going that far afield in the dark, alone."*

*"Ever make a wish there? On the stars, I mean?"*

*"Sure, I did. It's the very best place in the world to wish on a star."*

*On his cue, she'd passed him a nail, and he'd efficiently hammered another piece of lattice work into place.*

*"What did you wish for?"*

*"No way, Sid the Kid! I'm not telling."*

*"But it was a long time ago."*

*He'd shaken his head. "Doesn't matter. You're not allowed to tell until the wish comes true."*

*"Why not?"*

*"If you tell, it might not come true."*

"Oh my gosh! Is that a sword?" Danika clapped her hands together, but she did so carefully, fingertips splayed away from her palms to protect her inch-long nails.

"Sure is." Shaking thoughts of Scott away, Sid reached into the closet for the plywood cut-out sword with its black-painted hilt and silver-painted blade. "And that's just for starters. Wait'll you see the whole thing."

# – seventeen –

APRIL LOOKED around the Far South Barn. Happy orange pumpkins glowed overhead.

She didn't know why she was so darn nervous!

Wait. Yes, she did. Before the night was done, half of Harkness would have traipsed through. Not that the party had been all her doing. But it had mostly been.

It was early enough that it was mainly just the littlest kids. Hence, all the lights were on, blazing down on the transformed barn.

They'd gone sooo beyond the small event that had been initially envisioned. She shook her head. She'd actually thought those pumpkin lights were all there was to the decorating.

Ha!

Last night Ember and Jace, Titus and Ocean, and she and Scott had all made their way out to the barn after *Jeopardy!* to really deck the place out. Titus had brought a case of beer, which the guys and Ocean drank. April wasn't much of a beer drinker—or a drinker at all. But Ember had cracked open a bottle of wine after the work was done. April had allowed herself a glass. And she'd allowed herself to be happy, to join in on the fun. Relax for an hour. Afterward, she tried to think of another time when she'd enjoyed that kind of camaraderie, but couldn't dredge up a single instance.

This barn had absolutely come alive last night with laughter and teasing, friendship and love. It really had felt like the walls themselves had pulsed with life, not just from their exuberance as they worked, but from every gathering, party and dance the old barn had housed over the years.

Even now, those walls absorbed the high, excited squeals and laughter of the young ones. If they could talk, she was pretty sure the old boards would be saying *the more the merrier!*

Her gaze drifted up to the loft. If that loft could talk…

April grinned. And because the only other person who knew the full reason behind the smile on her face was standing right beside her, her grin broadened even more.

"You look happy," Scott said.

He put his arm around her shoulders and gave her a quick squeeze.

That was so Scott. He was happy to see her happy. No ulterior motive, just…Scott.

"I was thinking that as nice as the barn looked empty, it looks so much better with the kids, the costumes, the people."

"Looks alive," he said.

"Exactly."

"Well, congrats to you. You set the stage."

"This is hardly all my doing. You guys did more work than I did."

"Yeah, but we wouldn't even be having this party if it wasn't for you."

"And Sidney," she said, looking up at him with gratitude. "This means so much to her, Scott."

He smiled. "I'm glad."

"Oh, there's Ember." April gave her a wave.

The town's future doctor had been hectically busy setting up her new office. The shingle was already on the door, a nurse and office staff hired, furniture installed, supplies ordered. In a matter of days, the place would be open for business.

Ember waved back from the dessert table. In her hand she held a small orange paper plate with two pieces of April's Halloween squares on it. She pointed to the treat and mouthed, "These are to die for."

Beside Ember, with an assortment of squares on his own plate, Jace gave her the thumbs up.

Mrs. Budaker's divinity fudge was going fast. A perennial favorite of the townsfolk, April understood that Mrs. B brought it to every gathering. But she was pleased to see that her own chocolate cheesecake bars with their dusting of dark chocolate were equally popular, as were a number of the other standard goodies she'd prepared. But the cheesecake bars were her very own recipe, one she'd never served to a crowd before. To see them disappear so quickly was heartening. She'd so badly wanted to impress, not just the Standishs, but the whole town. It was her turn to shine—or not—under her own name. Not on behalf of the Boisverts, or one of the restaurants she'd worked at. *Hello, my name is April Dawn Morgan, and look what I can do.*

She liked it a lot more than she could have imagined.

Being around Ember and Ocean had stirred something in her. They'd become fast friends, of course, but it was more than that. Both women had very different but equally lofty goals—Ember with her passion for healing and Ocean with her love of story.

Once upon a time, April had had her own dreams…

"Scott, you old dog! When did you get back in town?"

April looked at the man who'd just spoken. He stood in front of Scott, wearing a wide, infectious grin.

"Good God, John? I haven't seen you in ages," Scott glanced at April. "April, this is John Redstone. John, April Morgan."

"Pleased to meet you, April." John extended his hand.

As April shook it, she noted how handsome he was. And just as tall as Scott, just as well-built. Probably a few years older. "Likewise."

“What are you doing here?” Scott asked. “And out of costume too.”

He chuckled. “My sister’s son.” He nodded toward the boy in the spaceship costume who was currently ladling some eyeballs—peeled green grapes—out of the punchbowl. Then she looked closer. The spaceship cleverly disguised a child-sized wheelchair.

“Is that Bruce?”

“Yup.” John nodded with pride.

“He was barely a year old when I saw him last.”

“He’s five now. And he was hell-bent on coming here tonight. Pamela’s studying, so here I am.”

“Pam still in nursing school?”

“Last year, thank God. She’s worked damned hard.”

Scott turned to April to give a quick explanation. “Bruce’s dad isn’t in the picture. John’s helped a lot with Bruce.”

“Helped? We’re family, bro. That’s how we roll.”

“Speaking of rolling, how’s that new Harley working out for you?”

And they were off, talking about their bikes. She held the sigh inside. Not that she didn’t like Scott’s bike. She did. But when it came to spark plugs and cylinders, she tended to tune out.

Pamela Redstone was a lucky woman, with a brother like John. A family like that. They hadn’t turned their backs on his sister. They’d embraced Bruce.

Ember joined them, having turned the dessert table over to Jace’s care momentarily. “Are you ready to see Sid’s costume?”

Finally! Sid had been working on it in secret, with only Ember privy to what it was. “I can’t wait. Where is she?” April scanned the remaining crowd.

“You have to close your eyes,” Ember said. “She wants to make an entrance.”

As instructed, she closed her eyes tightly.

"You too, Scott," Ember said. "Keep them closed."

April heard someone walk up—a couple of someones, actually—and knew it was Sidney and her friend Danika. "Come on, Ladybug," she said. "I'm dying to see your costume. Can I look now?"

"Okay, then…tada!"

April opened her eyes. "Oh, Sidney!"

There her daughter stood—a shield maiden ready for battle. The cutest shield maiden ever—April was sure of it. She wore a brown approximation of a Norse apron dress, and her hair had been plaited. The thick braids hung down below her Viking hat, complete with horns, which had been fashioned from a plastic popcorn bowl. In one hand she held a painted wooden sword and on her other arm, she bore a shield made from an old hubcap. That was pretty ingenious.

"Whoa, well done!" Scott said.

"A Viking!" April clapped her hands. "Sidney. That's inspired."

"I'm not just any old Viking." She turned around to reveal a patch tacked to her dress with a single word embroidered on it: *Minnesota*.

"I'm a Viking from Minnesota," she said, striking a proud shield maiden pose.

Scott chuckled. "Sid, that's absolutely the best—I mean, hands down *best*—costume I've ever seen."

"That's what I told her," Danika piped up. "Sid's so creative. Look at the sword!"

"Thank you," Sidney said. "And you are the most outstanding Sea Queen I'd ever seen!"

"I agree," a female voice said. "I'd say she looks positively royal!"

April looked over to see Faye Siliker smiling widely. Faye was dressed as an old granny—complete with round, wire-rimmed granny glasses and curly, gray-haired wig over her own sleek, blondish-white hair. Right behind her stood the big bad wolf. A very gray one. Arden.

April put her hand over her mouth to keep a laugh from escaping. A couple's costume? Could Titus and Scott possibly fail to appreciate the significance?

"Attention, everyone!" It was Ms. Makepeace in her unmistakable teacher voice. "It's time for the costume contest."

Scott leaned over to Titus, who'd just ambled over to join them with Ocean on his arm. "Guessing you won't win, bro."

Titus laughed. They all did.

"Oh, shoot," Ember said. "Customers at the dessert table. Looks like Jace could use some help."

Before April could offer to spell her, Ember zipped across the room to help Jace with the surge.

Then Ms. Makepeace spoke again, drawing April's attention.

"First, I'd like to thank the Standishs for hosting this party. I know it's been a long time since the community has had a Halloween party, so thank you for that." She looked over at April and her crowd. "Thanks, guys. The decorations are beautiful and the food—really superb!"

April smiled back at the teacher. They'd talked a couple of times since she'd taken Sidney to school. The last time they'd spoken, Ms. Makepeace—or Eden, as she insisted April call her—confided how delighted she was about the party. Well, she'd ostensibly called to speak about Sid's enrichment curriculum, but once that was out of the way, the conversation had turned to the Halloween event. It was something the community needed, she'd said. Some families were feeling the pinch of the economic times. And some kids had no friends to go trick-or-treating with. As if April didn't like her enough, the young principal had volunteered to look after the costume contest. As soon as Arden okayed the contest, April had given Eden the job.

There was a smattering of applause from adults and children alike, followed by it-was-nothing nods from the throat-clearing Standish menfolk while Ember smiled and waved from her position at the dessert table.

"Let's follow the same format that was used in the past," Eden said. "We'll get all the kids to gather at the front, then we'll call you up on stage by your grade. Those of you who are home-schooled, come right up when you see your friends. Or just whenever you like."

"Let's go!" Sidney said. She and Danika took off toward the front, along with every other kid in the place.

April so hoped Sidney won something. Not that it would be the end of the world if she didn't place. And not that she was one of those obnoxious parents whose kid had to be the best at everything. But Sidney was so happy. So alive. And she made a damned good Viking.

"For the adult contest," Eden continued, her teacher's voice cutting through the din without benefit of a microphone, "we've got three judges who've volunteered to roam the crowd—and by volunteer, I mean I cornered them and strong-armed them into it. Our judges are Donny Gravelle, Sissy Crocker and Buzz Adams."

"Chief Adams is blind as a bat," an unidentified voice called out from the crowd. "Why, he stopped me for speeding last week and I was practically crawling!"

April laughed along with everyone else, even harder still when Buzz called back, "Stop by my office for a ticket tomorrow, will ya, Earl? Save me the trouble of tracking you down."

Everyone laughed, none louder than a round-faced older gentleman with straw sticking out at the wrists and ankles of his scarecrow costume. Earl, she presumed.

Scott turned to Titus, who had packed all that muscle into a blue long-sleeved shirt and work pants. "So, tell me, bro, who are you supposed to be?"

"I'm a security guard," Titus answered, gesturing to his duty belt. But instead of a sidearm and a baton, it held a radio, flashlight, and other search & rescue gear. "Can I see your ID, buddy? Are you sure you're old enough to be drinking that?" He gestured to the plastic cup in his brother's hand, half full of punch. Nothing alcoholic in it, of course.

"Ask me later," he answered. "When this shindig is over, I might just crack open a beer. Two if I win best costume in the adult category. You know, to celebrate."

Ocean rolled her eyes at April. "Lame, lame, lame. Good thing you're a sport, Arden. Someone had to represent the Standish men."

Scott and Titus grinned at each other.

Scott himself had gone all out—that's right, he'd put on a cowboy hat and hauled on some old cowboy boots he probably used for biking. She had to give him points for the lasso, though. He'd braided some twine he'd found in one of the barns into a rope-ish thickness, looped it up, and secured it to his belt. April thought he made a pretty damned hot cowboy.

Ocean was dressed—unmistakably—as Mark Twain, right down to the wrinkles drawn on with a grease pencil, the bushy white hair and mustache, and the unlit cigar she carried. And just in case people didn't get the hint, she also toted a battered copy of *Adventures of Huckleberry Finn*.

Rounding out the Standish peeps, Ember made a beautiful, fiery-haired pirate. Not to be outdone, Jace had dressed as Jack Sparrow, complete with the dreadlocked wig, red bandana, and lavishly applied black eye makeup. She had to admit, the guy could give Johnny Depp a run for his money in the sexy department.

Then there was her own outfit… April ran her hands along the gypsy belt, heavy with its rows of dangling fake coins. It rode on her hips, atop her flashy, floor-length, orange and yellow skirt. She'd tied a matching strip of material—salvaged from hemming the skirt—into her otherwise loose hair. Completing the outfit, she wore a white peasant blouse beneath a tightly laced vest. The vest had been a loose, button-up affair, but had been cut down to size and modified with grommets to facilitate lacing up with a leather thong. And no, she hadn't done that all herself. Sidney hadn't been the only one to get a helping hand from Ember.

The effort had so been worth it, though. The look in Scott's eyes when he'd first caught sight of her in the costume had set her breasts and belly to tingling. Just like they were tingling right now as she looked her fill of him in those boot-cut Wranglers that hugged his butt so faithfully.

He chose that moment to look over at her. The eye contact was electric. Suddenly, it was as if all the air had been sucked from the room. She wanted to move closer, move into his arms. Close enough to inhale his smell, feel his heartbeat.

"Now, may I have all the pre-kindergarten through grade one students come to the stage, please?"

Eden's voice cut through the crowd, pulling April out of her trance. She tore her gaze from Scott's face and looked around. How long had she been staring at him? Had anyone noticed? They were supposed to be keeping things on the down-low. And hello? The room was full of kids.

She glanced back at Scott to see he was talking to Titus as though he hadn't missed a beat. Around her, people shuffled and chairs scritched on the floor as folks made way for the contestants. No one seemed to be paying the least attention to her. She let a sigh of relief escape.

Turning her attention back to the stage, she watched the little ones—most still holding their mothers' hands—move to the front. Cameras flashed. One photographer in particular caught April's attention. One of the few uncostumed people in the crowd was snapping pictures like crazy.

"That's Glee Henderson."

Scott's voice so close to her ear made her jump. He'd obviously left his brother to Ocean.

"Glee?"

"Her real name's Glenine. Everyone just calls her Glee. She's a local reporter for the Harkness newspaper."

How cool would it be for Sidney to get her picture in the paper? "Will she stay and take pictures of the older kids when they compete?"

"Absolutely. Adults too."

As if on cue, while waiting for the next little kid to make her way to center stage, Glee turned and snapped a picture of Stephen, the waiter from the tea shop, who was looking totally awesome as Vampire Bill from *True Blood*.

April felt a tap on her shoulder and turned to see Ocean. "I'm going to go help Eden wrangle up the little ones."

"Need some help?" April asked.

"I may need some security, actually." She looked up at Titus. "Looks like a particularly tough looking zombie Bo Peep up there, don't you think?"

"You're right," Titus eyed the tiny girl in her shepherd costume, carrying a wooden adult cane as her shepherd's crook. "I don't like the look of that staff she's carrying. And something about that bloody pink ribbon in her hair just doesn't feel right."

"Protect me, Titus," Ocean said, dramatically. Or as dramatically as a woman could through a bushy gray mustache.

"Isn't that the deal?"

"Why, Mr. Standish, I believe it is."

By the way the two of them were looking at each other, there was more to this casual exchange than met the eye. Titus confirmed it by kissing her, quickly, on the lips. He immediately lifted a finger to scratch over his own upper lip, clearly unused to mustache kisses.

Grinning, April watched Titus and Ocean head toward Eden.

No sooner had they left when Ember and Jace, dessert rush dealt with, came to stand with her and Scott.

"Nice shirt, dude," Scott said to Jace.

He smiled. "Yeah, the puffy sleeves really make it, don't they?"

Ember looked at April and rolled her eyes. "Boys, huh?"

April laughed.

"I'll tell you what *does* work, though," Jace said. "These brownies, April. Seriously, where did you get this recipe?"

"My own," she answered.

"Please tell me you've copyrighted it?"

She laughed. "Would that I could. No matter how new or novel, recipes are very hard to copyright. A list of ingredients and instructions on how to make the product are considered functional and thus not copyrightable."

"Too bad," Jace said. "I guess you could always keep the recipe secret?"

She grinned. "Exactly."

Jace's eyes widened. "I've just had the best idea. April, you've got to anchor a booth at the market and start selling some of this stuff."

"The downtown market?" Scott asked. "That's full up, isn't it? I know Duchess has had her name in for one of the outdoor stands for a couple of years now."

"Ah, but there's a new market in town," Ember said. "Tell her to give us a call."

"A new market?"

April listened as Jace explained about his plans for MacQueen Square. She'd known he bought it—Ember had been bouncing around these last couple days getting things set up for her new office, which was going into one of two larger suites that anchored the ends. Other tenants had made inquiries. But what was on Jace's mind now, and what was becoming more and more interesting to April as he spoke, was his plans for the area at the back of the building.

"Prince Region Wholesale used to occupy the space. Now it's just a large empty warehouse."

"Perfect for a weekend market," Scott nodded. "Damn, that's a good idea."

"We've already spoken to Mrs. Budaker," Ember said. "She's very keen to take a spot."

"Mrs. Budaker?" Scott's eyebrows rose. "Isn't she already at the downtown market?"

"They've upped the rent," Jace said, "and she's not happy about it. I'm offering her free rent until January."

"Two months," Scott said. "That's not bad. Especially considering the Christmas traffic."

"Then a year's lease after that, if she's interested."

"I've spoken to a couple of folks who have booths in Tynsdale," Ember added. "Not necessarily offering the same deal as Mrs. Budaker, of course; she'd be a bit of a coup. If we can get her, others will follow. But even so, a lot of the merchants told me they'd open a stand down here in a heartbeat."

Jace looked at April. "For you, April, I'd be thrilled to offer the same deal as Mrs. Budaker's getting. You could bring a lot of interest to this new enterprise."

*Yes!* she wanted to cry. *Yes, I'll take it. Yes, I'll do it.* For all of fifteen seconds. Then the old, cautious April Morgan—the one raising a kid on her own, trying to justify her work at the Standish farm—put the brakes on. Hard.

"It sounds great, but…" April shrugged. "If it were another time—"

"I think it's the perfect thing for you," Scott said. "And the perfect timing."

She turned wide eyes on him "Scott, I don't have the time. With work, and Sidney…"

"Don't dismiss it out of hand, April. Think about it."

"I *am* thinking about it. Sidney—"

"Yes, these past weeks have been busy, but planning for

this event has been a big time suck," Scott said. "It's not always like this. And hey, you pulled off the party and *still* got everything else done. You could do this, April. I mean, if you want to."

"But what about Sidney?" she said.

He smiled. "I seem to recall you telling me there's a certain young lady who owes you a debt. Put her to work in the kitchen with you. We both know she loves cooking, and she'd love to do this with you. What better way to work off what she owes?"

That niggling *I so want this!* feeling surged again. But still…it all seemed so sudden, so big.

"You'd be doing us a favor," Jace said. "I expect the place to fill up in a couple of weeks, and customers will follow. But we need some stable businesses to bring them back. That could be you, April."

"You've no idea what a great cook you are," Ember said. "Seriously."

"I don't know." She looked at Scott.

"I *do* know," he said firmly. "Trust me. You can do this. And I'll help." He raised his hands in a staving off manner. "Only as much as you let me. I've learned my lesson. But you can do this, April. And I know deep down inside, you want to."

Of course he knew that. They'd talked about everything under the sun and stars during those late nights in Montreal. He knew what she'd hoped for when she'd been young enough to hope. This was smaller scale than the grand plans she'd had at sweet sixteen, but it was still…something. Still bringing her cooking to the world.

"And the winner of the most historically creative costume goes to…Sidney Morgan!"

April looked up to see her daughter cross the stage to claim her prize—an orange bucket of candy with a blue ribbon attached. Whoa. She'd been so absorbed in the discussion, she'd totally missed that they'd awarded the prizes for the wee ones and moved on to the next age levels.

While applause—and a surprisingly piercing whistle from Danika—sounded, Sidney looked at April with sheer joy on her face. God, it had been so long since she'd smiled like that.

Maybe she *could* do it. With Sidney's help and Scott's support, maybe it was a real possibility.

# – eighteen –

"SO, THIS is the man you've been talking about," Scott said.

The young kids had long since left—including Sid, who'd gone up to the house with April—ceding the barn to the teenagers. Titus had just introduced him to David Hillman, one of the young bucks he'd hired to help spread straw on the berry fields.

"Yup. The hardest worker of the bunch," Titus said.

Scott extended his hand and the young man shook it.

*Strong grip.*

"Hi, Scott. How's it going?"

The perfect greeting. No *Mr. Standish.* Not in Harkness, where everyone knew everyone, at least peripherally. Now Arden would have rated a Mr. Standish, at least until his uncle swept the formalities away, but not Scott or Titus. There'd need to be serious seniority, multiple decades. Or the older party would have to be a teacher. Scott was still struggling with calling Mrs. Siliker *Faye.*

"Going great, David," Scott said. "I asked Titus to introduce us because I wanted to sound you out about a little part-time work at the farm."

"Titus mentioned it," he said. "And yes, I'm very interested."

"Did he tell you what the job entailed?"

Apparently he hadn't, because Titus immediately leaped in to elaborate on what helping around the farm for a couple hours after school three days a week at ten bucks an hour translated into. Which was just as well. Titus had a better grip on the day-to-day stuff than Scott did.

David nodded his head after every reference, not just automatically, but really taking it in, assimilating. Never breaking eye contact with Titus. Never shifting or showing the least bit of discomfort at the prospect of any of the chores. Yeah, he'd do fine.

"So how about it? Apple picking is still going strong, and cider-making. Then we'll need to sanitize under the trees. I think we can guarantee somewhere between ten and twelve hours a week until Christmas. Sound good?"

"Till Christmas? That should just about do it."

Titus grinned. "Saving up for something special?"

"Yeah, I am."

He didn't elaborate, but he didn't have to. The glance he sent toward his pretty girlfriend, Sally McAvoy, currently standing by one of the tables, looking anxious in her Anne of Green Gables getup, told the story. She twisted the brim of her straw hat in her hands.

"There's one stipulation," Scott said.

David frowned. "What's that?"

"Any day you're too busy after school with your studies—if you have an exam or paper due the next day—that comes first."

"Seriously?"

"Seriously. Just let us know as soon as you can. Fair enough?"

"Yeah," he answered. "That's more than fair."

"So, when can you start?"

"Heck, Monday, if you like."

"Monday's perfect." Scott extended his hand again. "See you then."

David shook Scott's hand, then Titus's. He walked right over to the girl with the straw hat and strawberry blond braids standing now at the edge of the dance floor. She threw her arms around him. As they stood there, the lights dimmed and a slow song started playing. With a cheer, the teens on the dance floor came together for the slow dance.

"You sure you know what you're doing, bro?" Titus said, now that David was out of earshot. "That's a lot of money going out. With April's salary and the extra mouths being fed around here…"

"Extra mouths?" Scott cut him with a glare. "Don't tell me you begrudge them being here? April's salary comes out of mine, remember?"

Titus's head shot back as though Scott had slugged him one. "Jesus, you know me better than that. I don't begrudge April and Sidney anything."

"Sorry." Scott rubbed the back of his neck, feeling like shit for lighting into his brother. On the other hand, if Titus was going to step back and take a break, he needed to let go and allow Scott to handle things. "David's wages will come out of the regular budget, but I've looked at the books. Ten hours a week for a couple of months won't kill us. And from what I recall, this wouldn't be the first time we hired a part-time person in the fall, over and above the pickers."

"True, but that was when I had to shoulder more of the domestic stuff on top of the chores. Hell, more of everything, what with Dad's depression."

There it was, right out on the table. When Margaret Standish had gotten sick, Scott had taken off. Titus had stayed. He'd stayed through their mother's illness, taking up the slack while Arden cared for her. And he'd continued to carry the load afterward when Uncle Arden got lost in his grief.

Some son Scott had been. Some brother. He'd failed them both.

"I'm sorry about that," Scott said gruffly, past the lump of pain in his throat. "I should have been here. Should have done more—"

Titus raised his hands in a stopping gesture. "Christ, Scott, that's not what I'm saying. Not why I brought it up. What I clumsily meant to say is that Dad's feeling a lot better—he can do more. And now that we've hired April—which I agree is a good thing—that takes the domestic pressure off. As much as I like David, and as glad as I am to be helping with his promise ring fund, I'm just asking, do we need it right now? Can we afford it?"

Scott felt some of the tension ebb. "In a word, yes. Between me, Arden and David, the farm chores will get done, and the repair projects will too. As for the repairs, I've done the math. Between my free labor, fabricating some of the materials myself and sourcing the rest wholesale, I won't break the bank. Okay?"

"Okay. You're the boss. Literally." Titus slapped him on the back and grinned. "Should be a fun couple of months."

The music changed, segueing from one slow song to another, the final *final* last waltz. That too was a Standish tradition from not-so-far-back. Years ago, Titus had finally worked up the nerve to ask a girl to dance at the end of the night. Watching Titus stiffly turning slow circles around the dance floor with her in his arms, Scott could see he was going to need some time to relax into it. So, being the kind of brother he was, he'd queued up a second last song.

Ocean had doffed her mustache since winning in the adult, non-zombie category, snagging the coveted box of Ganong chocolates, and most important of all—bragging rights. She'd also tossed aside the powdered wig, and thankfully, her attempt at a Mark Twain accent. She smiled sweetly at Scott then wickedly at Titus as she sidled over.

"Hey Mr. Security Man, may I have this dance?"

"Are you talking to me?" Titus said in his best Robert De Niro imitation.

"Oh, that's bad." Ocean laughed. "Worse than my southern accent." She grabbed his hand and led him away. Although "lee might not be the right word when his brother followed her so happily. Scott watched as they joined the other couples on the darkened dance floor. But unlike the other couples, there was no clumsiness or surfeit of teenage self-consciousness. Just effortless gliding, an easy belonging, an unmistakable tenderness…

"They make a striking couple."

Scott turned to see Uncle_Arden at his side. He'd lost the wolf ears somewhere along the way.

"They look happy," Scott said. "Finally. Ocean's had a crush on him for years."

"More than a crush, I'd say. I saw the way she looked at him every Christmas when she came home. And the way he looked at her when she wasn't looking at him." Arden chuckled.

"Been that obvious, has it?"

"Obvious enough."

Crap. If Uncle Arden had picked up on that from a few glances at Christmas parties, how obvious were he and April being?

The last strains of the *last* last waltz came to an end and the lights came up blindingly. Ocean and Eden started herding people toward the door.

"Been a pretty good night, huh?" Arden said.

It had. "Sidney certainly had a ball."

"She did." Arden agreed. "I liked seeing her hanging around with her new friend."

"Danika? She seems like a nice girl. Polite. Smart."

They stepped back out of the way so kids could grab their coats from the pegs behind them.

"Faye's having a great time tutoring them."

"It's not too much for her to handle both of them?"

"Not at all." Arden bent to pick up a scarf a young lady had dropped and handed it to her.

"Thanks, Mr. Standish."

"You're welcome, Sarah." He turned back to Scott. "Faye needed something to do. Something new. You know, son, a person just can't grow old and wither away."

"I'm really glad to hear you say that, Uncle Arden."

"Well, I never thought I would again after you mother died. But you know, life keeps going on. I've figured that out." He cleared his throat. "Faye has too."

Scott glanced around. "Speaking of Faye, did she head home?"

"No. Last I saw she was loading dishes in the dishwasher up at the house."

They'd used mostly disposable plates, but serving platters and bowls had come from the Standish kitchen.

Scott looked around the room, which was clearing out fast. "And where's my pirate sister? Don't tell me she cut out early?"

Arden sighed and shook his head.

Scott felt a shaft of anxiety. "What?"

The old man paused. "Ember was called away about fifteen minutes ago. An accident. Well, that's what they're calling it. There's trouble over at the Farmingham place. Ember had to go patch the young fellow up."

"Ig Farmingham's?" Scott bristled. "Please don't tell me she went over there by herself. Doctor or not—"

"Jace went with her."

Scott relaxed a little at that. "Trouble, huh? I'm guessing Ig was drunk again."

Arden shook his head sadly. Ig Farmingham was a bastard when he drank. An accident prone one. Scott remembered one time in high school, hearing how Ig had wrapped his pickup truck around a telephone pole out the Advail Road, then managed to find a very large tree to hit with his wife's car, all in the same night. Farmingham had walked away from the first accident without a scratch. The second time, he wasn't so lucky. He'd come out of it with a broken arm and facial lacerations. He'd also emerged to find himself on the fast track to divorce.

"It wasn't Ig this time," Arden said. "It was his young fellow, Jeff. He tripped on an old plow blade in the back yard."

"Was the kid drinking?"

Arden raised an eyebrow. "What did I always tell you kids about judging a person by the actions of another?"

Scott shrugged. "I'm just saying, Jeff grew up watching Ig drink. Not unheard of for a young man to follow in his father's footsteps, no matter where those footsteps lead."

Arden just stood there silently, not nodding in agreement, but not disagreeing either, as though waiting for Scott to find the fallacy in his own statement.

Rather than take the bait, he sighed. "Guess we'll have to get used to having a doctor in the family."

"Guess we'll have to get used to a lot of things around here," Arden said, his tone more cheerful now. "Things are changing fast. Ocean and Titus, for instance."

Scott searched them out. They were talking to a couple of young ladies who were getting their coats on. "Ocean's a great catch," he said. "I'm glad Titus has someone. She'll keep him on his toes."

"Then there's Ember and Jace," Arden said. "Ten years estranged, and they look like they never missed a beat."

Scott nodded. "He's a decent guy. Not like his brother."

Arden laughed.

"What?"

"I never thought you'd say something like that about anyone who was dating your sister."

Scott grinned. "Well, they are engaged. Even I know when to give up."

Arden tilted his head. "I don't suppose it hurts that he's giving April a deal on that rental space…"

"She told you?"

Arden nodded. "She wanted to assure me that it wouldn't interfere with her duties. Make sure it was all right with me before she fully committed."

Well, that was good news. She'd given Jace a tentative yes, but if she'd told Arden about it, she really was committed. "I'm sure she'll keep everything up."

"I told her I was glad to see her try to make something of her talent," Arden continued. "And something tells me she could use a break."

*More than you know.* The secrets she'd shared about her upbringing… Well, she'd had to be strong. Brave. She was overdue for a break. But Scott would never betray her confidence. He contented himself by saying, "She sure can."

"You're doing a good thing helping her out, Son. Jace too."

Scott shrugged, embarrassed. "She just wants to build something, provide the kind of security Sidney needs, a good future. If we can help that along, why wouldn't we?"

"Why indeed?" Arden turned his attention to David and his pretty girl, who were getting their coats on. "So you hired David."

"Yeah. I've already talked to Titus about the budget. If I'm going to get to some of the repair projects, we'll need the short-term help. And it might be tight, but I figure we should give a boost to a young man like that if it's mutually beneficial."

"Agreed. I had a few boosts like that myself in my younger days," Arden acknowledged. "But I don't suppose it hurts that the projects you'll be getting at are indoors?" He slanted a look at Scott. "You know, in closer contact with April while she's here?"

He should have known there was no fooling Arden. "Okay, yeah, that's part of it," he admitted. "But probably not how you think. I just want to be around to lend whatever support I can. This is April's chance, an opportunity to find out if she can make it on her own. With maybe some mentoring from Jace with that shiny MBA of his, and some encouragement from us, maybe her little business will take off. Harkness would be…"

"What, Son?"

"Safe," he said. "Good for Sid."

Arden nodded.

"So yes, I'm going to try to help her as much as she'll let me. If she could only see for herself how great she could be at this…" He swallowed. "Well, she just needs a little help, and I'm going to make sure she gets it."

Arden began to chuckle.

"What?"

"You'll have to be careful."

"Titus already gave me the employee-employer talk."

"I meant about trying to help her. When you're in April's kitchen, you'd better do it her way."

"I take it you heard about the Great Onion Fiasco?"

"I did."

"Well, I doubt she'll let me do anything of consequence in the kitchen, but I can lift and carry. Be a sounding board, if she needs it."

"Taste tester."

"Hell, yeah."

Arden laughed outright now. "Ah, it's good to see life coming back to the place."

Scott looked at the gleam in his uncle's eyes and couldn't agree more.

"Well, I'm going to collect Faye and drive her home. Between her and April, they should have the kitchen whipped into shape by now." He reached for his jacket and shrugged into it. "Don't wait up, as they say."

"Another night of Scrabble? Don't you two ever get sick of it?"

"Apparently not." Arden smoothed a hand over his silver

hair. "Are you good to lock the place up? Make sure no one sneaked up to the loft?"

Scott smiled. "Yeah, I'll double-check that."

Arden looked at him. "You're doing a good thing by April and Sidney. And you're doing a good thing by the family, giving Titus a break. Booker would be proud of the man you've grown into."

Booker Ward Standish—Scott's late father. It wasn't that they didn't talk about his father and mother, but they hadn't in a very long time.

"And I'm damned proud of you too, Son."

Scott knew he should say it—call the man who'd raised him *Dad*. It had been different with Margaret. He'd taken to calling her Mom within weeks of landing at the farm. But with Uncle Arden, he just couldn't. Maybe because he looked so much like Scott's father.

He drew a breath. Released it. "Goodnight, Uncle Arden."

# – nineteen –

APRIL COULD hardly keep up. No, correction, she *couldn't* keep up with her bouncing, all-over-the-room, excited-beyond-belief, non-stop-talking daughter.

Good thing tomorrow wasn't a school day. Sidney would have a hard time sleeping tonight. And it wasn't just the sugar rush. She was running on joy.

April had finally managed to get Sidney into her jammies, warm from the dryer—a touch that Faye assured her would help the little girl sleep. Her Viking sword stood carefully propped against the mirror. And every time she passed the vanity—which Ember was increasingly losing ground on—Sidney stopped to sort out a bit of candy.

"Sid, no more. You've brushed your teeth twice now."

"I know. I'm just looking at it." She glanced up. "Hey, should I save the caramels for cooking?" She plucked out a handful of the sweet, creamy treats.

Her first inclination was to decline the offer. Sidney loved her caramels. But she seemed to really want to be involved in the new business, and April wanted to encourage her.

"That's a great idea."

"So what will we name your company?"

"I was thinking Morgan's Edibles."

"Let's…um, pin that," Sidney said diplomatically. "I was actually thinking something else."

*"Pin that?"* Her daughter, the marketing advisor. "Oh, really?"

"Hear me out, okay?"

"Sure." She sat down on Sidney's bed. "What's your idea?"

Sidney finally lit on the edge of the bed beside her. "April Dawn's."

April frowned. "But that doesn't really say anything about—"

"About the business. But actually, it would, if you name the products right. Those blueberry coconut breakfast cookies could be *April's Blueberry-Coconut Dawn Breakfast Bars.* The maple ones? *April's Maple Dawn Bars.* Your hot pepper jelly? *April's Hot Pepper Dawn Jelly. S*ee what I mean?" Her daughter looked at her so hopefully.

April grinned. "Sid, that's pretty darned brilliant."

"You really like it?"

"I do. I can see it working especially well for the jams and jellies. They look so brilliant and bright in their jars, they might make someone think of dawn, as in daybreak…Grape Dawn or Chokecherry Dawn. But does it really work for the food?"

Sidney grinned. "It works for me."

April lifted an eyebrow. "So, you could really go for a Cranberry-Lemon-Honey Dawn Breakfast Bar?"

"Okay, maybe you need to lose the list of ingredients for some of them," she said. "Oh, wait! I have the perfect name for that one—April's Bee's Knees Dawn!"

"Bee's knees? Someone's been hanging around Arden."

"Don't you love it? He got it from his father. If something is really epic, you say it's the bee's knees."

"Really?" April suppressed a smile.

"Uh-huh." Sidney left her perch on the side of the bed and pulled out a pair of jeans and a long-sleeved shirt from a dresser drawer, placing them on the chair beside her bed. Tomorrow was a Sunday, not a school day, but it wasn't a bad habit for her daughter to prep for the morning, she supposed. Sidney kept talking while she grabbed fresh underwear and socks from a top drawer and plunked them on the pile. "You know what else would be cool?"

"What?"

"April's Bootilicious Dawn."

"Hmm, whatever that is, it's gotta be heavy on chocolate."

"And what about April's Energy Dawn. April's Lucky Dawn. April's I'm-Too-Tired-to-Cook-Breakfast Dawn."

April laughed. "Well, that last one might be hard to put on a label, but I like the concept. A lot."

The idea *did* have potential. At least she thought it did. She needed some adults to weigh in on it. But whether they ran with it or not, she loved seeing Sidney so enthused about her business. Correction—their business. "Did you just come up with all these names tonight?"

"No. I've been thinking on this for a long, long time." Sidney came to perch on the bed beside her again.

April frowned. "But I only just told you about Jace's offer."

"You used to talk about maybe starting your own business, when I was little."

April's eyes widened. "You remember that?"

"Yeah. And I've been thinking about it a lot, especially since Montreal. Since I messed things up and you lost your job."

"Sidney you didn't—"

"Dr. Boisvert fired you because of me," she said, flatly.

She couldn't deny it. "We'll be fine."

"Yeah, but what about that crazy lady?"

*Crazy lady?*

At April's blank look, Sidney added, "The woman who was coming to visit."

"Oh, you mean K.Z. Those are her initials—the letters K and Z—not Crazy."

"Ah, that makes more sense. K.Z. McCoy; not Crazy McCoy."

"What about her?"

"You missed your big opportunity. Mom, I *know* she would have loved your cooking. When I jumped into the back of Scott's truck, I knew she was coming. Knew you'd find me gone and worry. I shouldn't have done that." There were tears in Sidney's eyes now. "I'm *so* sorry. I really messed that up for you."

April's throat ached. "Oh, Ladybug, there were no guarantees with K.Z. It might not have come to anything anyway."

"Yeah, but it was a chance."

"There are always other chances."

Sidney brightened at that. "You mean like…other stars to wish on?"

"Exactly. And besides, this will be more fun. Doing it with you. Seriously, this is our enterprise, Sidney. We're in this together."

Sid bounced on the edge of the bed. "I'm helping in other ways too, don't forget."

"Of course."

Sid stilled. "About my debt… I was thinking, maybe ten percent of profits could go to paying it off. Does that work for you?"

*Work for her?* April suppressed another smile. "Right, but remember profit is after expenses, right? We have to pay for supplies, and set up, and—"

"And we want to set a fair price," Sid interrupted. "Especially just starting out, until we have lots and lots of customers and they really, really want our stuff and will pay more for it."

April looked at her daughter. "Wow, you're no slouch at this, are you?"

"Hey, I got another one! What about April's Heavenly Caramel Dawn?"

"For the salted caramel cupcake? I love it."

"Me too."

April glanced at her watch. This was the best, easiest mother-daughter talk they'd had in such a long time, but it really was late.

"Whoa, time for bed, Ladybug." She stood and held up the blankets. Sidney crawled in without complaint and let April snug the quilts around her.

"That boy, Roy—the one who won the grossest costumes—did you see him, Mom?"

"The guy with the cape and the sweater that read SuperGuts? Yeah, I saw him. He was a little hard to miss. Though I didn't know his name."

"He's in my class."

"Nice guy?"

"Yeah. But there's nothing *romantic* going on if that's what you're thinking."

April bit back a laugh. No, she had definitely *not* been thinking anything of the kind. Her daughter was in grade five, for pity sake! All of ten years old.

But wait, hadn't she had a ginormous crush on Corey Chapman at that age? And according to that note he passed her in Health class, he'd been "sweet on her" right back. Not that it had progressed even to hand holding. But romantic? Maybe it depended on the definition. She'd scribbled his name over every notebook she had. Drawn a heart around his photo on the class picture composite.

"Not like you and Scott," Sidney said.

April recognized a fishing expedition when she heard one. "We're friends, Sid."

They'd been careful to keep their romance to themselves—she hoped.

She rolled her eyes. "Right, like Arden and Faye are friends. Except…"

"Except what?"

She bit her lip and tears welled in her luminous brown eyes. "You guys are too chicken to…play Scrabble."

Whoa. "And by *play Scrabble,* you mean…?"

"You know…be girlfriend and boyfriend. Hold hands and stuff. Go to movies. Maybe…more than boyfriend and girlfriend someday."

April sighed. "Oh, Sidney, that's not going to happen. Please don't get your hopes up about that."

"But you guys like each other." Sidney's cheeks were red with embarrassment over the subject, but she persisted. "I know you do. More than I like Roy. I mean, *like* like."

"Yes, we do like each other. Maybe even *like* like." She sighed. "But, honey, this whole thing…being here…it's all temporary."

"'Cause you've got another job lined up."

*If only.* "That's…part of it."

"But what if you didn't take that job? What if we stayed here?" She looked up at April with such pleading in her eyes. "I'm staying out of trouble and I'm helping with Axl. Arden told me I'm not the least bit in the way. Scott always needs me to help him with something or other."

"Like when you guys painted the Far South Barn," April said. "You were a big help to him. And he enjoys your company."

"Really?"

"Yes."

"Did Scott say so?"

Well, not in so many words, but he'd insisted he didn't mind having her underfoot. She suspected he'd enjoyed teaching her a skill, and yes, even enjoyed her chatter. "Absolutely."

"See? We're not in the way here."

April cringed. Obviously, Sidney had felt in the way at the Boisverts'. And for good reason. They'd been good employers, but not the sort to be at ease with a rambunctious ten-year-old. She really had to do better with her next assignment, make sure it was a more suitable environment for her daughter.

"And, really, Mom, nobody on this planet can outcook you. Did you see how much spaghetti Arden ate the other day? And Titus just can't get enough of your apple jelly on homemade bread."

She smiled. "Ember really liked the flan you helped me make last Sunday."

"I know, right? And now, we're going to have a booth at the market!" Her bouncy daughter was back.

In fact, April was feeling pretty bouncy about the whole thing herself. But Sidney's expectations needed to be managed.

"I'm looking forward to it too. But don't get too carried away, honey. It's a Christmas booth, for a few weeks—Remembrance Day through to Christmas."

Sidney's pleasure dimmed. "Couldn't you keep it going?"

"The business? Maybe," April conceded. "But if it works out, we can always operate it wherever we go, our own little cottage industry."

"It could also work into something pretty fantastic right here in Harkness, couldn't it?"

"But I've—"

"Mom, I love it here. Can't I just…hope?"

April put her arms around Sidney, pulling her slight frame into a tight hug. Her inclination, her gut reaction, was to tell her daughter *no*. That she couldn't hope. It would be better in the long run.

She pulled back far enough to tuck a strand of Sidney's dark hair back behind her ear. "It's not like we're leaving tomorrow, Ladybug. We still have almost two months. But Scott's leaving in January. We are too, after Christmas. You know this."

"Right. That other job."

April bit her lip. She really was going to have to start combing through the want ads. But it would have to be a good job, with a good setup for Sid. One where she felt more—

"I'm pretty smart." Sidney pulled out one of her arms and lay back on her pillows.

*Pretty smart?* Did she know there was no job lined up?

"I know the difference between reality and make-believe. I really do, Mom. But…"

"But what?"

She shrugged her thin shoulders. Twice. And her breathing was fast and shallow. April recognized the signs. This was vitally important to her daughter, and she was searching for the right words. The magic words that would convince an adult.

"Go ahead," she encouraged. "Just say it."

"Can't I at least pretend? Just for a while? Just until I can't pretend anymore? Like, the very last minute."

Sidney's words slayed her. "Ladybug…"

"Deep down, I know that it's not going to last forever. Or very long at all. I know that, Mom. But for the little while we're here, can't we just pretend?"

April stood and walked to the window so Sidney wouldn't see the glint of tears. Pulling back the curtain, she looked out on the yard, only partially revealed by the sentinel light that stood midway between the house and the Far South Barn. As she watched, Scott came out of the barn. Axl materialized out of the shadows to join him and the two of them walked toward the house.

She turned to Sidney. "If I agree to let you pretend—"

"Thank you, Mom!"

"Whoa, wait a sec. I said *if.* I need an assurance from you. If we agree to pretend, that means I'll have to stop reminding you all the time that we're leaving after Christmas. But I need an assurance from you that you won't forget the reality. That you won't forget we're just pretending."

"I won't. Promise," she said gravely. "But I can't promise not to keep wishing."

She was a little girl growing up so fast, April was almost glad she could still believe in wishes. "Deal. Now I need something more from you."

"What?"

She heard claws on the steps and the labored breathing as Axl made his way up the stairs. "Ember's out again tonight, and Arden is at Faye's for a while. Titus is…well, I think he and Ocean went for a drive. I need to go out and help tidy up the barn, but that will leave just you and Axl in here. Which means I need you to promise to stay in bed."

"What if I need to pee?"

April rolled her eyes. "Okay, you can go as far as the bathroom if you need to pee, then right back to bed."

"Okay, I'll stay put. Promise. I don't like to disturb Axl anyway." On cue, Axl entered the room. "Come on, boy!" Sidney sat up to encourage the old dog as he climbed onto the bed. "Good dog."

Axl executed a couple of circles and settled himself gingerly on the empty side of the bed. Sidney gently scratched the thick ruff of fur on his neck and shoulders and he let out a groan of ecstasy that made Sid smile.

"So, you're all set?"

"Yeah, I'm good. And I'm not scared or anything, not with Axl here."

"Good. And we won't be too long."

"'Night, Mom." Sidney lay back on the pillows.

April drew the covers over her. "Goodnight, Ladybug."

At the door, she turned off the light, leaving just the night light beside the vanity on. Closing the door gently, she stood there a moment, listening to the silence of the empty house.

God, she hoped she hadn't made a mistake, agreeing to let Sidney pretend. It would make leaving that much harder. But her daughter seemed to need this.

And wasn't she basically doing the same thing with Scott?

She sighed, banishing those thoughts. There was no point second-guessing herself now. Like Sidney, she might as well enjoy the here and now, because it would be over soon enough.

She changed out of her gypsy costume quickly, then went down the hall to the bathroom and brushed her teeth. As she wiped her mouth, she caught sight of herself in the mirror. Her eyes were alight with anticipation, and it wasn't all sexual. She just couldn't wait to be with him.

Turning away from her reflection, she headed for the stairs.

# – twenty –

SCOTT FELT April's gaze on him as he rolled up the last strand of pumpkin lights.

"Sad to see them go?"

He looked up at her. "Who? The zombies?"

"The lights." She crossed to the table and opened the packing box.

"Rapunzel, Rapunzel…put those lovely orange locks away for another year." So saying, he dropped the pumpkin lights unceremoniously into the box. There. That was the last of the tidying. Taking stuff down had gone a lot faster than putting it up. It was all done inside of an hour. Of course, he'd had help. A couple of neighbors had hung around to help before heading home.

April closed the box's lid. "Did you see that little ginger-haired girl dressed as Rapunzel?"

"Yeah, I did. She's Albert and Debbie Saracen's girl."

"That was her real hair. Did you know that? I couldn't believe it when her mother told me."

She finished taping the box closed, and Scott shoved it beneath the table with the others he'd stowed there. Eventually, it would all go back in the sectioned off storage room behind the make-shift stage, but the area desperately needing a good cleaning first.

"I'll have the new guy put these away on Monday." It was as easy a way to approach the new hire as anything. He had to tread carefully to make sure April didn't think David's position was on account of anything to do with her.

"You hired someone?"

"One of the young lads who worked for Titus a few weeks ago."

"Why?"

*Damn.*

"We need a little extra help, and he can use the cash. Like I told you, we hire someone every year."

"So you said. But you hired *me*."

"We need more help."

She didn't look convinced. "I thought there wasn't that much to do, this deep into the fall?"

"We still have to get through apple-picking season," he pointed out. "But the kicker is that I've got some repair projects to do around the house. If I'm going to see to them and see to the farm too, I just need an extra body for a while."

She seemed to relax a little. "I just don't want to feel like a charity case."

"You're not." Quickly, to change focus, he said, "David was really happy to get the work. I'm pretty sure he's looking to buy a promise ring for his girlfriend, Sally, for Christmas. He's saving up, and well, the few hours we can give him—and they're only a few—are going to help."

"David I met. But Sally…" She frowned, obviously sorting through the image bank of new faces she would have seen tonight. "Wait, I think I saw him with a girl. Anne of Green Gables?"

He smiled. "That's her."

"I met her mom." April glanced around the barn. "So, I guess we're done in here?"

"Yup. So now what?"

April eyed him. "What did you have in mind? The night's not exactly young…"

"It's not that late," he said. "Besides, it's Saturday."

She grabbed his hand, turned his wrist to look at his watch. "It's after eleven."

"After eleven? Oh, well, then, we'd better head in, warm up some milk. Maybe break out the BenGay."

She laughed, but she didn't release his hand. He took that as promising.

"Okay, you have a point," She said. "But we really should go back to the house. Sidney's in there alone. Well, Sidney and Axl. Thank you, by the way, for letting him in."

"She's not alone anymore. Uncle Arden's home. Didn't you hear his Jeep roll in while we were packing up the lights?"

"Really?" She went to the door and cracked it. "You're right. I didn't even notice."

"The Scrabble game must have gone quickly tonight."

April laughed. "Yeah. Must have."

He didn't know what was so funny about that, but he did so enjoy hearing her laugh. She didn't do it often enough.

"Hey, why don't we head in to the Duchess Diner?" He would love to introduce April to the Duchess. "Best fish and chips in Harkness. Wait, what am I saying? Best in the province."

"Seriously?" She looked at him as if he were crazy. "I couldn't eat another bite. I'm sure I sampled a little bit of everything."

"Professional interest?"

"Naturally."

He felt her thumb move on the back of his hand and looked down at their now joined fingers. Then back up at her face.

"You know what I'd really like to do?" she said.

His heart sped up at the banked excitement in her eyes. "What?"

"Let's go for a walk."

That wasn't what he thought she was going to suggest. But now that she mentioned it, it was the perfect night for a walk. "Great idea." He looked at her appraisingly. "So, are you up for a little adventure?"

"Does it have to be little?"

His heart leaped again at the dangerous look in her eyes. This was a side of her he hadn't seen.

"Well?" She let the word hang there.

He pulled his phone out and hit Arden's number. "Uncle Arden, all good over at Faye's? Yeah? Good." He met April's gaze. "If it's okay with you, April and I are going out for a spell. Would you? That'd be great. I'll tell her that. And thanks."

She looked at him questioningly.

"We're good to go. He's in for the night and will leave the porch light on for us."

# – twenty-one –

DESPITE SCOTT'S assurances, April scooted into the house to check with Arden. Not because she didn't believe he was eager to help, but because it was the polite thing to do. The right thing to do. She found him in the living room in his easy chair with a book.

"April?" He looked up, surprised. "I thought you and Scott were going out?"

"We are. I just…are you sure you're okay with this?"

"Hundred and ten percent sure. I'll read down here for a while before I go up to bed. But don't worry; when I do turn in, I'll leave my door open. If Sid gets up, I'm sure I'll hear her. And if not her, Axl. He thumps around like a moose getting down those stairs."

She smiled. "Thanks so much. I'll just go check to make sure she's asleep."

He waved her on.

She ran up the stairs lightly and poked her head into Ember's bedroom. Axl lifted his big, boxy head briefly, then lowered it. Her little Minnesota Viking didn't stir. From the sound of her breathing, April knew she was sound asleep.

With a smile on her face, she went down the hall to her own room. Or rather, Scott's room. Except for a floral patterned comforter that Ember had tossed on the bed, the room looked pretty much the way it must have when Scott left at age eighteen, complete with football paraphernalia and heavy metal posters. So weird, glimpsing a teenage Scott. Weird, but undeniably sweet.

She was feeling pretty much like a teenager herself, getting weak-kneed over a boy. But so be it. She'd been over this mental ground a hundred times. She wasn't going to take herself to task for it. No point ruining the moment. Like her daughter, she knew the difference between reality and make-believe. The time to confront reality again would come soon enough, but until then, she intended to enjoy her time with Scott.

She decided against makeup—it was dark, after all—but put on some fresh lip gloss. Then, with excitement zinging through her veins, she swapped her old coat for her new leather bomber jacket, zipping it up snugly. It looked just as good as she remembered, perfectly tailored to flatter. Digging through a box in the corner, one of many she hadn't unpacked, she unearthed her red winter hat and mittens. She pulled the hat down on her forehead and checked her reflection in the mirror.

When it came to the clothing budget, Sidney's needs always came first. Always. But Ocean and Ember had taken April to an upscale second-hand store a couple of days ago, where she'd scored the new jacket for ten bucks. With her red hat and mitts, she thought she looked pretty good.

She'd had such fun shopping with the girls. They'd have to do it again. Ember had looked at everything, from jewelry to dishes, likening the search to treasure hunting. "You never know when you're going to find a jewel worth keeping."

Ocean had gone straight for the used books, delighting when she found a pristine copy of *Watership Down*. Apparently she'd loaned her copy to one of her New York friends. Greg Somebody-or-Other. From the girls' discussion, April gathered he was a famous music producer or something.

Ocean insisted the relationship, while close, was completely platonic.

Then Ocean casually mentioned she'd invited him to Harkness for Christmas.

Yikes! April really hoped that if this guy actually came, it wouldn't create any ugliness. In the world she'd grown up in—which admittedly was no model of normal, well-adjusted behavior—that would be like setting a match to a fuse.

Outside her bedroom window, April saw the headlights of Arden's Jeep swing from the garage toward the kitchen. Her ride.

She ran downstairs, stopping to say goodnight to Arden before letting herself out. She wanted to dash to the vehicle but managed a sedate, adult pace.

He leaned across the narrow vehicle and jacked the passenger door open for her.

"You look beautiful," he said when she jumped into the cab.

She laughed. "You're easy to please."

"Not at all. You look fantastic. I really like your new jacket. Very hot."

She'd hoped he'd like it, but now that he'd mentioned it, she felt a little self-conscious. "Just dressing for the weather."

"Yeah, it is getting chilly, isn't it? Give this beast a few minutes and we'll have some heat coming."

He drove slowly down the driveway, the lights uncovering the road ahead in a way April found almost mesmerizing. Which went to show how infrequently she'd dated. She could count on one hand the number of times she'd been in a car like this, in the dark with a boy, traveling toward a destination. That hadn't been allowed in the Morgan home. Not with her father's strict rules about girls and how they were supposed to behave.

Or *not* behave. That was more like it. No speaking unless spoken to. Blending into the background so as not to be seen. Definitely no laughing.

No. She would not let her thoughts go there. That world was behind her. Her father would not be ruining this night.

"So, when I suggested we go for a walk, what made you decide to get the Jeep?"

"Did you really want to walk this boring road?" He glanced at her. "I mean, you've been up and down it a dozen times already, right?"

"Yeah, but only in daylight." Even though it was technically within the Harkness town limits, the Shadow Road didn't have street lights like the more residential roads. "I'd never walk it at night. Well, not by myself."

"Smart decision," he said. "Also, thank you."

She frowned. "For what? Not walking alone at night?"

"Exactly." Signaling a right-hand turn, he turned onto the road at the end of the driveway. "Ember used to jog that road, back when we were in school."

"She's in great shape."

"Yeah, she's always been athletic. She used to go jogging in the early morning, at least five times a week."

April felt a twinge of envy. She'd always loved walking, but even in high school, her father wouldn't permit even that tiny bit of autonomy. To take a long walk alone—or run, as Ember had done—would have been the height of freedom. Pure luxury. As it often did, it struck her anew how abnormal what passed for "normal" in the Morgan household had truly been. She'd been permitted to walk only to the end of the driveway to catch the school bus. The only times she'd defied that restriction was when she fled the house to escape one of her father's drunken rages. Even then, she never went further than the vacant, overgrown, weed-choked lot across the street, sneaking back in while her father slept it off. Fortunately, he usually woke with no recollection of her flight.

Usually.

"At first, Axl would go with her, but he wasn't very keen on rolling out that early in the morning."

Scott's words pulled her back from those dark memories. She smiled. "I noticed he likes his comforts, but I thought that was because he's old."

"He's definitely arthritic now," he confirmed, "but he never did like to stir before dawn."

"So once she started leaving the guard dog at home, you took over the role, suddenly becoming an avid jogger yourself?"

"Not quite. I became a champion of stealth."

*Champion of stealth?* "A stalker, you mean?"

He took his eyes off the road long enough to give her a wounded look. "What is it with you and Ember? She called me a stalker too."

"Imagine that. A guy can't follow a woman down a long and lonely road, morning after morning, without being labeled. Hardly seems fair, does it?"

"Okay, when you put it that way, it sounds a little stalkerish," he admitted. "But there are things out here you wouldn't want to encounter alone, and I'm not just talking about the random, bearded, shaggy-haired whack-jobs of my imagination. Depending on the season, you might blunder into a bear with her cubs. Or a bull moose in rut. Hell, even a buck."

"I know. Just teasing."

They drove along in comfortable silence. April watched the trees whiz by. Alder bushes. "I used to hide in alders bushes as a child." The words were out before she could stop them. Before she could push back thoughts of Dick Morgan.

She glanced at Scott. His hands were white-knuckled on the steering wheel.

"I'm guessing you weren't playing hide and seek," he said.

"You'd be guessing right."

"I wish…"

"It's okay. I didn't mean to bring it up. It just slipped out."

"Don't apologize, April. I just wish those things hadn't

happened to you. I wish I could take away every bad memory you have."

"I know you do."

He offered her his hand and she took it. If the vehicle had had a bench seat instead of bucket seats, she'd have scooted closer, but just the warmth and strength of his hand was a comfort.

Silence reigned again and she went back to watching the vegetation in the ditch fly by. Then, out of nowhere, Scott braked hard. Her seatbelt didn't even have a chance to stretch and lock, because his arm was on her chest, holding her back as they decelerated.

Two deer bounded up out of the ditch in front of the vehicle. They stood for a few seconds, staring into the headlights. Then one of them hightailed it down the opposite ditch and into the woods. The second deer followed.

"That was awesome!" April said.

"It was pretty cool." He took her hand again.

She relaxed back in her seat, determined to memorize everything about this evening. The intimacy of the vehicle, the feel of her hand in his, the world rolling by, illuminated briefly by their headlights, then disappearing into darkness again. It would make a lovely memory. One of many she would tuck away for when she left this place.

# – twenty-two –

SIDNEY AWOKE to the sound of canine whimpering.

She opened her eyes, rolled onto her side and looked over at Axl. In the moonlight streaming through the window, she could see his eyes were closed, but his feet were paddling in short jerky bursts.

Ah, he was dreaming. Chasing a rabbit, probably. Or a squirrel.

As always, she wondered whether to wake him or not. The whimpering sounded pretty pitiful. On the other hand, if he could actually run hard in his dreams, why not leave him to it?

Axl whimpered again, but after a few seconds, the jerky leg movement stopped.

"Hope you treed that squirrel, Axl."

He went back to snoring gently.

Well, at least one of them was sleeping. The room was stuffy, she realized. That was probably why she'd woken up so easily at the dog's whimper.

She tossed back the covers, climbed out of bed and crossed the room to open the door. Fresh air hit her. Ah, that was better. She stood there for a minute and listened. The television was still on downstairs. That had to be Arden. When Titus watched TV late at night, she could barely hear it. But Arden's hearing obviously wasn't as good, 'cause he needed to turn up the volume. Right now, an infomercial was playing. Considering Arden probably wasn't looking to lose twenty pounds in only six weeks, and wouldn't be calling now—or ever—for that *special television offer,* no matter how much they urged him to hurry, she figured he must have fallen asleep in front of the TV again.

Just to make sure, she crept halfway down the stairs and bent to look. Yup, those were Arden's stockinged feet propped up on the arm of the old sofa. He was out like a light.

She went back upstairs. Leaving her door ajar, she crossed to the bed and climbed in, taking care not to jostle Axl. It was scary how much she loved that dog already. Titus was always saying he smelled, but he didn't. Well, not in a bad way. He just smelled like old dog.

Sid closed her eyes, but she didn't go right back to sleep. She'd been awake just long enough for the excitement to niggle back in again.

Halloween had been a blast—just as awesome as she'd hoped it would be. And she and Danika were becoming really good friends. The more they hung out, the more they realized they liked the same things. Like math! But even with all that, she was more excited about the business news. She'd gone to bed thinking of product names. She *was* going to be a big help, do more than a kid's share of the work, and not just because she was paying her mother back for that whole credit card mess.

She did not regret saving that dog's life. Not even for a second. Still, she had no right to take Dr. Boisvert's credit card. That part she did regret.

She turned onto her side to look out the window. She loved the way she could just reach out, pull back the curtains. From this angle, she could see the looming darkness of the Far South Barn. It had been so beautiful earlier, all lit up with lanterns. With all those people laughing, playing games, and having fun, it had totally lived up to the parties Scott had described for her back in Montreal. The whole night had been awesome, even though she'd had to leave when they turned down the lights for the older kids.

She pushed herself up on one elbow for a better look at the yard.

Yes!

Smiling, she let the curtain fall back into place. All the vehicles were gone. Well, the ones that should be parked in the yard. Her mom's car had been sitting in the machine shed for weeks now. Titus had set out to winterize it but discovered it needed some repairs and was waiting on parts. And Titus's old truck—the one she'd stowed away in to get to Harkness—was right there beside it in the old shed. But Titus's new truck and Arden's Jeep were definitely gone. Since Arden was asleep on the couch, that meant Scott had to be out with her mom in the Jeep. She knew it.

Everything was going to be okay.

Even when she closed her heavy eyelids to get back to sleep, she knew the stars were still shining there outside her bedroom window.

And if stars could give a thumbs-up, they would have.

# – twenty-three –

SCOTT STOPPED the vehicle and killed the lights. "We're here."

He watched as April leaned forward to peer out the window. "All I see is…darkness. What is that ahead? Trees?"

"It's Harkness Mountain."

Her jaw dropped. "Are you freaking kidding me? We're going to climb a mountain in the dark? All I remember suggesting was a walk!"

He laughed. "We won't be climbing the mountain. I wouldn't even try that in the dark, let alone subject you to it."

"Then what are we doing here? Unless…" Now that his eyes had begun adjusting to the darkness, he saw her turn toward him. "Scott Standish, did you bring me here to *park*?"

He grinned. "Do you want to?"

"I don't know." From the tilt of her head, he knew she was surveying the gear shift and the console between the seats and wondering how it could possibly work. Then she surveyed her surroundings outside, making sure they were truly alone. "I've never parked with a…gentleman before."

"Gentleman, huh?" He leaned across the console. Taking her face in his hand, he guided her chin up so he could kiss those perfect, full lips. When she leaned into the kiss, he dropped his hand to her chest, unzipping the bomber jacket to cup her breast beneath the soft material of her T-shirt and light bra. His fingers tightened on that luscious mound, and she shuddered, giving herself up to his touch with a sweet sigh. The sound sent a bolt of arousal straight to his groin. Before he could lose his head, he pulled back. He was *not* going to make love to her in Uncle Arden's ratty old Jeep. "How was that for gentlemanly?"

"Maybe I should have said I've never parked with a scoundrel before." She smoothed a hand over her hair. "Actually, I've never been parking with anyone—gentleman, scoundrel, or anything in between."

"Much as I'd love to correct that deficiency, I think we'd better wait until I have Titus's truck. It's a lot roomier."

If he turned the dome light on now, he was pretty sure he'd see her blushing.

"So what *are* we here for?"

"There's a place I'd like to show you." His eyes dropped to her open jacket in the moonlight. "Better zip up. It's cold out there."

By the time he rounded the vehicle, she'd already jumped out. While she zipped her leather jacket up as far as it would go and pulled her mittens back on, he pulled out a crushed cigarette pack, lit one, and took a long drag. Instantly, he felt the soothing effects of the nicotine roll over him.

"Why do you do that?" she asked. "I know you don't smoke enough to have a real addiction going on."

He shrugged. "I just enjoy it once in a while. But there's no danger I'm going to take it up in earnest. Especially not with Ember around. She gives me hell if she catches so much as a whiff of stale cigarette smoke on me."

"So the Standish women look after their men too."

He took another haul off the cigarette. "I guess."

She looked around. Now that they were outside the vehicle, there was a lot more to be seen in the moon's pale light. "Where are we going?"

"You'll see." He dropped his cigarette and ground it out

beneath his boot. Then he picked up the butt, stuck it in the empty pack and shoved it into his pocket. "Follow me. And stay close."

He struck out and she fell into step behind him. Instead of taking the trail that led to the mountain, he followed the one that carried them toward the river.

"Is that water I hear?"

"Yup. The Prince River. You doing okay?"

"I'm good," she assured him. "Lead on."

The path came to a T near the river's edge. As always, the glint of the water beneath the moonlight made something stir in his chest. Glancing back to make sure she followed, he turned and headed in an upstream direction. Before long, the low-level tumbling, burbling splash of the fast-flowing water grew louder and louder until they rounded the bend and were hit by the full roar of the rapids.

"I know what this is! It's Slamm's Landing, isn't it?" She pointed to a rocky ledge ahead. "That's got to be it. A view of the white water, open to the sky…"

"Yeah. That's the place. Come on."

The path was wide enough now that he could take her hand. They covered the last stretch until they reached the ledge. He led her to his favorite perch, a natural "seat" created by the stacked sandstone.

"It's beautiful. I can see why you love it here." She looked up and clutched his hand harder. "Oh, the stars! I'm almost dizzy looking up at them, with the water moving at our feet."

"You should see them when the moon's not so bright. It's unreal."

"I'll bet."

"I used to come here all the time. You know, most people think you have to climb the mountain to get closer to the stars, but you don't."

"It's not really about getting closer to them, though, is it?" she said. "Obviously, you just need the right vantage point."

"Exactly. And out here, there's nothing between you and just about every star in the sky."

She nestled closer, and he put his arm around her. "I'm so glad you brought me here." Even as she said it, she stifled a yawn. "Sorry. That wasn't a commentary about the view or the company. Just a long day. Sidney was so excited about the party, she had us both up a good hour before dawn."

Okay, so he wasn't gonna get lucky tonight. Oddly, he didn't mind. If that had been his sole goal, he could have swept her off her feet back at the barn. A few kisses and she'd have gladly climbed that ladder to the loft and his wide, welcoming bed. But he'd wanted to bring her out here, wanted to share this sacred place with her.

*Sacred place?* Jesus, he was starting to sound a lot like his embarrassingly romantic teenage self.

He cleared his throat. "So, how's Sid doing? She seems in good spirits these days."

April sighed.

"What?" He leaned back to look at her face in the moonlight, but she chose that moment to glance down at their linked hands. "Is something up with her?"

"She's playing a game of make-believe." She lifted her head to face him. "Pretending that this time in Harkness isn't going to end."

"Is that wise?" The words were out before he could consider them.

He felt her stiffen. "God, Scott. You think I haven't asked myself that question?"

"I'm sorry. Of course you have."

She sighed again. "No, *I'm* sorry. I shouldn't have snapped. It's the obvious question to ask." Some of the tension had left her limbs, but he could still hear the strain in her voice. "The thing is, she knows the difference between reality and pretend. No confusion there. And she's crystal clear about the timeline. I couldn't have been clearer that we're leaving after Christmas. But she asked me—*begged* me—not to keep reminding her."

He grimaced. "That's a tough position to be put in. What did you say?"

"I agreed to go along with it." She shrugged, a tight, jerky gesture that spoke eloquently to her ambivalence. "I don't know if it was the right thing to do or not, but she needs this, Scott." She looked up at him. "She knows she's buying these happy todays with the pain to come tomorrow, but what's the alternative? I just can't be the one this time to eclipse her happiness. To be constantly reminding her of the shadow on the horizon. She knows it's there. She just wants to make the best of every day until that day comes when we have to start packing."

His heart broke for her. For Sid too, but mostly for April. How hard it must be to carry that responsibility, to try to make the right decisions for your child. Her beautiful shoulders were so slim, so frail, compared to the burden she was forced to carry. But carry it she did.

Was it a good idea, letting Sid pretend it was never going to end? Hell if he knew. Although he did know a little something about living day-to-day, knowing the ax was soon to fall. Those months before his mother died…

"So, did I mess up? Did I make the wrong decision?"

"I don't know," he said honestly. "But I totally understand why you made it. She's been so happy, and you two are getting along so well. She's taken responsibility for the credit card caper and is working the debt off. Those are good things. Maybe giving her the space and happiness will be…restorative. Or will help her grow more resilient."

"Oh, God, that's what I hope. It's what I *pray* every day."

"Whatever happens, Sid will be okay because she's got you. You're a terrific mother, April."

"Thank you." She hugged him and he hugged her back. Then she pulled away, brushing her hair back under her cute red hat. "Whether it was wrong or right, at least it wasn't hypocritical. It's kind of what I'm doing too, isn't it?"

He held perfectly still. "Pretending?"

"Letting myself enjoy this. Enjoy *you.*" She laid a hand on his chest. "I won't lie. It's going to be a wrench when I leave. But I'm not about to let that steal the joy from today. I don't—and won't—regret a minute of it."

At her words, he felt a burst of fierce and warring emotions. Gladness. Desire. Sadness. Regret.

"Come here." He lifted her onto his lap and kissed her. Her arms slid around his neck and she kissed him back while the river roared beside them and the stars gazed silently down. When they were both breathing as hard as though they'd climbed Harkness Mountain, he tucked her head under his chin and pulled her close.

Slowly, his heartbeat returned to normal.

She nestled closer. "That was nice."

To his great pleasure, she sounded as soft and relaxed as her body felt. "Nice?" he huffed in pretend offense. "That's pretty faint praise."

She pulled back and he saw the gleam of her smile. "I can say without equivocation that that was the best riverside make-out session I've ever had. Is that better?"

"Um, since you've never even parked with a guy before, I'm guessing this is the *only* riverside make-out session you've had."

She giggled. "True."

"Want to hear something funny?"

"What?"

"It was my only river-side session too."

"Really?"

"Really," he said. "And it was fantastic."

She grinned again. "Yes, it was."

He pulled her back against his chest. They sat there in silence for a while. The cold of the rock beneath his butt was seeping into his bones, but he was loath to move. She felt so good in his arms.

"Hey," she said. "I was talking to Danika's mom at the party. She asked if Sidney could sleep over at their place next Friday night."

His pulse leaped. If Sid was away all night, April could spend the night in the Far South Barn with him. Well, until dawn, anyway. "What'd you tell her?"

"I said *yes.*"

"Good." He kissed her on top of the head. "Because you've got yourself a date."

"I do?" She leaned her head back. "With a gentleman or a scoundrel?"

"I guess you'll have to wait and see. But I'm not waiting until next Friday to do this." He kissed her upturned mouth and felt her shiver. "Come on." He put a hand on the small of her back. "We should head back before Arden's Jeep turns into a pumpkin."

Half an hour later, they kissed goodnight on the front porch. He opened the door for her and when she'd slipped in, closed it quietly behind her.

Scott had never needed much sleep, but he'd be glad for his head to hit the pillow tonight. After a quick smoke. Two in one evening. He really should throw the damned things away. Maybe he would…

He crossed to the front porch steps, careful not to let his boots clomp on the floorboards, and parked his ass on the top step. He lit up, took a drag, then looked out over the farm. Even with the moonlight, it was too dark to make out much, but he could picture the apple trees, heavy with fruit. David Hillman was going to be earning every penny of his paycheck.

He wasn't the only one who'd be busy. Now that the Halloween party was out of the way, April would be working like crazy to get stuff ready for her foray into business. He had no doubt she'd turn a tidy profit, but the timeline was so damned tight. Too tight to really launch a business properly. If she had a few more months, she could really establish herself and her brand.

Supposedly, she had a job lined up for after Christmas, in Northern Ontario. He wasn't entirely sure that was true. She might have fabricated it to limit her commitment to what she'd clearly seen as a charitable offer. She was far too proud to accept charity. Or maybe she'd invented it to coincide with his departure the first of January?

Could that be true? Could she have made up the job?

Dammit, it had the ring of truth. She'd only accepted the job here out of sheer desperation, to avoid having to go to live with her no-good brother. But she wouldn't have wanted to stay on past Scott's own departure. At least not when he'd first offered the job and she didn't know his family.

But even if the position in Ontario was real, wouldn't it be better for her in the long run to build her own job than go to work for yet another employer who might have a low threshold of tolerance for Sid? If the business took off, she might even decide to stay in the region, which would definitely suit Sid. But if she was still bent on leaving, taking the extra months to build her platform would still be a great investment. She could then port it over to wherever she wanted to go.

Now, all that remained was to make sure she would agree to stay.

He pulled out his cell phone, checked the time. There was a three hour time difference from New Brunswick to Alberta. Yeah. Georgie would still be up.

He descended the steps and walked out to the driveway before punching in the number. No need for anyone else to overhear this.

"Scott! How's it going, old man?"

"Can't complain. How about you?"

"Good, good. Hey, Tatiana had her baby yesterday."

"Yeah?"

"A boy. I'm an uncle, bro."

Scott smiled at the happiness in his friend's tone. He knew Georgie had been concerned about his sister, who'd had some issues with her blood pressure. "Awesome. How's the new mom doing?"

"Great. Her BP is still a little high, but they say it'll resolve in a few weeks."

The small talk continued and Scott listened patiently. For a while. The way Georgie was wound up, he could talk all night. So Scott brought the conversation around to work as quickly as he could.

"Yeah, yeah, it's still a go," Georgie said. "Everything's still cued up for January."

"About that..." Scott dropped the cigarette he'd neglected to smoke and ground it out in the dirt. "I might have to stay a bit longer."

A pause. "How much longer?"

"I don't know. Couple of months?"

"Jesus! A couple of months?"

"Or less. I'm not sure. But I could send my share of the money."

"It's not just the investment, Scott. I need you here if we're gonna do this. You know how much day-to-day oversight this project is going to take. So many details and moving parts. I can contribute a lot, but you've got the better brain for that part."

Scott raked a hand through his hair. "Can't we just defer it for a bit?"

"A little while, maybe. But Christ, we've got to move on this. If we don't do it, someone else will beat us to the punch."

"You really think our guy will walk over a two-month delay?"

"I don't know, do I?" The stress in Georgie's voice made his words clipped. "But even if he hangs in here with us, who's to stop someone else from beating us to the market with a different design?"

He paced. The project involved the construction of low-cost pod-type housing units that could be pre-assembled and quickly connected to a pre-built infrastructure to facilitate quick, functional housing where it was needed. "If they beat us by that much of a margin, they're already building them, Georgie. In which case, even our January schedule would be too late." It was the truth, but the idea of being beaten to the punch made him antsy. "Worst case scenario, if we're not first, we can still be best, right?"

There was another brief silence, then Georgie sighed. "I guess you're right. But don't take too long, bro. My brother-in-law is itching to get in on this. He's a dick, but he has construction experience. And if Tatiana sees the project is lagging, she'll be all over me to take Karl on as a partner. Don't make me do that buddy."

"Don't worry. I won't."

They talked a few moments longer about what a colossal pain in the ass Karl-the-brother-in-law was. Fortunately, Georgie got another call and said goodbye.

Shoving his phone back into his pocket, Scott headed for the barn. But somehow, he no longer thought he'd be asleep as soon as his head hit the pillow.

# – twenty-four –

*APRIL DAWN'S*

There it was in full, gorgeous color above her head. Titus had pulled some strings to get the sign done quickly, and April had expected to pay accordingly. But Titus insisted the bill was just thirty bucks. She doubted that, but he wouldn't take a penny more.

April smiled as she listened to the current customer discuss his diet. He'd started out strictly Paleo, but was now more focused on just eating real foods. She pointed out which products would fit his diet and which to avoid. He left with some coconut, date, and nut bars.

She'd answered so many questions, she figured she could now do it in her sleep: *Yes, I do put rum in the fruitcake, but ninety-five percent of it evaporates during cooking. That's right, it's all sweetened naturally. I mainly use coconut sugar, which has a lower glycemic index than cane sugar. Oh, and dates make a great sweetener. Raw honey? Not for baking. Heat tends to kill off the nutrients you're trying to get from it. Maple syrup's a better choice. Or molasses. Much more heat tolerant. Gluten free? Yes, I have some excellent options right here...*

She'd been there at the market since five-thirty. Now, as she stood chatting with a new customer, she stole a glance at the clock on the wall over Gladys's Henna Tattoo shop down the way. Gladys, who was experiencing a lull in business, leaned back in her lawn chair, reading. April hadn't had a lull since seven o'clock. It was now one o'clock in the afternoon. Three hours to go. Scott would arrive at four. He and Sid would help her look after packing up—which really didn't take that long. Then her daughter was going on yet another sleepover at Danika's house this Saturday night.

Sidney had put in just as many hours as April had today. Well, almost. April had let her daughter sleep in an extra twenty minutes while she loaded the truck herself. As it turned out, Sidney had been annoyed to no end to be left out of even that small aspect of their venture. She'd been a real trooper all day. At the moment, she was busily rearranging and compressing the remaining stock. April was proud of her and glad to see her so happy.

This business venture was pulling the two of them closer together. The naming of items, the measuring of ingredients, the baking. The way they both liked to good-naturedly tease Scott when they let him help out. And despite her protests that he must have something better to do, that was pretty much every day. Fortunately, he'd learned to confine himself to lifting and carrying stuff, or helping Sidney pack away the end products. Though she didn't want to pull him away from his duties on the farm, she had to admit it was kind of nice having him around.

Actually, it was nice having the whole clan around. Jace, sweetheart that he was, had shown her how to get her business registered and given her some priceless tips. Titus and Arden had eagerly tested each and every one of her products. Faye had brought over a large double boiler that had been lacking in the Standish kitchen. Ocean had printed the peel-and-stick labels on her color printer. Sidney and Danika had made an afterschool project of labeling all the jars. They look amazingly professional.

April bagged the gluten-free carrot muffins and cranberry apple jelly and handed it to her customer, a senior lady with an amazing mass of salt-and-pepper hair. "You'll have to let me know how you enjoy this combo."

"I will. You'll be here next weekend?"

April smiled. "We will."

"Then I'll be back!" She gave April a little wave and set off.

Finally, there was a lull. Not a customer in sight. Sidney stopped fussing with the merchandise and came to stand beside her at the counter.

"We're out of Almond Butter Dawn and Bootilicious Butterscotch Dawn," she reported. "I think we should double our product again next week."

"Yeah?"

"Yeah."

"Then we will." Bootilicious Butterscotch…that had been Sidney's idea.

It was their third Saturday at the market. If this kept up, by the time Christmas rolled around, they'd need a much bigger booth.

Sidney was such a quick study, jumping to do whatever April needed her to do, and always with a smile on her face. But it turned out her real gift was in sales and customer service. Her daughter was a natural. A ten-year-old natural.

Sidney reached for the order pad. "Lots of custom orders today, huh?"

"I'll have to get them into the spreadsheet so I'll know what to make and when it's due." April gestured to the pad. "There's a German chocolate cheesecake…I think that's for the 5th. Two Kalua cakes for an office party on the 12th."

Sidney flipped through the pages. "Wow, Mom, you just started this pad this morning, didn't you?"

April smiled. "Yup."

"I don't remember a bunch of these…you must have taken them while I was on my lunch break."

"Yeah, there was quite a rush." And lots of them were repeat customers, like Connie Lemon, who was currently bearing down on their booth.

"Hi, April."

"Hi, Connie. What can I do for you today?"

"I've been thinking about your Cranberry Oatmeal Dawn bars all week. Can I have four of them?"

April turned to Sidney. "How's our stock?"

Sidney came back with just three bars. "Sorry, this is all we have left."

"I'll take them," Connie said. "Quick, before someone else snatches them up."

April laughed.

"Actually, can I order a dozen of them for next Saturday? I want to give them out as Christmas gifts to my friends in Spanish class at the community center. I was telling them how tasty they were and now they all want to try them."

"Then you'll need sixteen, won't you?" Sidney said. "Twelve for your friends and four for you?"

Connie laughed. "Good thought, Sid, but I've already got it covered. There are only six in the class. The other six are for me."

"Twelve April's Cranberry-Oatmeal Dawn bars it is, Connie. I'll have them bagged and ready for you."

"Thanks, hon." Connie started to fish for her wallet.

"Hey, would you like to sample one of our Caramel Dawn squares before you go?" Sidney directed Connie's attention to the small sample jar on the counter.

"Don't mind if I do."

Sid carefully extracted one of the samples with the metal tongs and placed it on a napkin.

Connie picked up the treat and bit into it. "Mmm, this is so good!" She took another bite and chewed it slowly, savoring it. "Can you put six of these on the order for next week too?"

"Spanish class?" Sidney asked.

Connie grinned. "Knitting circle."

"Can do," Sidney said, scribbling the order on the pad. "Just give me a minute to do the math. Six caramel, twelve cranberry-oatmeal, ten percent discount for pre-order." With a glance at her mother, she said, "Let's knock off another five percent for being such a great customer and spreading the word about our products."

Connie smiled "Oh, that would be lovely!"

"Okay, so that's a full fifteen percent off…" Sid looked up at the ceiling as she did the mental math, then announced the total. April had already tallied the bill in her own mind, and the amount Sid arrived at was correct. No surprise there.

"That's a great price." Connie dug a bright green wallet from her burlap market bag. "And you, young lady, are quite the math whiz."

Sid was all smiles. "Thanks."

With a wave, Connie moved across the aisle to talk to Gladys, who happily ditched her book to chat.

April looked down at her daughter. "So fifteen percent, huh?"

"I know we said no more than ten percent for pre-orders, but just hear me out, Mom. If she's going to be handing our stuff out to her friends, that's like us giving out free samples, but they didn't cost us anything. We actually *got paid* for them! And she's reaching people who might not ordinarily come to the market and might never have found us, but maybe they'll come now if they have a good enough—"

"Relax, Ladybug. I was just going to say *good job*."

"Oh, good! We'll do that again, then. But I think it really should come from me, whenever possible."

"Excuse me?"

She bit her lip, a sure sign she was choosing her words diplomatically. "Mom, you are the greatest cook on the planet. And definitely chief cook and bottle washer of this whole operation—"

*Chief cook and bottle washer?* Which of the Standishs had she gleaned that expression from?

"But when it comes to sales, there's nothing like an earnest kid to land the deal."

April laughed. "Oh, Sidney, you're definitely a natural at this sales thing."

Sid shot her a sideways look, the kind kids give when they're trying to figure out if an adult is being condescending or not. "Seriously?"

"No question about it."

"Thanks." Sidney grinned. "You know, if this business takes off—I mean, really takes off—we could be all set."

Whoops. Time for some expectation management. "Nice thought, but we can't really judge by pre-Christmas sales, Ladybug. The Christmas season tends to bump up sales for all businesses."

"Duh. I know that, Mom. Nobody's going to want to buy a Christmas basket full of jellies and jams in July. But that just means we need to work super hard in November and December to offset the slower months. There are ways we could build business in those slower months too."

"How so?"

Apparently that had been the invitation Sidney had been looking for.

"Take Easter, for instance. We can set out a platter of samples of your Easter egg banana cake in February, so we can get people wanting our breakfast version. We'll have dozens pre-ordered for Easter. And hey, we can have a different type of fudge each week. It would sell even better than it's selling now if we made it into shapes—bunnies, and Easter eggs and stuff like that. Carrots, maybe, for the health nuts!"

April snorted. "A fudge carrot for the health conscious?"

"Okay, maybe not," Sidney allowed. "But the other ideas are great, aren't they?"

"They sure are." April had thought about trying a lot of

these strategies already, but that didn't take away from how impressed she was that Sid had thought of them. She didn't bother mentioning, either, that they'd have to put those strategies to work somewhere else because they'd be long gone by Easter.

"And listen to this, Mom. In August, we could have back-to-school sales. Think about it—individually wrapped breakfast bars sold in twelve- or twenty-four packs. Pre-orders welcome. Hey, maybe we could even approach Principal Makepeace! They have a breakfast club at school. Maybe she'd be interested."

April's heart sank. "That's another great marketing idea." She looked into her daughter's eyes. "But Ladybug, you know we'll be…"

"You promised!" Sidney said, her voice rising, her eyes suspiciously bright. "Just say *we'll see*. Okay?"

*Oh, Sidney.* What had she done, agreeing to let her daughter pretend? Except from the glitter in her daughter's eyes, it was evident reality wasn't far away. She knew what was coming.

April forced a smile. "We'll see."

"Um, I'd like to buy a Sunny Sesame Dawn. It's for my Mother."

April almost didn't recognize the young man at the counter plunking down a well-folded five dollar bill. Last time she'd seen Roy, he'd been wearing the banner of *Grossest Superhero* across his torso.

"Hey, Roy," Sid said.

"Oh, hey, Sidney," he said. "What a surprise. I'd forgotten you worked here." Considering how perfectly practiced that sounded, April doubted it.

Sidney frowned. "I saw you here last week."

"Oh, that's right," he laughed nervously. "Well, I've got a lot on my mind this weekend—you know, with football practice and all."

"Football? That's the bee's knees!"

Roy looked blank.

"I think it's pretty cool too," April said, to help him figure out whether bee's knees were good or not.

"Yeah? I mean, yeah. My big brother coaches it and this is my first year. I'm thinking I'll try out for tackle, but I've got a pretty good arm so I could see being put in the quarterback position."

"Cool." Sidney packaged up the small order, put it in a bag and handed it over to Roy. "Um, there you go. Hope your mom enjoys it."

"You forgot to take my money," Roy said.

"Right!" She picked the five up from the counter and started to make change in the cash box. "Ha ha…I should have brought a calculator."

Calculator? Playing dumb? About *math*? Her suddenly red-cheeked girl was just a little bit flustered.

Oh yeah, her daughter was crushing.

April watched the sweet, almost painful exchange.

"Say, Sid," she said. "We've been working so hard, I forgot lunch." This was true, she'd sent Sidney to grab a soft pretzel around eleven, planning to grab herself something less bready later when she had the chance. She hadn't had the chance. She opened her wallet, and held out a five. "Would you mind grabbing a couple veggie samosas for me?"

"Sure." Sidney took the money. "Though I'm not sure where the booth is…"

*Well played, Ladybug. Well played.*

"I can show you," Roy said.

"Oh? That'd be great."

Instead of lifting up the counter divide, Sidney crawled beneath it. She put April's money down on the counter and started to untie her apron, then thought better of it. Instead, she redid the tie at the back even more tightly. "Free advertising." She picked up the five dollar bill and tucked it into the apron's pocket.

The aprons had been Ember's contribution. One adult sized and one child sized, with *APRIL DAWN'S* printed across the front.

April gave her the thumbs up.

"So, back in…?" Sidney let the question hang.

"Take your time."

April watched the two of them head off, then glanced at the clock. It was 1:30. Two and a half more hours and she'd be done. She could use a nap. She'd sure give it a try when she got home.

*Home?*

Oh god, where the hell had that come from?

"Hey, sexy."

She turned to find Scott standing there, smiling. Her heart lifted at the sight of him. "You're early."

"I was in the neighborhood." His smile, the warmth and appreciation in his eyes, told her he was just as glad to see her as she was to see him. "Figured I'd come by and see if I could do anything to help."

She smiled back. "I'm glad you're here."

"Me too."

That was enough. For today, for this moment, it was more than enough.

# – twenty-five –

"SO, YOU'RE telling me you guys knew all along?" Scott sat with April on one side of the long bar table, a cold beer in his right hand, April's hand tucked in his left. Yes, holding hands.

Initially, he'd wanted to keep his relationship with April completely on the down-low. Since it had such a limited life expectancy, he didn't want to create any false expectations. But they'd been dating now for three weeks, and people were talking. It seemed easier to just concede the obvious, that they were seeing each other.

Telling his siblings had been no big deal, but telling Arden? That had been hard. Knowing his uncle would immediately start envisioning April as his future daughter-in-law, Scott had made it crystal clear that it was a just-for-now thing. Arden had nodded as Scott explained they both still intended to leave by the new year, April to her new job and Scott to his long-awaited project in Northern Alberta. His uncle hadn't said a single disapproving word, but Scott could feel his disappointment.

He'd been sorely tempted to defend himself. Dammit, he'd been so determined to leave her alone! But she'd worn him down. Of course, Uncle Arden would not have appreciated his passing the buck. And he'd be right.

"Yup," Titus said.

Everyone at the table looked at Titus.

"Oh, please." Ocean rolled her eyes. "You were nearly as oblivious about Scott and April as you were about Faye and Arden."

*Faye and Arden.* Jesus. Scott had just learned about their alleged romance earlier today. He huffed. "I can't believe I was the last one to know about Uncle Arden."

Titus turned amazed eyes on him. "You really thought he and Faye were playing Scrabble until midnight six days a week?"

Ocean laughed. "Um, you'd still be thinking that too, Titus, if we hadn't walked in on that lip-lock on the couch two nights ago."

*Uncle Arden and Ocean's mother making out on the couch?* Scott shook his head to dislodge the image.

"Hey, if I remember correctly, April was the one who pointed it out to *you*," Titus responded.

"True," Ocean conceded. "She saw instantly what we were too close—or too preoccupied—to notice."

"Seriously?" Scott looked at April with accusing eyes. "You knew all along and didn't tell me until today when I asked why we were buying Arden and Faye a joint Christmas gift?"

April grimaced apologetically. "We agreed to let folks figure it out for themselves."

"Don't blame April," Ember said. "It was my idea to see how long it would take you guys to twig to it."

"Obviously, a damned long while." Scott shook his head.

Titus grinned. "Don't worry, bro. I won't rub it in. Much. Just because I'm the more intuitive of the Standish brothers—"

Ocean snorted. "Don't let him needle you, Scott. When we walked in on them kissing, Titus was convinced my mother was having a heart attack and Arden was resuscitating her. I had to clamp my hand over his mouth and shove him down the hall to stop him from shouting 'I got this!' and going to her rescue."

They all laughed. Except Titus. "Hey, you weren't supposed to tell them that part!"

"Sorry. I couldn't resist," Ocean said apologetically. Except her eyes twinkled more with mischief than regret.

"You'd better be sorry," Titus said with mock sternness. "You just cost me bragging rights."

She laughed again and Titus kissed her. Nothing to elicit whistles or hoots of *get a room* from the other patrons. Just a quick, sweet kiss. His brother was in love. Scott still had a bit of a hard time wrapping his mind around it. But it looked good on him. Softened some of his too-straight edges.

A waitress stopped at their table. "Can I get you anything else?"

"One more round?" Scott looked around the table and received ready agreement.

"Thanks, Candy. Another Coke for me." Titus—the perpetual designated driver—tipped his glass toward her.

Ocean looked at Candy. "I'll have what he's having. Except put a belt of rum in mine."

Titus and Jace guffawed. Beside Scott, April laughed so hard, he could feel her body shaking. Across the table, Ember literally spewed her beer.

Scott's own face hurt from smiling.

These past weeks had been great. He'd taken April to the town's little movie theater twice—he picked the movie one night and she picked it the next time. They'd dined at a fancy restaurant in Crandler, and a few nights later, for a real treat, he'd taken her to the Duchess Diner for fish and chips. She'd concurred they were the best on the planet. They'd gone for moonlit drives along old country roads. One night, snow had been falling as they drove and they hadn't said a word. The comfortable silence had lasted more than an hour.

And they'd made love every chance they got, in Scott's bed in the loft.

So very often but not nearly enough.

Tonight, they'd opted for the company of Scott's siblings and their significant others. They'd actually gone for an early dinner, then Christmas shopping for Uncle Arden and Faye.

Jesus. *Arden and Faye*. He was still coming to grips with the idea of them as a couple.

For their gift, they'd collectively settled on a trip to Montreal to see a hockey game—the Toronto Maple Leafs at home to the Habs, courtesy of the Standish Siblings. Ocean was forking over for two nights' stay at a hotel near the Bell Centre. Jace had kicked in with Ocean to upgrade the hotel. And April had insisted on buying the tickets to the game. She'd been adamant that they not be in the nosebleed seats, and had wound up paying a fair amount. More than she could afford. But no amount of persuading would sway her. "Arden's been more than good to me," she'd said. "And Sidney adores Faye, who busts her butt with the enrichment tutoring. It'll be from the both of us."

And now the evening was winding down at the Ruby Slipper Pub.

"Crap." Ember wiped her mouth with a tissue, then dabbed at her shirt. "See what happens when you make me laugh? I got beer all over myself."

Titus grunted. "Sounds like someone has had one too many."

"Hey, don't bust my chops over a couple of drinks," Ember protested. "I'm on call so often, I rarely get to indulge anymore."

April leaned forward. "How does that work?"

"The on call thing?"

"Yeah."

"We share it. There are just three family docs in the immediate area, so eventually, I'll be on call one in three nights. But right now, Dr. McCann over in Crandler is in Paris for a week, so I'm on call every other night."

"That must be exhausting," April said.

Ember shrugged. "Sometimes. Other times, I don't get called at all."

As Ember and April continued to talk about the demands of Ember's practice, Titus leaned toward Scott.

"Guess my little talk about leaving her alone fell on deaf ears, huh?"

"Oh, I was listening, all right. But April wasn't."

Titus raised an eyebrow. "And you were powerless to resist?"

"Dude, you have no idea."

"You might be surprised." The sternness in his brother's face relaxed as his gaze went to Ocean. He turned his attention back to Scott. "I just hope you know what you're doing."

"Me too."

"What are you two talking about?" April asked.

"Just, you know, stuff," Titus said with his typical eloquence. "I was about to ask him how your business is doing, but now that Ember's no longer bending your ear, maybe you can tell us yourself."

Just then, Candy arrived with a tray of drinks, and Titus nodded to her. "We'll settle up when you're ready."

"Perfect. Be back in a few." Candy whirled off.

"So, how *are* things going at the market, April?" Titus prompted.

"Business is fantastic." April reached for her second cooler of the night. Never a big drinker, Scott knew she'd be feeling it. He also knew that it wasn't an alcohol buzz that put that smile on her face. She was high on her success. On this night. The fun of it. "We sold out of practically everything today," she said. "Some things were gone by *ten o'clock*. I couldn't believe it. Sidney and I ended up closing early."

"Good job," Titus said admiringly.

Scott lifted his beer. "Here's to booming business."

Glasses clinked around.

Ocean took a sip from her fresh drink. "Entrepreneurship suits you, April. I can see you're enjoying it."

"I am absolutely loving it. Harkness is such an awesome town. So many nice folks."

Her face was practically incandescent with pleasure. Scott found her hand again and gave it a little squeeze. "Told you you'd fit right in at the market."

"Well, I can't believe you've charmed Mrs. Budaker," Ocean said.

April frowned. "Why ever not? She's a sweet old lady."

"Ocean's just jealous," Titus said. "Mrs. B and I have this thing going. Have for quite some time now."

The way Titus said it, with such straight-faced intensity, Scott could see it gave April pause. Then Ember burst out laughing.

Ocean punched Titus's arm.

"Titus saved Mrs. Budaker's Westie a while back," Scott said for April's benefit. "She's still repaying him by delivering fresh-baked cookies every week."

April's confusion cleared. "Ah, those ginger snaps he's always carrying around."

"Exactly."

"What a sweet thing to do," April said.

"Sweet. Right," Ocean huffed. "She'd kill me in my sleep if she had half a chance."

Titus laughed.

So did Jace. "That's a little dramatic, isn't it?"

"Hey, I'm a writer. Drama is my stock in trade. But come on, have you seen how she glares at me? She's been downright hostile since I hooked up with this guy." She snuggled up against Titus.

Titus put his arm around her and pulled her close. "Well, *this guy* has you now. Mrs. Budaker'll have a helluva time prying you out of my arms."

Everyone fell silent for a few second. It was April who broke that silence.

“So, Ocean, tell me about your play.”

“It’s coming along like a house on fire.” Ocean extracted herself from beneath Titus’s arm to launch into an animated description of the scene she’d just finished writing—the moonshine-running Lovecraft sisters first brush with the law, an encounter that resulted in love at first sight for one of the sisters.

Since Scott’s grandmother had been one of the Lovecraft ladies, he knew the story well. Instead of listening attentively, he focused on being in the moment. As he sat there enjoying the company of his siblings and their significant others, with April’s small, strong hand folded in his on his thigh, he felt a sense of fullness in his chest. A strange contentment. Damn, it was almost enough to make a man want to stay.

*Stay?*

What the hell?

The warm feelings were instantly blasted away as the familiar, icy cold gripped his guts. The claustrophobia rising in his chest bordered on panic. He took a deep breath, held it a few seconds, and released it. *Breathe it out. It’ll pass.*

“It must be fun, writing about their adventures,” April said.

“Totally,” Ocean agreed.

By the time Ocean finished expounding on the exploits of the Lovecraft women, he’d conquered the claustrophobia. Jesus, he hated how out-of-control the sensation made him feel. A couple of episodes like that were usually enough to have him packing up and hitting the road. Even now, the urge to do just that niggled at him. Unfortunately, it was out of the question. He’d given his word that he’d stay until the new year. And hell, if he talked April into extending her stay to give her business a chance to really take root, he’d be stuck here even longer.

The thought made the ice stir in his gut again, but he

clamped down on it. Titus deserved this respite, and April deserved this shot at making something for her and Sid.

"With all this talk of adventure," Ember said, "I think it's time for me and Jace to head out. I can think of no better adventure than what awaits me under the covers."

Titus choked on his beer. "Jesus, Em!"

She batted her eyelashes innocently. "What?"

"I know you guys are engaged, but that's definitely TMI, at least when your brothers are at the table."

"Hey, get your mind out of the gutter, big brother." She balled up a bar napkin and tossed it at him. "The adventures I'm looking forward to are all in my dreams. I've been on my feet since before sunup, and I've just downed two drinks. I'm ready to pass out for about eight hours."

Everyone laughed, and Scott laughed along with them.

Jace took Ember's hand. "Okay, Sleeping Beauty, let's get your head on a pillow."

"Amen to that." Ember stood. Jace helped her into her coat.

"I can't believe you're leaving so soon!" Ocean said.

Ember looked at Jace. "You can stay if you want."

"Not a chance you're walking back to the apartment alone. Besides, I've got to be at the gym by six," he said. "Coach and I are just about to open the doors for business and we want to go over a few things."

"That's a damned good thing you're doing with the boxing club, man," Titus said. "The kids in this region really need something like that, and the schools just aren't resourced to do much anymore."

Jace shrugged. "Just trying to give them some focus, some discipline."

"Definitely needed," Scott agreed. "But it seems like the gym is just the beginning of your plans since you split away from your brother." He met Jace's eyes. "If we ever had doubts about you, you sure as hell erased them with your actions. Leaving WRP Holdings took a lot of guts, but you're not just standing up to Terry. You're taking the fight to him."

"Thanks." Jace smiled wryly. "And *fight* is the right word."

"You two still battling it out?" Titus said.

Ember snorted. "This is Terry we're talking about, so yeah. The battle won't be over anytime soon. Nor should it be after what he did to us. He's such a dick."

"That's too bad," April said, her voice wistful. Scott knew she was thinking of her own family.

"It is," Jace agreed. "But that's the cold, hard truth of it." He pulled his coat from the bench and shrugged into it. "Families don't always get along."

Ember hauled him close by the lapels of his coat and kissed him quickly. "Well, *this* family does." It was the way she said it, the way they locked eyes a few seconds longer than necessary, the almost conspiratorial smile…

Something was going on.

Jace reached in his coat pocket for his gloves. A white business card came out with them. "Oh, damn. April I meant to give this to you." He handed the card to her.

Scott felt his whole body tighten without even knowing why. "Who's it from?"

April read the card. "Someone named Stone Thibault." She passed it to him so he could inspect it.

The front of the card bore just the name and a phone number. No address, place of business, or anything, just a phone number with a 617 area code. The words *Please call me* were scrawled on the back. He gave the card back to April.

"Is this guy a friend of yours?" April asked Jace.

He shook his head. "Never meet him before today. He came into the office—I just happened to be there—and asked me to give this card to you."

"Are you sure he said me?" She turned the card over and over as though she might glean something more from it. "Oh, wait." She looked up at Jace again. "He probably intended it for Mrs. Budaker. We both sell sweets, we're both more or less at the south entrance…"

"No, it's definitely for you," Jace said. "He asked me to give it to *Ms. April Dawn Morgan*."

April's eyebrows lifted. "I wonder what it's about."

So did Scott. He wondered, too, why the hairs on his arm would not freakin' lie down.

Just then the waitress, wearing a smile that was getting a bit weary around the edges, came over with the bill. "And the winner is…?"

Jace, who was already on his feet, reached for his wallet. So did Scott and Titus.

"Ignore them, Candy," Ember instructed. "I've got this." She pulled a couple of bills out of her bag and dropped them on Candy's tray. "No change required."

Candy's eyes widened. "Thanks, Doctor Standish!" Tucking the bills into her waiter's wallet, she was off.

With the echo of Candy's words hanging in the air, the siblings looked at each other. *Doctor Standish.*

"Okay, I'll cop to it," Ember said. "I've been waiting a long time for that to happen. I mean, to hear it from a regular person who's not a patient."

Titus cleared his throat. "Better get used to it, Dr. Standish. You earned it."

Scott had to swallow too. "Proud of you, Kid."

"Kid?" Ember slanted him a reproving glance but didn't launch into her usual tirade about being just a couple of months younger than him. "This is your lucky day. I'm going to let that slide because I'm basically asleep on my feet. 'Night guys."

Hand in hand, Ember and Jace left. Their departure seemed to signal the end of the evening. Ocean drained her drink and Titus pushed his Coke away.

Scott looked around. "We about ready to call it a night?"

There was a chorus of agreements.

"I'll go heat up the truck," Titus said, rising.

Ocean scooted out right behind him. "I'll come with you."

Titus frowned. "But the whole point of heating it up is so you won't have to sit in the cold."

"Ah, but I intend to keep you warm while you're warming it up."

Titus's frown cleared. "Oh. Right." He looked at Scott and April. "Take your time, you two."

Scott turned to April, who was looking down at that damned business card again, her face serious.

"You okay?" he asked.

"What?" Her head came up. "Yeah, I'm fine. I was just wondering what this could be about."

He shrugged. "Seems weird that the guy would give it to Jace instead of just going to your booth and delivering it personally."

She worried her lower lip with her teeth. "Maybe I was away," she suggested. "I did take a couple of bathroom breaks and left Sidney in charge. Maybe he came by then and didn't feel comfortable leaving it with a non-adult?"

He shrugged. "Maybe."

"Should I call the number?"

"Well, *Ms. April Dawn Morgan*, that's entirely up to you."

"He must have got that from the company name. No one who knows me would call me April Dawn. I've always been just April."

"Right." Scott sure hoped that's where the guy got it. Otherwise, correspondence addressed to one's full legal name never boded well, in his experience. It usually came from the courts, like the time he'd gotten that summons to witness in a litigation involving his then employer.

Not that April would have reason to fear the law. Well, there was that credit card thing with Sidney, but the Boisverts had apparently agreed not to report it, and April had already made restitution…

Of course, the Canadian Revenue Agency used full legal names too, didn't they? But the CRA wouldn't send someone to personally poke around in a citizen's business. Not unless they suspected a big-time tax evasion or a tax fraud situation, in which case they might send an investigator. April was way too straight an arrow to engage in shady tax stuff, or any kind of illegalities. And even if she was, she was way too small a fish to warrant personal attention.

No, it must be business-related. Maybe she was being head-hunted for a job.

But that area code—617... It rang a bell. Wasn't that Massachusetts? He had a buddy who lived in Saugus, outside of Boston, and he was pretty sure that was his area code. Scott had stayed with the guy twice, once in the winter when he'd driven down there to see a Bruins/Rangers game, and once in the spring to catch the Jays at Fenway.

If he was right about that area code, it would definitely eliminate anything involving the CRA or the courts. He should have found that reassuring, but he didn't. It just made him more apprehensive. Who the devil was looking for her? From Boston? And why take this circuitous route?

"It could be about a job," she said.

"Could be," he agreed, having pretty much reached the same conclusion.

She looked down at the card once more before tucking it into her coat pocket. "I'll call after the weekend."

As soon as the damned card was out of sight, her face smoothed. He wished he could forget about it so easily. Unfortunately, that twinge of trepidation didn't want to go away.

"So, is it too soon to go out to the truck?"

"Let's give them another five minutes." Pushing the worry to the back of his mind, he smiled. "We can spend it making out in the shadows of the alley, if you're game."

Her dark eyes caught fire. "You're on."

# — twenty-six —

APRIL SMILED when Scott held the door open for her as they left the bar. There she was with a heart full of carnal intent, about to practically jump his bones in the alley, but he still treated her with respect. Arden Standish could be proud of the job he'd done raising his boys. In her admittedly limited observational experience, too many men abandoned all respect for a woman at her first display of sexuality.

She looked up at him. "Which way?"

He took her hand and led her around the corner of the building. It wasn't a dark alley at all; just a recess created by the L-shape of the building. From the paving stones illuminated by the nearby streetlight, it obviously served as an outdoor patio in the summer. But that same streetlight did create a narrow band of deep shadow near the wall, the perfect place for stolen kisses.

"Why, Scott Standish, have you done this before?"

He grinned. "I may have."

He pulled her into his arms, pivoting so that his back was against the hard brick wall. She splayed her hands on his chest and went up on tiptoe to press her mouth to his eagerly. He let her steer the kiss, following her lead in the now familiar dance. She loved when he did that, when he let her focus on exploring his body with her hands and tantalizing him with her mouth. But after a few moments, he growled and reversed their positions.

As much as she loved teasing him, she loved this even more—his hard arms boxing her in, the driving force of his passion trapping her. But his power never frightened her, which was a miracle in itself. It only made her feel feminine and powerful in her own right. The yin to his yang. A perfect physical match.

It was Scott who pulled away when things threatened to get too X-rated. He tucked her head under his chin and she nestled into his chest.

"God, you make me crazy," he said, his voice a rumble under her ear. "In the best possible way, of course."

"The feeling is mutual." She leaned back to look up at him in the darkness. "Think we've given them enough time to warm up the truck?"

Scott peered around the corner. "The windows don't look overly steamed, so I guess it's safe to approach."

Hand in hand, they crossed the street to the parking lot. Titus and Ocean sat in their respective car seats, talking easily. Still, he knocked on Ocean's window and said, "You guys decent?"

"Ha ha. Very funny." Ocean, who had very clearly been kissed, opened her door so Scott could open the rear-hinged back door.

He took April's hand to help her up into the truck, but before he could do it, his phone buzzed. Another phone buzzed inside the vehicle. Titus's, as evidenced by the way his hand shot to the right front pocket of his jacket.

The brothers exchanged a worried glance.

Why would they both be getting a text? Unless...maybe it was a search and rescue call. Neither of them had been called out on a mission since April and Sid had arrived, but Scott had told her about the family involvement in the regional S&R program.

Her worry was short lived.

"Ember," Titus muttered. "I swear, if her head wasn't attached…"

"What is it this time?" Ocean asked.

*"Missing my scarf,"* Scott read. *"Made a pit stop at the bathroom on my way out. Think I might have left it by the sink."*

"Just now, in the bar?" April handed her purse to Scott. "I'll run back in and get it."

"I'll go with you," Scott said.

"To the ladies' room?"

"Okay, to the door, then."

She'd sensed his concern earlier over the business card, and now he was fretting over her re-entering the perfectly safe bar they'd just exited? It was literally right across the street. It wasn't like she had to cross a lonely parking lot or dark alley. Did he think she was that helpless?

She rolled her eyes. "You want to walk me across the street? Because, you know, there's so much traffic." She looked left and right—pointedly—and there wasn't a headlight to be seen.

"Poke fun at me if you want, but I'm walking you to the door. Uncle Arden would skin me if I did anything less."

Well, since he'd invoked Arden, she supposed she could indulge him. "Okay, let's go."

As they started across the street, a young couple came out of the bar. They were laughing, holding hands, and more than a little inebriated.

"Hey, it's the lady from the market!" one said. "You make like the best cheesecake. Ever. April Dawn, right?"

"That's right." April smiled. Guess she'd better get used to being called April Dawn. "I recognize the two of you from the booth, but didn't catch your names…"

"Mackenzie," she answered. "Mackenzie Pace. This is my friend, Shelley West."

"Hey!" Shelley gave a half-circle wave. "I love your Bootilicious Dawn."

April laughed. "My ten-year-old daughter named it. I wanted to go with something else.

"Oh, no way! Bootlicious is the perfect name for it."

"I'll tell her you said that."

A taxi pulled in, right up by the door, and April was glad to see it. Neither of these young women was in any shape to drive.

"That's our ride." MacKenzie held the cab's back door open while her girlfriend slid in. "See you next weekend at the market, April Dawn," she said, then crawled into the taxi herself."

April waved them off. She had to admit it: life in Harkness was different. And no, it wasn't just the small town feel. It was Harkness itself—there was a heart to it. And she kind of liked it. Kind of felt part of it.

Just as Scott opened the pub door, another patron practically stumbled out, not because he was falling-down-drunk, but because he wasn't expecting the door to open so effortlessly and his momentum carried him out. That didn't stop Scott from razzing him.

"Whoa, Gareth, new legs?"

"Screw you, Scott." He laughed.

"Back atcha, G. What are you doing in town?"

Before Gareth could reply, April jumped in. "I'll just go grab Ember's scarf. Back in a second." She opened the door and let herself inside before Scott could register an objection.

The patrons had thinned out considerably, and for the first time this evening, no music boomed from the speakers. April didn't have a watch on but figured it must be close to closing time.

She made a bee-line for the bathroom, where she found the bright blue scarf on the vanity.

*Bingo.* And it was a nice one. Hand painted silk. No wonder Ember wanted it back.

Scarf in hand, April opened the door and slipped out of the brightly lit bathroom. But the previously well-lit hallway was now in darkness. What the hell? They couldn't be closing up yet. She had enough experience working in bars to know the lights always came up while people were ushered out and stayed up while the place got at least a cursory cleaning.

"Well, well, look what we have here."

"Oh!" Her hand flew to her chest. It took a few seconds for her eyes to adjust to the darkness, and when they did, she saw the man standing there was wearing an unpleasant smile.

She'd seen that look on men before.

She didn't like it one bit. Nor did she like the way he was blocking her passage back to the lounge.

"Excuse me," she said. "I'm just on my way out."

Instead of moving to let her pass, he leaned his hand against the wall, making an exit even more awkward. "You're the new girl staying at the Standish place, aren't you?"

"I'm *working* there," she said. "Not that it's any of your business."

"Oh, *working*…right."

He looked her up and down slowly and her skin absolutely crawled.

"I gotta hand it to Scott. I mean, he always was good at bird-dogging, but I don't believe he ever hired his lay before. What a great set up. Probably tax deductible."

April's blood froze. "You…creep! This conversation is over."

"Creep? It's Dundas, actually. Dundas Bloom."

*Dundas Bloom?* Her skin crawled a little bit more. This was the jerk the girls had told her about on one of their shopping trips. Jace's brother's henchman. Also, the guy who'd spread stories about Ember in high school. Apparently some people never outgrew being an asshole.

"I'm leaving." She stepped closer, hoping he would step back reflexively to preserve his personal space. He didn't. "Get out of my way, Mr. Bloom."

"Oh, I don't think so."

With the speed of a rattlesnake, he snatched her wrist. She gasped and tried to pull away, but his grip was painfully tight, unbreakable.

"Let me go!"

"April, is it?" His breath fanned her face. "Relax, April. Don't you know that any friend of Scott's is a friend of mine?"

She'd never actually kneed a guy in the groin before, but if he didn't back the hell up, she'd do it. On that thought, she shifted all her weight to her left foot…

"Get your filthy hands off her, Bloom."

Scott! Her aggressor's bulky body blocked her view, but she had no doubt who issued that icy command.

"If you don't release her this second, so help me God, I'll rip your fucking spine out."

Dundas let go of her wrist but didn't immediately turn around, which gave her a close-up view of his reaction. He hadn't moved, but those massive, sloped shoulders seemed to have drawn up. His lips drew thin. But then he turned around and huffed out a half-laugh as if it was some kind of misunderstanding.

"Just introducing myself to your friend." He moved aside, and April hurried past to Scott's side.

Scott looked down at her. "You okay?"

"I'm fine," she assured him.

He took her arm and she knew he felt the shudder that went through her. Fury sparked in his eyes.

"Really," she said. "I'm okay. Can we just go?"

He studied her for a few seconds longer. She held his gaze, knowing he needed to see the reassurance in her eyes. Apparently satisfied, he turned his now scathing gaze on Dundas.

"I think you owe the lady an apology."

It wasn't immediately forthcoming. And she knew why...Dundas was sizing Scott up. Sizing the situation up.

April was doing the same. Dundas was a big man.

"Go on out to the truck, April," Scott said, his voice a restrained monotone. "Please."

"I will if you will," she said.

"I have to have a little talk with my friend here. Seems he's a slow learner."

Dundas snorted. "You think you're man enough to teach me a lesson, do you?"

Scott's face was an expressionless mask. "Outside, Bloom."

Dundas's hands still weren't fisted, but he wasn't backing down. The slow grin spreading across his face told April he wasn't about to.

"After you, Standish."

April tensed. They were really going to do this. Go outside and brawl.

"Get to the truck, April."

"Scott—"

"Sweetie, this guy needs a—"

Dundas sucker punched Scott. With one lunge and flying fist, he caught him in the jaw. Scott flew back against the wall in the narrow hall. April scuttled out of the way. Scott regained his balance just in time for Dundas to plow into him, driving him backward and into the pub proper. With a roar, Scott grabbed the other man by his coat front and shoved him toward the exit. Then the two of them, trading blows, spilled out the pub's door.

*Shit!*

April ran out after them.

Outside, all she could do was watch as Scott and Dundas wailed on each other. In the periphery of her attention, she heard vehicle doors slamming.

A couple guys got out of a car parked near the building.

"Need a hand there, Dun?" One of them asked.

April didn't think it was possible, but her adrenaline went up another notch.

"Two-man fight, boys." The commanding voice was Titus's. "But if either of you want to go a round with me, I'm right here."

"Think you can take us both, Titus?" The shorter man said, drawing an alarmed look from his companion.

"Don't know." Titus cracked his knuckles audibly. "But I'm itching to find out."

"To hell with this," the bigger guy said. "I'm out of here."

Seeing his buddy climbing back behind the wheel of his souped-up Neon, the other guy swore and took off for the car.

Any relief April felt at their departure was overshadowed by the fight still raging on the sidewalk. Both men were down on the hard cement now, locked in struggle. Oh, God, because of her.

Ocean came over to her side, wrapped an arm around her.

"This is awful," April said. "How do we make them stop? I don't know what to do!"

"Just stand back," Ocean counseled. "They'll settle things."

Barely had Ocean got those words out when the two men broke apart. Scott levered himself to his feet. "Get up, Bloom."

On the ground, Dundas groaned.

"Go on, get up!"

Slowly, Dundas got to his feet.

Scott grabbed him by the shirt and slammed him up against the nearest car. Titus was on his brother immediately, dragging him off Dundas and holding him back. "Enough, bro."

"If you ever come near April again, I'll tear you limb from limb," he shouted over Titus's shoulder.

Dundas spat blood. "I wasn't aware you'd staked a claim."

"She's mine! And you sure as hell knew it, or you wouldn't be harassing her in the first place."

*Mine*? April felt the jolt of that word to the soles of her feet.

"Oh, I don't know," Dundas drawled. "She looks like a nice enough piece of—"

Scott lunged, almost getting away from Titus. Dundas took a few hurried steps backward.

"Dundas!" Titus barked. "Get the hell out of here before my arms get tired and I let him go."

"Yes, scurry away like the rat you are." Scott strained against Titus's iron grip. "And if you value your hide, you will never lay a hand on her again. Never so much as speak to her. You hear me?"

"You Standishs are all the same." Dundas managed to sneer even as he wiped away blood from above his left eye with the sleeve of his jacket. "But you'll get yours. And I'll be there laughing when it happens."

Ocean laughed sharply. "That's hilarious, Dundas. Even if that day came to pass, no one would hear you laughing. Not with your head stuck so far up Terry Picard's ass."

Dundas whirled toward Ocean. "Shut your mouth, bitch!"

Titus released Scott so suddenly, Scott almost fell. Then Titus started toward Dundas with deadly purpose. In a reversal of roles, Scott grabbed his brother's jacket and held him back. Well, slowed him down, at least.

Realizing the peril he'd put himself in, Dundas finally displayed the good sense to retreat. Hastily.

Heart pounding in her ears, April watched him jump in his old pickup and peel out, leaving the unpleasant smell of burned rubber behind.

# – twenty-seven –

SCOTT WOKE chilled. He'd kicked the blankets off his side of the bed in his sleep. Small wonder. He'd been dreaming of kicking the crap out of Dundas Bloom.

Actually in his dream, he kicked the crap out of him quite a few times, starting with that pimply-faced, lying jerk Bloom had been in high school. In the dream, he set the bastard on his ass with a wicked uppercut to the jaw. But when Bloom got up again, it was no longer the high school punk who'd made up those stories about Ember. This time, he had his filthy hands on April. Holding her by the arms. Leering at her.

Thank God he'd gone in to see what was keeping her. She'd looked so scared. He heard her voice again, high and thin with fear, but trying to sound commanding: *I'm leaving. Get out of my way, Mr. Bloom*.

Bloom barring her way. *Oh, I don't think so.*

Scott raked a hand through his hair. Jesus, it was amazing he hadn't done more than just kick off the covers.

He glanced at April. She lay on her side, facing him, her head nestled into her pillow. It was too dark to see much, but from the way she breathed, he knew she was asleep. He eased himself out of bed. She stirred briefly, then settled again. Exhaling the breath he'd been holding, he pulled the blankets up and tucked them closer around her.

Quietly, he dressed and descended the ladder to the barn floor. The tiny nightlight with its dusk-to-dawn sensor illuminated the way so he didn't have to count steps or feel for the floor. He'd installed it for April's safety, but had to admit it was convenient.

He shivered. The loft was nippy enough, but it was even colder down in the main barn's large, empty space. It wouldn't be empty for long. Soon it would be trimmed for Christmas. April seemed to be really looking forward to the party. Sid too. And Arden? Scott almost smiled—he seemed to be looking forward to everything a little bit more these days.

He opened the door and slipped out into the night.

Locating his cigarettes in his coat pocket, he shook the package open. One left. He looked at it for a moment. When had he bought this pack? Over two weeks ago.

At that rate, he might as well quit.

"Last one," he announced to the night. Yeah, it would be. It was a stupid habit. Stupider still with a child around. Yes, he was very careful to keep it well away from Sid so she wouldn't model his behavior, but kids didn't miss much.

Lighting up, he leaned on the barn door and stared out into the night. The yard light up at the house made it harder to see the night sky, but if he turned his back on it, he could still pick out plenty of stars. He waited for the peace they usually brought him, but all his mind wanted to do was run over earlier events, again and again. The longer he stood there—thinking, remembering—the angrier he got. At Dundas Bloom, certainly. But more so at himself.

He should never have let April go back in there alone.

Yeah, he got it. He *did* have a tendency to be overprotective. Sometimes oppressively so. Everyone knew it. It was damned near primal, the need to protect those he loved, especially women. God, how many times had he and Ember butted heads about it over the years?

But what people didn't know was that he did it because he was scared.

Scared? Hell, terrified. That he wouldn't get there in time if something went wrong.

When he'd walked in and seen April cornered by Dundas Bloom, adrenaline had ripped through him like a jolt of electricity. He'd never been so scared. And yes, he knew nothing too horrible would have happened. Much as he despised Bloom, he doubted he'd have been suicidally stupid enough to assault her physically. But he'd gripped April's wrist, actively intimidating her, making her feel trapped and vulnerable. He'd put that flicker of fear in her eyes and that quaver in her voice.

*Dammit, Standish, you almost failed her. She was with you; you're supposed to protect her.* Unacceptable.

He took another drag off the cigarette, but the scene kept replaying. Bloom's sucker punch. Dragging the bastard toward the door. The fight outside on the sidewalk.

His mouth went dry as he remembered what he'd said. Jesus. In the heat of the moment, he'd flat-out claimed April as his. For God's sake, what was he thinking?

Okay, he hadn't been thinking. Not with his brain, anyway. Those words had been torn from somewhere deeper.

The truth was, it wasn't just some he-man possessiveness thing. It was something more. April Morgan had somehow become…what?

*Precious.*

Yes, she was precious to him. Priceless. Irreplaceable.

Yet it changed nothing. April and Sid deserved a man who would never leave. Someone who would face the daily grind of life beside them. Scott knew himself too well. He wasn't that person.

So he'd have to let her think it was male pride that drove him to those words. Possessiveness. A macho reflex that—

"Scott?"

He glanced back inside the barn to see April descending the ladder.

He ground out his cigarette in the dirt as she came to join him at the door, arms wrapped around herself against the cold.

"Come here." He pulled her close. "You must be freezing."

She lifted a hand to touch his jaw where Bloom had landed that first punch. "I feel so bad that you got in a fight over me," she said, "But thank you. No one's ever come to my defense like that."

Christ, that just broke his heart. Her mother, her father, that useless brother. The man who impregnated her and abandoned her. The older sister's decision to leave, he could understand. But to never return to her sibling's life? April deserved better, from all of them.

"You should stay longer," he said.

"I will. Sidney's sleeping over at Danika's tonight, remember?"

"No, I meant you should stay in Harkness. Right here at the farm, if you want to."

Her eyes widened. "But I have a—"

"You have a job lined up. I know. But what better job could you have than April Dawn's? You could be your own boss, at the helm of something you created yourself. Anyone can see that you love it, and it's keeping Sid engaged."

She pulled back for a better look at his face. "Oh, I plan to continue building the business when I move on. In my spare time, as I'm doing here."

"Will you have the same supports in Ontario? A great spot at a market, at a preferred rate, to sell your wares? And hell, will your employer even give their blessing to a secondary enterprise?"

She pulled away completely. "I'd be working for myself. It's not like I'd be moonlighting for another employer, taking hours or energy away from the day job."

"I just think you've made a good start here. Why not stay

longer, and keep building? Maybe it can be more than just a cottage industry run in your spare time."

"But we agreed I'd stay until after Christmas. To stay longer…" She cleared her throat. "I don't want anyone's charity."

"Charity?" God, how many times did they need to have this conversation? "April, honey, that's the last thing this is. Do you have any concept how much your being here has helped? I've been able to focus on getting through the apple-picking and sanitizing the orchards. Not to mention the repairs I've been able to get done around here. It's meant that I haven't had to bother Titus, so he could have his break. Arden's been able to spend more time with Faye instead of trying to keep up on the domestic front. Ember's been able to give her full attention to getting her practice going." He reached for her hand. "And we've never eaten so well since before Mom got sick. Everyone feels better for it. Healthier, more energetic. Just ask any one of them and they'll tell you the same thing."

She lowered her gaze, but not before he saw a suspicious glint. "Thank you. I'm glad your family is happy with the arrangement. But—"

"No buts. Put this new job off until spring."

She bit her lip. "I've already delayed almost two months…"

"Well, if they won't wait, there are plenty of other employers out there who'd be thrilled to have you. If you still want another employer, that is. If you stay and build the business, you may find you have your hands more than full."

She looked up at him again and he could sense how torn she was, feel her indecision.

"But it wouldn't be fair to your family," she said. "I feel guilty enough already, using your kitchen as my production plant. If the business grows any more, I'll be out of room. I can't exactly install a commercial refrigerator in front of the window."

He frowned. "Well, we could always roll back your salary a little bit—say, five percent or something—for kitchen rental, if that makes you feel better. But I'm inclined to agree you'll outgrow the space if you keep expanding like you are. In which case Jace could likely find you some commercial space."

"I don't know…"

"I do," he said. "You should stay. Think about Sid."

Her beautiful, full mouth tightened. "I'm *always* thinking about Sidney."

"Sorry. I know you are. I just meant, wouldn't it be nice if she could stay and finish the school year?"

Her lips twisted with pain. "Of course I'd like her to be able to stay put. We've moved around so much over the years… But sometimes what we want isn't possible."

"This time, it's perfectly possible."

"I don't know. I'd feel…strange. You'll have moved on by the new year, and I have to too."

"Oh, didn't I tell you? I'm not leaving in January after all."

Okay, he'd done it, put that right out there. No taking it back now. But dammit, she deserved a chance. And he'd already forewarned Georgie…

"What?" Her head came up and she searched his eyes. "You're not leaving? I thought you had another project you needed to get to? The Alberta thing."

"That's on hold for the moment." Well, that wasn't a lie, exactly. Not as long as Georgie could stave off his brother-in-law's stacks of money and his sister's entreaties. "Not until June or anything like that, but for a month or two, probably."

"You're really staying? I mean, you didn't postpone that project because of me?"

He couldn't straight-up lie to her when she looked at him like that. So he chose not to answer her question. "Come here.

There's nothing to fret about." He pulled her back into his arms, and she went willingly. "The timing is great. I mean, there are so many more upgrades begging to be done around here. It'll give me a chance to tackle them. Plus Titus can enjoy a more extended break."

"Really?"

"So, will you stay through the spring?"

She took a deep breath and released it. "I'll think about it."

"Good." He slid a hand into her hair and tugged gently to lift her face. When he bent to kiss her, she went up on tiptoe to meet him. Her slim, strong body meshed perfectly with his and his arms tightened reflexively around her. God, he wanted to crush her to him. Wanted to take her in through his skin, absorb her. He just couldn't get enough of her.

He loved her.

He loved her more than he wanted to. More than he could fathom. Damn it, more than the world. And that terrified him, made him want to run like hell.

She pulled back and looked up at him. "Let's go back to bed."

"That's the best idea I've heard all night. Go on up and I'll be right there. I'm just going to close the doors."

He watched her climb the ladder safely before turning back to the door. With a last glance at the stars, he pulled the doors shut and latched them.

# – twenty-eight –

ANOTHER MARKET day almost done. Despite her exhaustion, April smiled. She'd been up and running since five a.m. But it was a good tired. She'd earned it. She'd also made a tidy profit, her biggest single day's sales yet. And she'd had a blast doing it. By now, she'd gotten to know, or at the very least meet, a good half of the population of Harkness. People loved her products. She hadn't felt so alive in years. But more important than anything, she and Sidney had gotten closer.

It was the last market day before Christmas. The lovely place would reopen, of course, in the new year, with "real" leases. God help her, she was leaning toward staying on, as Scott had suggested. She hadn't made a final decision yet, and he hadn't pressed her. But they both knew she'd have to decide soon.

She hadn't totally cut off her options. She'd applied for a couple of positions, and had strong interest expressed by a small, exclusive resort in the Niagara region. If she went after it hard, she figured she could land it. Thanks to the money she'd made from her little cottage industry, she had a bit of a nest egg built up. She no longer feared she and Sidney would be living hand to mouth.

But if she stayed, things would be so much easier. If she took a new job, she'd have to learn the ropes and get everything under control before she could expend any energy on a side business. She couldn't imagine another employer being as invested in her success as the Standish family had been.

Mrs. Budaker came to stand by April's booth to take up the conversation that had been interrupted by customers. The woman was relentless.

"So would you say it's *serious* between the two of them?" the older woman asked. Her penciled eyebrows rose with the question. After weeks of fishing for information about Titus and Ocean, she'd finally come right out and asked.

"Oh, yes, it's definitely serious."

Her lips thinned. "Why is it that all the good men are taken?"

April shook her head. "Isn't that always the way?"

Mrs. Budaker chuckled. "Oh, you're one to talk! That other handsome young Standish man is just sweet on you."

Of course, it was no secret in the community that she and Scott were seeing each other. After the initial relief of not having to hide it, April now felt a bit guilty. In a little town like Harkness, people tended to assume that dating would naturally lead to something more permanent. She and Scott knew better, but they could hardly come out and say that.

She grimaced. "It's complicated."

"Nonsense! Don't give me that. That's just young people speak for *we're slower than cold molasses!*"

April glanced at her daughter who was currently unpacking yet more of the popular breakfast bars at the back of the stand. From her failure to react to the "cold molasses" analogy, April knew she wasn't following the conversation. Sidney would have gotten a kick out of that folksy expression. She'd collected a whole slew of them from Arden and Faye, and even a few from Titus. Literally collected, as in writing them down on recipe cards April had given her for the purpose.

When she turned back to Mrs. Budaker, the older woman

was all smiles. It wasn't hard to see what had turned that frown upside down. A dashing and dapper gentleman had just stopped at her booth. He was tall, well-built, probably somewhere in his early sixties. He was bald on the top, but his silvering hair and beard was neatly trimmed, contrasting flatteringly with his deep tan. He wore casual jeans and leather boots, and a sharp looking gray jacket.

"Marcel?" Mrs. Budaker hustled back to her booth. "It *is* you! What a sight for sore eyes. How long has it been?"

"Too long, Nell. Far too long."

"Oh, my." She laughed, waved a flustered hand over her chest. "Are you home for Christmas?"

He shook his head. "No."

"Oh?" Her disappointment was palpable.

"I'm home for you."

April would have loved to listen in on the reunion—one that seemed to get cozier by the second—but three customers appeared at her booth at once. Sid took care of the first two while April looked after the third. By the time she'd finished helping the gal choose something suitable for her celiac daughter, Mrs. Budaker had closed shop, put up a Back Soon sign, and gone off with her handsome visitor. Presumably for coffee. Good for her!

April's feet were more than ready for a break too, but it was too busy to leave Sidney alone.

A customer approached—a girl from Sidney's class—and Sidney stepped up to serve her. April took the opportunity to sit on one of the two stools. She was going to need a foot rub tonight, something Scott was always quick to offer on market day.

She lifted her feet onto the rung at the bottom of the stool, flexing and pointing them by turns, and listened to Sidney and her friend, Courtney Pinnock, talk in excited tones about the Standish family Christmas party, set for the very next night. It would be a Sunday evening affair this year, and the Far South

Barn was all but ready. Brighter and more beautiful than April had ever imagined it could be.

As the domestic helper, April had expected the preparations would fall to her as part of her job. But Ember had insisted on doing it, and well, it *was* her prerogative to take over.

As strong and proud as the Standish men were, the Standish women were just as well equipped in that department. It was a matter of enormous importance for Ember that the barn be perfect, or as perfect as she could make it. Ocean had contributed a ton of time too. April had helped as much as they'd let her, which wasn't a whole lot. After an hour or two, they'd usually shooed her away, insisting she focus on making more product for the market.

She'd enjoyed working on the barn with the girls. They'd all been so busy lately, they hadn't had much time just to hang out. She'd missed their chatter, not to mention the trading of stories about their respective romances. Ocean had even pried a story out of April. Just the memory of that conversation made April grin.

April had learned something else from the chatter. Ocean was indeed expecting a friend from New York to visit over Christmas. It was a done deal. That should be interesting. According to Ocean, he was pretty famous. A sort of star-maker like Simon Cowell, but without the TV show.

April looked at her watch. Okay, more than *looked* at it. She counted down the seconds. Just a few more. Five, four, three, two, one. "Ta-done, Ladybug!"

"Done?" With her little friend gone, Sidney had gone back to work. Currently, she was opening yet another box of April's Bootilicious Dawn to put some more bars out. That had definitely been their best seller. "Sorry to disappoint you, Mom, but the market doesn't close for another three hours."

"I'm not talking about that. I'm talking about how—as of

right now—that Montreal credit card thing is behind us. You're all paid up."

"Oh, that was paid up last week."

*It was?* "Really?"

"Really. Do the math, Mom."

She did. And Sidney was right. "Well, that was anti-climactic."

"I sent a card," Sidney said.

"To whom."

"To Dr. and Mrs. Boisvert. I was feeling bad and I sent them a Christmas card apologizing."

April felt a lump in her throat. She was proud of her daughter. "That was really good of you, Sid."

She went to her daughter and gave her a hug. Sidney pulled back.

"After I put out this stock, mind if I take an hour off? I have some Christmas shopping to do."

"No problem, Ladybug. Need some money?" April had been giving Sid her allowance right along and her little girl was pretty good at saving, but still, she was guessing her gift-giving list was expanded considerably this year. April reached below the counter for her purse.

"Naw, I'm good."

She straightened. "Really?"

"Really." Sidney was smiling, but her eyes were no longer on her mother. They were on the football-jacket-wearing eleven-year-old approaching the booth.

Sidney crawled under the counter and joined up with him.

"Hi, Roy," April called.

"Hi, Ms. Morgan."

April watched the two of them until they disappeared from sight. Her daughter seemed pretty enamored of Roy. If she extended her stay, those bonds could deepen, as would her attachment to the Standishs, her friend Danika, the old dog Axl. The town. And if she left sooner rather than later…

Oh, who was she kidding? Whether they left after Christmas or in June, it was going to hurt like hell, for both of them. They might as well stay. The idea of building the business was too powerful a lure. And she could avoid uprooting Sidney during the school year.

Maybe she could build the business to the point that it could sustain the two of them without her having to hold down a full-time job. In which case, maybe they could stay in Harkness. Obviously, she couldn't stay on with the Standishs, especially after Scott left. But surely she could find a place for her and Sidney.

Could she really do that? Stay in Harkness, where she'd see Scott once or twice a year when he came home. Naturally, they'd break it off before he left. She had no expectations that he would live a celibate life between visits, and she had no desire to be his Harkness hook-up.

But would she have the strength to deny him if he waltzed back into town and decided he wanted her back in his bed?

Two elderly ladies approached her booth, saving her from any more soul-searching. Pasting on a smile, she threw herself into sales mode. When they left, she refused to let her mind go back there. Instead, she thought about the coming party.

She'd bought a new dress for the event. Just the thought of it gave her a little flutter of anticipation. She couldn't wait for Scott to see her in it.

She'd found it in a second-hand shop for gently used clothing a few weeks ago, on a trip to neighboring Crandler with Ember and Ocean. While Ember had scored a couple of huge hair clips and Ocean had picked up an antique broach, April had come face to face with the dress of her dreams.

She'd tried to resist it, enumerating all the problems: *Too red. Too expensive. Too fancy. Too gorgeous for you!*

Then Ember had declared it "Too perfect to pass up."

She could barely wait to slip into it tomorrow night. Scott would be so—

"Excuse me, are you April Dawn Morgan?"

The words jerked her out of her daydream. She hadn't even noticed the handsome young man approaching. "I am," she said. "What can I do for you?"

"I'm Stone Thibault." He passed her his card, identical to the one he'd left for her with Jace. "I've been expecting your call.

*Whoops.* "I'm sorry." She shrugged apologetically. "I meant to call back straight away, but things have gotten a little hectic around here."

"My employer is a very adamant that we make contact, Ms. Morgan."

"Please, call me April."

He lifted an eyebrow. "Not April Dawn?"

"That's my business name." Though come to think of it, more and more people in Harkness were greeting her as *April Dawn.* "But I'll answer to either. April, April Dawn."

He smiled, revealing even white teeth. He really was a very good looking man. Not in a rugged way, like Scott, but in a more polished, urbane way.

"As I've said, my employer is very anxious to make contact with you. She's a businesswoman, and she's had the opportunity to sample some of your product."

"At the market?" Her mind whirled as she tried to place who it could be.

"No, not in Harkness. Elsewhere."

Now she was really confused. "Mr. Stone, who exactly is your employer?"

He smiled. "K.Z. McCoy."

# – twenty-nine –

SID SAT on the edge of the bed in Scott's room, turning a small box in her fingers as she watched her mom get ready.

Her mom had never been happier. Sid was sure of it. She'd been happy all day. Actually, since yesterday afternoon. When she'd come back from her break with Roy, her mother had seemed almost dazed. Then a little excited.

Her mother had never looked more beautiful either. She looked more like a princess than a cook. Her new red dress had long sleeves and a high neck, but it was definitely *sexay*, as Danika would say. And thank goodness, she'd left her hair loose for a change. It looked really, really good. Ember had helped her do it so it had big, loopy curls liked a model on a shampoo commercial.

"Hey, Mom?"

"What is it, Ladybug?" Her mom had been checking her makeup in the mirror, but she turned to Sid.

"Can you come here for a minute?"

"Sure." She came to sit down beside her. "What's up?"

"I know it's not Christmas yet, but mind if I give you your gift early?"

"Mind? Sid you know I wouldn't."

Sidney pulled the box from behind her; she handed it to her mother.

It was earrings. In Sidney's mind they were the most beautiful earrings in the world, but would her mother like them?

Her mother opened the box and lifted one of the earrings. They were dangly silver stars on French hooks.

"Oh, they're gorgeous!" Her mother put them on. "How do they look?"

Sid smiled. "They're beautiful. Almost as beautiful as you."

"Oh, baby girl, thank you!" Her mom caught her in a hug.

Sid hugged right back. "I love you, Mom."

"I love you too, Sidney."

# – thirty –

SCOTT SHOOK David's hand. "Congrats, man. I'm glad Sally said yes."

"Me too."

"It's a big step."

"I know." David nodded his head gravely. "But I've loved Sally since fifth grade."

"Good stuff."

David shoved his hands in his pocket. "But her folks say we can't get married till after we're done high school."

"That's not a bad deal."

"Yeah, I know," he allowed. "It's just that…you know, we're both sure."

"Then you're a lucky man. Sally's a lovely young lady. I know you guys will be happy together."

David studied him earnestly. "Got any advice? Besides that we're too young to know what we want? We've heard a shit-ton—I mean, a lot of that already."

Scott smiled. Yeah, he just bet they had. But he wouldn't be piling on. Yes, they were young, but it was a rare thing to know your mind that well, at any age. Apparently, some people just knew. Hell, Ember might have been married right out of school if Terry hadn't sabotaged things between her and Jace.

"Take good care of her," Scott said. "That's about the best advice I can give a man. Take good care of the woman you love."

"I will." David looked across the room. "Hey, there's my aunt, Connie. I haven't seen her since Halloween. Mom told her about the engagement; I'd better go say hello."

"You'd better."

Seconds later, Scott watched as David got wrapped up in a huge hug from Connie Lemon.

"Scott?"

He felt a tentative tap on his shoulder and turned to see Mrs. Budaker and a gentleman. "Mrs. Budaker. Hello."

"Um, is your brother around?"

He gestured across the room. "He's over there, talking to Ocean and her guest."

Mrs. Budaker brightened. "Oh is that the New York fellow?"

Scott nodded.

"Which one is Titus?" the man with Mrs. Budaker asked.

"The hulking one," Scott said.

Mrs. Budaker grabbed the gentleman's arm. "Do you really think this is necessary, Marcel?"

"No," he said. "It's not necessary. But it is the right thing to do. Tell him man to man." He patted Mrs. B's hand. "Now that you're mine again, he should know. I want the world to know."

"Do be magnanimous, Marcel," Mrs. B said.

"Of course, my dear," Marcel said, tucking her arm beneath his. "It's easy to be magnanimous when you're the winner."

Scott shook his head as he watched Mrs. B and her new beau head toward his brother. Poor Titus. How awkward was that conversation going to be?

Trying to hold back a grin, Scott watched a series of expressions cross his brother's face. Confusion. Incredulity.

Horror. Then he produced a suitably chastised expression for Mrs. B. Mollified, Mrs. B and her beau strolled off.

Titus lifted his gaze and searched the room, stopping at Scott when he saw his wide grin.

"You knew?" Titus mouthed.

Scott shrugged, letting his grin widen. But then Titus's fierce frown dissolved and he started smiling. Scott didn't trust that smile one bit. Suspicious, he turned to see if someone was doing rabbit ears behind his head or something. That's when he saw her.

April stood there, holding Sid's hand. His breath stalled in his chest. Jesus, she was gorgeous. She wore a sinfully red dress that hugged her slight curves like a glove, and her hair was loose and full and soft looking. Her lips were touched with red gloss and her eyes looked huge.

With difficulty, he shifted his gaze to Sid. She wore a beautiful dress too. The long-sleeved top was black velvet and the skirt fell in tiers of white. Between the bodice and the skirt was a black velvet sash tied in a big bow.

"Wow. You two are the most beautiful ladies in the place. Wait, did I say in the place? I meant in the whole wide world."

Sidney beamed up at her mother.

"Like my earrings?" April asked. "An early Christmas present from the world's greatest daughter."

Scott winked at Sid. He'd actually taken her to the mall last week supposedly to pick up pizza for movie night later on with Uncle Arden and Faye. They'd gotten pizza, but they'd also made a quick stop at the mall's jewelry store. Sidney had picked out the dangling stars right then and there. *Do you think she'll like them?*

He'd been pretty sure she would.

"Oh, there's Danika." Sid nodded in the direction of a half dozen excited kids gathered around the dessert table. "And a bunch of my friends from school." She was off.

Scott watched—almost nervously—as Sid joined the

crowd. She slid right in with the others and they made room for her as naturally as though she'd always been one of them. Beside him, he felt April relax a smidge to see Sid taken into the fold like that.

Music filled the air and April's gaze shot to the source. "You hired a DJ?"

"Ember did. That's Tara Lee Doyle."

"She looks young."

"She is. But she has a great feel for music. Give her time; she'll have everyone in the place dancing."

"Why's she in a wheelchair?"

"Cerebral Palsy," he answered. "It affects mostly her legs."

"It's so cool that she DJs. Does she play mixes all night?"

"Just for an hour or so, until the talent show."

"That's right, the talent show! I'd forgotten." She smiled up at him. "So, do you and Titus have an act? A brotherly clog-dancing duo, maybe?"

He rolled his eyes. "Hardly. It's been a lot of years since I was up on that stage."

"Oh, I would have loved to have seen that! What was your talent?"

"Who said anything about talent? I was in charge of working the curtains."

Her gaze went to the stage, which was very obviously bereft of any type of curtain. "What curtains?"

"Well, here's the thing. I figured it would be so much more efficient if I motorized the whole operation. Unfortunately, the old curtains started smoldering. Talk about fabric coming down in a hurry."

"Omigod, you started a fire in the *barn*?"

He shrugged. "It didn't have time to turn into a fire. Uncle Arden saw what was happening. Those curtains got yanked down, rolled up and hauled out in no time flat. And they were never replaced, of course. Too much potential for disaster."

"Did the show go on, just like on Broadway?"

"Absolutely. With Mom running things, we barely missed a beat."

"I can just imagine." April smiled. "What about Ember or Titus? Do they participate?"

Scott snorted. "What would Titus do? Recite the *Motor Vehicle Act* regulations?"

She grinned. "I don't know. Bench press Ocean?"

He barked a laugh. "That he could do. Or tear a bike engine down and put it together again. But somehow I don't think that would hold anyone's attention but mine."

"So you Standishs really aren't going to participate in your own talent show?"

"Nope. But there's plenty of talent without us. Just wait till you hear Maddison Escher."

"Oh, I met her at the market. She works at the hospital or something, doesn't she?"

"Close. She has a social work background and works with a home for disadvantaged teens from all over the region."

Titus chose that moment to dim the lights, which made the red and green frosted bulbs running along the beams stand out all the more. Young David had strung them up and he'd done a fine job. Of course, Sally had come over and helped him do it. Had she held the ladder for David as April had for Scott when he'd put up the Halloween decorations?

The whole barn looked great. He had to hand it to Ember. She'd gone over and above this year. He especially liked the alder branches with the white mini lights. She'd used bales of straw as bases to "plant" the branches, placing them strategically to divide up the room. It was pretty damned magical looking, especially the grouping behind the punch table.

Punch. Crap. Where were his manners? Margaret would box his ears for neglecting a lady this long. "Can I get you a glass of punch?"

"Would you?"

"Of course." He squeezed her elbow, mainly because he couldn't resist touching her. "I'll be back in a minute."

By the time he got two glasses of punch, the DJ had segued into a fast Christmas song by some rock-and-roll artist and the younger kids had started dancing. Sid included! April's eyes were lit up with pleasure as she took the plastic punch glass from him.

"Oh, this is fun!"

Scott glanced around, trying to see things from her perspective. Dozens of kids, dressed in their Christmas finery, jumped and gyrated in front of the stage. The dance floor itself was ringed by tables and chairs, all fully occupied. The tables were all collapsible card table propositions gathered from around the community, but they looked so much better in the gauzy fabric Ember and Ocean had draped them in. And each table held a glowing candle. Not real ones, of course. Just the LED variety. But they looked quite elegant. Apparently that had been April's contribution.

Up on the stage, right in the center, sat Santa's chair. Santa had yet to arrive, but when he did, the little ones would queue up for a chance to sit on his knee and tell him what they wanted for Christmas. Scott looked around, noting that Chief Buzz Adams, who'd been there earlier, was now conspicuously absent, as were his deputies. He grinned. Santa would be putting in his appearance soon. It was a running gag, how the Chief of Police always managed to miss the big guy's appearance.

Suddenly, the young DJ changed things up. The soft strains of waltz music replaced the frenetic tempo of the earlier song. The kids drifted back to their tables and some of the adults got up. Scott wasn't much for dancing, but April looked so damned delectable in that dress. He would dance all night if it meant being able to hold her in his arms.

"I'm a little rusty, but would you like to dance?"

Her smile was dazzling. “I would love to.”

He led her onto the dance floor and took her in his arms. As they drifted around the floor, he knew he held the most beautiful woman in the world.

# – thirty-one –

APRIL WAS having such a great time.

The DJ was on break and people were milling around, talking. So many friendly faces.

She stood by the dessert table, having just tidied things up. She'd managed to remove four plates by consolidating the remaining sweets. She was pleased to see that her Christmas coconut macaroons had gone over very well. So well, there wasn't a single one left.

Unable to keep the smile off her face, she surveyed the crowd. There were a few faces she'd never seen before, but she was surprised by how many she recognized. Mostly from the market, of course, but also from other places around town. She gave a little wave across the way to Stephen from I'm a Little Tea Shop. Harkness, New Brunswick had to be the homiest place on earth.

Her gaze caught Scott's. He was over at one of the tables, talking to a pair of hand-holding old timers. He smiled at her over their heads and she felt a tingle of awareness. Earlier on the dance floor, it had been all she could do not to mold herself to him. His hands on her back had been light and not a bit inappropriate, but they'd nevertheless started a sweet hum of desire that vibrated through her still.

Then police sirens cut through the air and the barn doors

burst open. April started. Her hand flew to her chest, but when she looked to Scott, he winked.

The sirens cut out.

With a jolly "Ho, ho, ho," a very well-padded Santa strode through the doors, a uniformed police officer flanking him on each side. If there was one person in the whole place that didn't know it was Chief Adams, they were either very young or very new in town.

Fortunately for the children on hand, Santa's security detail was carrying bags of goodies. Ember had explained the gifts were just items from the local dollar store, but the kids loved it. With the help of two teachers from Harkness elementary, the littlest ones started lining up at the front of the stage. April watched as Sidney queued up with the other giggling older kids at the end of the line to get a gift. Noticing April watching her, Sidney smiled.

What a great night.

The food, the company, her happy little girl.

Stone Thibault's offer…

The next forty minutes passed quickly. Every kid got a treat of some kind, and the little ones who weren't too afraid to sit on Santa's knee had the chance to whisper their fondest wishes in his ear while their parents snapped pictures. Eventually, Santa departed. And of course, Chief Adams turned up shortly thereafter, saying he'd heard reports of a disturbance. The delighted kids rushed him to tell him he'd missed Santa *again*.

Scott came to join her as the music started up again. The dance floor filled up quickly. April caught Sidney's eye and pointed at her watch. She tapped it three times—Mom speak for it's almost time for bed. She then held up her left hand, splayed all five fingers three times—fifteen minutes.

Sid nodded. Most of the kids were gone by now and even as Sidney sat down on a bench beside Danika and Roy, their respective parents were heading toward the dance floor. The music had turned softer, proving once again that Tara Lee knew her stuff.

Scott took her hand. “Let’s go get some air.”

“I’d love to.”

They stopped to grab their coats. Scott helped her into hers, making her feel special. Outside, he pulled her into the shadows around the side of the barn. With the strains of the music in their ears, he drew her to him and kissed her. God, she was going to miss him. Miss *this*. But the opportunity was too good to pass up. Wasn’t it? Lord, she hadn’t even told Sidney yet. Thank God she hadn’t mentioned the prospect of staying until June.

Scott pulled back. “What’s on your mind?”

She blinked. “What do you mean?”

He cocked his head. “Either my kissing skills have suffered seriously overnight, or there’s another reason you’re a million miles away right now.”

She ducked her head, drew a deep breath. “I’ve got something to tell you.”

“I’m listening.” His voice was normal, but she felt the tension in his muscles.

“Stone Thibault came in to see me today.” Her words came out in a rush.

“The guy with the business card? Mr. Evasive. What did he want?”

“He’s offered me a job. In Boston. Working for K.Z. McCoy.”

He didn’t react at all.

“Say something, Scott.”

“Are you going to take it?”

*Ask me not to.* The thought came unbidden, yet right from the tips of her toes.

“I don’t know.”

“K.Z. McCoy,” he murmured. “That’s a big deal.”

“She sampled some of my cooking at the Boisverts’,

although I can't see Dr. Boisvert giving me any credit. Mrs. Boisvert must have done it. She was the one who told Stone where to find me."

"Well, I can see why she'd track you down, once she'd tasted your cooking."

"So what do you think?"

"Could be the chance you've been waiting for."

"It could. In so many respects—career-wise, and in regards to Sidney. To be able to give her a steady, real permanent home. That's been a dream of mine for a long time too."

"Salary's that good?"

The conversation had been brief, but Stone Thibault had made her a great offer. More than she could have ever hoped for. Certainly more than she would have thought to ask for. And the benefits? Again, more than she could have hoped for.

Then why had she dreaded answering Stone's last question—"*When can you start?*"

"The salary package is very good," she said.

"What about the other job you had lined up?" Scott asked. "Northern Ontario, wasn't it?"

She bit her lip; he had to know there was no job. "They'll have to understand."

"What's the time frame?"

"They want me to start as soon as I can."

He rubbed the back of his neck. "What's Sid think of it?"

April's happiness dimmed. Her little girl wasn't going to like being wrenched from this place. "I haven't told her yet." She looked up at Scott. "What do you think?"

"I think it sounds like a hell of an opportunity."

The barn doors opened and Sidney, Danika, and Roy spilled out, followed by their parents.

"That's my cue." She gave Scott a quick kiss, then started off toward the group.

Spying her mother, Sidney said goodbye to her friends and ran to meet April.

With a wave and a “Merry Christmas!” the others headed for their respective cars, carefully parked on the side lawn. As the two cars departed, April and Sidney started walking up to the house. Before they’d gone far, Sidney grabbed April’s hand, something she hadn’t done in ages.

“I can’t imagine it!”

“What can’t you imagine, Ladybug?”

“Being any happier than I am at this very moment. Christmas isn’t even here yet, but Mom, I’ve never been as happy as I am right now.”

*Oh, Sidney.* April’s stomach sank. So much for telling her about K.Z.’s offer tonight. She just didn’t have the heart to bring her daughter down when she was flying so high.

“And look!”

“At what?” April said.

Sidney held out her hand to catch a tiny flake of snow spiraling down from the dark sky. “It’s starting to snow!”

# – thirty-two –

IT WAS almost midnight and that had to have some kind of magic. And according to Danika, there was always an extra bit of magic in Christmas snow.

Sidney was sitting in the window seat of her bedroom looking out over the pristine grounds.

Two hours ago, she'd come over to the house and her mom tucked her in. Then Faye and Arden had shooed her mother out to the barn to dance the night away.

*Dance the night away?*

Oh, she hoped! She hoped Scott swooped her up into his arms and told her he loved her. Not just because of how much Sidney liked Scott and not just because she liked it here. Arden. Faye. Danika. The Farm. Her school. Axl.

But because her mom deserved it.

She pressed her cheek against the cold window pane. First snow of the season. According to Principal Makepeace, if you made a wish on the first snow of winter, it had a pretty good shot of coming true.

In all the excitement tonight, she'd missed her after-supper trip to the front yard to see that first star come out. She'd been wishing on that first star pretty much every night since she'd come to Harkness. Same star, same wish. But tonight, the sky-watching hour had slipped by her. That was okay, though, 'cause it was almost Christmas, so surely every star in the sky was a little more magic.

She would wish on a bunch of them now. Every single one she could.

# – thirty-three –

IT WAS just after seven on Christmas morning and Scott had been up since the butt crack of dawn making breakfast for everyone, trying to be quiet. *Trying?* Contrary to what his uncle may think, he was the epitome of stealth.

The hashbrown casserole was in the oven, the bacon was draining on paper towel, and he was about to tackle the quiche.

He cracked the eggs into the mixing bowl, added some heavy cream and grabbed the whisk from the drawer. The goat cheese, onion and olives would be next. This was one of his mom's own recipes, pulled from the recipe box Titus had made for her in an eighth-grade woodworking class. It was so rich, Margaret Standish only made it on special occasions. *For special people*, she'd said.

He'd actually improved his kitchen skills over the last while, from those times when April had let him help her out. Under her close supervision, of course. She was all business in the kitchen.

No, that wasn't quite true. She was all *passion*.

But this morning, the kitchen was his, and he would defend it to the bitter end—or at least until the coffee was ready.

April walked into the kitchen. She was still in her pajamas, with a robe wrapped tightly around her.

"Merry Christmas." She came over and put her arms around his waist. Squeezed him.

"Merry Christmas, April." He hugged her back and kissed her lingeringly.

When he released her, she pulled back to look around his kitchen.

"Hey, don't go getting any ideas," he said. "You have today off."

"This morning," she corrected. "I'm making Christmas dinner later, remember? That's my gift to the family. No interference on that one."

"I wouldn't dream of it." He'd seen the size of the turkey that had been defrosting in the refrigerator for the past few days, as well as the vegetables that were chopped and ready for cooking. No way would he get in the way of that.

She gave him a quick kiss on the cheek. "I'll go jump in the shower and be right back down. But first…" She pulled a CD from the pocket of her robe.

"What's that? One of your baking mixes?" He'd noticed April and Sidney always had music playing when they cooked. Not the radio—either a burned CD of their own making or a playlist cued up on the iPod.

"Baking mix? *A la* cake in a box?" She rolled her eyes at the pun. "This is a special Christmas edition. Sid made it for you." She popped it into the CD player on the island counter and hit a button. *Snoopy's Christmas* began to play.

He grinned. "That's one of my favorites."

She looked around the room, as though measuring his progress. "Okay, give me fifteen minutes and I'll be down to help."

He slanted her a look.

"Um, I mean, would you like a little help?"

"No, I would not. I've got this."

She looked at him a scrutinizing moment. "You just want all the glory."

He laughed. "You know it. Even though I'm sure it will be short-lived glory, once everyone tastes your Christmas dinner."

She smiled. "Fine, it's all yours. But…would you like a bit of advice?"

"Sure."

"Plug in the coffee maker. It works faster that way."

"Smart ass."

She giggled and headed off for her shower.

He found the cord to the coffee maker and plugged it in. The scent of brewing coffee filled the kitchen as he turned his attention back to breakfast. As he worked, the songs kept coming, making him smile. He didn't recall his mother ever playing music while she worked, but he had to admit it made the work go faster. He'd actually caught Uncle Arden playing April's tunes the few times he'd rustled up lunch for them while she was off to Saturday market. Maybe April had created a new tradition.

Fifteen minutes later, the quiche was in the oven and The Chipmunks were serenading him as he worked on the biscuits. He'd just turned the dough onto the floured counter when Sidney burst into the room, followed more sedately by April.

"Merry Christmas, Scott!" Sidney greeted him with a hug. "You're playing the tape I made."

He hugged her back, careful not to get his floury hands on her. "I am indeed."

"Awesome." She looked around the kitchen. "How can I help?" She was already tying on an apron.

April slid him a smile. She raised her eyebrows. It was one thing to fend her off, but sweet little Sid the Kid was another story.

"Do you know how to make butter curls?" he said.

"Puh-lease." She rolled her eyes. "I've been making those since I was five." She started toward the counter; then her face dropped. "Wait! I um…forgot something. Back in a sec!"

She shot out of the room and thumped back up the stairs.

He gave April an inquiring look.

She raised a shushing finger to her lips. "Listen," she whispered.

A moment later, he heard it—the ever-so-slight groan of that squeaking stair step as Sid crept back down, followed by the almost complete silence coming from the living room. Almost. They both heard the soft rustle of a plastic shopping bag.

Ah! The stockings. The stocking stuffing tradition was alive and well in Casa Standish. Everyone put something in each other's stocking. Sidney must be adding her contributions.

Seconds later, Sid popped back into the room, a mile-wide smile on her face. "So, where's that butter?"

"Right there on the table." He gestured toward it. "I've been letting it soften."

Both Morgan women gave him a look of mock horror. Or maybe real horror, he wasn't quite sure.

Scott was just pulling the biscuits out of the oven as Ember and Jace came through the kitchen door.

"You're just in time!" Sid said.

Jace snorted. "No risk of us being late. Ember had me up at five, I think."

"Quarter to six," Ember cut in. "And stop belly-aching. You love Christmas just as much and I do. And my family—soon to be our family—starts Christmas early."

She kissed him and he wrapped his arms around her.

"Did I hear *soon to be*?" Arden slipped into the kitchen, a wide smile on his face. "Have you two set a date?"

Faye and Ocean had arrived ten minutes earlier, just as

Titus was clearing the last of the snow left by the snowplow from the mouth of the driveway. The clan was all assembled now, and they all looked to Ember and Jace for an answer.

Ember and Jace looked at each other. “We have,” Ember said. “Next Christmas, right here on the homestead, in the Far South Barn.”

# – thirty-four –

APRIL SAT with Scott's arm around her. And nothing could feel more natural, right. Oh God, nothing could feel more *Christmassy* than this exact moment in time. It was the best Christmas of her life. She'd never seen Sidney happier. Never seen her so patient as she waited to open her gifts. Even though she did dive right into her stocking.

April absolutely loved the Standish Christmas stocking tradition. Thank God Titus had thought to tell her and Sid about it a good month before Christmas so they could start thinking early. Everyone put something in everyone else's stocking. But the trick was to sneak the gifts in when no one was looking, without getting caught. The penalty? Relentless, good-natured razzing. Everyone had succeeded this year in slipping those small gifts in unnoticed, except for Scott. Captain Stealth he was not. He'd banged a knee against the fire screen, clattering it against the stone. Sidney had run in and caught him.

And April herself? She didn't care if there was nothing but lumps of coal in her stocking, she loved seeing Sidney so happy. It was going to be so hard to leave here, for both of them. She'd have to tell Sidney soon.

But not just yet. This morning, she was going to savor the happiness. Hers, Sid's.

Scott squeezed her shoulder and she looked up into his eyes. "I forgot to say *Merry Christmas*."

"No, you didn't."

He smiled. "I just wanted to say it again."

"Omigod! Finally! Someone who appreciates my sense of style!"

Ember had just pulled from her stocking a bright beaded red poinsettia barrette. It was…big. Loud. And only took one try for her to guess who it was from.

"Sidney, this is beautiful," Ember said.

"I made it myself." She glanced at Faye. "Well, almost all myself."

Faye held up her hands. "I just supplied the craft books. A few small tools. You and Danika did all the work."

"You gave us most of the supplies."

She shrugged. "Leftovers from when Ocean and River were young."

April blinked rapidly. Life in Harkness was so wonderful.

What would it be like in Boston? Without this family? Without Scott.

"Well, I absolutely love it!" Ember's red hair had been up in a gorgeous mother-of-pearl barrette. She made short work of pulling that out and tossing it aside. A few seconds later, Sid's gift took its place.

"Lovely," Arden said.

Jace smiled. "I couldn't agree more."

Arden gestured to April's full stocking. "You haven't opened yours yet, April."

"Go ahead," Scott urged.

As everyone watched, she pulled the items out of her stocking one by one and unwrapped them. The first was a silk scarf in a merlot red with a gold floral pattern painted on it. April's gaze flew to Ember.

"I figured it would go nicely with so many of your sweaters."

"Thank you so much. It's beautiful."

She went on to open the gift she was most curious about. It had been rolled into a wrapping paper tube and poked down the sock. It turned out to be a gorgeous hand-stitched, lightweight apron from Faye. Arden's gift to her was a new paring knife. He must have been listening when she bemoaned the fact that while she could hone her chef's knives, it was futile to try to keep a paring knife sharp. Then there were the beautiful dangly earrings from Ocean, a small jar of cinnamon-infused honey from a local apiary from Titus, and from Jace, a vintage recipe box.

Sid's gift involved woodworking too, but as with all her gifts, she'd made it herself, no doubt after school under Faye's watchful eye. Sid came to perch on the couch beside her as she unwrapped it. Peeling the foil paper away, she found herself looking at a small wooden placard suitable for a desk, with *April Dawn's* etched on it with the aid of a wood burning tool.

Tears sprang to April's eyes. "Oh, Ladybug, this is priceless. I love it. Thank you!"

She hugged her daughter, and Sid hugged her right back.

Finally, there was only one gift left in the stocking. It had to be from Scott. She tore the wrapping off the small package to reveal a packet of kala jeera, otherwise known as black cumin seed. Her eyes widened. Harkness was a lovely town, but it didn't have much in the way of ethnic food or spices, and when it came to Indian spices, she was lucky to find cardamom or fenugreek.

She looked at Scott. "You didn't get *this* in Harkness."

He grinned. "That came all the way from New York with Ocean's friend, Greg."

The fact that he'd thought about what she might want, and then to ask Ocean to get her friend to pick it up… That kind of thoughtfulness was priceless.

"Thank you," she said simply, knowing her heart was probably in her eyes. "It's…perfect."

The whole morning had been perfect. Scott had acquitted himself fantastically in the kitchen. The biscuits had been awesome. His mother's recipe, of course. The quiche too. Predictably, the bacon and the hash brown casserole had been a hit with the men. But to Scott's chagrin—completely faked for comedic effect, of course—the real raves were reserved for the butter curls. Scott kept fishing for compliments to keep the joke going.

"Yeah, so what about those biscuits?" he'd prompted.

"A little dry," Ocean had teased. "Thank God for the butter curls."

Sidney had laughed so hard, she'd had to clutch her ribs.

That was the real gift—the laughter and the closeness.

But the other gifts had been pretty fantastic too. They hadn't even opened the "real" presents yet, but the thought and care that had gone into choosing the stocking stuffers absolutely blew April away.

"Your turn, Scott." Sidney brought his stocking.

April sat up straighter as Scott pulled the first gift from the stocking. From the wrapping, she knew it was Sidney's offering. He carefully peeled the paper back to reveal a gift box. He lifted the lid, peeled back delicate white tissue paper. "Chocolate cookies." He looked at April. "Are these from you?"

She shook her head.

"They're from me!" Sidney said. "Chocolate espresso shortbread cookies, made from espresso beans I bought at the market." She glanced quickly at her mother. "Don't worry, Mom. Faye helped. She melted the chocolate for me in the double boiler. But I did the rest, didn't I, Faye?"

"You certainly did," Faye said. "Including grinding the coffee beans."

"*You* made these?" Scott's amazement seemed genuine, and Sidney soaked it up.

"You're going to love them!" Sidney fairly bounced on her seat.

"I know I will," he said. "Thanks, Sid. That was a very thoughtful gift."

She beamed.

Scott pulled another gift from the stocking. It was the one April had put in there, she saw. He opened the small box and pulled out the black, grommet-studded leather belt, unfurling it.

"Damn, that's nice," Titus said.

"That one's from me," April said. She'd bought it from the leatherworks guy three booths down from hers.

He grinned. "It's perfect. Thank you."

It wasn't his main gift—no way would that fit in a stocking—but she was glad he liked it.

"Open another!" Sid urged.

He pulled out another gift, this one a neatly wrapped small box. He tore the paper off and opened the box's lid. "Tiny motorcycles?"

"Look closely," Ember said. "They're cufflinks."

April leaned closer. Yes, they were the ones she'd scouted at the market and almost bought. But they'd been too rich for her budget. Well, after she'd bought the other gift.

"They're kickass," Scott said.

"You can rock them at our wedding," Jace said. "'Cuz you know we'll be all tuxedoed out for that."

"Who knows?" Titus said. "Maybe you'll have occasion to wear them sooner than that."

Titus's voice was casual enough, but April caught the way he looked at Ocean and the way she looked back…

Ember and Jace. Titus and Ocean. Faye and Arden.

April and a fantastic new job in Boston. Enough money to finally provide her and Sid the financial security she so desperately wanted.

She leaped up off the couch, not even realizing she'd done it until everyone turned surprised eyes on her.

"The kitchen," she said. "I have to get the turkey in the

oven if we're going to eat on schedule. Excuse me for a few moments."

"Hurry back," Ember said.

"Take your time," Jace said.

"Jace!"

"What?" He looked at Ember. "This meal is going to be a work of art. I don't want her to rush a thing."

"Good point." Ember nodded. "Take your time, April."

On that compliment, she headed into the kitchen.

"Can I open my presents yet?" Sidney called after her.

She stopped at the door and fixed her daughter with a stern look. "No way. Wait till I get back, Ladybug."

"Aww."

That was the least heartfelt *aww* her daughter had ever uttered.

She'd just got the oven preheated and slid the turkey in when Arden joined her in the kitchen.

"How's it going in here?"

April closed the oven door.

"All under control, for now, thanks."

He nodded. "I've no doubt about that. I've never been so well fed since…well, since Margaret was well enough to cook."

"Thank you. That means a lot to me." It was one thing for Scott to sing her praises, but for Arden to do so—that was another thing entirely. "Scott's told me a lot about his mother. She sounds like a great woman."

"She was. We were very happy together." He looked reflective, both happy and sad.

"I'm guessing she'd be happy that you've found Faye."

Silence.

*Oh dear*. Had she overstepped her bounds? "Arden, I'm sorry. I shouldn't have said anything. That was awkward."

He shook his head. "Not at all. There was never a more loving woman than Margaret and I'm so grateful we had the time together that we did. Did you know that she and Faye were friends?"

"Scott mentioned it."

Arden made a bee-line for the coffee pot on the counter and refilled his mug. He turned and leaned on the counter in a way that reminded her strongly of Scott when he had something on his mind.

"You've got this place looking ship-shape, April."

"Thank you." She kept it short, hoping he'd get to the point.

"I know this is old-fashioned of me to say, but this place really needed a woman's touch. I'm really hoping…I mean…would you consider staying on?"

His words hit her square in the chest. Yesterday, she'd have jumped all over that offer. After Scott raised the possibility, she'd thought about little else, weighing the pros and cons. She'd all but decided to stay, but then Stone Thibault had made his bid…

"We've got the room," Arden rushed to assure her. "Ember's practically moved in with Jace now. And Sid loves it here. I don't know what you'd want for salary for a more permanent arrangement. Frankly, we'd be pretty strapped to continue paying you what Scott's paying you now. Once Scott leaves, the salary he's foregoing will have to be redirected to Titus when he takes up the farm management role again, but we can certainly offer something. Maybe we can figure out alternate terms that would fully replace any lost salary, like supplying you with all the free organic strawberries, raspberries, blueberries, and apples you can use for your business. We can even put in a vegetable garden or an herb garden…whatever you want."

Wait, *what*? Scott had been foregoing his manager's salary to subsidize her salary?

Arden was talking again and she forced herself to focus.

"…from what Sid's been telling me, your market business is booming."

Her ears felt like they were buzzing, but she managed to answer. "It's doing pretty well, yes."

"Well, just tell me you'll think about it, April." He pushed away from the counter. "There's so much room in this big old house. And it was all so stale before you and Sidney got here. The pair of you have been like a breath of fresh air."

"Hurry up, Mom!" came Sidney's shout from the living room.

She forced a smile. "I'll bet it was quieter before we got here, though."

Arden laughed. "A little." His face turned serious. "No, more than a little. It's been too quiet for too long. I'd really love for you to stay permanently. We all would."

"I don't know, Arden. Making things permanent…" She looked at the lovely bracelet on her wrist. "Does Scott know you're making me this offer?"

He shook his head. "Not yet. But I mentioned it to Titus and he thought it was a great idea."

"It's just such a big step. A big decision."

"It doesn't have to be." He sipped his coffee. "Maybe you can do it in increments. You know, stay till June so Sidney can finish out the school year, and then see how you're feeling about extending your stay."

She eyed Arden. "Are you sure you haven't been talking to Scott about this? Because he suggested the same thing—that I stay on until school finishes and focus on building the business."

"Did he?" Arden looked pleased. "The boy has good sense."

She huffed out a breath. "More like he knows my weak spot."

"It's never weakness to want to take care of your own," Arden said, his eyes kind and soft with concern. "You just need to decide what's best, for her and for you, in the long term. But in the short term, I think we can all agree it'd be easier on the girl if she doesn't have to change schools mid-year, but the decision is obviously yours."

And didn't that just encapsulate her problem? What was best long term? The position with K.Z. offered her the kind of security she'd always dreamed of, and if she took the job, it would cement her future. Careers had been made on nothing more than a passing comment from K.Z. McCoy. Once having worked for the woman, April would be a highly sought after commodity.

But she'd have to park her little business. Stone had been clear on that point. K.Z. expected undivided loyalty and attention from her employees, and she paid accordingly.

"Just think it over, okay?"

"Okay."

Arden drained his coffee mug, put it in the sink and headed back into the living room.

Not ready to rejoin everyone just yet, she rearranged some things in the refrigerator and put the few stray dishes in the dishwasher. Her thoughts kept going around and around, weighing the pros and cons of staying versus going. If they stayed until the end of the school year, Sidney would be so happy. It would be good for her too. She'd never had a better friend than Danika. And Faye Siliker was a godsend to her little girl. A surrogate grandmother. This old house? Sidney loved it. Axl. Arden. Even Titus, who she delighted in teasing.

But K.Z.-Freaking-McCoy? That was like having Oprah recommend your book or getting featured in Martha Stewart Living. It would be life-changing for her and Sidney. If she didn't go for it, she'd never know how far it could have taken her.

"Mom!"

"Coming!" She rubbed a hand over her forehead, consciously smoothing the frown lines. Putting a smile on her face, she walked back into the living room.

When she sat down beside Scott, he took her hand and squeezed it, then let it go.

Then there was Scott. Then there was *this*. If she stayed, she could have this, at least for a little while longer.

Sidney rushed up to her. "*Now* can I open my presents?"

"Go for it, Ladybug."

Sidney tore into the first gift, a medium-sized box. "A bike helmet?" She looked confused. "I don't get it. I don't have a bike."

"*Yet*," April said. "You don't have a bike yet.'

Sidney's eyes grew round.

# – thirty-five –

SCOTT WAS stuffed. Honestly, he did not think he could eat another bite if his life depended on it. However when April brought out the plate of bite-sized squares to the table… Well, a man only lived once.

The meal had started with prosciutto-wrapped scallops on a bed of arugula. Given how much food there was, an appetizer course was completely unnecessary. But damn, it was good.

The turkey, which Arden had carved earlier, had been perfect. The skin just as crispy and golden as his mother used to make it, the meat just as tender and moist. The herbed oyster dressing, while nothing like Margaret Standish's, was inspired. There'd also been garlic mashed potatoes, gravy, cranberry sauce made with Grand Marnier, a wicked acorn squash sweetened with maple syrup, buttery caramelized turnip, tender green beans, and roasted beets.

Dessert consisted of a choice of old-fashioned apple pie with ice cream or a traditional Yule log cake, or *bûche de Noël* as Sid called it, slathered with chocolate frosting. Scott's "choice" had been one of each. Titus had had two pieces of pie and one fat slab of cake.

When the dishes had been cleared away, April disappeared to the kitchen while the rest of them had sipped their wine, and Sidney enjoyed the apple cider she'd helped Arden make right here on the farm. Scott had wanted to help with the cleanup, but she'd insisted he relax with his family. This was her gift.

April had looked so happy, so alive and passionate, as she'd served the courses. Now they were having coffee and tea and—unbelievably—a plate of squares and sweets.

And conversation…

"So this time," Titus said, obviously reveling in telling the story, "Ember had actually climbed out the window and was halfway down the trellis when Mom came home from bingo."

Ember laughed "Oh, God, I was in so much trouble. She pulled into the yard and caught me in the headlights. Of course, she stopped right there, with me frozen mid-way down."

"Like the proverbial deer in the headlights?" Ocean guessed.

"More like a fly on flypaper—just stuck there."

Everyone laughed.

"And I was over in the apple trees by the road," Jace said. "My heart was beating out of my chest. It was one thing for Ember to get caught sneaking out, but to be sneaking out to meet me? I don't know who was more scared—me or her. Fortunately, Margaret didn't see me."

"I remember Margaret telling me about that," Faye said, wiping away tears of laughter. "She couldn't stop giggling." She turned to Jace. "She knew you were there."

"You're kidding!" Jace said.

"No."

"She never said a word to me."

"Well, she had plenty of them for me," Ember said. "She made me promise never to do it again, and I didn't," she said righteously.

Scott snorted. "Maybe you didn't climb down the trellis again, but you found other ways to sneak out. And I followed you every time."

"Did you?" Smiling enigmatically, Ember chose a square from the tray.

"Dammit." He injected the curse with more vehemence than it deserved after all these years. Everyone chuckled, which was his aim. Even Axl, who'd scored a few bites of turkey without skin or gravy or anything to make him sick, lifted his head and wagged his tail against the door frame. "You really got past me?"

She shrugged. "A time or two."

The family had spent most of the meal reminiscing about old times, good times. Christmas dances. There'd been lots of talk about the upcoming wedding, too. Happy talk.

Eventually, Faye jumped up and volunteered for dish duty.

Predictably, April protested. "Please, leave it to me, Faye. It's part of my gift."

"Yeah, and I'll help," Sidney said.

"What?" Titus said. "You want to be in here drying dishes when you got a brand new bike for Christmas?"

Sid rolled her eyes. "It's icy out there. I can't ride a bike on ice." Her eyes went to her mother. "Can I?"

"No, you most certainly cannot."

"No ice in the nursery," Titus observed, "and it's plenty big enough to do a few laps if I moved a few things out of the way."

"Oh, what a great idea!" Ocean said. "I'll help."

Sidney literally bounced in her chair. "Can I, Mom?"

April smiled. "Of course you can, Ladybug. But wear your helmet."

"I will!" She dashed off to grab her helmet and coat.

"And say thank you to Titus and Ocean for clearing that stuff away for you!" April called after her.

"Thank you, Titus and Ocean!"

"Can I give you a hand?" Ember asked.

April smiled. "No, I've got it. Why don't you and Jace take

your coffee into the living room? You too," she said to Arden and Faye.

Arden rubbed his belly. "That sounds like a grand idea."

Scott grinned. Uncle Arden would be dozing in his chair in ten minutes.

Ember insisted on helping clear the table, but then she let April shoo her out.

"Don't even try to chase me away," Scott said. "I'm helping with that mountain of dishes."

She eyed him. "Anyone ever tell you that you have a hard time accepting a gift?"

"It's a character flaw. One of many." He picked up a plate and scraped the few remaining food morsels off into the garbage disposal, then moved on to the next, stacking them as he went.

She opened the dishwasher and started placing the plates wherever she could fit them. Of course, the already partially loaded racks filled up long before the last plate. She started the machine, then turned to the sink. Filling it with dishes and hot, soapy water, she attacked the job. Scott grabbed a clean dish towel and started drying them and putting them away.

"So, Arden made me a very interesting offer this afternoon."

"Uncle Arden?" He looked at her sharply. "What kind of offer?"

"He invited me to stay on permanently."

"Really?" Holy crap. Where was the money going to come from to finance that? Once Titus took over the management role again, the money that had been going to April would have to be redirected to Titus. Of course, she'd made up her mind to accept K.Z. McCoy's offer, so it was moot anyway.

"Yes, really." She dropped the dishcloth and turned toward him, planting her damp hands on her hips. "He mentioned that there would be a salary cut once you leave, since apparently the stipend for the farm's management has been going to me instead of you."

Dammit. Busted. "What do I need a salary for? This is like a vacation for me, but with free room and board. And really, really good food."

"Be serious, Scott."

"I am being serious." He reached for another mug and dried it. "There's no way I could take that stipend anyway. I'd have felt guilty as hell accepting it since I left Titus here to manage alone all these years. The least I could do is roll that money back into the operation. Besides, I don't need it April. I've worked hard, saved plenty." He put the mug on its hook and reached for another. "I hope I don't have to tell you again how much you've contributed around here."

Some of the tension seemed to go out of her. "You should have told me."

He hung the second mug up, then draped the towel over his shoulder. "Would you have taken the job if I had?"

"Of course not."

"Well, there you go."

"You fibbed." She sighed and plunked more dishes into the water. "Maybe I did too."

"On the Northern Ontario job? Yeah. I figured it might be a…bit of a stretch."

"I guess I can't be terribly mad at you for—"

"Fibbing by omission?"

She smiled.

"So what did Uncle Arden say when you told him you're going to Boston to work for that McCoy woman?"

"I didn't tell him."

"No?" His heart leaped. Was she reconsidering? "Why not?"

She shrugged. "Arden made a good offer."

*What?* "Didn't you say your salary would be reduced?"

"Yeah, but he said the farm could maybe supply me with free organic fruit for my business to make up for it."

Way to go, Uncle Arden. "That's actually pretty smart. And it would allow Sid to stay in school."

"Oh, you can bet Arden didn't miss the chance to reinforce that." She plunged a pot into the dish water and attacked it with a nylon pad. "He suggested if I couldn't commit permanently, that I at least should think about staying until the school year is done."

She rinsed the pot and put it on the dish rack. He picked it up and dried it absently, his attention focused on her.

"That's not exactly a monetary win for you, though, is it, if they cut your salary? School's done in June, and you'd need to stay through July and August to benefit from the berry crops, and through to the fall for the apples."

"He said I could have my own garden too, for herbs and vegetables."

He smiled. "Mom used to keep a garden. I bet that would make him happy to see you resuscitate it." Her shoulders seemed to wilt, so he hastened to add, "Not that it's your responsibility to make Arden happy, or anyone else for that matter."

She turned to him, her face pinched. "What do you think I should do?"

God, she looked so lovely. It made his heart hurt to see her struggling. "I think you should do what's best for you and Sid. Period."

That produced a ghost of a smile. "Well, we're agreed on that. Now if I just knew which path would take us there, it would be a piece of cake."

He put down his dishtowel and pulled her into his arms. She went willingly, pressing herself to his chest. He rubbed her back. "You know, I read something interesting about making decisions like this, in a sciency article."

"Yeah?"

"Yeah. They say you shouldn't stress yourself out about trying to make the best possible decision in the history of decisions, as though the fate of the world depended on it. Instead, you should focus on making a decision that's what they called 'good enough'. The point being that your life won't be all rainbows and unicorns if you make one decision, and it won't be absolute crap if you make a different decision. Either way, you'll have heartaches and challenges. Either way, you'll have joys and triumphs. So a good enough decision is…well, good enough."

"Wow." She pulled back to look up at him. "That might be the wisest advice I've ever been given."

He grinned. "I did say I read it in a sciency article, didn't I?"

She went up on tiptoe and kissed him. "Thank you."

"So have you made a decision?"

"No, but I'll feel better about whatever choice I make."

"Good." He kissed the top of her head and released her, picking up his dish towel again.

They went back to work in silence. No doubt she was weighing the pros and cons.

One thing was for sure: he was going to have to call his partner again. Just days ago, he'd notified Georgie that he'd likely be staying in New Brunswick until February or March. Last night, after April had told him about the offer Stone Thibault extended on K.Z. McCoy's behalf, he'd messaged his buddy, saying he'd be there early in January after all. Now…hell, he didn't even know what he could tell his friend, other than that his departure date was up in the air again. He wouldn't blame Georgie if he decided to write him off and invite his brother-in-law into the project. At least then Georgie's sister would be happy.

But damn, Georgie was going to be pissed. Maybe Scott would wait until the new year to make that call, let his buddy enjoy his holiday. No point stirring up anxiety at this point.

April could yet decide to accept the Boston offer, in which case he'd have given Georgie an ulcer over nothing.

If she opted to stay, he'd stay too, at least for a month or two. He'd promised April as much when he'd made his own pitch for her to stay, and he'd keep that promise if it killed him. If that meant the Alberta project had to move on without him, so be it. And if his dawdling put Georgie in a tight spot financially, Scott would provide financing to bridge him until his brother-in-law could get his ducks in a row.

"There. The last pot," April said. "Thank you for helping."

"Least I could do after that dinner." He picked up the skillet and dried it, put it away, and hung the dishtowel on its peg. When he turned around, she was standing there with a Christmas gift in her hands.

"I didn't get a chance to give you your gift earlier."

He took it from her, noting it was heavier than he thought it would be. He hoped she hadn't spent too much money. He'd dropped quite a bit for that custom silver bracelet from that local jewelry designer Jace was helping get established, but he could afford to. In retrospect, he'd have happily paid twice the price for the pleasure that little bracelet had put on her face, the happiness in her eyes.

"Go on," she urged. "Open it."

He put the package down on the kitchen counter, tore the paper off. The smell of fine leather reached him before he'd even lifted the box's lid. "Jesus, April." It was motorcycle chaps. He pulled them out to examine them. "These are gorgeous. Fully lined, expansion panel in the thigh…"

"Titus helped me pick them out. He said you could use something warmer."

"I love them, but it's too much."

"I love that they'll help keep you safe and warm when you're cruising those highways."

She slid her arms around him and he tossed the chaps back in the box so he could gather her close.

"Now kiss me before I have to go out and watch Sid ride her bike in the plant nursery."

He did.

Oh, how he did.

# – thirty-six –

APRIL WAS enjoying having the house to herself.

Sidney was back in school after the Christmas break. Titus and Ocean had gone to Ocean's cottage at the lake where Titus was installing new fixtures in the bathroom while Ocean worked on her play. Arden and Faye had driven off for their Montreal hockey vacation and Ember had gone back to work at her practice. Even Scott had run out for a while. The dairy farm down the road was having a problem with the stainless steel piping system and had called Scott for help. Why was she not surprised that he had pipefitting skills?

The oven timer sounded. Humming, she pulled out the pan of breakfast bars. Or what would become breakfast bars when they cooled enough to be chilled, cut up and individually wrapped.

She put another pan into the oven and went to top up her coffee. Carrying it to the window, she looked out on the yard through a curtain of swirling snow. It had snowed every other day since Christmas, or so it seemed. Though it wasn't actively snowing at the moment, there was a good six inches of white stuff on the roof. When the wind gusted, that dry powder eddied around like crazy, making the world outside look like a shaken snow globe. She wrapped her hands around her warm mug, feeling cozy. Happy.

Scott had been right. Making a "good enough" decision had taken the pressure off.

Sid had been ecstatic, of course, when April had told her they would stay on until she finished the school year. So ecstatic that April had felt the need to remind her that they would definitely be leaving in June.

Scott had been happy too. At least, she thought so. Since his project out west was on hold, he'd be staying until the end of February himself. Sometimes, though, when he didn't know she was watching, she sensed he was battling with himself. Apart from those short few days in Montreal, he'd been in Harkness since the Thanksgiving weekend in October. The urge to be moving on was probably right there all the time, under the surface.

Most of the time, though, he seemed very present. Tonight after supper, he was taking her and Sid skating. The community didn't have a real arena, but the Furrow family on the other side of Harkness turned their old, unused pig barn into a rink every winter. She grinned. Skating in a pig barn! Scott had assured Sidney that it no longer smelled of pigs after all these years. April hoped he was right.

She'd yet to communicate her decision to Stone Thibault. Her happiness dimmed a little. She knew it was too much to hope that K.Z. McCoy would wait six months for her, but as Scott said, it would work out one way or another.

She'd call Stone this afternoon after the baking was out of the way and the kitchen cleaned up.

Decision made, she drained her coffee. Bootilicious bars were next. They were still her bestsellers, despite being almost identical to her regular breakfast bars. It was all in the name, evidently.

She was reaching for the dried cranberries when she heard a cell phone ring over by the sink. Scott's phone, she realized from the ringtone. He must have left it when he'd headed out to the Eschers'. It rang a few more times, then stopped.

She'd just uncapped a huge jar of raw honey when the house phone started ringing. She answered it on the second ring. "Hello."

"I'm looking for Scott," a male voice said. "I just tried his cell phone, but there was no answer."

"Oh, was that you a moment ago?" she said. "Sorry about that. He got called out during breakfast to help a neighbor and forgot his phone."

"Can you have him call me? Like, as soon as you can. Name's George Hemsworth."

The tension in the man's voice wiped the smile off her face. "Is something wrong?"

"I just got Scott's text putting me off until the end of freakin' February."

"Umm…"

The caller sighed. "I'm sorry. That was rude. Is this April?"

"Yes."

"Sorry, April. Didn't mean to take it out on you." The edge of exasperation in his voice was replaced now by anxiety. "I just don't think this project will wait that long, know what I mean?"

"Of course." Her stomach felt like a tight, hot ball of lead. *Scott had lied to her about the delay.* Or if not outright lied, he'd allowed her to believe the delay was for other causes—permits or approval or financing or something like that. She took a deep breath. "Actually, I could use a little clarification. Is the project being delayed because of Scott?"

"To be fair, he gave me his blessing to go ahead and bring another partner on if I can't wait, but it's not that easy." His tone was almost apologetic now. "I don't have Scott's track record with a project this size. Without him on board, I just don't know if I can pull it off. This is the biggest thing we've ever undertaken. Hell, it's the project of a lifetime. A real game-changer for us. Well, for me, anyway. So you can see why I need to talk to him."

"I can definitely see." The words came out so normal, so calm. "I'll let him know you called the moment I see him. I'm sure you'll hear from him soon."

"Thanks, April."

"No problem." She hung up.

*Big fucking problem.*

Scott's presence in Harkness through to the new year had factored into her taking the job in the first place. And his continued presence for the next couple of months had tipped the balance of her recent decision to stay on. But she never would have stayed if she'd known she was holding Scott back from…what had George called it? *The project of a lifetime.* Here she was collecting what should effectively be Scott's salary while simultaneously allowing him to jeopardize his big break.

The phone rang. Probably Scott checking on the whereabouts of his phone. She snatched the receiver up. "Hello."

Her terse tone must have taken the caller aback because there was a few seconds' silence. "Is this April Morgan?"

Definitely not Scott. But the female voice sounded vaguely familiar. "Yes, it's April." She leaned closer to look at the call display. The school? "Is everything okay with Sid?"

"It's Amanda Carr, the school secretary. Principal Makepeace would like you to come down to the school as soon as you can."

April's legs went weak. She pulled a chair away from the table and sank down on it. "What is it? Is Sidney all right?"

"Your daughter is fine, Ms. Morgan. But Ms. Makepeace would like to speak to you in person. When can you come?"

Eden wouldn't be asking her to go to the school for a social visit. Something was wrong. That ball of lead in her stomach suddenly felt the size of a bowling ball.

"Give me fifteen minutes."

She hung up the phone. Grabbing an oven mitt, she yanked

the partially cooked breakfast bars out and plunked them on the stovetop. She turned off the oven and tore off her apron. With a last look around the kitchen, she grabbed her keys and coat and headed for the door.

# – thirty-seven –

APRIL TWISTED the leather handle of her purse nervously as she waited in the school's outer office.

The door to the principal's office opened. "Thanks for coming in, Ms. Morgan," Eden said. "Right this way."

*Ms. Morgan?* They'd worked together so closely on the Halloween party, and Eden had been very friendly at the market. April had a feeling this sudden formality didn't bode well.

It didn't.

April entered the room to see Sidney, her head hanging down, squirming in a black plastic chair. Several chairs over, another kid and a man she presumed to be his father sat in identical chairs. And oh, crap, the kid—Will Peterson—had a swollen lip. She glanced at his dad. His name was Tim, she was pretty sure. An accountant, maybe? Definitely a professional, judging by the suit he wore beneath his wool car coat. And actually, the kid looked almost like a replica of his father. Well, except for the fat lip.

April looked at Eden, catching a flicker of sympathy on the other woman's face. This was so not looking good.

April trained her attention back on her daughter. "Sid, do you want to tell me what this is about?"

Deliberately, she directed the question to Sidney rather

than the principal. She wasn't so far removed from Morganville—aka that family from hell—that she didn't remember what it was like to be sitting right where Sidney was now. But in April's case, she'd sat in front of her accusing father rather than a school principal. Small, alone and voiceless. She was determined that her daughter would never feel that way. Not while she was around.

Will came to his feet. "She smacked me, that's what happened!"

"You had it coming!" Sidney shot back.

"Sidney, Will! Enough."

The room fell silent again at Eden Makepeace's command.

"What happened here, Eden?" Tim demanded. "Why are Mrs. Morgan and I—"

"Ms. Morgan," April corrected quickly.

"Sorry," he said. "No offense…"

God, he looked half flustered. His son, on the other hand, snickered behind his hand.

"None taken," April said.

"I called you both down here because your children were fighting this morning."

Tim looked at his son. "Will, if you hit a girl, you are in some kind of trouble, young man."

"I'd never do that!" He pointed to his lip. "She hit me!"

April looked at Sidney. "Is this true?"

"Like I said, he had it coming."

"How about we give a better explanation than that, Sidney?" Eden said.

Will sat up in his chair. "She jumped me, that's—"

"You'll have your chance, son."

"Yes, you will," Eden said. "Now, Sidney, you first."

Her bottom lip trembled. Her eyes filled with tears. "Will was saying stuff."

April immediately stiffened. Saying stuff? What kind of stuff? She was well aware of the kind of tales boys could tell.

But in grade five? Oh God. How awful that would be for Sidney. She wanted to throttle the little brat.

"What was he saying?" April asked.

She sniffled. "He called me a bad name."

"Is that true, buddy?" Tim Peterson asked. "Did you call Sidney a bad name?"

The young boy hesitated a good three seconds before he answered. "No." His words were barely audible. He looked down at his feet.

"You did so!" Sidney said, her little fists bunching. "You called me a bastard!"

Tim looked shocked. "Is that true, Will?"

"What? It's the truth! She doesn't have a dad."

Tim clamped a hand on his son's shoulder. "Ladies, if you'll excuse us a moment, I need to speak to my son privately."

"Of course." Eden gestured to the door.

"I'm so sorry, Ms. Morgan." Still with his hand on young Will's shoulder, Tim escorted him from the room.

After a moment, Eden rose from her chair. "I'll give you two a moment, as well," she said. She left, closing the door behind her.

A second later, Sid sobbed and leaned into her mother. Because she finally could, she let the tears fall.

And April held her like she hadn't in a very long time.

Sidney let her.

# – thirty-eight –

SCOTT HAD just toed off his boots on the porch—after spending half the day at the Escher dairy farm, they could use a good airing out—when the door opened. He looked up to see April standing there holding his cell phone out toward him.

"You forgot your phone."

"Yeah, I noticed." He shrugged out of his coat and hung it on a peg, then reached for the phone. "Did I miss a call?" He powered it up to look at the call log. Shit. Georgie.

"Yes, but he called back right away on the land line."

"You talked to him?" Scott frowned, stepping into the house. "Did he leave a message?"

She laughed, but it was a harsh sound. "Yeah, he did. He'd like to know why you're hanging around the farm in the dead of winter while the deal of a lifetime hangs in the balance out there."

Oh, man. Busted. "I don't know that I'd call it the deal of a—"

"And guess what? I'd like to know the answer to that question too. What *are* you doing here, Scott?"

He reached a hand out to touch her arm, but she backed away. "April—"

"Don't say you're relieving Titus. He'd be the first one to

tell you he's sufficiently relieved. There's so little to do now, it hardly makes sense."

His lips tightened. "We've talked about this. The projects around the house—"

"The critical ones are already done," she said. "At this point, anything else is pretty much a make work proposition to keep you busy. Which was fine when I thought you were killing time until the Alberta project came on line, but now..." She went to the sink and poured herself a glass of water. Turning toward him, she leaned against the counter, glass in hand. "Why, Scott? Why couldn't you have been honest with me? I told you from the start that I didn't want to be anyone's charity case, but that's exactly what you've turned me into."

"Charity case?" For about the millionth time, he cursed those parents of hers, who'd made her feel like a terrible burden instead of a blessing. "You're anything *but* that, April. What you did for us this fall..."

She waved him off with her water glass. "Okay, maybe I was earning my keep—our keep—back then, when you were still busy with the orchards. But you don't need me here now. And you don't need to stay here and jeopardize your future. I don't want that for you, and I sure as hell don't want it for me and Sid."

Scott heard feet thundering down the stairs and Sid burst into the room. "Mom, what's going on? What are you guys fighting about?"

"We're not fighting," April said. "I was just explaining to Scott why we have to leave."

"Leave?" Sid practically shouted the word. "But you said we were staying until school finishes."

"I know, sweetheart, but there's been a change of plans." She pasted on a bright smile. "Remember K.Z. McCoy, the Martha Stewart-type lady we talked about? The one who came to visit the Boisverts? Well, she's offered me a job with a fantastic salary and I've accepted. This is the big time,

Ladybug. We're going to Boston. We're going to have our own place, a nice one, and we'll enroll you in a really good private school."

"No," Sid protested. "I don't want to go." She turned to Scott. "Tell her to stay. She'll stay if you ask her."

Scott's heart was breaking. "I'm sorry, Sid. This thing with K.Z. could really launch your mother's career. It's a real good thing for both of you."

"But this is where we *live*. Where Arden and Faye are, and Ember and Titus and you. And Axl and Danika. It's where all my friends are. I don't want to go to stupid Boston."

April looked positively sick. "Honey, you've always known we were going to have to leave Harkness. Remember? I told you it wasn't permanent. I know I let you pretend it would last—and yes, I've done some pretending too—but it's time. We've already stayed longer than we planned." She finally put the glass of water down without ever having sipped from it. "Pretending was nice, but we can't pretend anymore. This is really a big break for me and I have to take it."

"But we were building our business." Sid's face was flushed, her eyes hot with anxiety. "It was really growing, wasn't it?"

April's smile was tremulous. "It sure was. And we make a great team. But this job might wind up being the best thing for the business in the long run. For now, though, we'll have to park it for a while."

Sid's lip trembled. "Is this because I gave Will Peterson a fat lip at school 'cause of what he said?"

*What? Sid had been fighting?*

"Oh, no, baby," April hastened to assure her. "Don't think that for a minute."

Sid glanced from her mother to Scott, then back to her mother.

"How about I stay here with Scott while you go to Boston?"

April looked like she'd been gut-punched to hear her daughter say she'd prefer to be separated from her than to move. Then she took a deep breath. "Scott's not staying, either. He has a big project that's been waiting for him out west."

"You're just making that up!" Sid accused.

"Sid—"

Sid turned huge, tear-filled eyes on Scott. "You're staying here, right, Scott? To do all that work you talked about. I was gonna help you strip that ugly wallpaper in my room, remember?"

Jesus, she was killing him. "Your mother's right," he said gruffly. "I have to leave."

"But I don't want to go!"

If Sid's wail tore at his heart, it was absolutely shredding April.

"Please, Sidney," April said. "We have to go."

"Why? You don't need that job. We can stay here and keep doing the market thing." She turned desperate eyes on Scott. "Arden wouldn't mind, would he, Scott?"

Christ, he felt gutted. He looked to April for direction.

"No, Sid. We have to go. We can't keep imposing on the Standishs. We've got an opportunity for me to stand on my own two feet and make enough money to secure your future. That's what we have to do."

"But—"

"Sidney, we don't belong here. We're moving and that's that."

She looked to Scott again, tears welling in those brown eyes that were so like her mother's. "Tell her we do belong! Tell her she's wrong."

He cleared his throat. "Your mother knows best, kid. You have to trust her. She's looking out for the both of you."

Sid whirled on her mother. "I can't believe you're making us leave. *I hate you!*"

With that, Sid whirled and raced up the stairs, her feet pounding on the steps.

Scott turned to April, who looked absolutely stricken. "She didn't mean that. She's just upset."

"This is all my fault, letting her pretend." She hugged her arms around herself. "It was going so well until…" She shook her head. "No, it was wrong, not forcing her to face reality. And I let it go on too long."

Her pain made him feel so helpless, so inadequate. There was nothing he could say to ease it. He reached for her, intending to fold her into his arms to comfort her. Or hell, maybe to comfort himself. But she pulled away, stepping back out of his reach.

"Just go, Scott." She hadn't shed a tear, but he could hear how close they were in her voice. "Don't you have a phone call to make?"

His hands fisted at his sides. Dammit.

She turned away. "I have to start supper."

He watched her go back to her preparations. Well, that was that, wasn't it? There wasn't a damned thing he could do here. Except leave.

And hey, wasn't that what he was good at? His specialty?

Without a word, he left the kitchen.

# – thirty-nine –

THE GARLIC bread was burned around the edges. The lasagna? Not April's best effort by any means. And no wonder. She'd put it together so hastily, she'd used the wrong onions. And she'd completely forgotten the anchovy for the Caesar salad. Bacon bowls for that salad? Not tonight.

She looked down at her plate. The lasagna with its wrong onions sat there growing colder by the moment.

With Arden and Faye still off in Montreal and Titus at the lake with Ocean, it was a small group at the table tonight. Scott, Ember, Sidney and herself. Ember was full of chatter about her new practice, and Scott nodded and interjected appropriate words at the right spots. *Really? Wow. Proud of you, Sis.*

Finally, Ember put down her fork. "Okay, what's wrong?"

Scott's glance shot to April. She knew he'd make the explanation if she wanted him to. Just like he'd supported her earlier during the confrontation with Sidney. He'd backed her up, refusing to make her look like the bad guy. Her throat ached just thinking about it.

"We—that is, Sid and I—are going to be leaving sooner than I thought." She twisted the napkin on her lap so hard, her fingers hurt. "I've had a job offer, one I can't turn down. A once-in-a-lifetime opportunity."

“Wow, how exciting!” Ember said. “Where is it?”

Sidney replied before April had a chance. “It’s in Boston. Some stupid job for some stupid rich lady.”

“I’m sure she’s a perfectly nice lady, Sid,” Ember said. She put her hand on Sidney’s shoulder. “And she’s certainly got good taste if she wants your mom to come cook for her.”

April was grateful for Ember’s effort but Sid was clearly not impressed, judging by her deepening scowl.

“It means security for us,” April reminded her daughter. “It’s a good job. A good opportunity. And it’s…reality.”

“When are you leaving?” Ember asked.

She sucked in a breath. “The day after tomorrow.”

“That soon?” The shock on Scott’s face pierced her.

“I thought it was best.”

“Yeah, day after tomorrow,” Sidney repeated. “Can you believe that? I get exactly one measly day at school to say goodbye to everyone.”

“Sidney, I…I’m sorry. We can’t stay longer. We need to get on the road.”

“Danika’s having a pajama party for her birthday next week,” she said dully. “But I’m not going to be there for it. I didn’t even buy her a present yet.” She dipped her head, sniffling.

“I’m so sorry, Sidney.” She was. She was so very sorry about everything. Sorry for herself too.

Sid’s head came up, her eyes pleading. “Can’t you just call that guy again and tell him you changed your mind? Just…give us a little more time?”

“You know I can’t.” April’s voice broke. “We talked about this. There’s not really enough work to warrant me staying in the job, and I’m not one to stick around once the job’s done.”

Sidney whirled toward Scott. “Tell her that’s not true. There’s other stuff my mom could do outside the kitchen, like helping with those renovations.”

He shook his head. “Sorry, Sid. Your mom did a fantastic

job for us, and you were a great help too. But like she says, the job here is done."

April felt a fresh spike of pain. Not from Scott's words, but from the fact that he was saying them for her. Being the heavy, absorbing some of Sid's anger.

"*The job is done*?" Ember had been taking this all in with an expression of shock on her face. "That's kind of a hard line, isn't it?" She turned her gaze from her brother to April. "For God's sake, April, don't feel you have to rush off. I'm sure Dad would be cool with—"

"Thank you, Ember." Scott's words cut across his sister's, and he sent her an unmistakable *cool it* look. "It goes without saying that Uncle Arden will be disappointed to lose April, as am I. And I know we'll all miss Sid the Kid. But this chance to impress K.Z. McCoy is something April has been actively seeking for quite a while." He sat back in his chair. "Opportunity knocks when it wants to. We don't get to control that."

"Like your project out west," Sid said.

"Exactly like that."

Ember shot a look at Scott. "Wait, you're leaving too?"

"That's why Mom's leaving," Sid blurted out. "I heard her say she wouldn't have stayed this long if she'd known he was postponing that job on her account."

"I'm lost," Ember said. "What job?"

"In Alberta." April and Sid said the words at the same time.

"Yes, Northern Alberta," Scott said. "A buddy and I are partnering with an architect to build some affordable, pod-type housing units that will stand up to the bitter cold, but that can be deployed quickly at pre-engineered sites."

"To cope with the growth in boom towns?"

"Yeah, but they can be made to work anywhere emergency or overflow housing is needed, including First Nations reserves. Depending on how you set up the infrastructure, you could stack them, or lay them out like petals on a daisy."

"That's cool," Ember said. "Don't you think that's cool, Sid?"

"I suppose," she conceded. "But I don't see why we have to leave." She looked at April. "Are you sure it's not about decking Will Peterson? 'Cause I promise I won't fight anymore, even if he calls me that bad name again. He can call me all the bad names he wants."

"Oh, sweetie, no. It's not about that. I promise."

"What bad name?" Scott asked.

"It doesn't matter," April said quickly. "It's over and dealt with. And I'm telling you it's not a factor. K.Z. McCoy made me a ridiculously good offer that I couldn't say no to. That's it, that's all."

Scott turned to Sidney. "What'd he call you, kid?"

"He said I was a bastard, 'cause Mom's not married to my dad."

"He did not!" Ember sounded aghast. She looked at April with concern in her eyes. "I hope you had a talk with his mother."

"His father, actually," April said. "He seemed to take it pretty seriously."

"Tim Peterson?"

April nodded.

"He'll straighten the kid out." Scott gave Sidney a sympathetic look. "Sorry that happened, Sid. Some people are just asshats."

"Scott!" Ember reprimanded.

"I mean jerks," he corrected quickly. "Some people are just jerks."

"Small towns can be like that," Ember said softly. "Everyone knows, or thinks they know, everyone else's business. Sometimes names fly, or in my case, rumors." April met Ember's eyes and saw the intensity there. "But please don't let that sour you on Harkness. Yes, there's some of that, but there's so much more love and acceptance and warmth. You might have more anonymity in Boston, but you won't find this kind of community."

"That's what I'm trying to tell her!" Sidney said.

April sighed, "We've talked about this, Sid. It's not about what happened at school."

And it wasn't. Well, not really. It might have been the straw that broke the camel's back, but it was Scott's deception that really mattered.

"Then what's it about?" Sid demanded.

"It's about facing reality," she said crisply. "We're not really needed here during the quiet winter months, and it's not really fair to stay under those circumstances. Meanwhile, we have this other great opportunity that could set us up for life." She put her balled up, wrinkled napkin on the table. "We talked about this, Ladybug. I'm sure—"

"Don't call me that!" Sidney leaped up from her chair, tears coursing down her reddened face. "Don't call me that ever again!"

She turned and ran out of the room and up the stairs. Axl, who'd been snoozing in the living room during the meal, lifted his head and watched her retreat woefully. With a sigh, he got to his feet and climbed the stairs after her. A moment later, when the old dog had had time enough to reach Ember's bedroom, the door closed with enough force to qualify as a slam.

*Ember's room.*

Sidney would have her own room in Boston. A permanent one. The improbably big signing bonus Stone Thibault had offered on K.Z.'s behalf would assure that. It would be plenty enough for a down payment on a condo in a very, very good neighborhood. But she wouldn't rush into anything. She'd rent first, make sure she knew the area, make sure Sidney was happy at her private school—tuition to the same another signing bonus. She could finally give her little girl a proper home.

*Except the only home Sidney wanted was right here.*

And April herself?

"Well, I have to scoot." Ember pushed back her chair and got to her feet. She touched April on the shoulder, looking down at her kindly. "Please don't think I'm fleeing from the drama, April. I just promised Jace I'd come to see his boys do a sparring demonstration at the gym and I'll probably stay over. But you'll be here tomorrow, right?"

"I will."

"Mind if I bring Ocean over for one last coffee klatch before you go?"

April smiled up at her, blinking back tears. "I'd love that."

"I'll see you tomorrow then."

"Perfect."

She gave April's shoulder a last squeeze, cleared her dishes to the sink, then, with her usual breakneck pace, was out the door.

Scott and April sat in silence. Or rather, near silence. The *tick tick tick* of his mother's clock in the living room marked every second.

April's throat ached with tears. *Just a little bit longer.* She had to hold off just a little bit longer. She'd cry later. When she could.

"So, the day after tomorrow, huh?"

"Yes." Feeling the heaviness of his gaze on her, she looked up to meet his eyes. He'd been so supportive during the discussion with Sidney, she was startled to see the expression in them now.

"I wish you'd found the time to tell me beforehand that you were leaving so quickly, instead of springing it on me like that."

Her lips thinned. She didn't have enough on her plate dealing with Sidney, she had to think about his sensibilities? It wasn't enough coping with her own devastation at the thought of leaving Harkness—of leaving *him*—while simultaneously trying to hide it?

"Why?" She lifted her chin. "It's not like it would have changed anything."

He lifted a hand to rub the back of his neck, a gesture she'd grown to know and love. "Well, no, it wouldn't have changed anything, but I thought we meant something to each other."

She sucked in a tight breath. "I thought we were pretending."

If she'd slapped him across the face, he couldn't have looked any more startled. Not that the look stayed long. It was gone in a flash.

"Right. That's what we were doing in that loft with the doors flung open to the stars. Pretending."

Did he want it all from her? Everything? Would he not be content until he'd wrung from her an admission of love? Because God help her, she loved him. A rambling man who would never stay.

"Don't," she pleaded, poised on the brink of shattering. "Just…don't."

Her throat ached unbearably. Almost as much as her heart did. She stood and started gathering the dishes from the table, then turned to the counter, away from Scott.

She'd been pretending all right. Pretending she'd be able to walk away with her heart intact.

*You've been dreaming, April Dawn Morgan.*

Living the life of another woman—one who hadn't gotten pregnant at seventeen and had to fare for herself and her child. One who hadn't come from a family with archaic, hateful notions of womanhood. She'd behaved like a woman who could afford to dream. She'd dreamed—*pretended*—and look where it had gotten her.

Oh, God, look where it had gotten her little Ladybug.

*Don't call me that ever again!*

And Scott…

She closed her eyes. If he touched her now, the dam would

break. The tears would spill. She'd fallen in love with the wrong man again.

He put his hands on her shoulders and it was all she could do not to wilt under his warm grip.

"Tell me you don't love me," he said against her ear. "Tell me you were pretending all of that. Really pretending. And I'll let you go, April. Right here and now, tell me."

She wouldn't turn around. Through her closed eyelids, the tears spilled.

"I was pretending."

He walked away.

# – forty –

SIDNEY BIT her bottom lip as she leaned close to the window to peer out at the ground below.

*Heck.* It was a long way down!

It was also very dark out there. Then again, why wouldn't it be? It was almost eleven o'clock.

Axl whined softly beside her and she looked down at him. Even in the dim bedroom lit only by the tiny nightlight in the far corner, she could see the worry in the old dog's eyes.

She stepped back from the window, and lowered her backpack onto the floor, careful to avoid the strapped-on telescope making contact with the hardwood. The telescope was in its case, but still she wanted to be careful.

Well, careful would be to *not* sneak out the window in the first place, *not* climb down the shaky looking trellis. But Ember had done it like a zillion times. If Ember could do it, so could she.

Of course, Ember had been a teenager when she'd done it, Sid was pretty sure. A teenager sneaking out to meet a boy. Not a ten-year-old kid all by herself.

She was stalling. She knew she was. She just needed to gather her courage.

The house was perfectly quiet. Her mother, who'd gone to bed super early, had to be asleep by now, and Scott would be out in the hay loft where he always slept. Ember hadn't come home yet, which meant she wouldn't be coming home at all.

So here she stood, the only one awake in the whole house. Well, besides Axl.

She'd gone to bed fully dressed. When her mother had looked in on her on her way to bed, Sid had pulled the quilts up around her neck and pretended to be sleeping. She'd bent and kissed Sid's forehead and whispered goodnight. Her voice had sounded so sad, Sid had wanted to reach up and hug her, but she couldn't. Not without giving away that she was fully dressed. So she'd lain there without moving a muscle.

She'd set the alarm for eleven. Not the clock alarm, but the one on her phone. And she'd set it to vibrate so it wouldn't wake anyone else. But she'd been so anxious, so afraid she'd fall asleep, miss the alarm and sleep the night away, she hadn't slept at all. She'd wound up shutting the alarm off at ten fifty-five and climbing out of bed.

Her coat was at the ready, slung over the vanity seat. She'd stashed her boots beneath the chair. All she needed to do was put them on, strap on the backpack and make the climb.

Turning, she examined once again the Sid-shaped lump she'd made under the quilts with pillows and sweaters. Pretty convincing, if someone just poked their head in the door. *Yup, nothing unusual to see here. Just Sid asleep in her bed.*

Her bed?

Nope. Not her bed. Not even close. Ember's bed in Ember's room, in the Standish family house. Where hobos were hobos and bastards had to move along.

And on that thought, Sidney grabbed her coat, pulled it on, and zipped it right up to her chin. She pulled on her boots and went back to the window, and this time—ever so quietly—she slid the window up.

Axl stood. He made a sound somewhere between a woof and a whine.

"Hush, Axl. It's okay, good dog. Be nice and quiet, okay?"

She stroked him on his bony head where the fur that was so wiry on the rest of his body was smooth and soft as silk.

He nudged her with his nose. Whined again, just a little bit louder.

Oh crap, he might give her away! She hadn't thought of that.

"Come on, Axl," she said. "You can sleep in Titus's room tonight."

He followed her to the door. But when Sidney opened it and let him into the hallway, Axl didn't make his usual beeline down the hall. Instead, he just sat on the cold floorboards, facing her. To shut the door now would mean shutting it in his face, literally. So Sidney listened. Nothing. She slipped into the hallway herself. The door to Titus's room was open.

Grasping Axl's collar, she led him into Titus's empty bedroom, wincing at the sound of the old dog's claws on the wooden floor. Once in Titus's room, she patted the low bed, encouraging him to jump up. He obliged. When he'd settled himself, she sat down on the edge of the bed beside him.

"Don't worry, I'll be okay," she whispered. Gosh, she hoped that was true! "It's just something I've got to do. I really don't want you to worry."

Axl lifted his big head. She stroked his fur. "I always wanted a dog. Thanks for hanging out with me. Seriously, you're the best. I'm glad we could be friends. But if there's one thing I wanted more than a dog, it was someone who could love my mom, and maybe me too. But especially her. Someone good enough for her. Someone who would love her and take care of her. Someone who would look at her cooking as more than just what she puts on the table, but for everything she puts into it. Like love.

"I know Scott loves her, and she loves him too. And if ever I could have wished for a dad, I'd want it to be him."

Axl's response was to lick her face.

She smiled, wiping the slobber with her coat sleeve. "Hey, want to know a secret?"

He just gave her more of those woeful eyes. She took that as a yes. "Every night since I got here, I've been wishing so hard that things would work out with Scott and my mom. I've been out to catch sight of that first star every evening. Well, almost every evening. I missed a couple of times but made up for it by wishing on hundreds of other stars. And I've been wishing like *really* hard. Hard as I could. But it hasn't worked. So the way I see it, I've got one shot left."

Axl lowered his head to the bed. After a few minutes, he began to softly snore. She got up carefully, missing his warmth immediately. Biting her lip, she tiptoed back into Ember's bedroom and closed the door behind her.

She grabbed her backpack and slung it on, steadied her breath, and moved toward the window. "Here goes."

She straddled the sill, then moved her second leg outside the window. Feeling for the trellis, she finally breathed when her right boot made contact. Supporting herself partially with her grip on the sill and partially with her toes, she lowered herself, one toe-hold at a time. Then came the point where she had to let go of the sill.

Oh wow! She shouldn't be doing this! It was dark and dangerous, and okay, maybe even a little bit stupid for someone like her who was supposed to be so smart. What if the trellis came loose? What if she slipped and broke a leg? Or cracked her head on the frozen ground? What if there were bears down there in the dark?

Yet she knew what was at stake, and despite everything, she hadn't been wishing hard enough.

There was this one shot left. One wish left, and she was barely holding on.

Sidney took a deep breath, then reached for the trellis with one hand. Securing her grip, she let go of the sill and reached for another handhold. Whew! The trellis held! Scott must have built the darned thing. It barely even creaked under her weight.

Slowly, carefully, she descended it.

# – forty-one –

APRIL WOKE with a bad feeling in the pit of her stomach.

She'd crawled into Scott's old twin bed with its extra-firm mattress just after nine o'clock. She'd let the tears come then, crying as she hadn't done since she was a new mother alone in the world. Crying like there was no tomorrow.

In a way, there wasn't.

When the tears finally dried up, she'd closed her eyes, more because they were painfully swollen than because she was tired. She wasn't sure she'd actually slept.

She glanced at the bedside clock. The digital readout read 1:32.

Okay, she'd definitely slept.

She was wide awake now, though, with that awful feeling gnawing in the pit of her stomach. Had all the tears she'd cried just distilled her misery? Solidified it? As she lay there analyzing the terrible dread, she felt it slithering up into her chest, pressing down on her like a weight.

She tossed the covers back, swung her bare legs out of bed. From this position, she could see her reflection in the dresser-top mirror. The moonlight streaming in through the window illuminated her eerily in shades of black, white and gray as she faced herself.

Or rather tried to face herself.

This was what she got for pretending.

Somewhere along the line, she'd fallen in love with Harkness. With the Standish clan.

Those *Jeopardy!* nights, Ember's quick wit. Her friendship, and Ocean's. Jace's kindness and mentoring. Titus's slightly uptight, by-the-book outlook. Oh, how Sidney loved to tease him! Then there was Arden and the care he took with everyone, including Sidney. And Faye. What she'd done for her little girl with the after-school tutoring was nothing short of amazing.

And they'd all loved her cooking. The Standishs had enjoyed it around the dining room table, and the wider community had snapped it up at the market.

*April Dawn's*. It might not have been the business success she'd dreamed about as a teenager, but it was hers and it was awesome.

She'd have to give that up too, for now. But she would make boatloads more money with K.Z. McCoy. After years of poverty—of food insecurity and not knowing if she'd be able to keep a roof over Sidney's head—the appeal of that kind of income could not be overstated. It meant security, something they'd never truly known. Not long term, anyway.

But worst of all, she'd fallen deeply, irrevocably in love with Scott. And she'd done it with such abandon.

She'd known all along. On some level, she *must* have known. Must have felt herself falling. She'd used logic to talk herself into the affair—no, to talk *Scott* into it. But then it had become something else.

Somewhere along the line, she'd moved from allowing herself the heady pleasure of intimacy with someone for whom she felt a rare attraction, a rare safety, to…well, to this. The point where contemplating never seeing him again—never having him smile at her across a room, never going into his arms at the end of the day, never running her fingers through that glossy, springy hair—made her feel bleak and empty.

But there was no help for it. Life was back to black and white. She and Sidney had to leave. April was going to work for K.Z. McCoy. That was settled. No room for negotiation. This…interlude, lovely as it had been, was over.

As much as her heart ached for herself, it hurt so much more for Sidney.

As adamant as her so-smart daughter had been about knowing the difference between pretending and reality, she really hadn't. Not deep down in her little girl heart.

Her little Ladybug.

Sidney had been four when April had dressed her as the world's cutest Ladybug. Sid had loved it. And she'd loved it all the more when April pretended she'd made the metamorphosis to a real red and black bug. But that was a Halloween long ago and far away from the Viking shield maiden from Minnesota she'd played just a few months ago.

Her precocious ten-year-old no longer believed in Santa or the Easter Bunny or any of that stuff. But *wishes*? Those she still believed in. She'd always been hardcore about not telling what she wished for when she blew out the candles on her birthday cakes, insisting the wish wouldn't come true if she told. And how many times had she turned her face up to the evening sky and said those words. *Star light, star bright, first star I see tonight. I wish I may, I wish I might, have this wish I wish tonight.*

Axl whined outside her door, and it was the most lonesome sound she'd ever heard. Then he whined again and chuffed out a tentative bark with it. More urgently.

That dread she'd awoken with suddenly took a bounding leap.

*Sidney.*

She was across the room and out the door in a flash. Axl, who was standing there in the hallway, turned his big worried eyes toward her. She hurried down the hall. Before she even opened the door to Sidney's room, she knew something was terribly wrong. Knew it from the temperature of the room.

She snapped on the light, hoping against hope. "Ladybug?"

Silence.

The bed. The Sidney-sized lump on the mattress looked sickeningly familiar. Two seconds later her fear was confirmed. She tossed the blankets back and the pillows rolled out. A small cushion from the downstairs sofa, Sidney's Canadiens jersey.

"No, no, no! This can't be happening."

She went to the open window, poked her head out and looked down. "Sidney?" There was no answer. And thank God, no broken child on the ground below.

Racing back to the bed, she pulled the bundle of blankets right off and shook them. Something hard hit the floor. Sid's phone. With a hideous sense of *déjà vu,* she tossed the bedding and bent to pick up the phone. After the last experience, she'd ensured the lock feature was disabled, so when she switched it on, she had no trouble getting into it. It opened to a picture. It was from Christmas—another strategically posed selfie. Sidney smiled in the foreground and just behind her, April and Scott sat on the love seat in the living room, looking into each other's eyes. The Christmas tree sparkled beside them.

She flipped through the other photos, but they were mostly of Axl, a few from around the farm, and a bunch with Sid and Danika acting silly.

She went back to the Christmas selfie. She knew it was no accident that she and Scott were framed in the background exchanging that intimate glance. And the look on Sidney's face was positively radiant, as though she were bursting with happiness.

Had her little girl imagined they'd become a family? April, Scott, and Sidney?

The thought made her want to burst into tears again, but she couldn't afford that luxury. She had to find Sid. "Think, April, think!"

*What else was missing*? She threw open the closet doors, looked high on the shelf. More *déjà vu*. The sleeping bag was gone. Shit! Not good.

What else? She looked around the room quickly. What had she taken last time she'd run away?

The telescope. It wasn't perched by the window where it should be.

"She took her telescope?"

The voice came from behind her. She whirled to see Scott standing in the door frame.

"Yes, she did. Her sleeping bag too. But how did you…?"

He reached down to soothe an anxious Axl with a pat on the head. "I was awake and saw the light come on. Then I saw you at the window," he said. "I knew something was wrong."

"Sid's gone," she said. "She's run away again."

"Let's not jump to conclusions. Let's check her friend's house."

"You think she might be at Danika's?" April dared to hope it. She'd still be pretty pissed, but it was better than stowing away in a vehicle and traveling hundreds of miles. Oh God. What if she had done that? Gotten into someone's car? She battled a surge of nausea.

"I'll call her father." Scott stepped out of the room and shot down the stairs to the house phone.

She went to the window and looked out on the yard below. Yes, there was some moonlight, but there were many more patches of impenetrable darkness where the light didn't reach. "Oh, Ladybug where are you?"

Below the kitchen door slammed, and April's heart leaped in her chest. *Oh, please let it be Sidney*.

She ran to the top of the stairs. Scott stared back up at her.

"She's not with Danika. Her father even woke her up to see

if she knew anything about Sid's whereabouts. She says she doesn't."

"What else?" There had to be a *what else*. She could tell by the look on his face. "What were you doing outside?"

"Her bicycle's gone."

# – forty-two –

THIS WAS it. The special place Scott had told her about. The place where the stars seemed close enough to pluck right out of the sky. The place he'd gone when he was sad. If ever there was a place to make a last-ditch, desperation wish, this was it.

She wished he'd told her how far it was, though. She'd almost turned back so many times, thinking maybe she'd set off in the wrong direction. But then the trees on the side of the road parted and she'd caught a glimpse of Harkness Mountain, much closer up than it looked from the farm. So she'd pressed on.

There was a little skiff of fresh snow on the shoulder of the road, and she found that offered better traction to her fat bicycle tires than the slicker, snow-packed pavement. But even at that, she'd spun out twice. The last time, she'd kinda hurt her elbow a bit breaking her fall. It still burned a little, which made her think she might have skinned it. Considering that she now had a tear in the elbow of her coat, that was a real possibility. But she hadn't quit.

Thankfully, she hadn't encountered any traffic. If she'd seen headlights, her plan was to hop off the bike, toss it up on the snowbank, crawl up there herself, and hope they drove on past without seeing her. No way would anyone in Harkness drive past a kid on a bike at midnight and just keep going.

They'd figure out who she was and take her back to her mother.

After pedaling for what seemed like forever, she found the turnoff to the mountain. She was relieved to see the road had been plowed recently. They usually kept it up pretty good so families could get out there for sledding, but it didn't always get plowed as quickly as the main roads.

Ten minutes later, she'd found the parking lot at the base of the mountain. The trails were well marked, so it was easy to find the one that took her to the river. She'd had a moment of panic when she reached the river's edge.

She would have to be very careful. The river was only partially frozen. It was sort of open right at the edge, then there were sheets of thin-looking ice stretching part way across from each side, but they didn't quite come together in the middle. When the moon came out from behind a cloud, she was able to see the current in the middle of the river. She turned left and headed upriver. And she did so on foot.

There the path had been beaten down by snowmobile traffic. Good for walking, but not so good for a bike. Not that she'd risk riding her bike so close to the river's edge anyway. If she took another spill, she might wind up in the water.

She'd never been to Slamm's Landing before, but she knew it even before she got there. Knew it from the increasing loudness of the river. Scott had said it was right beside a rapids where the river narrowed. Because the water rushed so fast, there wasn't much ice at all. Just a little at the edges.

Then she spied the rock. Scott had told her it was pinkish sandstone, but in the dark, all she could see was the parts that were snow-covered. She'd have to be careful. It was likely to be slippery, and her tired legs were turning to rubber.

She made it up onto the big rock without too much trouble. Without trees to shelter it, the powdery snow had pretty much blown clear, leaving the rock exposed. Moving gingerly, she found a place to sit down. She brushed a bit of snow from the perch, then took her sleeping bag from her backpack. Folding it into a thick cushion, she put it on the rock, then parked her butt on it. Perfect. Later she might climb inside the bedroll, but for now, she'd just sit on it.

She took a moment to glance up at the sky. It looked pretty clear, but she knew there were some drifting clouds up there. They'd blocked the moon plenty of times on the drive out here. But right now, it was clear and stars shone like diamonds.

She hopped up and assembled the telescope. As she was preparing to look through it, one of those clouds drifted over the moon. She tipped her head up, knowing the stars would seem even brighter without the moon's wash of light. And darned if Scott wasn't right! The whole sky was strewn with stars. Totally plastered from horizon to horizon! Their cold pinpoints seeming to grow bigger, closer, with the moon's retreat.

Forgetting about the telescope for now, she went back to sit on her sleeping bag. Her plan was to stay there until dawn, wishing on every star she could. And then she'd wish a while longer, because even when you couldn't see the stars anymore, they were still there. Scott said so. He'd promised it was true.

She turned back, intending to try out the telescope, but the sleeve of her jacket hit the tripod. Before she could grab it, it fell off the rock, landing on the thin ice inches from the rushing water.

Oh, no! Not her telescope! Scott had given it to her. She couldn't lose it.

She *wouldn't* lose it.

Setting her mouth like Scott did when he tackled a tough job, she slid down off the rock the same way she'd clambered up. Then she made her way around it and down to the water's edge. The telescope lay just out of her reach, frustratingly close but just a bit too far. She stepped one foot onto the ice and pressed. It creaked but didn't give. If it would just bear her weight for a second, she could lean down, snatch the telescope, and leap back.

She put a little more weight on the ice. It creaked again but held.

Maybe if she took her coat off, she could use it to try to snag the telescope and pull it closer. Except what if her coat got wet? She was already colder than she could ever remember being after riding her bike all the way out here. If she got her coat wet, that would suck. Same with the sleeping bag.

And what if she missed and knocked the telescope into the water?

Maybe she should go break a branch off a tree and use that instead. A branch would offer more control than a floppy coat or the sleeping bag. Except she'd have to trek quite a ways back or forward along the trail to reach a tree. There were no trees close to the water right here. Because, duh, if there were trees overhanging the river, it wouldn't be the perfect place to look at the stars.

And she was getting tired, really tired now. She really didn't want to walk way back to the trees.

She heard a splashing sound and looked down to see that a tiny rogue wave had caught the edge of the telescope, spinning it closer to the water. Shoot! If she left now to get a branch, it could be gone by the time she got back, swallowed by the Prince River.

Okay, she'd do it really quick

Taking a deep breath, she stepped on the ice and reached for her telescope.

# – forty-three –

"WHERE DO you think she'd go?"

April shrugged helplessly. "I don't know. But Scott, look at this."

She passed him Sid's phone. His heart squeezed in his chest when he saw the photo. Him and April trading a lover's glance on Christmas day, and Sid smiling almost slyly in the foreground.

He gave the phone back to her. Clutching it, she looked up at him, a world of agony in her eyes. "God, this is all my fault. I let her play that pretend game."

"Don't beat yourself up," he said gruffly. "If you want to start down that road, there's no end to it. If I hadn't offered you the job, if I hadn't practically twisted your arm to make you stay, both of you would have been gone from Harkness the day after you landed here."

"Yeah, but we'd have been in Dartmouth with my brother." She grimaced. "There's no way *that* would have been better for Sid than the months she's had here. I just wish…"

Her voice broke. She looked so miserable, he couldn't resist the urge to comfort her. He put his arms around her and she pressed herself against his chest.

"I'm so scared," she said. "Should we call the police? Search and rescue?"

He could have pointed out that Titus represented the better part of S&R in the region and he was off with Ocean. He'd come at top speed, though, if Scott called him.

"Before we hit the panic button, let's go see if we can track her," he said. "She's on her bike; maybe Axl can help us determine direction of travel."

Two minutes later, they were both bundled up against the cold. It wasn't a terribly bitter night, thank God, but Scott knew how cold it would be on a bicycle. Granted, it wasn't as dramatic as on a motorcycle, but the wind generated by speed still stole your body warmth.

Scott had also paused to grab a search and rescue bag. Titus always kept several of them at the ready.

Axl tromped out the front door ahead of them. He circled around, then headed down the hard-packed snow of the driveway as fast as his arthritic old legs could carry him. At the mouth of the driveway, he did another circle, then took off down the road.

"Good boy," Scott called, and they loped after him. After about a hundred yards, a bicycle track appeared in the loose snow on the shoulder.

"Look!" He pointed to the tracks. "She must have found it less slippery on the shoulder. We'll be able to follow her now."

"Oh, thank God!"

He called Axl back. Reluctantly, the dog returned, but he made a weird yodeling noise at Scott as though to tell him he was making a mistake.

"It's okay, boy. We're going after her, but we'll do it in Uncle Arden's Jeep." He turned to April. "Can you wait here with Axl while I go get the vehicle?"

She was already reaching for Axl's collar. "Got him. Hurry!"

He raced back down the road, sticking to the shoulder as Sid had done. The driveway had never seemed so long. Then he had to duck into the house to grab Uncle Arden's keys. With zero regard for the engine, he fired up the old Jeep, put it in gear and shot off down the drive.

When he stopped for them, Axl was unable to get up into the vehicle by himself. April went to lift him, but Scott told her to hang on; the old dog was heavier than he looked. He hopped out and helped Axl into the back seat while April jumped into the front. He was back behind the wheel and letting out the clutch while April was still fumbling with the seatbelt.

He glanced at her. "Can you get it fastened?"

He heard the seatbelt click home.

"Yeah, got it."

"I've got to keep an eye out for deer and moose," he said. "I can still scan back and forth and see her bike track, but if it changes, make sure I don't miss it."

"Like that?" She pointed, but he'd already seen it. A patch on the shoulder of the road where the snow had been scraped down to the gravel beneath.

"Looks like she wiped out."

"Oh, no!" She put a hand to her mouth. "She must have skidded on the ice."

"It's okay," he said. "Her trail starts again up there. See?"

She looked further down the road to where the tire tracks resumed. "I hope she's not hurt."

"Doesn't look like anything too serious," he said. "She probably tried the snow pack on the road a while after her spill, but decided to get back on the shoulder."

About a mile down the road, they found another wipeout spot. This time, Sid had obviously just gotten up and continued on the shoulder. Good girl.

"How far could she have gone?" Beside him, April was getting tenser by the moment. "And where the heck could she be headed? She's got to be so cold."

Up ahead, his headlights illuminated the sign for Old

Mountain Road. As he drew closer, he could see Sid had taken it.

*Shit*. He knew where she'd gone. *Shit, shit, shit.*

He started braking.

"Oh, God!" April said when she saw the road sign and the evidence of Sid's wobbly turn. "Does she know where Slamm's Landing is? That you used to go there for the view of the stars?"

"I've told her about it," he said, cursing himself. "Enough that she can probably find it."

*Or get herself in trouble trying to find it.*

He took his eyes off the road long enough to glance at April. She looked grim, her face ghostly white.

"How fast can we go on this surface?" she said, her voice eerily calm.

"We're about to find out." He punched the accelerator and the Jeep leaped forward. Thankfully, Uncle Arden believed in studded winter tires. They gripped the snow-packed surface as he sped along. In the back seat, Axl whined anxiously.

In just under six minutes, they pulled into the parking lot at the base of Harkness Mountain. Sid's bike track led straight across the parking lot to the big sign with the trail map. And there it was! Her bike. She'd obviously abandoned it.

He brought the Jeep to a skidding halt and they piled out. There was enough snow that they should be able to track her without the aid of a dog, but Axl wasn't about to be left behind. He yipped sharply. Scott opened the door to grab his S&R backpack and Axl leaped out. As Scott strapped the heavy bag on, the old dog loped toward the river trail.

He turned to April and offered his hand. "Come on."

She took it, and together they sprinted off after Axl.

"We're almost there," he told April after a few moments. "She'll be all right."

"Oh, God, she has to be. If not…God, Scott."

"She's fine. Bound to be cold. I'll give her my coat. And

she'll warm up quickly in the Jeep. It's got a good little heater."

He thought some of the tension went out of her, so kept it up. "You said she took her sleeping bag, right? So it's not like she doesn't have something for extra warmth. And—"

A sharp, short scream rang out. Sidney's scream.

April yanked her hand free of Scott's. "Go!" she shouted. "You can reach her faster. Help her, Scott."

"I'll get her."

He took off, racing as fast as the footing would allow. His breath sawed in and out as he ran, the cold air searing his lungs, and his muscles screamed from the exertion.

*Don't let me be too late. Please God, don't let me be too late.*

# – forty-four –

SCOTT'S HEART leaped into his throat when he rounded the bend and saw Sid stand up in frigid knee-deep water and try to step out. Before his horrified eyes, she slipped on the ridge of ice at the edge and went down again, right on her butt. Even that close to shore, he knew the pull of the rapids would be strong, especially with the weight of Sidney's waterlogged wear. Axl had reached her and was barking frantically up on the bank.

"Hang on, Sid!" He called, putting on an extra burst of speed.

As he covered the last few yards, he saw Axl wade partially into the water. His back feet were on the snowy bank, but his front end was submerged to his chest. Sid clutched at his fur and the old dog held his ground. Seconds later, Scott arrived. The water was shallow at the edge but deceptively fast-moving. And Sid was sitting in it, soaked to the skin, trying not to get pulled away by the current.

He waded in, pushing past Axl. Quickly, he scooped her up. Instantly, his own clothes were soaked, but he didn't give a damn. She'd probably been pretty damned cold before she fell in. Now she was in immediate danger from hypothermia.

Axl backed out of the water and shook himself. Dammit, he'd be a hypothermia risk too.

"I'm sorry, Scott." The words came out through clacking and chattering teeth. "I lost the telescope. It f…f…fell off the wishing rock, and I t-t-tried to get it back, but the ice broke."

"Oh, honey, don't worry about that. We can get you another telescope any old day. But we can't get another Sid the Kid." He looked up the trail. April was running toward them as fast as she could.

"I think you brought a sleeping bag, didn't you?" he asked, glancing around.

"It's up there." Her voice sounded a little slurred.

He had to move fast. "I'm just going to put you down a second so I can get at my stuff. I've got a really great space blanket in here and some warming packs. Does that sound good?"

"Y-y-yes."

April skidded to a halt beside him before he could put Sid down.

"Oh, Sidney. You must be freezing."

"Can you take her?" he said. "I've got to get the stuff out of my pack."

She took Sidney from his arms.

As he shrugged out of the pack and started assembling what he needed, he heard Sidney chattering out broken apologies while April hugged her tight and assured her everything was all right.

"Okay, let's get her out of her clothes," he said. "We need to get her dry and get her body temperature up as fast as we can."

April met his eyes, her own rounding at the seriousness in his.

"Come on, Sidney, let's get this stuff off." She sank down on the snow so Sid was sitting on her lap. Between April's efforts and Scott's, they got her boots and pants off. Scott immediately swaddled her lower half in a dry blanket before they removed her coat. He'd hoped she could keep her sweater on, but the lower hem was wet too, so off it came. He pulled the blanket up to cover her bareness.

"We need to wrap her in this heavy duty space blanket, but let me fetch the sleeping bag first. We'll get her swaddled in three layers."

April nodded, pulling her daughter closer. "Hang in there, Sidney. Scott has a plan. He's got all the search and rescue stuff. It's going to be all right."

"I know," Sid said simply.

He bounded up onto the rock. Her sleeping bag was there and reasonably dry. It looked like she'd been sitting on it, using it for insulation against the cold rock. He hopped back down. By the time he reached the girls, he had the sleeping bag unzipped. He dug out the heavy duty Mylar blanket and lined the sleeping bag with it. Then he reached for Sid. She was shivering rhythmically now.

"Come on, sweetheart. Time to bundle you up like a burrito."

He took a blanket-wrapped Sid from her mother's arms and placed her on the Mylar. April started to tuck the crinkly blanket around her, but he stopped her. "Just a sec. We need to put some of these in with her." He handed her a couple of heat packs. "Just tear the package open and they'll start heating up."

When they had a couple of body warming packs started, he tucked them around her. With April's help, he swaddled her with the reflective blanket, then zipped her into the sleeping bag. Within minutes, she was wrapped up as snug as he could make her.

"Can you feel the warmth yet, Ladybug?" April asked.

Sid nodded sleepily. "I think so."

Scott's own feet felt like blocks of ice. He couldn't imagine how cold poor Sid was.

Working quickly, he gathered stuff up and shoved it back in the search and rescue bag, then strapped it on securely.

He'd leave the damned thing there, but if Sid ran into trouble, he might need some of the other supplies.

"How are we going to get her back to the car?"

"I'll carry her." He bent and took the precious load from April. "I'll get her back as fast as I can and get the heat blasting in the Jeep."

Tears sprang to her eyes. "Thank you, Scott. I'll be right behind you."

She would have to be. She was pretty wet now too.

"Can you dig my phone out of my coat's right-hand pocket? You'll need to call Ember and tell her what's happened."

"Of course." She took off her wet glove and fished his phone out.

"Ask her to meet us at the house," he said. "She'll know if Sid needs a hospital or whether she's okay at home."

"I will. Now go! Run!"

He did.

# – forty-five –

APRIL WAS still shivering when they pulled into the yard. For that matter, so was Axl, sitting on the back seat beside her.

They were met at the door by Jace and Ember.

"Bring her right up to her room," Ember instructed. "Jace, can you get the blankets out of the dryer?"

"On it."

By the time Scott got her up to the room, Jace was there with flannel sheets hot out of the dryer. While he spread one on the bed, Ember stepped in to help unwrap Sid. Feeling useless, April watched as Ember directed Scott to deposit Sidney on the warm blanket. Immediately, she pulled it snugly around her. Jace then piled on several more hot blankets and he and Ember tucked them around Sidney.

"How you doing, Sid?" Ember asked. "I hear you went for a polar dip."

"Only by accident," she said. "Polar dips are stupid."

"I'm just going to get your vitals, but I'll be real quick about it." Ember dug one of Sid's thin arms out of the warm cocoon of blankets, took her pulse and a quick blood pressure reading. She removed her stethoscope and tucked Sidney's arm away again.

"How is it?" April asked anxiously.

Ember glanced up at her and smiled reassuringly. "So far,

so good. You've got a strong kid here." She produced a digital thermometer and applied it to Sid's ear. It beeped right away and Ember checked the readout. "Whoa, you're a pretty cool cat, Sid."

April twisted her hands together. "Does she need to go to the hospital?"

Ember shook her head, stashing her medical stuff back in her bag. "No, she's going to be just fine, thanks to you guys. We need to bring her body temperature up, but that first aid wrap was outstanding. Getting her out of her wet clothes and bundling her like that…well, it made all the difference. Good job, guys."

"That was all Scott." Tears welled in April's eyes as she turned toward him. "I don't know what would have happened if you hadn't been there…"

"Hey," Ember jumped up from her perch on the edge of the bed. "I think you guys both need to get under a hot shower yourselves." She ushered April and Scott toward the door. "I'll stay with Sid until you guys are warm and dry."

"Axl needs attention too," Scott said. "He was first on the scene and waded in to give Sid a hand."

"I'm on it," Jace said, then turned to Ember. "What do you recommend? Towel him off and give him the hot blanket treatment?"

"I'm no vet, but that sounds good to me. If he gets too hot, he'll let you know by crawling out from under the quilts. Right, Sid?"

"Right," Sid confirmed.

Clearly her daughter had tried to snuggle Axl under her quilts a time or two.

"Titus keeps Metacam for when his arthritis flares," Scott said. "I'll dig it out and make sure he gets a full dose. He's going to need it with all the running he did tonight, never mind the cold dip."

"That'd be great," Ember said, waving them all out of the

room. "Now everybody, go and do what you need to do. That's an order."

Jace hustled downstairs to deal with the dog, leaving Scott and April standing outside Ember's bedroom door, which Ember had firmly closed behind them.

April promptly burst into tears.

"Whoa, honey, it's okay." He pulled her into his arms. "You heard the doctor. Sid's going to be all right."

"My poor girl." She drew a deep breath and let it shudder out. "She must have been so scared when she fell in. God, she'll probably have nightmares about it for months to come. She's still half frozen, and there I was, reminding her what might have happened…" She made a choking sound, half laugh, half sob. "No wonder Ember ejected me."

"That's her job as Sid's doctor." He tipped her chin up forcing her to meet his earnest eyes. "And your job as her mom is to hop in the shower right now, then get into your warmest pajamas so you can go curl up with her."

"I know." She reached up and touched his face. "I'll pull myself together. For her sake, I will. But it just scares me so much when I think about it. If I hadn't woken up, and if Axl hadn't whined and paced in the hallway, I wouldn't have noticed that she'd run off. And if we didn't know she was missing, we wouldn't have gone out in search of her. She might have died out there from hypothermia. With wet clothes and nothing but that sleeping bag…"

"I know." He pressed her head into his chest and hugged her tighter than he'd ever hugged her. Hard enough to drive half the breath from her lungs. Close enough that she felt the emotion vibrating through him. "Jesus, April. I don't think I've ever been so scared."

Knowing that he was just as shaken up as she was actually helped calm her. Or maybe it was the tightness of the hug. They clung together for long moments until finally, he loosened his grip. But he didn't let her go entirely, keeping a grasp on her shoulders, gently massaging them. A shiver went through her. He must have felt it because he released her.

"What am I thinking? Go hit the shower," he said gruffly. "I'm going to check in on Axl and give him his meds."

"Okay."

Feeling a little less shaky, she made her way down the hall.

The hot water felt like pure heaven, but as soon as she was reasonably warm, she shut it off. Scott had gotten much wetter than she had. She wanted to make sure there was plenty of hot water left for him.

God, he'd saved her girl. His foresight to bring the search and rescue kit, his knowledge of first aid. His strength and stamina to get her back to the car so quickly. Even thinking to call ahead to put Ember on alert. April wasn't sure she'd have thought of that. She'd been so frantic.

Realizing that she'd been staring at herself in the steamed-up mirror for God knew how long, she gave her still damn hair another toweling, hung the towel up, cinched her robe, and left the bathroom.

She almost bumped into Scott in the hall as she stepped out of the bathroom. "How's Axl?"

"Feeling pretty good under all those heated blankets, I think. Jace missed his calling. I predict that when the meds come on line, old Axl will sleep like a puppy."

"Thank God for that dog." She blinked rapidly. "Now it's your turn to get warm. I think I left you lots of hot water."

"I'm pretty sure you did. I expected you to be in there a lot longer. I hope you didn't cut it short for me. I was just on my way to shed these wet clothes and get into something of Titus's."

She grinned. Obviously, dipping into Titus's closet was a better solution than running out to the loft in the cold to change, but the idea of him wearing his brother's clothes struck her as comical. Scott was nicely muscled—just the way she liked, in fact—but Titus was wickedly ripped from all that gym work and the S&R training.

He laughed. “I know what you’re thinking. But I’m hoping he has some older clothes from before he went crazy with the weights.”

Her smile faded. “I don’t care what you look like, just come to me when you’re done, okay? To me and Sidney.”

“Just try to stop me.”

He put a hand on her warm nape, which made her shiver, but not from the cold. He leaned in and kissed her, careful not to get her robe wet. It was a quick, fierce kiss.

He released her and strode away seconds later, leaving her reeling. But she didn’t know what affected her more, the kiss or that very emphatic statement.

# – forty-six –

SCOTT'S HEART pounded ridiculously hard as he made his way down the hall to Ember's room toward Sid and April. Toward everything that mattered. How could he have been so stupid? So blind?

So scared.

He'd made a freakin' career out of scared. Running from strong emotion, from attachment. From love, dammit. But he was done with that. No more.

The only thing he was scared of now was that it might be too late.

The door to Sid's room was closed. He tapped on it and April called for him to come in. He did. The reason for the closed door became quickly evident. They'd plugged in a fan-forced portable heater. Sid lay in the middle of the bed, bracketed by April on one side and Ember on the other. She now wore fleecy pajamas. Scott was willing to bet Jace had pre-heated the PJs in the overworked dryer too. She sat reclined against the pillows, with both arms out from under the blankets, which he took as a very good sign.

"Good grief!" Ember said. "You look like a scarecrow."

He looked down at the sweats he'd dug out of Titus's room. The athletic pants weren't too horrible. They were loose at the waist, but the drawstring solved that. At least he hadn't had to roll the bottoms up. He couldn't say the same for the Title Boxing classic hoodie. Without his brother's bulk filling it out, the sleeves reached his fingertips and the waist hung so low, it looked like he was trying to conceal a muffin top. Which he sort of was, with all that material bunched under the drawstring of the athletic pants.

"That'll be enough out of you," he said, giving Ember a stern look. "Have you forgotten that I lived through the nineties with you? I mean, crimped hair? On a redhead? Scrunchies? That weird lip liner thing…"

"Enough said." Ember held up her hands.

He went to the foot of the bed, rolling up his sleeves as he went. "How you doing, kiddo?"

"Better," Sid said, dipping her head almost shyly. "Jace brought that hot fan and some hot water bottles." She lifted the blankets to look under. "I've got one on either side. Oh, and a heating pad at my feet, but I have to wear some of Mom's big wooly socks to make sure I don't get burned. I think I'm finally warmed up."

He looked at his sister. "What do you say, Dr. Standish? Is Sid the Kid no longer a cool cat?"

Ember smiled. "I'm happy to say she is not. Temp's very acceptable. I'd like to see an adult sleep with her tonight, though, to share body warmth. She shouldn't have any trouble regulating her temperature, but it couldn't hurt."

"Oh, I planned to do that," April said.

Ember nodded. "I knew you wouldn't let her out of your sight. Just wanted to make sure you'd snuggle in the same bed." She glanced around the room. "I'd take that heating pad out before you settle down, and maybe even ratchet that heater back a bit at the same time."

"Would you and Jace consider staying?" Scott asked. "Titus's bed is free."

"Of course we will. I expect Jace has already changed the bedding." She grinned. "I'm not really worried. I mean, Sid's doing great, as you can see. But if you do have any questions or concerns, I'd rather be on hand, you know?"

"Thank you." April reached across Sid to squeeze Ember's hand. "You don't know what this means to me."

"Happy to do it," she said. "But again, you guys did all the heavy lifting with the pre-care." She squeezed April's hand back, then slid out of the bed. "I think I'll leave you now, if you're good?" She glanced at April for her approval.

April nodded. "We're good. Go take care of Jace. He's been running himself ragged looking after everyone else."

"I will." Her smile was a little too wicked for Scott's taste. "He's certainly earned a special reward, I think."

"Whoa." It was Scott who threw up his hands this time. "TMI."

Ember laughed, then batted her eyes innocently at him. "What? I meant a relaxing massage."

"Of course you did."

"Or a game of Scrabble," Sid offered, quietly.

Everyone laughed, and it was more with relief that the little girl had made a joke than the joke itself.

"See you in the morning, Sid the Kid."

"'Night, Ember. And thanks. Those warm blankets were the best thing I ever felt."

"They are pretty awesome, aren't they?" Still grinning, Ember left, closing the door behind her to preserve the heat. Or maybe their privacy.

Now that he had the girls to himself, Scott felt awkward. Tongue-tied. He moved around to the side of the bed Ember had just vacated.

Sid looked up at him with those big, luminous eyes suddenly brimming with tears. "How's Axl? He got awful wet helping me."

"He's doing great," he said. "Jace dried him really well—even used a hairdryer on him. His hair kind of looks a bit fluffy now. Then he gave the old boy the same warm blanket routine you got. We also gave him some pain medicine in case his bones ache from all the excitement."

"I'm so sorry." The gathered tears spilled. "I didn't mean for him to get wet or worn out. I didn't mean for anything bad to happen. I just wanted…" Her words trailed off and she looked away, blinking rapidly.

"I think I know what you were doing up there," he said gently, as she dashed away tears. "You went up there to wish on the stars, right? Because of the story I told you about how they're so close."

She nodded. April handed her a tissue and she blotted her face.

"Blow," April instructed.

Sid blew her nose noisily, then crumpled up the tissue. "I know it was dangerous. But it was my last chance. I was going to wish on all the stars I could until they faded away, and then I was going to wish and wish some more, as hard as I could. Because the stars are still there, right? Even when we can't see them?"

He recognized the words as his own. "They are," he said, sitting down on the edge of her bed. "I promise you they're always there."

She ducked her head again and her lower lip trembled. "So when we're in Boston and I look up at the stars, they'll be the same ones as you'll be seeing in Alberta?"

"Absolutely. But about that…" He looked across Sid to her mother. "Would you mind if your mom and I talked privately?"

Sid looked up, her incredulous gaze going from one adult to the other. "Uh…you want me to leave?"

April's eyes had widened at Scott's words, but she had to smother a smile at Sid's reaction.

"No way," he said. "You stay there with all that heating apparatus. Your mom and I will just step into the hall for a few minutes. Would that be okay? We'll be right outside, and I won't keep her too long."

"Take your time," Sid said, a completely different gleam coming into her eyes, one that owed nothing to the shimmer of tears. The kid was sharp. "Keep her as long as you like. The heat is making me sleepy anyway." She produced a convincing yawn.

He stood, looking at April. "Shall we?"

She gave Sid a kiss on the top of her head. "Be right back."

He followed her out of the room, pulling the door closed behind him.

April could feel her pulse throbbing in her throat. What could he have to say that he couldn't say in there?

"Marry me."

*What?* Sudden tears stung her eyes and made her throat ache. "That's not funny, Scott. I've had a long day and I can't…" She shook her head. "I just can't."

He took her hand. "I'm serious, April. I love you. I love you so damned much."

"I love you too." The tears she'd been holding back for the whole tension-fraught night finally spilled. "But that's not the only consideration here, is it?"

"Come here, baby."

He pulled her into his arms, crushing her against him. A powerful tremble went through him, so strong she felt it in her own bones. Her tears just kept coming.

"It's okay," he soothed. "I've got you. And I'm not letting you go."

*Not letting her go?* She pulled in a deep breath and let it shudder out. If only he meant that. She pressed her face to his shirt—Titus's shirt, she supposed, but it smelled already of Scott—and drew another breath. If only she could stay here in his arms. But she couldn't. She needed to stand on her own.

She pulled back. He loosened his grip but didn't release her entirely.

"I do love you, Scott Standish." She looked up into his warm eyes. "I really do. I said I was just pretending, but I think we both know that for the fiction it was. But I can't marry you. Sidney needs—*I* need—stability. Permanence. Security. Belonging." She blinked away fresh tears. "We can't follow you from pillar to post. I can't have Sid switching schools every whipstitch, making new friends only to leave them behind. And I won't sign up for a relationship where we see you between jobs or on major holidays." God, this was killing her. She wanted so badly to stay in Harkness and do just that—take whatever crumbs he could give her—but she and Sid deserved better.

He tipped her chin up. His expression was so tender, she wanted to cry again. "Are you finished?"

She took a deep breath and exhaled. "Yes."

"Good. So now you can listen to me."

Her brows shot up.

"I don't want that either, and I wouldn't ask you guys to sign up for it. I want to marry you because I want to spend every day of the rest of my life with you. You and Sid."

Her heart twisted in her chest like it was being squeezed by a vice. She stepped back, out of his arms. "Don't say that."

"Why not? I mean it."

"I'm sure you do. At this moment, with that close call with Sid, I'm sure you—"

"I know my own mind, April." He raked a hand through his still damp hair, making it stand up. "And yes, it took a kick in the ass to wake me up. It took seeing Sid out there…" His voice broke.

She wanted to take him in her arms, pull his head down to her breast. She wanted to hold him close and comfort him as he had comforted her so many times. But she didn't move a muscle. She was afraid it would stop his words altogether.

She wet her lips. "It took seeing Sid out there to what?"

He swallowed, his throat moving convulsively. "I lost my parents when I was just a kid. I survived the accident, but they didn't. There wasn't a damned thing I could do to save them, or to change that. Then I came here and everyone tried so hard to make me feel like part of the family. My adoptive mother became my new mom." He smiled faintly. "Of course, I tried to resist, but she was having none of that."

She blinked. "I'm glad."

"I definitely had my issues with belonging, but not through anyone else's fault. Not my family's, not the community's. But it seems like I circled and circled but never settled in quite the way they wanted." He rolled his shoulders. "Uncle Arden calls me son, but I was never able to call him dad. And Ember and Titus…"

"I know that Ember and Titus count you as their brother," she said softly. "Surely you don't doubt that?"

"I don't. And life was good. Well, until Mom got diagnosed with cancer. It wasn't so bad the first time. Or maybe I was too young to know how bad it really was. But then it came back again… Jesus—*metastatic breast cancer*." A muscle leaped in his jaw. "Those words make my stomach knot up even now. I read up on it by then, after she had the primary cancer. When it came back, I knew it was going to take her, probably sooner rather than later. And I felt so helpless. I just couldn't watch it. I couldn't. I was so…powerless. So I cut and ran.

"Except the Standish code is to take care of our women. That was not so much drilled into me as modeled by Uncle Arden and Titus. Not that Mom and Ember needed coddling. Mom was one of the strongest women I'll ever know, and well, you know Ember."

April laughed, but it came out more like a choked sob. "Yes, I do."

"But regardless, that was the code: protect the women.

Take care of them. But I defaulted on it. I couldn't stand to see my mother suffering, to witness that horrible decline. So I…took off. I ran away."

She'd known some of this stuff since Montreal. Scott was not the type to spill his guts, but one night after she'd given him the highlights from her train wreck of a childhood, he'd opened up about losing his parents and then his second mother. But she hadn't realized how badly he thought he'd failed everyone.

"I feel like I abdicated my right to be called a Standish."

His words broke her heart. "Oh, Scott, no! No one believes that."

"Maybe not. But I did. That's why it's always been so hard to come home, even though home never lost its pull. That's why it's been hard to stay, here or anywhere." He took a deep breath and looked her straight in the eye. "But not anymore."

Her heart pounded in her throat. Was he saying that he was done wandering? "Scott, there's no need to—"

"There's every need, April. And I mean it. I'm a changed man."

"I don't understand." She pressed a hand to her chest, as though she could calm her crazily beating heart. "I mean, what changed? This is just so fast. How…?"

"It *was* fast," he agreed. "But sometimes that's all it takes for your world to shift—a matter of seconds."

Despite herself, she felt a wild spurt of hope. "Go on."

"It hit me as I was running along that path by the river, desperately trying to get to Sid, that the only thing worse than the hellish torture I was suffering at that second was the thought of *not* being there to try. Not being here to keep the both of you safe, to take care of you."

She heard his words, but she heard one louder than the rest. *Here.*

She wet her lips. "You said not being *here* to keep us safe. Do you mean *here* here, as in Harkness?"

"Harkness, Boston." He held her gaze with blazing determination. "*Where* is up to you. If you want to jump on the offer from K.Z. McCoy, I'll move with you. I have dual citizenship, and with my construction skills, I'd have no problem landing work."

Her head still whirled with questions, but there was no denying the happiness rising in her chest. *Rising?* God, it was unspooling in joyful ribbons and shooting streamers, filling her to bursting. Escaping, finally, in tears.

"You'd really go to Boston?"

"I'd go to the ends of the earth with you if you'll have me," he declared. "Because wherever you are will be home. We can make it home."

The tears streamed down her cheeks. "Are you sure?"

"I've never been more sure of anything in my life." He took her face in his hands and kissed her tear-wet cheeks, her nose, her eyes. Then he lifted his head. "I love you, April Dawn Morgan. I love you so damned much. I want to be with you and Sid, wherever you choose to make your home. Marry me."

The door to Ember's bedroom flew open and Sid, clad in her fleecy pajamas, burst into the hall.

"Say yes, Mom! Say yes!"

April choked back a laugh even as she stepped back from Scott's arms. She should have known Sidney would be eavesdropping. She wiped her damp cheeks. "So, you think I should accept?"

"Yes!" Her daughter's face looked sharp with excitement, but it was also kind of pinched with anxiety, as though she was afraid April could still mess this up. "You *have* to," she said earnestly. "It was in the stars, right?"

April blinked, then turned back to Scott with a tremulous smile. "Well, in that case, what can I do but surrender to fate?"

He grinned. "You'll marry me?"

"I will."

Scott hauled her into his arms for a crushing bear hug. Then he pulled back a few inches and held an arm out to Sidney in invitation. “Come here, Sid. Family hug.”

Sidney flung herself at them, hugging both of them around the waist as hard as her little arms would allow.

♡

Scott couldn’t remember feeling fuller, happier, more at peace with himself than he did right now with his arms securely around the woman he loved and her precious, funny, smart daughter. And for the first time since childhood, he no longer felt that chill that had been part of him for so long. Miraculously, he’d finally found his home, right here in this circle of arms.

Then Sidney shivered, reminding him she needed to be in bed.

He rubbed his hand over her back. “Hey, Kid, you’re still cold. Let’s get you under those blankets again.”

She leaned back to look up at him. “Will you help tuck me in?”

He looked to April for direction. She smiled and stepped back.

“Sure thing,” he said to Sid. “Want a lift, or want to do it under your own steam?”

She held her arms up in answer. Scott scooped her up and carried her back into Ember’s bedroom. April pulled the blankets back and he lowered his burden into the bed. She gave him a last hug with her thin arms before releasing his neck, and his throat tightened.

He helped April tuck the covers around Sid.

“So, if you’re going to marry my mother, does this mean you’ll be my dad?”

That tightness in his throat became an ache. “I’d like that,” he said, realizing just how much he meant it. Realizing finally on a bone-deep level how much Uncle Arden had meant it when he'd spoken those words to Scott all those years ago. "And if you're comfortable calling me Dad, I'd like that too."

"Oh, yes! I really want that."

"Good." Beside him, he heard April sniffle.

"But maybe not right away." Sid looked from Scott to her mother, then back again. "Maybe I could start calling you that after you guys get married, if that's okay with you?" She looked up, searching his face nervously as though gauging his reaction. "I'd feel like you were really my dad then."

He nodded gravely. "I think that would be perfect timing. It would be official then, don't you think?"

Sid's relief was palpable. "Exactly! That's what I meant—official."

April sent him a grateful look. Her face was blotchy and her eyes a little bloodshot from the tears she'd shed, but he'd never seen anything more beautiful.

"So where are we going to live?"

Scott looked down at Sid, then back at April. "That Boston offer sounded like a once-in-a-lifetime opportunity," he said. "If you want to pursue it, I'll go with you."

"Turns out I've had a better offer." April smiled at him, her heart in her eyes, then looked down at her daughter. "I think we should stay right here in Harkness, don't you?"

"Yes!" Sid's thin arm emerged from the blanket to do a fist pump. "Thank you, Mom! I mean, anywhere would be okay if we're all together, but I really wanted to stay here with Arden and Axl. And Titus and Ember, of course. And my friends at school."

"I'm glad, Ladybug." April pulled back. "I mean…if it's okay I call you that again."

"You know it is. I…I should have never—"

"It's okay, Ladybug. It really is."

"Whoa!" Sid's eyes widened and she sat up. "I just thought of something."

"What?" April asked.

Sid turned her eyes from her mother to Scott. "Do you think Arden would mind if… I mean, when everything's *official*, do you think he'd mind if I called him Grandpa Arden?"

Scott's aching throat closed. He had to swallow before he could answer. "I can safely say he'd be honored, Sid. Really."

She looked pleased, but then her brows drew together in a frown that reminded him so much of her mother. "Do you think he'll mind waiting until after the wedding? I probably shouldn't start calling him Grandpa until after I start calling you Dad."

There he went with the feels again. He took a breath and let it out. "Honey, Arden is the most patient man in the world. He'll wait as long as it takes. That's a promise."

Her frown deepened. "But you're not going to wait a long time to get married, are you? Like Ember and Jace? I can't believe they're waiting a *whole year*."

"I hope not," he said. "I'd marry your mother tomorrow if I could."

"That could work. I'm free tomorrow," Sid said.

April laughed. "That might be a little soon." A delicate blush rose into her cheeks as she met Scott's gaze. "But no, I don't wait to wait a long time, either. We can talk about it later."

They'd definitely be doing that. Now that he'd made up his mind, he wanted to hustle her to the altar before she could change hers.

No, he hadn't "made up" his mind. It had been made for him. It was like a missing piece of him just slid into place tonight. The missing piece that had let the chill in.

Jesus, he'd come so close to making the stupidest mistake of his life.

"Could you guys stay with me for a while, until I go to sleep?"

"I'm not going anywhere," April said, stroking her daughter's hair. "I'm sleeping right here tonight."

Sid rolled her eyes at her mother. "I know you're going to sleep here to help keep me warm, but you don't have to come to bed right away. You probably want to kiss and stuff."

Scott grinned. "I definitely want to kiss your mother, but it'll wait."

"Then hop in." Sid patted the bed on either side of her.

April climbed onto the bed beside her daughter, on top of the quilts, but instead of lying down, she sat with her back against the headboard. Scott did the same, leaning in so he could put his arm around April's shoulders.

"How's that?" Scott asked.

"Perfect." Sid yawned and burrowed down. "It's completely perfect."

# – forty-seven –

"MY SOUL." Uncle Arden, who was sitting in his chair at the kitchen table, dabbed at his eyes. Faye sat across from him, a ball of tissues clutched in her hands. The two of them had gotten in about an hour after supper, after a leisurely drive back from Montreal in Faye's Audi. They'd been surprised to find the house full—Titus and Ocean and Ember and Jace were there, along with Scott, April, and Sid. Everyone had wanted to be there to see their reaction to the happy news.

Scott had just finished telling them about the events of the last twenty-four hours, and there wasn't a dry eye in the house.

Uncle Arden put his handkerchief away. "Go away to take in a couple of hockey games and come back to a daughter-in-law-to-be. That's a pretty good deal."

"And a granddaughter-to-be!" Sidney said, from her position beside Arden's knee.

"Gracious, yes! That's the best part." Arden smiled at Sid. "But there's a special condition attached to being my granddaughter. Did anyone tell you about that?"

"There is?" Sid's face sobered. "What is it?"

"You have to promise me you won't go off like that on your own again. Not until you're a lot bigger."

Sid ducked her head. "I'm really sorry. But I already told

Scott that I won't do anything like that again. Didn't I?" She lifted her head to look at Scott.

He looked down at her grave brown eyes. "You did."

"So, does that mean I make the cut?" Sid looked back to Arden for his approval.

Arden laughed. "Sweet girl, you'd make the cut for anyone with a brain in their head. It's just this old heart…I don't think it could stand it if anything happened to you. That's why I needed you to make that promise."

"I love you, Arden." She put an impulsive arm around his neck and hugged him. "Even though I already promised Mom and Scott, I promise you too. No running away, no sneaking out."

Uncle Arden hugged her back. When he released her, there were fresh tears in his eyes. Even Titus at the far end of the kitchen had to clear his throat.

Sidney must have seen the tears in his eyes for she said, "Seriously! I'm not half as bad as Ember was at my age."

"Hey!" Ember said.

They all chuckled. Sid especially.

"Well, if we're done with all this touchy-feely stuff," Titus said, "I have to take a shower. I've been working on the plumbing at Ocean's cottage, and we've been making do without water in the bathroom."

"I wasn't going to say anything," Ember said, wrinkling her nose, "but I endorse that plan."

"Hey!" Titus protested.

Ocean laughed. "It's true. We're both a little ripe." She glanced at Faye. "Speaking of which, if you're ready, Mom, maybe we should head out?"

"That's a good idea, sweetheart," Faye said. "After that drive, I'm ready for a soak in the tub myself."

"Great." Ocean helped her mother up and escorted her toward the door. "We can thumb wrestle to see who gets to go first."

Faye stopped short of the door. “Why would we do that? We have two bathrooms and plenty of hot water.”

“Aaand there goes my punch line.” Ocean looked back over her shoulder. “Congratulations again, guys. I couldn’t be happier for you. April, let me know when you have a date. It’s never too soon to start planning, right?”

“Right,” April said, looking bemused.

“Come on, Ma.” Ocean steered her mother out the door, explaining as they went why the image of the two of them physically vying for dibs on who got to bathe first was funny.

Scott met April’s eyes and grinned.

“We’re out of here too,” Ember announced. “Because…reasons.”

Scott turned to see her looking up at Jace wickedly. He had a pretty good idea what those reasons were. As did Titus, from his groan.

“Oh, grow up,” Ember said. “We’re going to unpack some equipment that came in for the boxing club. Aren’t we, Jace?

He waggled his eyebrows. “Eventually.”

Laughing, Ember went to hug April. “I’m so glad you’re going to be joining the family. I always wanted a sister.”

When April emerged from the hug, her eyes were damp.

Jace gave Scott a shot to the arm on the way past. “Congrats again, man.”

“Thanks.” Scott had a feeling he was grinning like a fool, but he couldn’t help it. Didn’t really care.

“Okay, I really do need a shower,” Titus said, as soon as Ember and Jace were out the door. “But I’ll expect the scotch to be broken out when I come back down. The good stuff.”

Scott had gone to the liquor store earlier for a bottle of The Maccallan. “Deal.”

When Titus left, April came over to Scott’s side. He put his arm around her and drew her close. Sid came up on the other side, and he pulled her into the hug.

“This has been the best day,” Sid said.

"Agreed." Scott ruffled her hair.

"Can I tell Danika the news tomorrow?"

Scott looked at April. As far as he was concerned, he didn't care who knew, but women could be funny about that stuff. "I have no problem with folks knowing, but it's up to your mom."

"Can I, Mom?"

"Sure."

"Can I call her tonight? Like, right now?"

"It's almost bedtime, Ladybug."

"Danika doesn't go to bed until nine, so there's still time. And everyone in the family knows now. So can I?"

April groaned. "Okay, sure. But you'll make the call from your bedroom, and I'll be timing you. Tomorrow's a school day. We'll have to start getting ready for bed as soon as you hang up."

"Okay. My phone's upstairs. Let's go." She tugged at her mother's arm.

April smiled at Scott. "I'll take my time up there. You can come find me after you've had that manly drink of scotch."

"Try and stop me."

Smiling, she let Sid lead her away.

Uncle Arden cleared his throat, looked around the empty room. "Was it something I said?"

Scott laughed. "Yeah, it cleared out pretty quickly, didn't it?" But he was glad they were alone.

He went to the cupboard, grabbed three glasses and brought them over to the table. Retrieving the scotch from the cupboard over the refrigerator, he went to sit beside his uncle.

"I'm so happy about this, Son. I thought April was perfect for you from the first, but I didn't dare hope."

Scott rubbed the back of his neck. "Well, I've never given you much reason to hope, have I? A rolling stone gathers no moss, right? No marriage prospects, either."

"Scott, you don't owe me anything, not even

grandchildren. If you'd wanted to keep rolling—if that's what you needed to do to find peace—well, that would have been okay by me. But for your sake, I'm so glad you found April and Sid."

"I want to adopt Sid," he said in a rush. "April's on board."

"Good for you." Arden grinned. "I'm guessing Sid approves?"

"We haven't raised it with her yet, but I want her to feel like my daughter, as much my child as any kids April and I might have."

Arden nodded. "That's important, taking the legal steps. And I know you'll work at making sure she knows it, *feels* it."

"I get it now." Scott picked up the whisky bottle and cracked the seal, but made no move to pour it into the glasses. "I mean, I always knew you wanted me to be a real part of this family. You did everything right. It was just me. I couldn't—"

"Don't beat yourself up about anything, Son. You had a traumatic loss, followed by being jerked out of your city life and plunked down on a farm with relatives you didn't know. No one could blame you if—"

"Just listen, okay?"

Arden lifted his eyebrows but he nodded for Scott to continue.

"What I'm trying to say is that I knew all of that *intellectually*. But it wasn't until I realized that I wanted to make a family with April and Sid that I really understood it on an emotional level. A gut level. I just want to say thank you. What you and Mom did for me…there are no words. You made me feel at home, feel loved, but you gave me the room I needed. I was so afraid you'd be mad at me or disappointed if you suspected that sliver of loneliness I was hiding. But you knew all along and you gave me space and freedom…" Scott swallowed. "Just…thank you."

Arden's eyes looked damp again, but his voice was strong. "You're welcome. Literally. You've always been welcome."

"Thanks." It took everything he had not to cry. "Sid and I have had the dad talk. She's decided she'll keep calling me Scott for now, and will call me Dad as soon as her mother and I are married. And she wants to call you Grandpa."

"Grandpa?" Arden grinned. "I like the sound of that. And it's a good plan. A logical time for the transition."

"I was thinking…" Scott looked down at his boots. "I know it's a couple decades late, but how would you feel if I started calling you Dad?"

Arden closed his eyes. For a second, Scott thought he was in physical distress. Then he opened his eyes, climbed to his feet and held out his arms.

Scott stood and embraced his father. "Dad."

"Thank you, Son." Arden returned the hug, thumping Scott on the back.

Scott released him. "It'll probably come out *Uncle…er…Dad* for a while, but I'll get there."

"I know you will." With a last clap on the shoulder, Arden stepped back. "We've got plenty of time."

They both retreated to their chairs in time to hear Titus thumping down the stairs. He rounded the corner into the kitchen and spied the scotch and glasses.

"Good, you waited for me."

Scott and Arden laughed uproariously.

Titus frowned. "What'd I miss?"

"Not a thing," Scott said, reaching for the whisky bottle. "Grab a glass."

# – forty-eight –

APRIL'S HEARTBEAT slowly returned to normal. She and Scott lay in his bed in the lovely old hayloft, arms wrapped around each other.

They'd sneaked out after everyone else was down for the night around eleven o'clock. April had been so ready. Scott's mouth had been redolent of scotch, with his own bold, exciting taste just beneath it. He'd kissed her dizzy, then kissed every inch of skin he exposed as he stripped her clothes off. Despite the heat thrown off by the space heater, she'd shivered hard. He'd shed his own clothes and they'd dived under the goose down duvet he'd brought out the beginning of January to supplement the Hudson's Bay blanket.

"Hey, how're you doing?" He lifted a finger to push a strand a hair back behind her ear.

"Fantastically." She smoothed a hand over his back, loving the warm solidity of him beneath her palm. "You?"

"Never better. Although I'm thinking it's getting a little cold for this."

She smiled, recalling the way her skin had broken out in gooseflesh when he'd kissed his way up her thigh. "A little."

He nuzzled her chin. "If we were married, we could sleep inside."

She pulled back to see the grin on his face. "Are you

seriously suggesting we get married sooner for your *comfort*?"

His smile faded. "No, I'm suggesting we get married as soon as possible because I cannot wait to be your husband. Sid's father."

She blinked. "Good answer."

"I know you and Ember and Ocean have to dig your calendars out and pick a date that works for your business, for the farm, and all that. I'm just saying March has a lot to recommend it, as opposed to, like, June. Or September."

"I'll take that under advisement." She brought her hand around to his chest. "Any other considerations we should be mindful of?"

He captured her hand in his. "Here's the thing—whether it's next month or next year, I'll be okay with it, if it's what you want. I'm in this for life, April Dawn Morgan, soon-to-be April Dawn Standish."

*April Standish.*

Yes, she was taking his name. Sidney would too when the adoption went through. She couldn't wait to become an official part of this family she'd found. To love this Standish man, and live here on Standish ground. Though maybe not in Arden's house. At least not forever. Scott was already talking about building them a new, energy efficient home on the south side of the main house's driveway, one with a kitchen to be designed to her specifications.

She smiled at him, her heart in her eyes. "I'm in it for the long haul too."

He kissed her tenderly, then relaxed back onto his pillow. "You're going to be so good for this community. I can see your April Dawn's business really taking off. It could be so much more than a cottage industry, if you want it to be."

His faith warmed her. "Thank you. I *do* want to see what I can do with it, see how far I can take it. I've already mentioned to Jace that I'd like to pick his brain, avoid as many pitfalls as I can."

"He knows what he's talking about," Scott said. "He's done a ton of consulting for start-ups, or so Ember tells me."

"Yeah, but could he help the Eschers when they need a pipefitter who can work with stainless steel?"

He grinned. "True that."

Her own smile faded. "I know we talked about it, but are you sure about passing on that Alberta project? It sounds like the kind of thing that could make a big impact, get you noticed."

His answer came instantly. "As sure as you are about turning down K.Z. McCoy."

"So, that would be *very sure*."

"Exactly." He rolled onto his side, his hand coming to rest on her belly. "Now that I'm here…present and committed to being here…I can't stop thinking about stuff to be done. Not just building a house for us, but the farm."

"What kind of things?"

"For one, I'd love to look into controlled atmosphere storage for our apple crop. We're a pretty small operation, too small to afford CA technology. We rely solely on refrigerated storage, such as it is. But if we got together with a few other organic apple farmers, maybe we could do something collaboratively."

That's when she knew it. That's when she allowed herself to fully, wholeheartedly believe that he was here to stay. There would be more nights like this, with them curled up together in bed talking. Nights after Sid—or their kids, plural—had gone to bed.

Her heart swelled with such happiness, she just couldn't contain it. Pushing up on her elbow, she leaned over and kissed him.

"Mmm, where'd that come from?"

She grinned. "Must be all that sexy controlled atmosphere talk."

"Yeah?" He waggled his eyebrows. "Then maybe you'd

like to hear my ideas about using lava rock as a growing medium for the strawberry plugs?"

Her lips quirked, but she managed not to laugh. "Oh, yeah," she said in her sultriest voice. "Like that, lover." In one quick motion, she slid her knee over his groin and moved astride him. The blankets slipped down to her waist. His eyes widened and his breath caught. And dear God in heaven, he'd never looked more gorgeous to her than he did right now with his dark head on the pillow, passion flaring in his eyes. "Talk horticulture to me."

"Are you sure you're ready?" He lifted his hands to her breasts with their nipples pebbled from the cold. "Because it gets dirty. Really, really dirty."

She couldn't hold it in any longer. Throwing her head back, she let it out in a joyful laugh.

He curled up to cradle her in his arms.

"That," he said gruffly. "If I can just hear that laugh…" He brought one hand up to cup her chin. "See that smile, that face, every day for the rest of my life, I'll die a happy man. I love you, April. I love you more than there are stars in the sky."

There it went again, her heart swelling and swelling with emotion.

"That's all I need too." She touched his hair, his forehead, then bent to kiss his eyelids closed. "I love you, Scott Standish, and I'll love you until those stars burn out."

Then there was silence in the barn. Outside, the cold winter sky blazed with the glittering of a thousand stars.

## – message from the author –

Thank you for investing that most precious of commodities—your time—in my book! If you enjoyed *Promise Me the Stars*, please consider helping me buzz it. You can do this by:

• *Recommending it.* Help other readers find this book by recommending it to friends or by sharing about it on social media.

• *Reviewing it.* Nothing carries as much weight as a happy reader's review. Posting a short review at the vendor site where you bought this book, or at readers' sites such as Goodreads, can really help a book gain visibility.

Again, thank you for choosing to read my book!

If you don't want to miss future releases, you can sign up for my newsletter at **www.norahwilsonwrites.com**.

Please turn the page to read about my other books!

# – other books –

ALSO IN THIS HEARTS OF HARKNESS CONTEMPORARY ROMANCE SERIES:

A Fall from Yesterday, *The Standish Clan #1*
Ember's Fire, *The Standish Clan #2*

ROMANTIC SUSPENSE

Fatal Hearts, Montlake Romance
Every Breath She Takes, Montlake Romance
Guarding Suzannah, *Serve and Protect #1*
Saving Grace, *Serve and Protect #2*
Protecting Paige, *Serve and Protect #3*
Serve and Protect Box Set

PARANORMAL ROMANCE

The Merzetti Effect—A Vampire Romance, #1
Nightfall—A Vampire Romance, #2

DYSTOPIAN ROMANCE W/ HEATHER DOHERTY

The Eleventh Commandment

DIX DODD COZY MYSTERIES BY N.L. WILSON

The Case of the Flashing Fashion Queen (#1)
Family Jewels (#2)
Death by Cuddle Club (#3)
A Moment on the Lips (a Dix Dodd short story)
Covering Her Assets (#4)
Dix Dodd Mysteries Box Set 1 (#1-3)

BOOKS BY THE WRITING TEAM OF WILSON/DOHERTY

YOUNG ADULT

Comes the Night *(Casters, #1)*
Enter the Night *(Casters, #2)*
Embrace the Night *(Casters, #3)*
Forever the Night *(Casters, #4)*
Casters Series Box Set *(#1-3)*

Ashlyn's Radio

The Summoning *(Gatekeepers, #1)*

# – about the author –

NORAH WILSON is a USA Today bestselling author of romantic suspense, contemporary romance, and paranormal romance. Together with the very talented Heather Doherty, she also writes the hilarious Dix Dodd cozy mysteries, exciting YA paranormal, and even dystopian romance.

The tenth child in a family of eleven children, Norah knew she had to do something to distinguish herself. That something turned out to be writing. She finaled three times in the Romance Writers of America's prestigious Golden Heart ® contest, and went on to win Dorchester Publishing's New Voice in Romance contest in 2004. A hybrid author, she now writes romantic suspense for Montlake Romance and also self-publishes.

She lives in Fredericton, New Brunswick, Canada, with her husband, two adult children, two dogs (Neva and Ruby) and two cats (Ruckus and Milo).

**Connect with Norah Online**

*Twitter* http://twitter.com/norah_wilson

*Facebook* http://www.facebook.com/NorahWilsonWrites

*Goodreads*
http://www.goodreads.com/author/show/1361508.Norah_Wilson

*Norah's Website* http://www.norahwilsonwrites.com

*Email Norah* norahwilsonwrites@gmail.com